WHITE RABBIT

WHITE RABBIT

CALEB ROEHRIG

FEIWEL AND FRIENDS
NEW YORK

A Feiwel and Friends Book
An imprint of Macmillan Publishing Group, LLC
175 Fifth Avenue, New York, NY 10010

Our books may be purchased in bulk for promotional, educational, or business use. Please contact your local bookseller or the Macmillan Corporate and Premium Sales Department at (800) 221-7945 ext. 5442 or by e-mail at MacmillanSpecialMarkets@macmillan.com.

Library of Congress Cataloging-in-Publication Data is available.

ISBN 978-1-250-08565-8 (hardcover) / ISBN 978-1-250-08564-1 (ebook)

Feiwel and Friends logo designed by Filomena Tuosto

First edition, 2018

10 9 8 7 6 5 4 3 2 1

fiercereads.com

For my mother, Kay Nichols.
You once said, “A book is no fun unless everybody’s dying all the time.”
Hope this body count passes muster!

and

In memory of my Aunt Holly and my Uncle Andy,
gone too soon, but together forever.
Thank you for believing in me.

There is nothing more deceptive than an obvious fact.

—ARTHUR CONAN DOYLE

1

THE PHONE GOES DEAD IN MY EAR. THE SUDDEN SILENCE ON THE line is so total, so ominous, that a cold surge of adrenaline brings goose bumps to my flesh in spite of the thick and sticky heat that lingers in the night air. "Hello?" I say stupidly, hearing the raw agitation in my own voice. "Are you still there?" A quick and pointless glance at the display assures me that the answer is, indeed, *no*.

"What's going on?" The boy standing behind me asks, his ancient Chucks scraping against the rough pavement of the street. Sebastian's "lucky" shoes are so worn out, they're literally falling apart, his dark socks peeking through frayed holes in the graying canvas. I used to think it was cute. "Who was it?"

I wave him irritably into silence as I dial my cell, calling the number back. It rings repeatedly on the other end, but no one picks up. "Come on," I urge out loud. "Answer your damn phone!"

"Rufus, who was it?" Sebastian repeats as I give up in frustration, jamming my cell back into my pocket and turning to face him. His wide, dark eyes are filled with obvious concern, and it makes me angry. He has no right to be worried about me—not now, not after everything he's done—but I'm suddenly too confused and anxious to summon up the righteous fury I'd been feeling just a few minutes earlier.

"It was April," I report stiffly, feeling a twinge of self-directed anger as I indulge his solicitude. *Why am I answering him?* My life is none of his business. Not anymore.

"Your sister?" He wrinkles his nose in genuine bewilderment, eyebrows scrunching together. It's a familiar sight, and another thing about him I used to think was cute—back before he broke my heart.

"She's the only April I know."

"Why was she calling you?" He isn't asking for a summary of our conversation. What has him so perplexed is the simple fact that my sister has called me *at all*—and I'm just as baffled as he is.

April is only ten months younger than me, fifteen to my sixteen, but we barely know each other. I'm her brother only in the most technical sense, and we're hardly even what you might call friends; *friendship* is something our controlling and self-important father, Peter Covington II, would never tolerate between us. And while I do not personally give two flying shits what that hypocritical dickbag will or will not tolerate, neither do I especially want anything to do with *any* of the Covingtons.

But April has a way of worming into your heart, no matter how many obstacles you set before her. She's outgoing, fun-loving, and bold, and so far has never met a rule that doesn't have an April Covington–shaped loophole. There's a sweetness to her that even her cold-blooded parents have failed to stamp out—and you can bet they've given it their best shot. Peter and his wife, Isabel, *have* succeeded in passing along some of their more dismal qualities, though; and to that end, likable though she may be, April can also be calculating, manipulative, and spoiled. Her company often comes at a price, and I'm pretty sure my account with her has just been called up.

"She's in trouble," I hear myself saying to Sebastian, the words sounding surreally technical, my brain already spinning faster and faster as I try to figure out what I'm going to do next. "She—she needs my help."

"April needs *your* help." He tries the words on for size, but they make no more sense to him than they do to me. And yet, not two minutes earlier, it was exactly what she said.

"Hello?" My voice was testy, my patience threadbare when I answered her call. I was already regretting it—already wishing I'd just continued with the angry speech I'd been about to give Sebastian—even as the greeting left my mouth.

A strange, shuffling silence came back, a susurrant nothingness on the line that was slowly replaced by shallow, labored breathing. Then, just as I was starting to think it was a prank: "Rufus?"

Her voice was quavering, distant, my name sliding around in her mouth like a sliver of ice, and in that instant, I forgot my anger. "Yeah, it's me. What's . . . what is it?"

"Rufus," she repeated fretfully. There was more breathing—stiff and unnatural—and then her distant voice again. "I need . . . I need help, Rufus."

"What are you talking about? What's going on?"

"I'm at . . . Fox's c-cottage," she said next, the words jerky and disjointed, as if they had taken colossal effort to put together. "Fox's parents' cottage. You have to help me. Please."

"What's happened?" I demanded, still too innately suspicious

about anything to do with the Covingtons to take my half sister's plea at face value. "Tell me what—"

"You're the only one I can trust!" She blurted in a kind of high-pitched whimper. "You have to come, Rufus. You have to! Please promise me . . . promise me." Garbled words followed, a string of nonsense, like English spoken backward, and then, "I don't know what to do. I'm so scared. I think I—HELP ME!"

And the line went dead.

I recount this for Sebastian in broad strokes, not really wanting to share, but too upset not to. We're standing in front of his car, amber streetlights casting his stupidly gorgeous face in sepia tones, and the heavy, still air that settles around us is redolent of gunpowder. A block away, my best friend, Lucy Kim, is hosting her Fourth of July rager; it's our pathetic attempt at living up to all those iconic Hollywood teen movies, where no parents and lots of beer is the only formula necessary to create one perfect, life-changing night for a handful of feisty, lovable underdogs—but so far we've only succeeded in creating buckets of puke and a few scorch marks on the back of a couch, which Lucy's going to have a hell of a time explaining to Mr. and Mrs. Kim when they return from Boston on the sixth.

"What are you gonna do?" Sebastian asks worriedly. He moves closer, like he's going to touch me, and I step back. He registers the rebuff and stops, but his eyes stay on mine, his gaze soulful enough to stir a feeling to life inside me that I long ago drove to its grave with a stake through the heart.

"I don't know," I mutter, glancing up toward Lucy's place to avoid his gaze. I can hear shouts, music, and laughter, fireworks still cracking and booming intermittently from somewhere along the lake. It's nearly ten . . . Would anyone at the party even be sober? "I don't— Maybe I should call Peter."

"Your *dad*?" This statement confuses him even more than April's request for my help. "Is that a good idea?"

"No," I admit, feeling my face color. "But what else can I do? I don't have a car, all my friends are shit-faced, and I don't even know where April is! 'Fox's parents' cottage,' I mean, where the fuck is that? It could be anywhere!"

"South Hero Island," Sebastian responds promptly, because of *course* he knows. "I've been there a couple times. It's only like thirty minutes from here—I'll drive."

"No, thanks," I say in a cold voice, summoning up as much dignity as I can, even though it's obvious that I'm just cutting off my nose to spite my face—a tacit and embarrassing confession that I'm still hurting. That I still care.

"How're you gonna get there, then?"

"I'll figure something out."

"Yeah?" he challenges, a small spark of irritation at last flickering to life beneath his perennially cool facade. "You gonna walk out to the island? Knock on every cottage door you see until you find her?" He takes a step back and gestures to his Jeep, four feet away. "My car's right here, and I know exactly where we're going. You want to yell at me, I can tell, so do it on the way and kill two birds with one stone."

He concludes his proposition with a rakish grin—the smirky, vulpine look that melts underwear across all four grades at Ethan Allen High—and I will the ice to thicken over my heart against its fearsome power. Even so, with an anxious glance at my phone's display, I can see that time is already slipping past; I don't actually know what kind of help April needs, how serious a situation she's in, and I can't be sure I have the time it'll take to go back to Lucy's and search the party for somebody still clearheaded enough to take me on a half-hour excursion to the middle of Lake Champlain.

Plus, despite my antipathy toward Sebastian Williams, having him along might end up being a good thing. April's crowd is his crowd, too, and if this *does* turn out to be some kind of trap, his presence might fuck up their plans a little. Maybe.

Feeling shakier than I care to show, beginning to grow truly worried about my sister in spite of all my misgivings, I give a curt nod and wordlessly start for the passenger-side door. Sebastian's smile broadens as he blips his locks open, but I pretend not to notice, busying myself with an explanatory text to Lucy. I've been out of the house for less than ten minutes, but she's already written me a (very drunk) message inquiring after my absence: *WHERE ARE YOU, RUFUS HOLT?? IT IS TIME FOR TEQUILA SHOTS AND I NEED MY BESTIE!!!*

Three years earlier, when I was suffering the slings and arrows of a really shitty coming-out process, Lucy Kim was the first friend to rally to my side, communicating her allegiance via a series of effusive texts. First: *JUST FOUND OUT MY BFF IS GAY OMFG SUPERCOOL WOW LET'S GO BUY SHOES!* Followed by: *jkjkjk u know I love you to death Rufus and I am in your corner 110% no matter what mwah xoxo.* And: *I will fight a bitch for you if I have to just say the word.* Then, finally: *Srsly tho I really do need new shoes so how about it?*

Lucy is high-energy, high-maintenance, and often just plain high, but I love her to death. As I clamber into Sebastian's Jeep, I use my thumbs to hammer out, *Had to leave. Something's up with April?!? Call you tomorrow bae.* I'll get at least seventy more messages from her before the night is over.

The streets of Burlington sweep by in a leafy, starlit blur as we speed north toward Winooski and Malletts Bay, heading eventually for the narrow causeway that connects the shore to the chain of islands in the middle of the serpentine lake separating Vermont and New York. Sebastian was absolutely correct—I really *did* want to yell at him—but I'm too preoccupied with April's summons to shift my mental gears back to the recriminations I've been stockpiling for the guy who so readily volunteered to be my chauffeur. The guy who, not so long ago, was also my first boyfriend.

Dating Sebastian Williams was both the best and worst thing that ever happened to me. In a lot of ways, being with him made me feel as if maybe I'd never really been alive at *all* before. I was like a violin—an object that hasn't much purpose until someone touches it, fills it with resonance, draws things from it that it can never produce on its own. Sebastian had been the one to draw music from me, and it's why the end was so bad; before him, I'd never actually realized how painful the silence was.

But the hardest part of our breakup was also the hardest part of our entire relationship: having to keep it all a secret from everyone we know.

I cast a glance in his direction as we loop through a traffic circle, light gliding across his face in a way that I've tried to capture in photographs a million times without success. He's so good-looking it still takes my breath away, even when I'm wishing I'd never known him. With dark skin, flirty eyes, and a cocky smile, he's too handsome for his own damn good—and that's before you consider his long-legged, slim-hipped, and perfectly toned body.

Fuck.

It's only been six weeks since he suddenly, and without explanation, stopped answering my texts; five weeks since he officially stomped my heart out like a spent cigarette in the most painful way imaginable; and only one week since I stopped entertaining pointless fantasies that, one day, he would take me back again—or at least give me the chance to tell him to his face exactly what I think of him. Imagine my surprise, then, when he turned up out of the blue at Lucy's house, saying that he needed to speak to me, that it couldn't wait. But we'd barely gotten into the subject before my phone began ringing in my pocket, April calling with her baffling emergency, and now here we are, sitting mere feet apart in an uncomfortable silence as the night gets weirder and weirder around us.

Whatever's on his mind, I know it has to be something big—big enough for him to figure out where Lucy lives, anyway, since he always made an emphatic point of avoiding my friends throughout the four months we dated. Even so, I'm determined to have my say first, to unburden myself of all the poisonous, caustic feelings that have eaten their way down into my marrow over the course of six long weeks. I've rehearsed this scene so many times in my head that delivering my righteous rebukes should be simple . . . only, seven days of training myself not to think about it at all—out of some asinine, self-helpy notion that all the negative emotions were hurting me—has caused my crystal-clear accusations and arguments to become hopelessly tangled together. Answering April's call had partly been a simple play for time to sort my thoughts.

"It's gonna be an hour to get out there and back," Sebastian remarks conversationally, his voice jarring in the silence. "You can't ignore me the whole time."

"Challenge accepted," I return icily, instantly indebted by my own perverse stubbornness to suppress the vengeful words a little longer. It's so stupid; I *really* want to tell him off, but if it's what he wants, too, then I'll be damned if I give him the satisfaction. I once grudged my way out of tickets to see Death Cab in concert because they were a peace offering from my friend Brent—with whom I was in the midst of a Blood Feud—and I didn't want him to feel better about whatever it was that he'd done to piss me off.

I can't fathom what Sebastian has to say to me after all this time, though—what could possibly have compelled him to track me down so late on a night when he should, by all rights, be at a party with all his cool friends—and I admit that I'm more than a little intrigued. Even if I don't want to be. And neither can I begin to fathom the reason why April called *me* of all people, said *I'm* the only one she can trust. None of it makes sense; the whole evening has turned so bizarre so quickly that I actually squeeze my thigh until it hurts, just to remind myself that I'm really awake.

"This isn't some kind of a trick, is it?" I finally ask, my voice rusty as Sebastian steers the Jeep onto the two-lane causeway. The sky is freckled with stars, and the lake is a sheet of rippling black metal spreading out to either side of us.

"What do you mean?" He wrinkles his nose again.

"I *mean*, I'm not being lured into some kind of ambush, am I?"

"April wouldn't do that to you," Sebastian answers assuredly.

"Yes she would. She has."

When I was in the fifth grade, before I knew enough to truly distrust the Covingtons, April approached me outside of school one day following the final bell. I had just unlocked my bike when she appeared at the end of the long metal rack, looking tense but excited.

"Rufus, I need to talk to you!" She hissed urgently, glancing about with her large, robin's-egg-blue eyes. We weren't supposed to speak to each other, and I assumed she was nervous we'd be seen. "It's really important. It's . . . it's about my dad and your mom?"

"Um, okay," I said, only a little suspiciously. She was acting oddly, the words not sounding entirely natural, but I didn't know what to make of it. "What about them?"

"Not here—in private!" She started backing away. "Meet me behind the gym, okay? I don't want anyone else to find out."

"April, what—" I started, but she was already running across the playground, heading for the large brick extension that housed our elementary school's gymnasium. After a short inventory of my doubts, I secured my bike again and trotted after her.

Rounding the corner, I walked straight into a trap. April stood against the wall, her blue eyes wide and solemn, and she watched with silent fascination as our older brother, Hayden, and two of his friends spent the next four minutes beating me into a quivering, bloody pulp at her feet.

"You guys were little kids back then," Sebastian says, familiar with the story, dismissing the experience as if it were no big deal—as if it weren't just one small part of a very big hell from which I have literally no escape.

"Some people don't change," I reply rigidly. How can I explain to him, for all her winsomeness, how dangerous April really is? How she was raised in such a bubble that she's simultaneously helpless and ruthless, immured from the consequences of her actions by a family that refuses to see her actions in the first place?

"It would be kind of a shitty trap. I mean, she knows you don't have a car, so how could she be sure you'd—"

He stops short as he finally catches up to the rest of my insinuation, and his voice takes on a thorny quality that is immeasurably more pleasing than his attempts at friendliness. "You think maybe I'm in on it." I respond to the charge with silence, and he states gruffly, "I wouldn't do something like that, Rufe. Not to you. You know I wouldn't."

"I don't know *what* you'd do," I shoot back, and six weeks of hurt and doubt and raw anger break the surface like an underwater explosion, venom scorching my throat and pricking my eyelids. Embarrassed, I turn my face to the window.

We leave the causeway and head inland on Route 2, rolling past the apple orchards and farmhouses of South Hero Island, the *crack-boom* of fireworks still intermittently punctuating the night. Presently, Sebastian turns off the main road and onto a narrow lane, heading toward the western shore through a corridor of lushly overgrown trees. The darkness is total, isolating, and the island suddenly feels terribly remote. My hands drift to my seat belt, worrying the fabric with rhythmic motions as the road turns from pavement to hard-packed dirt beneath the Jeep's tires. *Where the hell are we going?*

Eventually, the tree line breaks before us, Sebastian's headlights stabbing out into the moonlit void of Lake Champlain, and he turns north again to parallel the water. We pass a few cottages—mostly vacation rentals—before we finally reach our destination and the Jeep begins to slow.

On our left, a gravel drive snakes through a copse of aspens and pines, leading to a craftsman-style cabin with peaked gables that form an upper half-story. Massive bushes cluster beneath a wraparound porch, and a detached carport shelters a black Range Rover. A Playboy bunny decal on the imposing vehicle's tailgate flares under Sebastian's headlights and, recognizing it, I shift in my seat. The SUV belongs to April's superdouche boyfriend, Fox Whitney.

Fox is seventeen, a senior-to-be at Ethan Allen, and an absolute prolapsed rectum of a human being. He's also the youngest of three boys, sons of a corporate attorney and a dermatologist, and is therefore nearly as spoiled as my sister. I blink in confusion at his car, even more ill at ease than before we pulled up; if Fox is here, why does April need me? And, come to that, why *me* and not the brother she's allowed to associate with—or one of her many popular friends?

"This is it," Sebastian says a little uncertainly as he shoves open the door of the Jeep and jumps out. I follow suit, a welcome wagon of mosquitoes instantly gathering around me, and I almost regret my choice to wear a tank top to Lucy's party. I say "almost" for two simple reasons: 1) my arms and legs are already stuccoed with bites, so what can a few more hurt? and 2) I've been working out *a lot* over the past six weeks, determined to be hot as fuck the next time I crossed paths with Sebastian, and my arms actually look pretty good.

My ex-boyfriend leads the way to a set of wooden steps that ascend to the porch, and I try to ignore how good *his* arms look—how the muscles in his calves flex before my eyes, how the scent of his dumb cologne still makes me dizzy in a treacherous way after all this time—and concentrate on what I might be walking into. Lights burn in the cottage, every window ablaze, and I can hear music pumping from inside.

Sebastian knocks at the front door and peers through the beveled glass insets, and I feel like telling him not to waste his time; I've been calling and texting April repeatedly on the trip over and haven't gotten any response. If she's in there, she's not going to answer. Reaching past him, I try the knob, and the door swings open.

"April?" I call out apprehensively. A pinewood foyer extends into a family room decorated in a style an obscenely wealthy person might call "rustic"—the kind of down-home, country charm that requires raw silk slipcovers and *objets d'art* imported from Provence—but it hasn't been treated well; the furniture is out of alignment, red Solo cups and abandoned bottles are everywhere, and fragments of broken glass and ceramic litter the floor like bloodthirsty confetti. My sister is nowhere in sight.

Cautiously, I step over the threshold, my concern mounting. Still, I'm hyperaware of Sebastian's presence immediately behind me, and I wonder—not for the first time—how he intends to explain what he's doing here. There's still a chance this is a ruse, that he's tricked me into another ambush to prove something to his asshole friends—who, for all I know, have somehow sussed out the truth of our relationship. Maybe he's about to pass some kind of ruthless social test at my expense. "April, it's Rufus. Are you here?"

A highly polished staircase rises on my right, climbing to what I suspect is a loft-style bedroom or study, and I cock an ear toward the upper story. The soft noise I then hear, however—a cross between a sigh and a whisper—comes not from above, but from somewhere else on the ground floor.

As I move forward out of the foyer, a dining nook appears to the left off the family room—and then, just to *its* left, the kitchen. This is where I find April at last, when I round the corner, clearing the central island so I can look down at the floor.

My sister is slumped against the cupboards beneath the sink, her head bowed forward, her skin as white as candle wax against her purple bikini; and Fox lies sprawled across the tiles beside her, half-curled into the fetal position, his face nightmarishly slack.

Both of them are drenched in blood, and the fingers of April's right hand are loosely wrapped around the hilt of a massive butcher knife.

2

"APRIL!" I GRIP HER BY THE SHOULDERS, HER FLESH FRIGHTENINGLY cold and sticky to the touch, and drag her forward, straightening her up. The knife slips from her right hand as my knee jostles a discarded cell phone resting by her left, and her head lolls and swings on her neck, heavy as a sandbag. Frantically, I give her a hard shake. "April!"

"Holy fuck, dude." Sebastian's eyes are huge with panic as he prowls Fox's body, searching for a pulse. "Holy *fuck*, Rufus, I think he's dead!"

Willing myself not to lose it, I press my fingers against April's carotid, holding my breath. When I feel the faint and erratic undulation of blood moving beneath her pallid skin, I emit a primitive noise of relief and squeeze my eyes shut tight. "She's alive."

"What the fuck happened here, man?" Sebastian asks me, deathly serious. His face is stricken as he backs away from Fox's corpse, the Whitneys' favorite son stretched across the slate floor tiles, his T-shirt so saturated with blood that its true color is impossible to determine. *"What the fuck happened?"*

He jolts to his feet and stumbles a little, eyes still getting wider. His anxiety is so sincere that, I finally realize, if this *is* some twisted prank, he is certainly not in on it. I search my sister's body, looking for wounds or some other sign that she's been hurt, but I can't find anything. The blood doesn't seem to be hers.

"April, wake up," I command sharply, sweeping her auburn hair out of her face and tilting her chin to the light. She mumbles something unintelligible, and I pry one of her eyes open. Her pupil is a tiny dot in a pool of aquamarine, her gaze glassy and unfocused as it drifts up into her skull. "She's on something."

"*Shit*, man!" Sebastian paces agitatedly, but he can't stop staring down at Fox's body. "We have to call someone."

"Not yet," I tell him firmly, giving April another hard shake. With a guilty feeling, I swat her lightly across the face. She gives a sharp snort and her eyelids lift unevenly. "April! April, can you hear me?"

". . . Rufus?" Her voice is a breathy whisper.

"Yeah, it's me."

Fat tears roll down her cheeks as I watch, and then, to my complete surprise, she tosses her arms around me in a flaccid, desperate embrace. Her forehead thuds against my shoulder, and she begins weakly to sob. I let it go on for just a moment before I straighten her back up again, flustered. "April, what happened?"

"I-I don't . . ." She starts to look toward Fox's body, but I take hold of her chin again and force her to face me. I can't afford to lose her concentration now.

"Focus on me, April. Tell me what happened."

She licks her lips, her eyes clouding for a moment before she seems to will them clear again, but her voice is a faded, broken whisper as she moans, "I don't remember. I don't . . . there was . . . all that blood . . ."

With Sebastian's help, I haul her to her feet, and the two of us start walking her through the dining room and living room, hip-hop music blasting from speakers I can't see. She's like a newborn colt, her legs rubbery and untrustworthy, and her chin keeps dropping to her chest. I ask her what she's taken, but her answers are unintelligible, and I feel the quick heat of impatience snapping under my skin. I try to quell it, recalling my therapist's advice: *Take a deep breath and step back.* Over April's head, I ask Sebastian, "Do they have a shower? Maybe it'll wake her up."

"There's a bedroom through there," he answers after a beat, his face alarmingly gray, and gestures to a door set in a small vestibule beside the stone-fronted fireplace. "It's got a bathroom. I don't think there's a tub, but—"

"Let's get her in there."

The Whitneys' master suite is cozy in size and luxurious in appointment—Egyptian cotton sheets, a hand-carved headboard, priceless antique armoires—but an open doorway leads to a surprisingly spare bathroom with a shower stall.

I shove April into Sebastian's arms while I kick my shoes aside, strip off my tank top, and crank the cold water to full blast. Then I pull my blood-soaked, half-dead half sister under the hard spray with me, holding her upright while she squirms and mumbles, pink water sluicing off her and swirling ominously down the drain. Her bare skin becomes slippery as the drying blood loosens up, and I have to hold her tighter. Eventually, her struggling grows more forceful, her protests more lucid, and I slap the water off at last.

With most of the blood washed away, it's even more apparent that she's physically unharmed, her slight, pale frame streaky and textured with goose bumps but otherwise pristine. I sit her down on the lid of the toilet, and she stares at the white tiles of the floor, shivering and blank. Breathing hard from the exertion of holding her up, I ask, "Are you feeling better?"

A long second passes where she just gazes up at me, and then she gives a faint nod. "Yeah."

"Where are your clothes?"

She raises her arm like it weighs two hundred pounds, and points vaguely into the master bedroom. "In there. Is . . . is Fox—"

"Get yourself cleaned up, put your clothes back on, and then I'm gonna need you to tell us what happened tonight, okay?" I try to deliver it like a statement, mimicking the way my mom "asks" me to do chores—*I need you to mow the lawn, okay?*—but my voice is shaking. I clamp down hard against the fear. I cannot lose control. *Take a step back.* "Can you do that for me?"

April nods again, and mumbles, "Yes."

As I herd Sebastian back into the chaos of the living room, shutting the bedroom door behind us, I hear the shower turn on again. My ex-boyfriend gives me an incredulous look, his soft, kissable lips scrunching up like a cat's anus. "You're letting her take a freaking shower, man? She's covered in evidence!"

"This whole *place* is covered in evidence," I fire back, waving my hand around the connected rooms. We've tracked Fox's blood across the pinewood floors, and streaks of it cling to Sebastian's clothes, arms, and face. I'm standing there, trying to compartmentalize, fighting to think, when I notice his eyes bob up and down the length of my torso and I finally remember that I'm still shirtless. Even in the midst of all the shock and disorder, I feel a wave of wildly inappropriate satisfaction as my ex-boyfriend gets a look at how toned my chest and abs have become in the weeks since he dumped me.

I had this whole plan to turn into a crazy-hot sex god over the summer, to build muscle like an underwear model and then have Lucy take some "candid" photos of me that I could post on Facebook and Instagram and anywhere else Sebastian might see them and realize how awesome I was doing without him—so he could see the newer, hotter Rufus Holt and eat his heart out. My biology proved unequal to the fantasy, however; my upper body hardened a bit, but after putting on exactly two extra pounds of muscle, my narrow-shouldered physique seems to have just plain given up. No matter what I try, I appear to be stuck permanently on lanky. Still, I look way abs-ier than I did the last time Sebastian saw me without a shirt on, and I guess that's all that matters.

"We have to call the police," he insists next.

I shake my head. "Not yet."

"What the fuck do you mean, *not yet?*" Sebastian demands, his voice climbing into the realm of hysteria. "Why not? Fox is fucking *dead*, Rufus!"

"Not until we hear what April has to say! We need to know . . ." *We need to know what we've walked into.* "We need to know what happened first."

Something's not right. On the surface, it sure as hell looks like April killed her boyfriend with a big old knife . . . but why? And why did she call *me* for help? At the risk of sounding selfish, this is the real reason I don't want to involve the police just yet. Instead of her doting parents or her close friends or even our take-charge asshole of a brother, she's involved *me* in this thing, and I want to know exactly where I stand before I start getting all reporty with the cops. My recent history with the law is dodgy, anyway, and I can't exactly afford any misunderstandings.

"Just wait until she's told us, okay? Just *wait*." I try to sound authoritative again as I turn and start for the front door, my brain speeding while I struggle to close off any avenue of thought that doesn't lead directly forward.

"Where are you going?" Sebastian asks, indignant.

"I just want to have a look around outside. I think— Let's just know as much about what's going on here as we can, okay? Before we call anybody?"

Sebastian is silent for a moment, his lips still pursed tightly. He looks more than a little freaked, but he gives me a short nod. "Okay. Okay."

The second the door closes behind me, I sprint to the porch rail, barely covering the three steps before I start to heave. Nothing comes up but an unearthly retching sound, my stomach convulsing, drool running over my bottom lip as I struggle to breathe and fight my nausea into submission. The air outside is still heavy and warm, but it's not until I start sucking in great mouthfuls of it that I realize how good it smells. For all its rarified trappings, the lake house reeks inside with the metallic stench of blood.

I will my stomach to settle, my head to clear. When I'm finally breathing evenly again, I step back and begin a methodical circuit of the house, eyes sweeping left to right as I look for something I can't even begin to anticipate. Nothing special catches my eye, though—just more Solo cups and cigarette butts—and I soon reach the end point of the porch. A set of steps descends to the yard on my right, while on my left, a patio door affords me a full, Technicolor view of the kitchen and Fox's body—still swimming in a lap pool of his own congealing blood.

With a shudder I quickly reverse course, tugging my phone out of my shorts. It's damp from the shower but seems to have avoided the worst of the spray, and it still works. I'm definitely not ready to talk to the cops, but I haven't totally lost my mind, either; I know an adult needs to be involved in this slasher-movie nightmare. But it has to be one that I trust.

My mom answers on the fourth ring, her voice groggy and thick. I can picture her lying on top of her bed, a paperback splayed across her chest, fumbling for her glasses on the nightstand. "Hey, kiddo, what's up?"

"H-hey, Mom, I—" My voice chokes off, the reality of what I have to say slamming into me like a crosstown bus. *April might have murdered her boyfriend.*

"What is it? What's wrong?" She's immediately alert, her hair-trigger panic tripped by my hesitation. "Did you and Lucy have a fight? Do you need a ride?"

"No, it's nothing like that," I assure her in a quiet hurry, feeling my way through my own words. "It's . . . actually, it's, um . . . April?"

"That girl." Mom's tone becomes as hard and sharp as a broken tooth. "What did she do this time? Did she crash your party tonight? Listen, if she said . . . if she said something about my calling Peter—"

"No, Mom, it wasn't—" I stop short, her words hitting their target. "Wait, what do you mean, 'calling Peter?' Did you talk to him?" She stays silent, and I feel the back of my neck prickle. "Mom?"

"I *might* have phoned your sperm donor today," she admits at last in an aggrieved huff. "It was a moment of weakness, and I'm not proud of it."

"Why?" I ask, surprised to find that it's actually still possible for my night to get worse. With one possible exception—me—nothing good has ever resulted from any kind of contact between Peter Covington and Genevieve Holt.

Sixteen years ago, my mother was a bright-eyed, twenty-five-year-old interior designer and art consultant, new to the city of Burlington, Vermont, and the proud owner of a small firm bearing her name. She'd done three years of art school, dropping out when an internship with a major decorator in New York turned into a full-time job she couldn't refuse, and then eventually followed her heart to New England. Thanks to a modest inheritance from my grandparents—a, by all accounts, quirky and lovable couple who ran a country store in a small Maine village, taught their kids to pursue their dreams, and unfortunately died before I could ever meet them—she was able to rent an office, hang out her shingle, and take on private clients.

It wasn't always easy. Work came in when the economy was up, and vanished when it went down, leaving her scrambling to cover the bills; and so, when a law firm by the name of Pembroke, Landau, and Wells offered her a massive chunk of cash to help them choose a few impressively priceless works of art for their offices, she was overjoyed to accept. When she met their junior partner, a Harvard legacy by the name of Peter Covington II, she was quickly swept off her feet. He was tall and handsome, with blond hair and gray eyes, and he was utterly charmed by the bohemian and unpredictable free spirit that was the young Genevieve. They were a total mismatch, his white-collar starchiness at complete odds with her offbeat *joie de vivre*, but—in my mom's mind, at least—the sparks their differences generated were what fueled their romance.

The sparks worked their magic for approximately two weeks before my mom discovered that Peter Covington was in fact married, that he had a toddler at home—a little boy named Hayden—and that most of the things he'd said to her in private were a pack of lies. She ended things immediately, with a fiery speech that she has a tendency to recount verbatim whenever she's had a little too much white wine, and then spent a few months debating whether or not to rat the man out to his wife. When she learned that she was pregnant, it was merely the icing on the cake.

I was born into the midst of an ugly war that continues to this day, erupting in periodic skirmishes as Peter Covington tries to ruin my mother's career and life, and she sues him repeatedly for slander and back child support. Peter's wife, Isabel, amazingly has stuck by him through the whole lengthy ordeal; supposedly, April was born to save their marriage, but I suspect a prenup is the real reason their matrimonial bonds have never been torn asunder.

Peter wouldn't have anything to do with me; in sixteen years, I've never received so much as a birthday card from him. When I was a kid, he fascinated me—my wealthy and elusive father, who lived in a beautiful home and drove a fancy car—but I only made the mistake of calling him Dad once, when I was five years old and he came by our house to deliver some personal message to my mom; his reaction, which was swift, furious, and terrifying, permanently cured me of my misplaced affection. In an emergency, my mother would have turned to the *Cloverfield* monster for help before asking for a favor from Peter Covington—and if she'd called him now, it could only mean one thing.

"How broke are we?" I ask flatly, when her silence becomes unbearable. My thoughts fragment inside my skull. Fox's corpse is practically looming over my shoulder, but the poverty my mom and I struggle against is a black hole with its own inescapable gravity; I can't avoid it, so I might as well dive in instead and give myself a little more time to think about how I'll bring up the *dead body* I've just discovered.

She takes a hesitant breath. "It's not for you to worry about, kiddo."

"Mom."

"I've got it under control, Rufus."

The lie is so threadbare, it's impossible to let it pass unchallenged. "You said you'd rather take a bath with a lawn mower than ask that ass-butt for money again! You'd never have called him unless it was really serious." More silence follows, and I bite the inside of my cheek as the bottom drops out of my stomach. *How much worse is this night going to get?* "How bad is it?"

"Ruf—"

"Please, Mom, just . . . tell me." I've made my way to the rear of the cottage now, and I lean tiredly over another porch rail, crickets underscoring the deceptively tranquil view of dark water spreading toward the far shore. The moon glares brightly down at the Whitneys' cottage like the spotlight from a police helicopter, and I duck my head. "Whatever it is, my imagination'll only make it worse."

"We owe the bank about eight grand," my mother confesses miserably, "and, okay, it's kind of . . . urgent." It's only the fourth of the month, and she's already panicked enough to appeal to my father; that means this is an old debt, a compounded one, and she's starting to get desperate. "I can scrape together about a quarter of it if I can get your uncle Connor to pay back the money I loaned him last Christmas. But . . ."

She trails off, my stomach heaves again, and just like that I feel the phantom grip of Fox's cooling fingers at the base of my neck. I called my mom about a *murder* and now we're talking about the chance that we might lose our house? The ground seems to tilt sharply under my feet, pressure grips at my chest, and I struggle for air.

My mom's all I've got; my whole life, it's just been the two of us, holding hands to ride out the storm; and too often, the storm has been *me*. Somewhere inside me lurks a volatile Mr. Hyde, an alter ego driven by an engine of combustible anger I've only recently found any success in mastering. Swept up in the inner hurricane of my rage, I've screamed and ranted, broken dishes and bones, terrorized my teachers—and provided my father with ammunition in his agenda against us. How many phone calls has she gotten from school officials over the years because I lost control and broke the glass on a trophy case or attacked someone in class?

And she's stood by me through all of it. I owe her so much. I owe her everything. How much more can she take? My mouth clicks dryly, my free hand tightening on the wooden rail. "I've been working all year, Mom. I can help—"

"*No.* Absolutely not, no way!" She's so vehement I can practically hear her hand karate-chopping the air. "I will *not* let you spend your money on this, Rufus Holt. Do you hear me? These are my mistakes, not yours, and if—if—"

She stops altogether, and I can picture her again: glasses in her lap, fingers pressed hard against her lips, mouth trembling as she tries not to cry. The lake smears in front of me, black and gray and blue all running together, and I blink hard. None of this is fair. "It affects me, too, Mom. It's my house, too."

"I'll take care of it. If I have to sell my organs on the black market, I will handle it. Okay?" She puts some steel in her tone. "Your shithead sperm donor owes us so much by now I would own this fucking place outright if he'd pay up."

"Don't hold your breath," I mumble weakly.

"I'm sorry, kiddo. All that . . . let's strike it from the record and start over. What did April do this time?"

Reflexively, I turn around and peer back into the cottage through the broad French doors of the family room. The fixtures of the kitchen gleam menacingly at the front of the house, and Sebastian stands near the fireplace, watching me with brightly nervous eyes and radiating an inarticulate terror of being alone inside with a corpse. I know I should tell her what we've found . . . but how can I? She's already in a lousy place; the first thing she'd do would be call the police—or, worse, Peter—and there would go any chance for me to take control of my involvement in the situation.

I'm not exactly one of the Bad Kids, but my history of anger-related behavioral issues are well documented, and cops don't really seem to care much about your GPA when they already remember you from the time you lost your shit in the eighth grade and knocked a bully's tooth out with the back of a chair. Especially when your own father prosecuted the bully's subsequent lawsuit against the school district and publicly called you a "dangerous animal." Thanks to a good therapist and the right medication, my moods have stabilized a lot since then, but the president of the school board is just waiting for the proper excuse to expel me—and having been suspended once this year already, my situation is precarious.

I haven't thought things out, I realize; once my mom learns what's happened, there will be no taking it back. I need to know more. I just need a little more time.

"It's nothing," I mumble at last. "Don't worry about it."

As I disconnect, though, it is with the distinct sensation that—somehow, in some way—the Covingtons have just ruined my life yet again.

3

"WHO WERE YOU TALKING TO?" SEBASTIAN DEMANDS THE SECOND I let myself back in through the doors of the family room, stepping carefully around the glass fragments that litter the glossy floorboards. The music is off now, and so is the sound of water rushing through the pipes in the bathroom April is done with her shower. "I thought you said we shouldn't call the cops!"

"Five minutes ago, you wanted to call the cops," I point out, startled by his about-face. From my new perspective, in the middle of the family room, the disarranged furniture looks like evidence of a struggle; the chairs have been knocked rather than pushed aside, and the glass inset of the coffee table is feathered with cracks.

"Five minutes ago, I hadn't had a chance to look around yet," Sebastian counters with quiet urgency. He comes closer, his soft, dark eyes gazing steadily back into mine, and a painfully happy memory zings through me like an electric shock. "Rufus, who were you talking to?"

"My mom, all right?"

"You told your mom?" Aghast, he stares at me, his face turning gray again in an instant.

"No, I didn't. It was just . . . forget it, it doesn't matter. What did you mean about having a chance to look around? What did you find?"

Wordlessly, he leads me away from the scattered furniture and into the dining nook. There are paintings on the wall of sailboats and harbors, a sideboard with bric-a-brac and iron candlesticks, and a blocky wooden table holding up a bounty of all sorts of things kids our age are not supposed to be into. There are jugs of cheap wine, an open case of cheaper beer, and about a half-dozen bottles of liquor that are nearly empty; an ashtray bristles like a porcupine with cigarette butts; and a broad hand mirror shows unmistakable traces of white powder, a tightly-rolled dollar bill resting alongside it.

Mr. Hyde is already fighting to surface within me, some hot, dark emotion clawing at my chest like heartburn, when Sebastian directs my attention to the small white pills that lay scattered everywhere across the floor like rice at a wedding; there are so many of them, strewn about so haphazardly that they're impossible to count. With shaking fingers, I turn one over, revealing the telltale stamp pressed into the top side of the tablet: the outline of a rabbit.

"White rabbits, man," Sebastian notes the obvious. "A shitload of them."

Rage sweeps over me so fast that lights actually flash in my eyes. My brain feels like it's spinning, exploding, and melting all at the same time, and I become dizzy from the heat building in my face and neck. *What the fuck has April gotten me into?*

Migrating from the New York club scene, "white rabbit" is a designer drug known to cause euphoria, heightened sensory perception, and hallucinations. The pills have also been linked, notoriously, to acts of extreme violence—like, trying-to-exfoliate-your-neighbor-with-a-belt-sander extreme—and parents everywhere are terrified of them. We had two assemblies about drug abuse at Ethan Allen this past spring alone, after white rabbits turned up in a couple of arrests on campus at the university. Get caught smoking a joint or taking some of your best friend's Adderall and you'll be in trouble; get caught with white rabbits and you're *fucked*. They've replaced bath salts as the latest version of History's Most Dangerous Substance Ever, and local authorities come down like a guillotine on anyone caught buying, selling, or using them.

Rumors make the rounds at Ethan Allen all the time about the various losers and burnouts using hard drugs, blotting out dismal visions of their uncertain futures with a chemical assist; and the bored, rich kids are notorious for spending their unwieldy allowances on recreational substances, counting on their trust funds and connected parents to protect them in the event of "legal complications." But what Sebastian and I stare at now is an order of a different magnitude.

Lucy and I swore a blood oath to each other, once upon a time, that we would never ever so much as *touch* white rabbits. For one thing, my brain chemistry is unpredictable enough as it is without adding hallucinogenic nightmares to the mix, and for another, I absolutely cannot afford the trouble that getting caught with white rabbits would bring me. My mom and I have no money and no prestige. My life would be ruined.

And April has invited me to a murder scene decorated with enough of them to fill a fucking beanbag chair.

"Hey—hey, Rufus? I need you to breathe, man, okay? Slow breaths. Like me, right? Do what I'm doing." Sebastian's voice penetrates the fog of my rage, his eyes level with mine again, his right hand locked with my own. "Take a step back, right? Say it."

"Take . . . a step back," I repeat, forcing myself to focus—on his face, on his touch. I struggle to control my breathing, and he moves my free hand to his chest, holding it there. He's done this for me before when my anger has taken over, talking me down from the ledge when I was perilously close to losing it, and the routine is heartbreakingly familiar. It felt so huge, so significant, to share such an awful part of myself with him—to be so unbalanced, and to know that I could trust him to be my counterweight.

He's looking at me, looking into me, and his eyes are warm, dark pools full of our shared history—windows into a past that's still too painful to touch.

The first time I really met Sebastian "Bash" Williams, it was at a meeting for the Front Line, *our school's sorry excuse for a newspaper. Everybody knew who he was, of course; Bash was too good-looking and his dad too important for him to fly under anyone's radar for long. But he and I didn't become personally acquainted until September of our sophomore year.*

I'd been working on the paper ever since I'd started at Ethan Allen, writing occasional editorials, but mostly serving as a photographer. Bash joined the staff as a sports columnist—a position for which our supervisor, Mr. Cohen, felt he was eminently qualified, based solely on the fact that 1) he played lacrosse, and 2) the guy's father was the athletic director at the university. It didn't make a lot of sense to me, but everyone on the Front Line *was so impressed by*

Bash's lacrosse stats—and his looks—that they didn't really care. For some even less explicable reason, Mr. Cohen assigned me *to act as Bash's personal photographer, shooting the pictures that would accompany his articles.*

It was not an easy partnership in the beginning. Bash's popularity elevated him well above my own meager social standing, putting him into the orbit of Ethan Allen's student royalty. He hung out with guys like Fox Whitney and Race Atwood—and, thusly, my brother, Hayden, as well. Natural enemies, Sebastian and I were antagonistic from the moment we were introduced, boring holes into each other with iron glares.

Over the course of the next two months, however, things slowly changed. Our mutual hostility proved too difficult to maintain when we were forced to sit together in the same car for hours a couple times a week, driving back and forth to different away games. I started to realize that he actually was *a pretty good sports writer after all, and the atmosphere between us gradually shifted from open animosity to resentful cooperation to a grudging but necessary pact of silent non-aggression. Finally, at a football game in Brattleboro the week before Thanksgiving, Bash Williams actually spoke to me in a genuinely friendly way for the first time ever.*

I was rummaging through my bag, digging for a camera lens that had gotten lost in the other useless crap that I kept in there, and I had hauled a bunch of items out in order to make the search easier. Right on top of the disordered pile I was creating beside me sat a battered and dog-eared copy of Love*—the fourth volume from the most badass manga series of all time.*

"Dude," Bash blurted unexpectedly, a spark of something unfamiliar glimmering in his eyes. "Are you seriously reading Death Note?"

"Uh . . . yeah?" Aware that this might be a trap, I kept my answer guarded. But Bash surprised me.

"That story is the shit!" He couldn't keep his excitement under control. "I don't want to give anything away or whatever, but by the time you finish that? You're gonna have lost your mind. What part are you up to?"

"Actually? I'm kind of rereading it. For the third time," I admitted, eyeing him with a curious level of newfound respect. I didn't think popular kids were into anything except the Top 40, other popular kids, and ganging up on nerds. "You like manga?"

"I mean, sorta." He shrugged sheepishly. "My girlfriend's little brother, Javier? He's, like, nuts about anime and stuff. All last summer he was bugging me to read Death Note." Bash was in a very high-profile on-again-off-again relationship with Lia Santos—the kind of obnoxiously torrid love affair that involved tons of handsy PDA in school hallways, followed by tons of screaming arguments also in school hallways, a breakup, a make-up, lather, rinse, repeat. Paying attention to them was exhausting. "I finally agreed, just to get him to lay off, and . . . man, once I started it, I stayed up for thirty-six hours straight and finished the whole series. I mean, I think I literally know what it feels like to come down off a meth binge now."

"I know what you mean," I said with a short laugh. "The first time I read it was back in the seventh grade, and I didn't sleep for about a week, because I was convinced that maybe it was really possible to kill somebody just by writing it in a notebook."

He grinned. "You did?"

"It's really embarrassing." I felt my face turning red, but I smiled anyway, because he didn't seem to be mocking me.

"I get it. I, uh . . . I actually maybe kinda slept with the light on for a few days after I finished?" he confessed, rubbing the back of his head. "And that was last August."

"It's freaky as hell," I agreed.

"It's awesome," *he returned, seriously. "Have you read Blue Exorcist? It's wild—it's all about the son of Satan learning to fight demons so he can bring down his dad. The action sequences are rad as hell."*

"I've heard of it."

"You should check it out," Bash said, his eyes not quite meeting mine. "I'm, like, obsessed, and . . . and I'm sick of not having anybody to talk to about it."

For a second, I wasn't sure how to react. This sudden and unexpected olive branch was difficult to process and harder to trust, given our history; but at last, I said, "I will. It sounds really cool."

He looked at me then, and smiled; and there was a quality to it that was shy and sincere and searching, and I felt something warm flip over in my chest.

And, just like that, I realized the horrible truth: I had a crush on Bash Williams.

As soon as the spinning in my brain begins to slow, the throbbing fire in my chest to subside, I break my contact with Sebastian and step away. No matter how much I trusted him in the past, I can't anymore—and maybe never should have.

"You okay?" He asks gently, and the compassion in his voice is almost more than I can bear.

"I'm fine." I look past him to the kitchen, where Fox's head is just visible behind the island, a dark mass in a spoiling pool of scarlet-black blood. Weirdly enough, it helps me get a hold of myself, like a sudden cold-water bath. "I'm all right." Stiffly, but not without real gratitude, I mutter, "Thanks."

"Did you find anything outside?"

"Not really. No bloody footprints or whatever, and pretty much every room in the cottage has a door that opens onto the porch. This place is at the ass-end of nowhere, though. No one came in off the street and did this. Either it was April, or . . ."

Only I don't have an *or.* At the moment, there's no better explanation. It's pretty obvious that April and Fox weren't alone in the house all night; in addition to the massive supply of drugs and alcohol on the dining table, grocery bags heaped atop the kitchen island disgorge a sick-making bounty of junk food. Brightly colored packages of chips and candy have been ripped open, many of them half-empty, and crumbs litter the counter. There were people here—but who and when and how many, we won't know until April comes out of the bedroom.

I turn to say something and catch Sebastian flicking his eyes away. "What?"

"Huh?" He glances back, trying and failing to effect an innocently blank expression—his who-me? face. He used it all the time when we were together, and he was terrible at it.

"You were looking at me. What?"

"Nothing, it's just . . ." Sebastian shrugs, and his eyes do that down-up thing over my torso again. "Have you been working out or something?"

My face heats up again, this time with embarrassment, and I cross my arms self-consciously over my bare chest. I wanted him to notice, of course; this is basically the moment I've been imagining, repeatedly, for the past six weeks: Sebastian seeing the hot new Rufus Holt, wishing he could have me back and hating himself for letting me go. Only the situation is all wrong, Fox's grisly death crowding the moment, and my ex-boyfriend's puzzled eyes seem to track the changes to my body with only clinical interest.

And, just like that, I feel humiliated all over again. Even standing in the middle of an *actual crime scene* I can't escape how much I've let him get inside my head. How much I want Sebastian Williams to still want me, and how much it hurts that he doesn't.

To my utter relief, the door to the master suite pops open at just that moment, and April sidles meekly into the room. She's wearing jean shorts and a loose-fitting shirt, her auburn hair falling to her shoulders in damp, tousled ropes. Her face is still drawn and colorless, but her eyes look way more alert.

"How are you feeling?" I ask neutrally, moving toward her through the wreckage of the family room.

She stares, her expression flat. "Better, I guess. Um . . . thanks." Her gaze drifts toward the kitchen and fixes in place, like a missile system locking onto target. There's no way she can see Fox from the little vestibule, but the presence of his body commands attention nevertheless. "Is, um . . . is he still . . . ?"

"You want to go into the bedroom to talk?"

April gives a minute and almost frightened nod, and then the three of us retreat through the door, shutting it again for good measure. My little sister sinks down on the edge of the bed, letting her hair fall into her face, while I straddle a shabby-chic chair placed in front of a shabby-chic vanity. Sebastian stays close, breathing more easily now that a physical barrier stands between Fox and him.

"What happened tonight, April?" I prompt.

She sniffles, picking at the dark polish on the nails of her right hand, and says, to my left kneecap, "I'm not sure. I mean, I don't really remember."

"Try to think," I suggest through my teeth, already thin on patience, just like that. "You called me for help, right? I can't help if you don't tell me anything."

"But I don't *know* anything, Rufus." Her voice shakes, her big blue eyes meeting mine, filled with tears. "We were having a party, and I got tired so I came in here to lie down, and then . . . when I woke up, I was in the kitchen, and . . . and Fox, he, he . . ."

She starts to cry, dropping her head forward as her shoulders quake and loud, mucusy snorts sound from behind the curtain of her hair. April wipes her face with her hands over and over, until Sebastian leans past me to swipe some tissues and hand them to her. She accepts them wordlessly and, after a few moments, lifts her chin again.

I'm not sure what it says about me as a person, but I spend a good, long moment studying her expression for possible evidence of bullshit before I speak again. "What were you on when we got here?"

"Nothing," she declares, impossibly.

My jaw goes tight. "Don't lie."

"I'm not!"

"April, when we found you in the kitchen, you were so fucked up, you couldn't even walk," I remind her, heat slowly turning my brain into a tropical greenhouse. "There's an avalanche of coke and pills in the dining room that you could slide down with a toboggan, and you want us to believe you were sober?"

"I didn't take anything!" She practically screeches it this time, and I almost think she's telling me the truth. "I never use that

stuff! Fox . . . I mean, okay, he got me try some things once or twice—but I *hated* the way they made me feel!"

"Even white rabbits?"

"Especially that shit." She shudders. "I took some once and I thought plants were growing under my skin. I almost cut my arm open trying to let them out."

Sebastian and I exchange a perplexed glance, and I turn back to my sister. She looks me in the eye, her expression level and grim. If she's lying, she's gotten a lot better at it than the last time we faced off—but if she's telling the truth, it makes no sense. "Look, just . . . let's start from the beginning. Who was here tonight, and what happened?"

April takes a breath. "We were having a Fourth of July party, you know? Fox's parents went to New York so he knew the cottage would be empty, and he told everybody to come over."

"And by everybody you mean Race and Peyton?" I venture, naming Fox's and April's respective best friends—who also happen to be a couple.

She nods. "And Arlo Rossi, and . . . some other people."

Her eyes dart to Sebastian when she says this, but just as quickly drop back to my kneecap. I'm intrigued, but decide not to press her on it. At least, not yet. "Okay, so Peyton and Race and Arlo came out here, and you guys had a party, and then what?"

"And then I don't know," she says helplessly, her voice small and shaky again. "Honestly, Rufus, I didn't take anything—all I had was a couple drinks, but maybe they were stronger than I thought, because, like . . . there's just this big *blank*! Last thing I remember, everybody was over here, and then . . . then I wake up in the kitchen, and Fox is on the floor next to me and, and . . ." She trails off, hiccupping, and slaps a hand to her mouth. For a moment,

I'm afraid she's about to barf, but then she asks, "Is he really dead?"

I shift in the stupid little chair. "Yeah, April, he is."

She shakes her head in disbelief, auburn tresses swinging, and squeezes her eyes shut. A couple of tears roll silently down her colorless cheeks. "I didn't kill him. You have to believe me."

With some difficulty, I ignore her grasp for my heartstrings, determined to stay clearheaded—to not let my creeping sentimentality for April Covington get in the way of my judgment. I'm rattled enough as it is, with pink shadows of Fox's blood still dappling my wet shorts, and I can't afford to be softhearted right now. I try to remember all my reasons not to trust her, but our past keeps intruding on my perception.

In the eighth grade, when the stage-whispered rumors of my sexuality were publicly confirmed, April stunned me by being the second person—after Lucy—to voice her support. The day I learned that my secret and I were both officially *out* was horrific, and after the final bell rang, I fled our school for the privacy of a wooded rise behind the soccer field. All I wanted was to finally get a chance to cry without an audience of jeering, scornful thirteen-year-olds, but my half sister somehow managed to track me down.

"I don't care," she blurted in a quiet rush the second I noticed her, copper sunlight gilding her face as she looked up at me. "I don't care that you're gay, I mean. It doesn't make any difference to me. I don't think there's anything wrong with it, and I think Cody and Eric are shitheads for making fun of you and stuff."

"Thanks," I answered awkwardly, befuddled by her sympathy and lacking for anything more meaningful to say. Cody Barnes was

one of Hayden's many acolytes, willing to hurt me in any number of trivial ways if it would catch his hero's attention, but Eric Shetland had—until that very morning—been one of my closest friends. I was so stung by his betrayal that no one's actions seemed to make sense to me anymore.

"Hayden's a shithead, too." April's cheeks flushed with the guilty pleasure of saying it out loud. "He's so mean. All the time. I mean, you're lucky you don't have to live with him." She glanced over her shoulder instinctively, as if afraid saying his name might actually conjure his presence, and then went on in a fervent undertone, "Honestly, Rufus? Sometimes I wish he was dead. Sometimes I wish you *were my real brother and Hayden didn't even exist!"*

Without warning, April suddenly threw her arms around me—our first actual embrace—and then, while I was still reeling from the unexpected show of affection, she turned and dashed away toward the school.

Willfully blanking the memory, I ask April, "Where was your phone?" The question seems to confuse her, so I back up. "You woke up next to Fox, and then you called me. Where was your phone?"

She makes a bewildered face. "I guess I had it with me. I don't really know."

"You didn't have to go looking for it?"

"I don't think so. I mean, if I had, I wouldn't have still been sitting next to Fox when you got here." She shivers a little.

"So why did you call me?" I finally ask, after tallying up everything she's said. I'm pretty sure I have the reason figured out, though, and am anticipating her answer with a growing sense of prickly unease.

"Don't you get it?" She fixes me with a haunted look. "All my friends were *here*. The last thing I remember, we were all having a big party; and then all of a sudden, I'm waking up, my boyfriend is *dead*, and I'm here all by myself? They *left* me, Rufus." With both hands, she drags her hair back from her face, and whispers, "I didn't do it. I know I didn't. But that means . . . it means—"

"One of them is the killer," Sebastian concludes, rubbing his eyes. "Fuck." I can tell he's regretting whatever impulse compelled him to seek me out tonight, whatever guilt or curiosity made him so eager to drive me to South Hero Island so he could stumble over the dead body of one of his friends.

"I didn't do it," April repeats insistently, searching my face with the piteous desperation of an orphaned beggar. "You know me, Rufus, I could never have done something like this!" The point is, frankly, equivocal, but before I can address it, she's already moving on to the true purpose of her summons. "You have to get me out of here, okay? I've already bagged up my bikini—we can throw it in the lake, and—"

"April—"

"They left me here to take the blame for something I didn't do!" My half sister's pitch begins to rise, her cheeks becoming blotchy. "This isn't like getting caught drinking with your loser friends, *Rufus*," she fires at me stingingly, a weapon tailored to fit my dubious record. "I could go to fucking *jail*! Actual fucking *jail*!"

"And if I do what you're asking me to, *I* could go to fucking jail," I shoot back, my vision starting to shimmer as my anger soars above and beyond the call of duty. "Even if you throw out your bathing suit—even if we wipe your prints off the knife and every other damn thing in this place—Fox's parents are *still* going to find him dead in the kitchen, the cops are *still* going to find a metric shit-ton of drugs in the dining room, and all your friends are *still* going to say that the last time they saw your boyfriend alive, he was *alone in the house with you*." I guzzle air into my lungs, having ranted all that in a single breath. "Don't *you* get it, April? You can't cover this up, and if you try, it's only going to look worse!"

She goes quiet again, her lips clamping into a narrow line, and we glower at each other for a long moment. I know her better than she thinks; I can see the wheels turning behind her lucid, blue eyes. Most of the people in her life are susceptible to her manipulations because they want to please her, but her tears and tantrums won't work on me. She's actively calculating my weaknesses, looking for another access point.

"Okay, you're right," she finally says. "I guess I wasn't thinking. But you can't just call the cops, Rufus. Dad—*our* dad—will kill me. You know he will."

This is also debatable. Peter's rages are infamous—and I would know, having both suffered and inherited them—but he and Isabel treat April with the care and handling of a holy relic. The man would lose his shit if his daughter became implicated in a murder, but it's hard to picture him actually taking it out on her. However, the fact of the matter is that I really have no idea what goes on behind closed doors in the Covington household.

"So what exactly are you suggesting?" I ask warily.

"I know about your mom's phone call today," she reveals, having found her access point at last, and I feel a metaphorical trapdoor swing open under my feet. "I know you guys need money, and I'm willing to pay you—"

"I'm not taking money to help you cover up a murder," I declare hotly, thrown off-center by how humiliatingly accurate her read on me is.

"Not for that," she insists, leaning forward, the tendons in her hands standing out in high relief as she grips the coverlet. "You're smart, Rufus—everybody knows it. Remember when we were in that summer reading group thing, and you solved all those little mysteries or whatever? Maybe you can figure out what happened tonight!"

"April, I was *eleven*," I splutter, appalled, "and they were just a bunch of dumb riddles with the answers already built in!" The "summer reading group thing" was an activity sponsored by the public library, a way for parents to ditch their kids for a couple hours a day and feel good about it. A condescendingly perky volunteer read us a bunch of two-page mystery stories—tales of theft and people being bonked over the head—where finding the solution was as easy as identifying simple inconsistencies woven into the narrative. A man claims he was getting the mail when his neighbor was robbed, for instance, only this supposedly happened on a Sunday, when there is no mail delivery. It was kid stuff, and I only succeeded where the others failed because the others didn't try. "This is real life—this is a *real fucking murder*—and I wouldn't even know where to start! Even if I could figure it out, we'd have to go to the police anyway."

"I know," she whispers defenselessly, her chin wobbling. "But just . . . please, Rufus. *Please*. I don't mean you need to catch whoever did it, but I need help. Really, really bad." Tears splash down her cheeks, and I suddenly realize how authentic her fear is. "All I want you to do is talk to the people who were at the party and see what they say. Maybe you'll be able to tell if one of them is lying, you know? Maybe somebody will, like, give themselves away? And then we can go to the police and tell them what we know. Everything. That's all I'm asking."

I sigh, a headache beginning to beat at my temples like a blacksmith pounding out a horseshoe. "April—"

"I've got two thousand dollars, in cash, and I'll pay you all of it if you help me figure out who really killed Fox." She cuts me off decisively, and my jaw lands in my lap. "Two grand, Rufus—no questions asked—if you agree to go talk to everyone. Just talk. And then, no matter what, we go to the police. Okay?"

I can see in her eyes that going to the police scares her beyond measure; I can also see that she's dead serious about that two grand. I know it would be lunacy to agree—and my permanent record doesn't really have the cushion to absorb a lot of cataclysmically bad life choices—but she's nailed my Achilles' heel on her first try. Even as I tell myself I need to say no, I'm mentally reviewing the reasons to justify saying yes.

My eyes fall to the clock on the Whitneys' bedside table, bright red digits reminding me of our limited time. "When are Fox's parents due back from New York?"

"Not for a few days," April answers, studying my face with quiet intensity.

I nod. No danger there. I won't be interfering with a police investigation because, as yet, there *is* no investigation; I won't be removing or destroying any evidence; and we'll ultimately go to the police and report the crime ourselves anyway. More to the point: *April* will report the crime—and any theoretical damage done by her leaving the crime scene was already done by my dragging her into the shower in order to wake her up, anyway. There's no way to undo that, but we can still mitigate how guilty it looks by calling the police before they even know there's been a murder in the first place.

But all that is incidental. The only thing that truly matters is that my mom owes the bank eight thousand dollars, and doesn't know where to get it. She has a little less than two thousand at hand; I have a little more than two in my savings—which I'll make her accept, no matter what she says; add April's two and, even though it won't hit the target, it'll still bring us to within a respectable margin. Maybe even close enough to buy a temporary extension on the remainder.

Even if it doesn't pan out that way, though, it's worth the gamble. It's all worth the gamble. Even if I'm ultimately expelled for getting involved in whatever psychotic drama has unfurled at Fox's cottage, it's still better than being homeless—and if we get evicted anyway, my transcript will be the least of my concerns.

Squeezing my eyes shut for just a second, I take a deep breath and then nod at April. "Okay. I'll do it."

4

WORDLESSLY, MY SISTER BENDS DOWN AND DRAGS A BACKPACK out from under the bed, where it's been hidden by the lacy curtain of a dust ruffle. She rummages through a couple of pockets before finding and extracting a fat wad of paper currency—rolled into a rubber-banded cylinder thick enough to choke a zebra—which she then hands over to me. "You can count it if you want, but it's two grand. All yours, no matter what."

She probably means it to sound comforting, but I'm starting to feel the dry heaves coming on again. Nobody just carries around two thousand dollars in cash like that. It was either intended for something illicit, or was already used for something illicit, and as I sit there adding the tens to the twenties to the fifties, my misgivings redouble. It didn't escape my notice that April had to search the backpack to find the money, or that from one of the bag's zippers there dangled a highly recognizable keychain—a cast-pewter emblem of two intersecting lacrosse sticks. It was Fox's bag, and Fox's cash, and the less I knew about it the better off I'd be.

"Okay," I begin unevenly, cramming exactly two thousand dollars into the driest pocket of my damp cargo shorts, "how many people were at the party?"

"Six," April answers promptly. The math is easy, but the equation puzzling nonetheless: April + Fox, Peyton + Race, and Arlo + "some other people" = six. Before I can ask who the sixth person is, and why she's being so deliberately evasive about it, she's already continuing, "It was supposed to be low-key—just our group, you know? Fox was sick of having parties where half the school showed up and somebody broke something or spilled beer on his mom's work stuff, so this was only our inner circle."

"So what happened?" Sebastian asks carefully, having not missed the defensive inflection in April's voice. Clearly, there had been some sort of trouble even before she supposedly slept through a gruesome murder.

My half sister goes quiet for a moment, just long enough for me to realize that what she plans to tell us will be edited somehow, and then she admits, "There was a fight. Arlo and Fox . . . got into a fight."

"About what?" I ask.

"I don't know." She shrugs, appearing truthful enough. "I was out back, in the hot tub, and we heard the two of them shouting. By the time we made it up to the porch, they were throwing punches and stuff. Then Fox told Arlo to get out, and he left."

"What time was that?"

"I don't know," she repeats guiltily. "Maybe, like, a half an hour before . . . before I blacked out or whatever?"

The ending of the statement is so blatantly hijacked and

directed away from its initial destination that it leaves me momentarily at a loss for words, allowing Sebastian to interject, "So, as far as you remember, Arlo was long gone by the time you fell asleep?"

"Maybe. I mean, I guess?" Immediately, April starts retreating back into Little Girl Lost mode, all Bambi eyes and self-deprecating chagrin, and I have to fight the urge to shake her again. "Like, I don't actually remember hearing his bike leave, but even if he did take off, he could have come back while I was passed out, you know?"

"Look," I state, partly unhappy and partly relieved, "if Arlo killed him, you might as well take your money back. That dude fucking hates me, and he's not going to tell me shit. *Especially* not if he did it."

Arlo Rossi had just graduated from Ethan Allen that spring, alongside Hayden, and he could quite possibly be Mother Nature's most egregious act of criminal malpractice. Where Hayden effects the self-consciously preppy look of a sex-murderer from the 1980s, Arlo is equally committed to inhabiting the role of the stereotypical local badass; he has a motorcycle, an ugly haircut, and a tattoo on his neck that looks like a leopard barfing flames. He and Hayden had never exactly been friends, but they were both popular and feared—and their own personal Molotov-Ribbentrop Pact, dividing the school and its student body into spheres of influence, had designated me a zone of mutual hostility. Accidentally-on-purpose slamming me into walls for fun was one of the few things they enjoyed doing together.

"You can at least try, though, right?" She demands indignantly. "It's not like he's gonna beat you up just for asking him a few questions!"

I grit my teeth, exasperated by her cluelessness. "April, Arlo would beat me up for no reason at all, let alone if I start asking questions about a party where he might have just killed somebody. He's not going to let me get past 'Hey, how's it going?' before he puts a steel-toed boot up my ass!"

"He'll talk to me." Sebastian says, surprising us both. I glance over at him, but his gaze is fixed on the floor, his posture taut as a leather strap. When he looks up, I see conflict swimming in his eyes—fear and conviction chasing each other on an endless loop—and he takes in a deep breath. "We get along okay. We're not, like, *friends* or whatever, but he'll probably answer the questions if I'm the one asking."

"You don't have to do that," I say automatically, the rejection backed by a symphony of collaborating motives. Where not so long ago I was full of excuses for why I wanted to see Sebastian one more time, I now only want to get him out of my life again. I'm still angry, still hurting, and—worst of all—still attracted to him, even after one week of panic, four weeks of tearful misery, and another week of trying to pretend he'd stopped existing. I'd convinced myself I could be over him, but now every time he looks at me, smiles at me, touches me, it feels *good*—which feels horrible; I'm starting to realize that I've never stopped missing him after all, and it terrifies me. "If you drop me off at my house, I'll get my mom's car. I'm pretty sure she's in bed by now."

"You just said yourself that Arlo won't talk to you," he counters, scrubbing his palms up and down his thighs in agitation, "and Race probably won't, either. I'm cool with those guys, though. Face it: You need me."

April watches this exchange with narrowing eyes, and finally, she gives voice to the question that I've also been wanting to ask all night long. "Bash, what are you doing here, anyway?"

"Um . . ." Sebastian freezes, blinking a distress signal. "We were . . . I was at a party—at the same party as Rufus when you called. And I've been out here before, so I offered to give him a ride."

The explanation clearly doesn't make sense to her. "But—"

"Where does Arlo live?" I interrupt, seizing the reins of the conversation. There's a lot I want to know about Sebastian's reappearance in my life—in spite of my better judgment—but I sure as hell don't need for it to come out in front of April. Besides, no matter how much my ex-boyfriend may have hurt me, I still feel the need to protect his secret. I had the right to come out on my own terms taken away from me, and it was devastating; no amount of self-righteousness would make me feel good about watching it happen to someone else. "Because, believe it or not, he's never invited me over before."

April just looks at me blankly, and then alley-oops the question to Sebastian, who offers a bewildered shrug. "I don't know, man. I've never been there, either."

"Awesome." I give an acerbic sigh. "We're off to a great start—we've got no idea where our prime suspect even lives. Not to be pessimistic, but what if we finally figure it out, and then he's not even home because he's lying low somewhere? You know, trying to avoid getting pulled into a murder investigation?"

"I can call him," April suggests.

"Don't." My tone is so forceful that she actually recoils. "April, if Arlo is the one who murdered Fox, then he's also the one who expects you to take the fall for it. Whoever left you here made sure your phone was sitting right next to you. Don't you get what

that means?" My response is another empty look. "It means they *wanted* you to call the police! They wanted the cops to come out here and find you all stoned out of your mind and covered in blood, lying next to the dead body of your boyfriend in a house filled with drugs known to cause violent episodes!"

"I told you I didn't *take* anything—"

"Fine! Whatever," I snap irritably, deciding not to make an issue out of it. There's no time. "Whoever did this is pretty confident the evidence will incriminate you, and they're expecting you to wake up and use your phone. If Arlo did it, and you call him, acting all casual, like, 'Oh, I was just curious to know where you are right now—no reason!' he's gonna know something's up. You've gotta be radio silent, April. I *mean* that."

"*Okay.*" She puts her hands up in a sulky surrender. Strangely, then, her eyes slide to Sebastian again before darting back to me. "There is someone else who would probably know where Arlo is. Who might even . . . you know, be with him."

"Who?"

April fingers a silver charm bracelet that encircles her wrist. "Lia."

Sebastian and I both stiffen at the same time, and I feel my eyes turning to granite as I refuse to look his way. His voice is guarded and perplexed as he seeks to clarify, "Lia *Santos*?"

"Yeah." April winces apologetically. "She and Arlo came here together. They're . . . well, anyway, I didn't know if you knew about them."

"No." Sebastian sounds totally hollow. "I didn't."

On the last Friday in May, I emerged from seventh period like a zombie, the act of putting one foot in front of the other requiring a superhuman effort. I trudged heavily through the halls to the classroom where the writers and editors of the Front Line *met after school, and slumped into a chair. There was nothing I wanted less than to spend one more hour sitting in a room full of oblivious people, pretending not to be heartsick and destroyed, but my mom couldn't pick me up until after the meeting—and it wasn't as if I'd have felt any less terrible in a different environment.*

And there was always the chance, I pathetically allowed myself to believe, that Sebastian would show up this time.

It had been exactly six days and nineteen hours since the last time I'd heard from him—six days and nineteen hours of unanswered texts and phone calls, of obsessively checking his Twitter, Instagram, and Facebook accounts for some indication of what he was thinking, of trying to figure out how I could fix whatever I'd done wrong.

I was literally nauseous. We'd been together for four months— four months! *The surreptitious smiles when no one else was looking, the heart-pounding kisses stolen in empty hallways or at our secret spot behind the theater, our date nights watching dumb horror movies and eating pizza, making out in his bedroom while his parents thought we were studying for a quiz in biology; it had all been so great and so exciting, an endless series of doors opening onto more meaningful, more important kinds of happiness. How, after all that, could he just shut me out with no explanation?*

Sebastian was a no-show at the meeting that day, though, and I placed my cell phone on the desk in front of me where I could see it in case he decided to text, the minutes ticking by unbearably as boring story ideas were pitched, reviewed, and assigned. There was a pep rally taking place in the gym, concurrent with our meeting, and the occasional interruption of cheers and rhythmic foot-stomping underscored our incongruously dull debate over whether it was appropriate for the Front Line *to openly criticize the actions of certain faculty members.*

Mr. Cohen was in the midst of splitting the finest of ideological hairs, simultaneously extolling the virtues of free speech while imploring us to keep our opinionated pieholes shut, when the urgent and approaching shriek of tennis shoes against linoleum in the hallway outside grabbed our collective attention. Two seconds later, Ramona Waverley—a pushy junior who was inexplicably, fiercely dedicated to the cause of our crappy high school newspaper—exploded into the room. Her face flushed and her eyes wild, she immediately exclaimed, "OMG, you guys! Oh em fucking *gee!"*

Mr. Cohen frowned with his entire body. "Ramona—"

"I'm sorry, Mr. C.," she apologized gravely for the profane outburst, "but this is, just, like, I mean. *I was at the pep rally, okay? And, like, we* have *to write about this in the paper, Mr. C., because* literally everybody *is going to be talking about it!"*

"Talking about what, Ramona?"

And so she told us. "Okay, you know how, like, at the rallies, teachers and players get up and say stuff to pump up the crowd? Like, giving speeches and whatever? Well, right after Coach Kowalski spoke, Bash *got up and took the microphone—even though he wasn't supposed to—and right in front of* literally everybody, *he* begged *Lia Santos to take him back! He said he'd never stopped loving her, and that breaking up with her four months ago was the biggest mistake he ever made, and then he* got down on his knees *and asked her to be his girlfriend again! And he actually started* crying *when she said yes!" Ramona could barely breathe. "It was* the *most romantic thing* ever. *Seriously, I almost died.* Everybody *almost died. This* has *to be in the paper."*

The room burst into conversation. Some girls up front cooed about how they wished a guy felt about them the way Bash felt about Lia, and a few cynics placed bets on how long this particular on-again phase would last for the mercurial supercouple.

I just stared at my cell phone through a solid, shimmering wall of unshed tears, aware that something meaningful and important had just broken inside of me.

Into the dead silence that follows April's unexpected disclosure, as she avoids looking at Sebastian, and Sebastian avoids looking at me, I speak through wooden lips. "Well, then, I guess our first step is talking to Lia."

Without another word, I get up from my chair, march to the bedroom door, and stomp out into the wrecked family room, where the air still reeks of Fox's curdling blood.

5

THE EFFECT OF MY FURIOUSLY DRAMATIC EXIT IS UNDERCUT pretty quickly when I remember that my shoes and tank top are still in the bathroom, and I have to go back and get them. I instruct April to collect her cell phone from the kitchen and, before either Sebastian or I can react, she snatches up a hand towel from the countertop and wipes her prints off the hilt of the knife. Defiantly, she announces, "I'm *not* going to jail for this. I didn't kill him, and I'm not going to let anybody frame me for it, either!"

It's too late to stop her, and I don't have the energy to speculate about what will happen if the cops learn what she's done, so we just usher her out of the cottage and down to where Sebastian's Jeep is parked. As we back our way into a three-point turn, the Whitneys' cottage looks eerily inhabited, windows spilling warm light onto the porch and bushes, and I can't suppress a small shiver as I think about what waits inside.

My fingers bother the seat belt again as I wonder how much time we've got. Every minute that passes is another opportunity for someone to find the body, someone to call the police. I'm pretty confident no one has alerted them yet; if any of the neighbors had heard the murder being committed, the place would have been swarming with cops way before Sebastian and I made the thirty-minute drive out here. And, to that point, the prospect of the hour here and back will probably discourage the party's guests from returning to the lake house so late at night, on the off chance anyone forgot something.

I repeat these facts to myself like a mantra, trying to stifle my anxiety, but it doesn't help much. Whoever punched all those holes into Fox is someone whose behavior I'm not sure I can predict; they left April's phone where she could reach it, presumably hoping she'd do the obvious—call her parents, or the police, and put Fox's murder on the map—but there's no way to be absolutely sure they don't intend to drop a dime on her and tip off the authorities themselves. What I've agreed to do is a huge gamble.

How far, I ask myself, am I really willing to take this quixotic performance before I hold April to her promise of going to the police, anyway? And how much do I really expect to learn from the cast of stuck-up, hostile characters who attended Fox's party? Next to nothing, if I were to be honest; but for two thousand dollars, I'd be willing to bang my head on a literal brick wall, so I figure I might as well give it a shot.

As the Jeep glides down that darkened tunnel of trees leading back to Route 2, I sneak a glance at Sebastian out of the corner of my eye and feel a perverse wave of pleasure when I see the tense and brooding look in his eyes. A malicious part of me—a part I'm not so proud of—gleefully anticipates what's about to come.

It was difficult, not being able to tell people about dating Sebastian—and lying to Lucy, in particular, was excruciating—but

I knew how sensitive the subject was. I understood the fear of damaged friendships and sobbing parents, the dread of the world turning against you because a twist of biological fate makes you Different. Keeping our relationship hidden wasn't always easy, but I did it because I cared about Sebastian. I did it because he needed me to, and because I'd have done almost anything for him.

By the time the Front Line *reconvened for its first meeting after winter break, I'd come to a horrible realization: I had fallen—* hard*—for a straight boy.*

The more articles Bash and I worked on together, the more I learned about him, and the more I began to let my guard down. He started laughing at my jokes, sharing secret thoughts, and even teasing me in a way that made this squirmy ribbon of warmth begin twisting in the pit of my stomach. I'd begun looking forward to those after-school meetings—to seeing Bash Williams smile as I walked through the door, to feeling the buzz of goofy self-consciousness if I caught him looking my way when somebody else was speaking. I'd really *begun looking forward to watching his cute, perfect butt move whenever he happened to be walking in front of me.*

It was awful. Bash Williams was not only friends with my sworn enemies, he also had a girlfriend*—and everybody knew he and Lia were epic. The problem was that I couldn't avoid him without quitting the paper, which I really didn't want to do, and I couldn't be close to him, either, because my stupid feelings kept getting worse.*

I had been silently agonizing over my frustrating crush for weeks before a fateful day in February when the two of us found ourselves alone in the office of the Front Line. *Unprompted, and after a long, curious silence, Bash rather awkwardly announced, "I broke up with Lia again."*

"Oh?" I looked up at him from the screen of my laptop, where I'd been toggling between two photos I was considering for the next issue, and tried to sound nonchalant. "Um . . . I'm sorry."

He shrugged, the motion stilted and off. "It's okay. I mean, it's . . . like, we've split up before? But this time I think it's for good. You know? I mean, I think I want it to be for good. I've started thinking . . . I don't know." He took a breath, and for a long, speechless moment, he seemed inexplicably terrified. He licked his lips, took another breath. "I think . . . I think maybe I'm kind of into somebody else?"

The whole time he'd been speaking, he'd been fumbling with his phone, twisting it around and around in an agitated motion, like he couldn't figure out which way he wanted it. And then he glanced over at me, and I saw something in his eyes that made my stomach wonky and my neck hot. We just looked at each other for what felt like a hundred and fifty years, my heart thumping so hard my eardrums almost blew out; and then he moved closer, until I could smell his citrus and vetiver cologne . . . and then he kissed me.

It was a revelation. I was one of, like, three openly gay kids at our dumb school, and I had literally never had a real kiss before. It was almost aggressive, like he was afraid I would bolt and he wanted to make sure it happened before I could escape; and then he drew back and we just stared at each other some more in startled silence.

And then he kissed me again, and it was even more *aggressive, and my pulse went so fast I could hear it hum, my lungs empty and full all at once, and in my head I just kept thinking,* This is real, this is happening, I can't believe this is really happening.

A second later, we heard footsteps outside the door, and Bash jerked away from me just as Mr. Cohen entered the room. I was dumbstruck, the afterglow of our kiss burning on my lips, while

Bash snatched his backpack up from the floor like a thief startled by flashing blue lights.

"I gotta run," he announced in an unnaturally thin voice. "See you later."

And then he was out the door. I was so thrown by what had happened, my thoughts such a maelstrom of hope and glee and confusion that I couldn't concentrate on anything Mr. Cohen asked me for the next ten minutes. I ended up choosing one of the photos at random, my heart smashing around my ribcage like a wrecking ball.

That was only the beginning. After that first amazing kiss, Sebastian was always finding excuses for us to be alone together, pressing his mouth to mine the second we had a little privacy, and not stopping until both of us were lightheaded and short of breath. He wasn't ready for people to know yet, and begged me not to tell anyone about us. Eager to make him happy—and not especially anxious to deal with the added attention such news would bring me—I promised him it would be our secret.

In a way, the clandestine nature of our relationship made it even more exciting. The coded glances in public, the way his foot would find mine under the table during meetings for the *Front Line*, the way we'd arrange to request bathroom passes at the same time so we could meet behind the theater and make out—all of it felt supercharged and sexily dramatic. It bothered me that Sebastian still flirted openly with girls, even right in front of me, because I knew he still actually *liked* girls; but I also knew why he felt the need to do it, and I believed all the things he said to me in private—how special I was, how happy I made him, how good he felt when we were together—and so I plastered over my jealousies and let myself fall into him.

It feels pitiful to admit it, in retrospect, but I never thought he would dump me—not the way he did, and certainly not so he could get back with Lia again. He'd told me so many stories about their squabbles and embedded resentments that I honestly thought he'd worked his way free of their mutually destructive relationship for good. And to find out about it like I did, to have to hear it from the ecstatic mouth of *Ramona fucking Waverley* and not even from Sebastian himself . . . it tore me in half.

So it's with malevolent pleasure that I look forward to seeing him confront Lia now—to watching him face her with the fact that she's been cheating on him with Arlo. I'm not proud of it, but it's the truth.

The Santos family turns out to live in a tidy Cape Cod–style house on the south side of town, in a neighborhood of similar homes that all seem eerily desolate. It's just midnight as we pull up, and even on a national holiday, there are precious few signs of life. Light, however, flickers in one of the dormer windows facing the street, and Sebastian shifts apprehensively behind the wheel. "That's Lia's room."

"So she's here?"

"Looks like."

We all stare out from the Jeep. Suddenly, I'm wondering what we'll do if she refuses to speak to us; she has no reason to give me the time of day, and if she's been seeing Arlo behind Sebastian's back, she probably isn't too eager to face him, either. A glance up and down the street shows me no signs of the tattooed miscreant's motorcycle, so at least he doesn't appear to be here with her.

From the backseat, April violates the silence of our indecision with a grousing sigh. "Are you waiting for her to come out and confess, or what?"

“Text her,” I instruct Sebastian. “Tell her you’re out front.”

With obvious dread, he pulls out his phone and thumbs in a message, which I read over his shoulder: *Need to talk. Can you come outside? I’m at the curb.*

He sends it and we wait, watching the flickering light, seconds stretching into minutes. From the backseat, April murmurs in a devious undertone, “Maybe she’s avoiding you.”

Sebastian tries again. *Lia it’s B and I’m outside your house. I’m not going home till you come out here.*

“Are you serious?” I ask him incredulously. “You sound like a stalker—she’s gonna call the police!”

“Not if she killed Fox,” April interjects, but I’m already grabbing the phone from Sebastian’s hand and typing in a message of my own.

I know where you were tonight. Either you come outside or I bang on your door till your parents wake up and I tell everybody.

A half second after I put the phone back in Sebastian’s hand, the light in the dormer window vanishes. Three more minutes pass—during which time I picture her doing everything from calling Arlo for help to slipping into some MILFy lingerie to greet her cuckolded boyfriend—and then the front door eases open, and Lia Santos starts down the front walk.

She’s one of those girls who’s so wildly beautiful that it’s almost frightening—all bee-stung lips and smoky eyes and flawless brown skin; even the way she moves is impressive somehow. Wearing a rumpled T-shirt and cotton running shorts, her thick, black hair swinging loose in her face like velvet curtains, she *still* looks like she’s storming the runway at New York Fashion Week, and there’s unmistakable fury in her stride as she approaches the Jeep.

"Stay in the car," I command April. "Don't let her see you. We don't want anyone to know you're awake yet."

"I get it." She frowns peevishly, but ducks down out of sight as Sebastian and I open our doors.

Lia, who was clearly not expecting her boyfriend to have company, draws up short when she reaches the end of the walk, standing in the darkness that pools between streetlights. "What the hell do you want?" she hisses, her arms and shoulders tensed. Then, recognizing me with a startled look, "And what the hell is *he* doing here?"

"Nice to see you, too," I offer, but she ignores me.

"What the fuck does this text mean, *I know where you were tonight*?" She thrusts her phone into Sebastian's face. "This has got to be the saddest, most pathetic attempt you've made yet to get my attention, Bash Williams. Seriously, truly pathetic."

The air practically crackles in the silence that follows, Lia's eyes flashing in the shadows as she stares daggers at the two of us. Sebastian lets her outburst ring in the air for a moment. "Are you done?"

"Screw you," she spits.

"Great. We've got a couple questions—"

"You know what? Fuck your questions, Bash! I am so sick of you jerking me around, making promises and messing with my head! I'm done with all of it, so . . . you know, whatever *this* is, you can shove it up your ass."

She turns to march back up the walk to her house, and I blurt, "Where's Arlo?"

Lia freezes and pivots back around, eyeing me warily. "I've got no idea. Why are you asking me?" Then, as if she's suddenly confused, "You mean Arlo Rossi?"

"Oh, gimme a break," Sebastian scoffs. "*You mean Arlo Rossi?* You are the worst liar."

"You would know," she shoots back, immediately venomous, "lying was always *your* special talent!"

"Stop it, both of you!" As much as I'm enjoying their tiff, I'm anxious to get to the point; Fox is still lying dead in a cottage some twenty-five miles away, and every other second I seem to have a different, heart-stopping vision of the police finding out about it before we have a chance to tell them ourselves. "Listen, Lia, this is actually important. We know you and Arlo went to a party together tonight, so just level with us, okay?"

"We didn't," she returns adamantly, flustered again, just as bad at lying as Sebastian pointed out. "I've got no idea what you're talking about. Who even told you that?"

I weigh my options. "April. She was texting me about Fox's party, and said she'd call me when it was over, only now she's not answering and I'm getting worried."

Lia actually squints at me. "Why would she call *you*?"

"Because I'm the only other person she knows who's still into *Supernatural*, and she wants us to write some fanfic together," I retort acerbically. "What she wanted to talk to me about is none of your freaking business, but you were with her tonight, so I want to know what happened."

She looks between the two of us, vibrating like a tuning fork, and directs her next question to Sebastian. "So what are *you* doing here? What do you have to do with this?"

"Just answer him, okay?" Sebastian sighs. "Please?"

"She's probably boning Fox." The answer comes quickly, and with purposeful bluntness. "Nothing like a little make-up sex to keep you away from the phone, right? Hope that doesn't scandalize you."

I'm trying to figure out if this is a real guess, or if she's simply trying to distract me with the unwelcome mental image, when she gives her long hair a defiant toss, exposing her face fully to the light for the first time. A nasty purple contusion arches along her left cheekbone and eye socket, stippled with broken blood vessels, and she only seems to realize what she's shown us a second before Sebastian reacts, lunging forward. "What the hell happened to you? Did Arlo fucking *hit* you?"

"No." She shoves him away, ducking her head down and letting the shadows conceal her injured eye again.

"Don't lie for him!"

"I'm not lying!"

"I'm gonna fucking kill him," Sebastian fumes, his face darkening with rage, and I watch as his fists tighten and veins pop up along his forearms. "Where is he?"

"Oh, get over yourself, Bash!" Lia suddenly snaps. "This 'jealous protector' crap isn't gonna work, so you can just drop it, okay? I am so sick of you thinking you can totally ignore me when we're together, and then make some great big gesture once we've broken up, and that that'll be good enough—that I'll just take you back because I'm that desperate for some dude to validate me."

"That's not—"

"I told you the last time that we were over for good and I *meant* it." She makes an emphatic gesture with her hands. "I wasted enough of my life dating you, and you can literally go fuck yourself for all I care."

Crickets saw away into the charged stillness that follows, and

I turn to Sebastian in surprise. *He and Lia broke up again?* He won't look at me, though; he's still glowering at his—apparently—*ex*-girlfriend. Through gritted teeth, he says quietly, "If you think the only reason I'd go after a guy who hit you is because I want to impress you, then you don't know anything about me. Any guy who beats up girls deserves to get his fucking ass kicked. I don't need another reason." Then, "And, for the record, I *don't* want you back, anyway."

"Great, then we finally agree on something," Lia snaps, although her relief doesn't seem entirely genuine. "Besides, like I was saying, it *wasn't* Arlo—and it wasn't even on purpose. Arlo and Fox got into a fight, I tried to break it up, and Fox hit me by mistake. No big deal."

"What were they fighting about?" Sebastian asks next, and then stuns me by suggesting, "Drugs?"

A security shutter drops down in Lia's eyes, and she takes a step back. "I've got no idea what you're talking about. *You've* got no idea what you're talking about."

"Please. Everybody knows Arlo and Fox deal shit," he says, totally matter-of-fact, but I give him another wild-eyed look because—of course—I knew no such thing. As I digest it, though, the statement isn't so hard to believe; Arlo's family isn't wealthy, and he only works part-time at a grocery store, but he'd managed to buy himself a very expensive motorcycle a few months back. I'd never bothered to wonder how he'd pulled off such a trick. And Fox . . . well, I've overheard him and his friends make enough casual remarks to understand how disturbingly fluent they are with drugs.

"I've got nothing to say about that," Lia avows firmly. "Arlo is a good person, okay? And *if* he and Fox got into a fight about . . . *that*, then it would've been because *Fox* was trying to do something shady and *Arlo* didn't want any part of it. But I didn't say that, because I don't know anything about any of it. Okay?"

"Understood." With thoughts of Lia's bruise in mind, I shift out of the light myself. My shorts are still clammy with moisture, and I'm aware that I have bloodstains on my tank top. "So did Arlo leave after the fight?"

"Yeah, basically." If she finds the question odd, she doesn't challenge me on it. "He went to go cool down and stuff, but the party . . . it kind of broke up a little while after that anyway, and we all left."

"All at the same time?"

Now she seems baffled. "Pretty much, yeah. What difference does it make?"

"I'm worried about April," I repeat, as if that explains it.

Lia sighs extravagantly. "Race took off first, and then Peyton, and then Arlo and me a few minutes later. We passed both of them on the road."

"So where's Arlo now?"

"At home, probably." She's clearly tiring of the conversation. "Not like I keep tabs on him, but that's where he said he was going when he dropped me off. Why?"

"I don't want to go all the way out to Fox's lake house if it turns out nothing's up, so I just want to hear what Arlo has to say first. Where does he live?"

"He's not going to have *anything* to say except for what I already told you. And April was hitting the bottle pretty hard tonight, you know? She probably passed out."

"Humor me," I propose. "Give me his address, and we'll leave you alone."

"Promise?" She asks sarcastically. It does the trick, though, and she directs us to a neighborhood that's conveniently close by. With a pointedly coquettish smile for Sebastian, she purrs, "Tell him I said hi, okay?"

There's still one thing I don't understand, though. Something about the timeline that's coming together doesn't quite add up, and it's begging for attention like a mosquito bite. If Arlo got kicked out, and was so pissed he needed to "cool down," then why was he last to leave? "It's not like Arlo to just back down from a fight like that. To let Fox kick his ass and walk away."

A curious thing happens; Lia goes completely still, her eyes flashing open wide for a split second before she gets her reaction under control. Her tone is so casual it's almost flippant when she asks, "What the hell would you know about it?"

"Considering that I'm one of the guys he beats on the most, let's just say it's something I've noticed about him," I return coolly, studying the forced blankness in her expression. There is no smoke without fire, or so they say, and Lia's shabby performance of indifference is giving off smoke like a few hundred acres of smoldering California brush. "Arlo doesn't like losing face. He's a score settler."

"Oh, please, like you'd even know." She speaks quickly, tossing her hair again, an agitated gesture. "They got into a fight. Boys fight sometimes. They got into it, he got over it, we left, and we came straight here. Ask him when you see him—he'll tell you the same thing."

I'm sure he will, I think, but do not say out loud, *because you're going to text him the second you get back inside your house.*

"Thanks for answering our questions," I reply instead.

"Don't come back," she instructs imperiously. And then she spins around and sails up her front walk without a backward look.

6

SEBASTIAN IS QUIET AS WE TURN AND START FOR THE JEEP, HIS eyes downcast and troubled. Before I can stop myself, I blurt, "You and Lia broke up?"

It sounds so needy and weak that I curse myself the second the question is out of my mouth, but Sebastian doesn't even look at me. "Yeah. A few weeks ago. It was kinda ugly."

I set my jaw. If he wants sympathy, he's not going to get it; I spent the entire month of June indulging in lurid, punishing fantasies about Sebastian and Lia groping each other and sharing their Starbucks and shouting a lot right before they went back to groping again, and the whole time I was wishing a plague on both their houses. Finding out their reconciliation barely lasted until summer break should feel rewarding, but in fact it does nothing to assuage my anguish. I still hurt inside.

As soon as we're back in the Jeep, April straightens up behind us. "What did she say? Did she know anything? Was she lying?"

"She said a lot of things." I turn around to face my half sister, indignation kindling quickly to life in my breast. “What did you and Fox fight about tonight?”

Even in the dim light, cast sideways through the Jeep by amber streetlamps, I can see April blanch. “I don’t know what you’re talk—”

“Stop.” I cut her off. “Lia said she figured you and Fox were having ‘make-up sex.’ You wouldn’t be making up unless you’d had a fight, so what was it about?”

She squirms. “Nothing. It was just a stupid argument.”

“If it was nothing, why didn’t you tell us about it before?”

“Because it was fucking *private*!” She glares at me. “And because it doesn’t even matter what we fought about, because *I didn’t kill him.*”

She slams herself back against the seats, turning her face to the window in a tacit display of resentment. Childishly, I mimic her, facing front with a darkening mood. I try to remind myself that April is the one who expects results out of this pointless enterprise, and if she’s going to withhold information, it’s her own damn funeral. Peter will undoubtedly do whatever he can to bail her out—he’ll probably be mortified by the inevitable publicity and will do what it takes to protect the Covington family name—and maybe I should just let her play these stupid games with him instead. I have my two grand whether this wild goose chase pans out or not, so what do I care?

Only I *do* care. That’s the problem. Reckless and selfish though she may be, April still has a good heart, and she’s the only branch of my Covington family tree that I’ve never wanted to summarily saw off and burn. “Well, she was definitely lying about stuff.”

“She didn’t kill him, either,” Sebastian interposes sullenly. “Lia couldn’t do something like that.”

"Oh yeah, no, she's a real sweetheart," I remark caustically, sounding like an asshole. "By the way, did you happen to notice how she *freaked out* and *lied her face off* when I called bullshit on Arlo just letting Fox off the hook?"

"She didn't want to get him into trouble! That doesn't mean she killed anyone."

"I never said she did," I shoot back, and I can feel ugly demons slipping up through my veins, my personal feelings about Sebastian's history with Lia Santos swiftly making the disagreement into something entirely other than what it is. Taking a deep breath, I add, in a more level tone, "I don't care why she lied—the point is that she *did*, and she did it *obviously*, which makes Arlo look even guiltier."

"Do you think she knows he killed Fox?" April asks from the backseat, her curiosity overcoming her resentfulness.

"I don't know," I say after a moment. "I don't think so. She wigged out when we mentioned the drugs and when I talked about Arlo liking to settle scores, but when we talked about you and Fox it didn't seem to hit any particular nerves. I mean, I don't think." Rubbing my face, I sigh. "She was all edgy and upset, so her reactions were hard to gauge. Maybe she thinks Arlo did *something*, but she doesn't know what."

A minute of uncomfortable silence passes in the Jeep as all three of us sulk independently, and then Sebastian cranks the engine to life. "Well, I guess we might as well just go and ask the fucker."

The Rossis live in a narrow Victorian that peaks like a witch's hat beneath the heavy canopy of a massive oak, its facade decorated with intricate woodwork and a shield of trellises that fence in the front porch. Mr. Rossi is an electrician who actually came out to our house one time when a lightning strike blew several of our fuses, but his home has not a single bulb lit as we coast to a stop out front. Even the curbside streetlamps are utterly defeated by the oak's overgrown pelt of leaves, and the shadows are so dense, we can barely read the address through the gloom. Arlo's house is a glaring black gap in the bright smile of the neighborhood.

"Well, shit, he's *obviously* the murderer," April squeals breathlessly. "Look at this place! Frigging *Dracula* wouldn't go in there."

"It's just a house." I give her a sharp frown, although I'm not exactly charging up the walk myself. The Victorian looks deliberately uninviting, and I can see no sign of Arlo's bike anywhere. "Maybe Lia warned him we were coming, and he took off."

"Maybe," Sebastian grumps. It's about as close to a peace accord as we're going to get on the subject, and I accept it for the sake of the task ahead.

"Only one way to find out, I guess." With great reluctance, I shove open the door of the Jeep and step out onto the street. The whole block appears deserted, and a gust of wind pushes the paper remnants of a few fireworks up the sidewalk. Peering into the uncompromising darkness beneath the oak's overhanging branches, I squint at the narrow gap in the trellis that opens at the top of the porch stairs—a forbidding black socket, inside of which hides the front door. April is right: It looks like a haunted house.

The distance between Arlo's neighborhood and the Whitney cottage can be best measured in tax brackets, and I have to wonder what it must be like for him: a poor kid hanging out with such a privileged clique. What do they talk about? All they have in common is bullying. Is he fascinated by their wealth? Are they fascinated by his blue-collar authenticity? I can't picture snobs like Fox or Race or Peyton hanging out at a place like this, with its dark, weedy lawn and peeling paint.

Sebastian comes around the front of the Jeep, and we share a wordless glance before starting up the cement walkway. We barely make it five feet before a figure materializes out of the black shadows of the porch, looming into view at the top of the front steps. "I don't know what's going on with April, and I don't care, so you two dipshits can just fuck right off."

Arlo's voice is so loud against the still night that it actually causes me to jump; my heart is done no favors, either, by the object the guy has casually propped across his shoulder. His booted feet resound heavily against the wooden steps as he descends to the walkway, and there he stops—feet apart, one hand holding a cigarette, and the other wrapped possessively around the stock of a hunting rifle.

"Is that meant for us?" I squeak stupidly, nodding at the weapon while just managing not to pee myself.

"Depends." Arlo gives me a sharp-toothed grin. He's added a few more tattoos since the last time I saw him; bare-chested and muscular, his arms and torso are wallpapered with a hodgepodge of images—daggers and roses, sugar skull girls, frigates under sail—and a metal stud shows like a bulbous growth beneath his bottom lip. "Are you planning to ask me a whole bunch of dumbfuck questions about where I was tonight?"

Obviously, he got the memo from Lia. His posture is casual, the firearm pointed vaguely skyward—but there's a menacing tension in his stance that's impossible to disregard. Licking my lips, I venture, "Look, I'm just worried about April, okay?"

"I don't give a shit what you're worried about," he retorts. As my vision continues to adjust, I notice Arlo's eyes moving as he speaks; he's looking past us, at the road, scanning left and right along its desolate length as if he suspects we might have backup on the way. "I'm not gonna help you two, so piss off."

"C'mon, man. She's his sister," Sebastian intercedes on my behalf.

"Barely," Arlo snorts, "and I *still* don't give a shit. What are you doing hanging out with this faggot, anyway, Bash? Lia mess you up that much when she dumped your sorry ass?"

It's a schoolyard taunt, crude and unimaginative; but it's also the very question my ex-boyfriend was always the most terrified of having to answer, and it shuts him up. For my part, I'm not exactly fond of being called a faggot, and I'd love to try to take one of Arlo's tattoos home with me as a trophy—but even though it wouldn't be the first time I'd given in to my anger and picked a fight with someone I had no hope of beating, I'm not quite reckless enough to take a swing at someone toting around an *actual fucking rifle*. Instead, I take a deep breath and struggle to remain focused. *Breathe and take a step back.*

"Lia said you two were the last to leave Fox's cottage tonight. Did you happen to notice what sort of shape April was in at the time?"

"Man, I could not give less of a fuck what Lia told you!" He chucks his cigarette to the ground, swings the rifle down off his shoulder, and grips it with both hands; the barrel nudges in our direction, and Sebastian and I both take an unconscious step backward. "You're so worried about April? Go drive the hell out to South Hero and see what she's up to. But leave my ass alone. And get the fuck out of my yard, too."

"Or what?" I challenge, my intelligence ebbing as my anger

mounts. "You'll shoot us? I'm trying to make sure my fifteen-year-old sister didn't OD at a coke party you and your *business partner* were throwing, and all you've got to say is 'fuck off'?"

He takes one step forward, eyes flashing, and points the rifle at me. "What I've got to say is, get off my property, you pussy-ass faggot, or I will *blow* you off it."

"Well, thanks for all your help, man." Sebastian reanimates swiftly, grabbing me by the shoulders and dragging me back to the Jeep on legs that are suddenly surprisingly cooperative. "Enjoy the rest of your night. Happy Independence Day!"

He practically shoves me into the passenger seat, then darts around, jumps behind the wheel, and takes off from the curb with a high-pitched squawk of the tires. I can just barely make out Arlo's pale figure in the gloom at the foot of his porch steps, the rifle trained lazily on Sebastian's taillights as we drive out of sight.

7

"ARE YOU OUT OF YOUR FUCKING *MIND*, RUFUS?" SEBASTIAN demands as soon as we're out of the Rossis' neighborhood. He hurls me a look full of furious disbelief. "Were you trying to get yourself killed back there?"

"He wasn't going to shoot me," I mutter with far more conviction than I feel. The truth is that Arlo, I am fairly certain, would love to use me for target practice—and wouldn't require much incentive to go for it. But at the moment, I need to hear somebody say out loud that I hadn't actually been in mortal danger. "I mean, if he killed Fox, the last thing he wants right now is to attract attention from the police."

"Or maybe he could figure he's got nothing to lose by upping his body count a little, so why the hell not?" Streetlights flash across Sebastian's angered features, gold flecks sparkling in his dark eyes. "And what the hell do you mean '*if* he killed Fox'? Were we talking to the same guy? Because the guy *I* was just talking to was a homicidal whack-job who threatened to *shoot us in the face.*" He takes a breath. "I mean, I've known Arlo for a while, and dude is definitely a little messed up in the head, but he's never gone fucking *Westworld* like that on anybody before. This is next-level shit, Rufus! You said yourself the guy is a 'score settler'—your words—and now he's threatening to kill people just for asking about where he was tonight? Sounds guilty to me!"

"I think he did it, too," April interjects in a small, quiet voice. "He's not like the other guys, you know? He's always getting into fights and stuff, and he completely loses his shit when he thinks someone is screwing with him. Like, why else would he have grabbed a freaking *gun* when Lia told him you guys were coming?"

I don't answer right away, because both of them have excellent points . . . but a tiny, confounding worm of doubt is slowly nibbling its way toward the center of my brain, nonetheless. Yes, Arlo has a reputation as a brawler, preferring to solve all his problems with fists whenever possible; and even though I hadn't exactly been expecting a warm welcome, my fairly basic questions about April provoked a disproportionately combative response. This is all true. It's also true that he advised me to drive out to the lake house—perhaps growing tired of waiting for April to wake up and call the police, already—and that his bare chest has me wondering whether he had to get rid of a shirt that would almost certainly be soaked in blood after stabbing his buddy to death.

But the more I think about it, the less I like it. "I don't know," I admit at last, the words escaping in a disgruntled huff.

"*What?*" April and Sebastian react in unison.

"What are we?" I ask rhetorically. "We're a nuisance, showing up and pestering him with stupid questions in the middle of the night. We're not the cops. From his perspective, what could we possibly know that would get him in trouble? And *if* he killed Fox, then he should *want* us to be asking about April; he should've told us that the last time he saw her, she was taking white rabbits and flipping out and making threats—this was his golden opportunity to start selling the frame-job he set up at the cottage!" I comb my hair back with my fingers. "But he couldn't wait to get rid of us, and he didn't want to answer any questions at all about April *or* Fox."

"And you think that means he's innocent?" April's disgust is plain.

"I don't know what it means," I answer honestly, "but I know he didn't need a rifle to scare us off. That house looked abandoned, you know? He could have just pretended he wasn't home and waited for us to leave. And—let's be real, here," I add, directing this part to Sebastian, "he could have kicked *both* our asses empty-handed, and we all know it."

"So what are you trying to say?" Sebastian asks tersely.

"I'm saying maybe *we're* not the ones who had him sitting in the dark on his front porch, holding a rifle in his lap. Did you notice that he wouldn't leave the foot of the steps? That the whole time we were talking to him, he was watching the street, like he expected more people to show up?" I look from one of them to the other, to see if they've understood. "Arlo was scared."

April practically gasps. "Arlo doesn't *get* scared."

"Scared of *what?*" Sebastian's incredulous question comes almost simultaneously.

I make a helpless gesture. The answer isn't likely to be either of the party guests we haven't spoken to yet. Peyton Forsyth, April's best friend, is no fragile flower—she's one of the taller girls at Ethan Allen, and an athlete in her own right—but she's no physical match for Arlo Rossi; and Race Atwood, marginally closer to the tattooed bruiser's size, is a notorious pretty boy who's never been in a fair fight in his life. The thought of Arlo being afraid of either of them, or even both of them together, seems absurd. But if it's not them, then who does that leave?

"April, are you *sure* that no one else came to Fox's party tonight?" Even before I've finished asking the question, I know how pointless it is. My half sister is trying to clear her name—and whatever it is that she's still not telling me, if there were more suspects to consider, she'd have identified them by now.

"I told you, Fox wanted to keep it small. It was just the six of us." She's clearly not ready to give up on Arlo. "Maybe he was scared of the cops. Maybe he's afraid he left some evidence behind, or that I'll remember him doing it."

"Maybe." I take a look at the digital clock display set into the dashboard and feel a tremor of anxiety; it's late, and Fox is still lying dead on his kitchen floor, the trail growing colder while we waste time with speculation. The longer it takes us to get to the police, the worse things will look. "We still have to talk to Race and Peyton; maybe they'll tell us something useful."

"I already texted Race," Sebastian reports as he navigates the Jeep around a corner and onto a narrow street drenched in darkness by overgrown trees that crowd at the curb like shapeless ogres. "He's at home. I didn't tell him what I wanted to see him about, but he says it's cool to come over."

"Let's hope he's still feeling cooperative once he knows what we want," I remark pessimistically. "Just out of curiosity, how's he feel about guns?"

Race lives in a sprawling McMansion near Oakledge Park, not far from the shore of Lake Champlain—which seems appropriate, as

Race is the McMansion equivalent of a person: pompous, generic, and transparent in his need for admiration. The Atwood home, located halfway along a curving street, is an elaborate mess of sloping, shingled roofs, wooden siding, and pointy dormer windows. There are two chimneys, a widow's walk, and a three-car garage, with a contiguous row of bosomy, ornamental shrubs hugging the perimeter of the house. Sebastian pulls into the driveway, stopping beside Race's flashy white Camaro. "He says he's out back and we can just walk around."

It's a fancy address, but in the shadowy silence of the blind avenue, it's no less foreboding than Arlo's place was as we get out of the car and shut the doors. April watches us apprehensively from the backseat of the Jeep while we set off to navigate our way to the rear of the property, her expression haunting. I can see that the awful night is taking its toll on her, the circles under her eyes darkening by the minute, and I hope for all our sakes that it will be over soon. I can still smell the tangy, metallic odor that filled the lake house, and Fox's body flashes in front of me every time I blink—like an afterimage burned into my retinas—and I'm starting to feel guilty about leaving him there.

I need this to be over soon.

As Sebastian leads the way to a tall gate tucked out of sight behind the house, I steal a glance at my phone. There are eleven missed texts, all of them from Lucy, and I feel something deflate in my chest. Not two hours ago, I was hanging with my best friend, having a great time and congratulating myself on how much I *wasn't* thinking about my ex-boyfriend. Now I'm troubled and moody again, following him onto the Atwoods' rear patio, an irregular peninsula of sandstone pavers that juts out into the lushly quiet backyard. There's an enormous propane grill off to one side, a covered hot tub off to the other, and a straight-from-the-showroom cluster of expensive outdoor furniture grouped around a glass-topped coffee table dead center. Ensconced on a sofa of weatherproofed wicker and stain-resistant cushions, we find—conveniently enough—both of the remaining people on our list.

As individuals, Race Atwood and Peyton Forsyth are both terrible people, and anything less than two thousand dollars in cash wouldn't entice me to voluntarily share oxygen with either of them; mean, shallow, and self-absorbed in equal measure, they are, in a perverse kind of way, the perfect couple. It's how they refer to themselves, too. *The Perfect Couple.*

The thing is, I'm fairly certain that neither of them has much in the way of original thoughts to share with the world; from the music they like, to the clothes they wear, to the people they accept as equals, their opinions have all been formed and handed to them by Fox—the gravitational center of their social circle. Certainly April's been guilty of this, too, but from where I stand, currying his favor seems to be a full-time job for Race and Peyton in particular—and they've always appeared to think quite highly of themselves for doing it.

As we cross the stone flooring, the so-called Perfect Couple turns to watch our approach, and I nearly stumble as I walk into a force field of awkward tension as thick as a brick wall. Race and Peyton are seated at opposite ends of the sofa, their faces drawn, their body language as stiff and detached as strangers forced to share a bench at the bus stop.

"Hey, guys," Sebastian offers experimentally as we sit down across from them.

"What the hell's he doing here?" Race asks inhospitably, scowling at me through the shock of strawberry blond hair that tumbles over his forehead. Evidently, they were not forewarned of our nocturnal door-to-door. A nice surprise.

"I know you guys were with April tonight," I begin without preamble, just as happy to dispense with meaningless niceties, "and I'm worried about her."

The couple exchanges a quick look, but neither of them answers me right away. They're both smoking, and the mass of butts crowding the shared ashtray sitting before them on the coffee table suggests that they've been at it for some time. Peyton takes a long drag on her cigarette, curiosity and suspicion flickering in her catlike green eyes. "Why?"

"She was supposed to call me tonight, but she never did, and now she's not answering her phone." By this point, the lie comes out as easily as if it were the truth. "When's the last time you saw her?"

They exchange another look, and Race gives an uninterested shrug. Once again, Peyton answers for both of them. "None of your fucking business."

"Please?" Sebastian intercedes in a far friendlier tone than I personally think is warranted, and the girl rolls her eyes impatiently.

"When we left Fox's lake house. We were having a party out there." She turns back to Race for confirmation, but his gaze is fixed firmly on the coffee table. "It was a few hours ago."

Sebastian waits for her to add more, and when she doesn't, he leads, "Which was . . . ?"

"I don't know," Peyton replies with an aggrieved look, "maybe nine fifteen, nine thirty?" Leaning forward to knock some ash off her cigarette, she then asks antagonistically, "Seriously, Bash, what are you doing with him?"

Sebastian squirms again, his eyes zigzagging miserably from

one person to another as he seeks a refuge that simply isn't there. "Um, we were both at—"

"How did she seem?" I interrupt, steering deliberately away from Sebastian's secret for a second time. The strange, schismatic energy surrounding Peyton and Race—who have left enough space between them on the sofa to land a Black Hawk helicopter—intrigues me. As sure as I am that Peyton really wants to know the answer to her question, it also feels like she's changing the subject to avoid discussing the party. When neither of them responds to me after a long moment, I ask again. "How was April when you left?"

More silence, and this time Race shoots a look to Peyton that isn't returned. My sister's best friend leans forward to stub out her cigarette, offering a cryptic "Not very happy."

Moonlight glows against the pale skin of her face as she shoves her platinum tresses behind one ear and grabs for the pack of Camels sitting on the coffee table, and a wave of déjà vu crashes over me; it's like Lia all over again as the sudden illumination reveals a dark, ugly bruise on Peyton's jaw. I almost pounce. "Is that compliments of Fox, too?"

"What?" Peyton glances up, startled, and then she covers the injury with her hand, shrinking back from the light instinctively. "No. What do you mean?"

"Fox and Arlo got into a fight and we heard there was some collateral damage," I explain judiciously, watching Race out of the corner of my eye as he puffs mechanically at his cigarette. "It's part of the reason I'm worried about April."

"She didn't have anything to do with that," Peyton states restlessly. Then: "Wait, how did you hear about it?"

"Lia told us."

Peyton shakes her head, lips pursed, annoyed at the lack of discretion. "Then she should have told you that Race, April, and I were all out in the hot tub when that whole thing went down. We don't even know what it was all about, all right? One minute we're having a good time, and the next minute those two drunk shitheads are trying to throw each other through a window. By the time we made it up to the porch, it was all over, and Arlo was on his way out the door."

"So what happened to your face?" It's a pretty tactless question—but then, Peyton is a pretty tactless person, in my experience. Like the daughter of Regina George and Voldemort, she's made a lifelong hobby out of inflicting her point of view on others, no matter how abusive or unsolicited it is. I've gone to school with her since kindergarten, and cannot remember the last time she was remotely nice to someone who wasn't rich and/or popular.

"Fuck off," she answers promptly, living up to my low expectations. "Fuck all the way off." Angling a glare at Sebastian, she shakes her head. "Honestly. What is he doing here? Why is he talking to me?"

"Peyton." Sebastian meets her gaze imploringly. "People were throwing punches at this party, and he's worried about his sister. Just tell him what he wants to know and we can *all* fuck off, okay?"

The girl doesn't exactly signal her agreement, but neither does she hurl the ashtray at my head, so I repeat the question. "How'd you get hurt?"

She doesn't answer right away, taking her time lighting another cigarette while her boyfriend turns and stares daggers at her across the sofa. At last, in a sulky and almost accusatory voice, she says, "Ask April."

"I'd love to, but she's not answering her phone." My delivery is so smooth, I doubt that either of them can sense how pissed off I have suddenly become.

Peyton shifts, her mouth twitching down at the corners. "She hit me, all right?"

"Why?"

"Because she fucking flipped out!" Peyton's eyes flash, and she skewers me with that look that popular kids always have on hand for guys like me—that hateful who-gave-you-permission-to-exist? glare—and I can tell her tolerance of our exchange is reaching its true terminus. "How is it any of your damn business, by the way? Go out there and talk to *her*, if you're so concerned with how she's doing. Not that I can understand why you even give a shit. April doesn't even *like* you." She's worked her way onto more familiar ground, now, sneering at me contemptuously. "She thinks you're a freak. I mean, *everybody* thinks you're a freak, but April talks about it all the time. She says you used to stalk her and Hayden."

"Is that why the party broke up so early?" Sebastian forces the conversation back on topic. I can't tell if it's because he's afraid I'm going to lose control of myself—which I'm not, thank you, having endured far worse than Peyton's weak game—or because he's deduced, correctly, that my usefulness as an interrogator is *finis*. "Because April took a swing at you?"

"Yeah," Peyton confirms shortly. "Fox kicked Arlo out, and then April went psychotic, and it kind of put a damper on things, you know? You asked how April 'seemed' the last time I saw her? She *seemed* like a crazy fucking bitch who was trying to rip my head off my shoulders. So forgive me if I don't really give a crap what she's up to or how she's doing right now."

"You guys should've called me," Sebastian admonishes Race blithely. "Jake Fuller was having a thing at his place, and it was totally wild. You could've come over there instead."

"We sorta weren't in the party mood anymore." Race speaks through locked jaws, as if the words hurt coming out.

My ex-boyfriend gives a vigorous nod, playing dumb to the unfriendly mood that hangs in the air like smog. "So what'd you do?"

"Came back here." Race gazes off into the trees, black shapes in the darkness that obscure the view of nearby homes and offer the Atwoods a natural privacy screen. "My parents are with my sister in DC, so we've just been sort of chilling."

He won't look at us, and I struggle to tell if this means he's lying. Frankly, I can't quite figure out why he's answered the question at all; if it had come from my mouth, I'd have been lucky to get so much as a middle finger in response. But he isn't acting as if he finds Sebastian's interest odd or intrusive. It's impossible to figure out if this is because he has nothing to hide or because he's been rehearsing his story, waiting for the chance to provide it.

On the other end of the sofa, Peyton gives a corroborating nod. "We should've just stayed here all night. You didn't miss anything, trust me. Fox's party sucked."

Her expression is a little too earnest to be entirely genuine, and the silence that follows her remark is choking. Something's not right, but I can't put my finger on it, and I can't challenge their story without tipping my hand. If I bring up the drugs, they'll go as cold as Lia did—colder, probably—and our conversation will be over; and there's nothing I can say about the real reason we want them to account for their evening, because to do so would mean revealing everything we're trying to cover up with this awkward Q&A in the first place. Sebastian saves me from a clumsy attempt at grilling them further by noting casually, "Lia said you guys were the first to leave."

"More or less." Race shrugs. "Lia was still trying to calm April down when I took off. But she and Arlo passed me on the road before I made it to the causeway."

"I waited until she gave up, and then I followed after him," Peyton chimes in cooperatively. "Arlo and Lia couldn't have stayed behind long, though, because I wasn't even back on Route 2 when they passed me." She stabs her cigarette out with a vengeance. "Fucking Arlo was going, like, ninety—almost took off my side mirror. He's gonna die on that bike."

There's more silence, then, that oppressive sense of awkward discomfort building over the patio like a weather front. I'm all out of benign questions, out of ways to make my curiosity sound appropriate and nonthreatening, and they've barely told us anything of value. Desperately, I try, "How did Fox seem when you guys left? Was he still pissed about the thing with Arlo? Was he mad at April?"

"Fox is mad at anybody who doesn't kiss his ass," Race retorts harshly, spitting out the name of his best friend as if it were poisonous, "but April knows how to handle him by now. She's probably the only person he's actually afraid of—her and Hayden." Agitated, Race leans forward and snatches his cigarettes from the table, then slumps back against the cushions to light up. "Fox had his lips so far up Hayden's ass tonight, he could've kissed the roof of the guy's mouth."

Sebastian and I straighten up at the same time, but it's my ex-boyfriend who follows through with the obvious question. "Hayden was at the party, too?"

“Only for a minute.” Race’s expression turns abruptly serious, as though he’s afraid he’s just put his foot in his mouth. “Just to . . . pick something up.”

He’s clearly talking about drugs—making Hayden one of Fox and Arlo’s customers. It’s a turn of events I should have seen coming . . . and yet I’m rigid in my seat, anyway, my eyes locked on the surly boy sitting across from me.

When Race reached for his cigarettes, I caught a split-second glimpse of a dark stain on his right index finger—a dark *red* stain. His movement was too quick, the light too dim, for me to be certain . . . but it sure as hell looked a lot like blood.

BEFORE I CAN COME UP WITH SOME SUBTLE WAY OF DEMANDING TO get a better look at Race's fingers, Peyton jumps to her feet, instantly breaking the moment apart. "Well, I'm tired, and I'm sick of talking to you guys, so I'm going home."

She lingers for a moment, her eyes sweeping from one of us to the other, waiting for someone to challenge her; but I can't think of any way to make her stay, and her boyfriend barely even spares her a glance. Silently, then, she turns and marches off into the shadows that loom near the gate. Race stands up the second we hear the latch release. "Look. The next time you want to ask stupid questions about Fox's girlfriend? Just text me. And don't bring *him* to my house again."

"Listen, man—" Sebastian starts, rising from his seat, but Race cuts him off.

"I don't know why you're hanging out with this freak in the first place, Bash, but you should quit before people get the wrong idea." He turns to me, then, drawing himself up to his full five foot nine—giving him the one extra inch he needs to glare down at me along the length of his pointy nose. "Next time *you've* got questions, just remember I don't give a shit, butt-boy."

The pejorative is so ridiculous that I wouldn't be able to take it seriously if he didn't look like he was ready to punch my face off at the same time. At any rate, I'm more than ready to leave, and Sebastian and I reenact Peyton's exit forthwith.

The blond is nowhere to be seen when we return to the front of the house, but I don't waste any time trying to figure out which way she's gone. I'm tired of this snipe hunt for facts no one wants to give me. It requires more nerve than I've got left to keep acting like I *don't* know that Fox is dead and lying in a pool of his own blood right now, and I can feel my karma spoiling the longer I try. As far as I'm concerned, I've lived up to my end of the bargain I struck with April, and I'm very much looking forward to washing my hands of the entire ordeal—and then drying them on a giant pile of money. Not to mention the fact that I am also starting to get entirely sick of being jerked around by people I despise.

When I climb back into the Jeep, I slam the door so hard that the vehicle rocks. The motion stirs April who, lying across the backseat, appears to have rather improbably fallen asleep while we were in the Atwoods' backyard. Snapping awake in an instant, she sits up and fixes me with an anxious look. "What did he say?"

I don't answer right away; I *can't*. I'm too busy counting my breaths and fighting back the throbbing red mist that is stealing its way across my brain. It's Sebastian who informs her, "Actually, it was *they*. Peyton was with him."

"Well, what did *they* say?" April rephrases, annoyed by the correction. "Did one of them do it?"

"I don't know," I finally manage, speaking through my teeth.

"They basically gave us the same story Lia did—Race left first, then Peyton, then Lia and Arlo together."

"But obviously one of them is lying," she insists, and that's when I finally lose it.

"They're *all* lying!" I explode, twisting around in my seat so I can murder her with my eyes. Rage sputters in my heart like hot grease in a pan. "*You're* lying, April! Not a single person has told me the whole truth all night long. I almost got fucking shot for you, and it turns out you've been lying to me!"

"I-I didn't *lie*—"

"Did you just *forget to mention* that Fox and Peyton hooked up tonight? That you went berserk on them? That you have a pretty damn obvious motive for wanting your boyfriend's head on a fucking stick?"

It was a guess—an educated one, but a guess all the same—and I receive my confirmation in the way April's face goes first white and then crimson. Her mouth flaps open and shut a couple of times, and then she asks, with difficulty, "They told you about it?"

"They didn't have to. You left a bruise the size of Connecticut on Peyton's jaw, Race will barely look at her, and Lia already said you and Fox were fighting about something," I enumerate the evidence. "You should have told me, April. You should have fucking told me!"

"If I had, you'd've just thought I was guilty!" She shouts back thickly. "Crazy, out-of-control April does it again, right? Fox cheats on me, so I stab him a hundred times? You'd've had no trouble believing that, because you hate my whole family—you always want to believe that we won't do anything unless we know it'll hurt somebody else! Admit it: If I'd told you about all this stuff back at the cottage, you wouldn't have agreed to help me at all, because you'd've just figured I killed him." Her blue eyes are wet and stormy. "I know how it looks. I didn't tell you, because *I didn't do it.*"

"Well, let me just take your word for it, now that I know you've been hiding stuff from me all night long," I retort weakly, the wind somewhat taken out of my sails by the fact that she actually has a point. If she'd admitted to me up front that she had such a compelling reason to be furious with Fox, I might easily have just dismissed her tearful claims of innocence as nothing but theater.

Then again, maybe that's all they are. Maybe accusing me of being eager to believe the worst in her is just the latest weapon in April's ever-evolving arsenal of manipulations—preying on my guilt so I'll second-guess my instincts and ignore my growing doubts. Is she that clever? Am I that gullible? Or am I so caught in my own mental cogwheels that I can no longer see what's right in front of my face?

Neither of us says anything more as Sebastian starts up the Jeep, pulls out of the Atwoods' driveway, and heads along the curving street. Finally, April speaks again, her voice resentful and halting. "It didn't happen tonight. I mean, them hooking up. It happened a few weeks ago. I guess." She has her chin tucked down, so I can't see her expression. "I only found out about it at the party, and, yeah, I went a little nuts. Fox can be a dick—could be a dick—" Her voice hitches and she stops, caught horribly on her mistaken use of the present tense, and when she looks up for a moment her eyes swim. Blinking, though, she forces herself to continue, "But Peyton's supposed to be my best friend. I was *furious.* So I kind of . . . hit her in the face. With a bottle."

I fight the urge to roll my eyes. The gene carrying Peter

Covington's notoriously short fuse must be a particularly dominant one. "What about Fox?"

"I would've gone after him, too, but Lia stopped me. And then he and Race were getting into it, and then . . . I don't know." She looks up again, and her expression is utterly guileless. "Honestly, Rufus, I don't know what happened after that. That's where it all just goes blank. Until I woke up and called you, I mean."

"How did you find out about Fox and Peyton?" I ask. "Did he tell you?"

"No, Lia did. She . . . well, she found out about it from Arlo."

This raises questions I know April won't be able to answer, so I move on to one she can. "Why didn't you tell me that Hayden was also at the party tonight?"

"Because he wasn't." She looks at me like I'm nuts.

"Race said he came by, and that Fox was kissing his ass."

"Oh, *that.* He was just buying some pills. He had his own party, as usual."

"White rabbits?"

"I guess." She shifts uneasily, just like Race did, and I know the reason. Hayden doesn't tolerate people talking about him, and if he finds out we've been discussing his fondness for controlled substances, he'll put all of us in intensive care. "I stayed out of Fox's business, and I stay *way* out of Hayden's business. You know what he's like. Anyway, he was only there for a few minutes, and then he took off. He didn't even say hi."

But he was there, I note in my mind. My personal knowledge and healthy fear of Hayden Covington run too deep for me to dismiss his presence at the lake house as unimportant or coincidental. Guys like Race and Fox, perpetually drunk on their own mean-spirited testosterone, love to push around anyone they're sure they can take; a guy like Arlo, better with his fists than his words, will eventually stop whaling on you when he's finally sure his point is made. But Hayden is different from all of them.

The day I started kindergarten, I still didn't know enough to be automatically suspicious of anyone named Covington, so when Hayden—in the second grade, and already shining with the irresistible light of popularity—sought me out at recess, telling me how cool it was to finally get to know me, I felt warmed and exalted by the attention. On the pretense of wanting to show me "something awesome," Hayden then led me behind a screen of bushes, punched me in the face as hard as he could, told me our father wished I was dead, and then walked serenely away. It was my first bloody nose, and the last time I ever trusted my older brother.

Peter and Isabel have made an art out of ignoring or excusing Hayden's violence, and April, a convenient target for his lazy cruelty, has told me she avoids him as much as possible. He hurts people because he *enjoys* it, and if he's also in the habit of using drugs that are known to cause violent outbursts . . .

I stop there, knowing I'm getting way ahead of myself. I've already got more suspects than I know what to do with, and not nearly enough information to keep them sorted. The blood on Race's finger had seemed significant in the moment, but I'm no longer so sure; while he has a motive for wanting to put his alleged best friend in the morgue, that doesn't mean his hands are stained from stabbing the guy. April said the two boys scuffled after she took her own swing at Peyton, and considering that Fox had already taken a beating from Arlo, it makes sense that Race would have some blood on him.

And then there's Peyton; but if she has a motive for wanting

Fox dead, I can't quite see it yet; however, if she felt sufficiently guilty for cheating on her boyfriend, she might have been willing to help him frame April—and to vouch for his cover story later.

"The problem is," I finally say out loud with a dispirited grunt, "that as far as I can tell, both Race and Peyton are in the clear. Lia said they left the party first, and they gave us the same story independently—so unless she texted *them*, too, and told them what to say to us—"

"She wouldn't do that," Sebastian interrupts sullenly.

"She did it for Arlo." I swivel to face him, aggravated by the reflexive defense of his ex-girlfriend. "We don't really know what went on up at that party—aside from, you know, *drugs* and *murder*; Lia could have a million reasons for making up bullshit and then warning her friends to stick to an established version of events!"

"I'm telling you, I *know* her. She couldn't kill anybody, and if she knew Race or Peyton had done something to Fox, she wouldn't be helping them with a fake alibi."

"Well, I hate to break it to you, but your girlfriend—excuse me, *ex*-girlfriend—seems to have a problem with the truth!" I shoot back, my heart beating in my face. "She broke up two fistfights tonight, but she only told us about one of them. Why?"

"I kinda wondered about that, too," April admits softly. "I was sure she'd tell you guys about me clocking Peyton. Actually, I'm surprised she didn't."

"Exactly," I say, with more than a little satisfaction. "She was so worried about us persecuting poor little gun-wielding Arlo that she called ahead and told him we were on our way over, but when she made the conscious decision to edit one of tonight's free-for-alls out of her story, it was the one that involved April,

Peyton, and Fox—the one that actually ended the party—not the one between Fox and his business partner. She handed us a clear motive for Arlo but glossed over the rest of it."

Grudgingly, Sebastian allows, "It doesn't make sense."

"No, it doesn't," I agree, suddenly tired. If Arlo really had gone back into the house and murdered Fox, and Lia knew about it and wanted to protect him, why didn't she try harder to draw our attention away from him? Why didn't she make it a point to implicate someone else?

I shuffle Arlo's piece to the center of my mental game board again and frown at it. He's mean, he's violent, and he picked a fight with Fox not long before his grisly demise . . . What do I really have that testifies *against* him as the killer? My sort of vague impression that he was scared of something when we made our unannounced visit to his house? He's a freaking drug dealer, for Pete's sake—there are any number of people he might have good reason to be afraid of, and who might drop by with less-than-friendly intentions in the middle of the night.

"Fuck, maybe they *all* did it," I finally exclaim in a frustrated huff. "Maybe the fight kept going after April blacked out, Fox ended up dead, and they all just panicked and decided to pin it on the most convenient scapegoat."

"They wouldn't do that," April hazards, sounding entirely unsure.

"How well do you really know those guys?" I counter. "How long have you been hanging out with them? Two months? You're the new kid, and I guarantee you they don't care about you half as much as they care about themselves."

"He's got a point, April." Sebastian's glumly supportive interjection takes me by surprise, considering that I'm in the midst of shit-talking his friends. "I mean, I've got a longer history with this crew than you do, and I'm *still* an outsider to them. Plus . . ." his eyes flit nervously to my sister and then to me. "You know, don't take this the wrong way or anything? But Fox has had a lot of girlfriends. Being with him doesn't buy you any loyalty."

The problem with the Everybody Did It theory, though, is that the lot of them seem to be doing a piss-poor job of presenting a unified front to bolster the April Did It narrative. If they're all covering up a murder they each had a hand in, and they intend to pin it on my sister, then their stories should be identical; each one should feature some variation of "April was high off her ass, waving a knife around, and threatening to stab her boyfriend a bunch of times." Instead, I've been getting nothing but feeble alibis and vaguely contradictory accounts. As far as conspiring goes, they seem really shitty at it.

I let out a troubled sigh, aware that both April and Sebastian are watching me, waiting to see what I'm going to do next. But my head is starting to hurt. Fox is still dead, and only getting colder; nothing I've done has turned up the answers my sister wanted; and the killer is still at large—a killer we may have *spoken to* tonight. We can't keep this up. My sister is counting on me, but I can't take the ghostly touch of Fox's fingers on the back of my neck any longer. The fact is, I know what our next move has to be, and suggesting it isn't going to make me very popular. Not looking at either of them, I announce, "We have to go to the police."

"No!" April stares at me, stricken. "We haven't figured anything out yet. If we go to them now, they'll think I did it!"

"April, if we don't go to them soon, they're going to think you did it anyway, *and* that you hired the two of us to help you cover it up. Even if I think your friends are all hiding something, we can't prove—"

"But I'm innocent!" she shrieks. "You can't just hand me over to the police when I didn't do anything! They'll put me in jail, Rufus!"

"Nobody is handing you over!" I yell, but my sister's panic mounts like a thunderhead right before my eyes, and I'm not sure there's anything I can say to soften this blow. I doubt I'd be much calmer if our roles were reversed, and I don't feel very good about myself for what I'm volunteering her to do. April might be guilty of a lot of things, but I don't believe she killed Fox, and I don't think she deserves to go through this nightmare—but I can't see any choice other than what I'm proposing. "The whole point is to make you look innocent, here. If you report the murder before they find out about it, they might actually be willing believe your story," I assert, hoping it's the truth. That's how it works on *Scandal*, anyway, although I'm not sure I'm going to admit that that's where I'm cribbing my plays from. "The longer you wait, the more they're going to think you're hiding shit."

"You were supposed to help me!" she screeches, thrusting an accusatory finger at me from the backseat. "I fucking *paid* you to help me! You took two thousand dollars from me and now you're just going to throw me under the bus? I should have known I couldn't actually trust you! You're a liar and a freak and all you've ever wanted to do is ruin my family. You and your greedy fucking mom—"

"Stop right there," I interrupt, fury instantly forking my tongue. "April, if you say one more word about my mom, I swear I will go straight to the police and tell them you did it—that you confessed and tried to bribe me to lie!" Sparkling white pinpoints dance before my eyes. "You called me for help tonight because you didn't have anybody else to turn to, because your friends are all garbage people and your family's even worse. *They're* the ones ruining you, and you can't even see it!" My ears are ringing and my throat burns. "You paid me to talk to your lying, backstabbing, shithead friends, and I held up my end of the deal. Now you hold up yours!"

I swing back around in my seat, blinking and breathing hard, trying to unclench my fists, and April is quiet for a moment. I wish I could believe she feels chastened, but more likely, she's just recalculating, planning a new attack. Her voice is plaintive when she finally speaks again. "Look, I'm sorry I said that. I-I didn't mean it, okay? I'm just . . . I'm really scared, Rufus. There has to be something we haven't tried yet—"

"There is," I cut her off, brutally. "We haven't tried the cops yet. Call Peter—tell him he needs to get a lawyer and meet us at the police station." Then, because I'm feeling vengeful and particularly cruel, "And tell him it had better be a really *good* lawyer."

April bursts into tears.

9

THE BURLINGTON POLICE DEPARTMENT IS LOCATED IN AN unassuming brick building next to Battery Park—a pleasant expanse of grass and trees near the lake, where tons of people had probably gathered earlier in the evening to watch fireworks bloom against the stars. At one-fifteen in the morning, however, the only folks still hanging around are probably shooting up in the bushes, either too high or too stupid to realize that they're all within moaning distance of being arrested. As Sebastian steers the Jeep into the parking lot, all three of us are as tense and silent as a German horror film.

It's been about thirty-five minutes since April's sobbing subsided enough for her to make the necessary phone calls. Lacking anywhere better to go, Sebastian drove us to the parking lot of Silverman's, a twenty-four-hour diner that's popular with his crowd, and we positioned ourselves in a remote corner while my sister phoned our father and told him she needed an attorney. As soon as she hung up, she dialed my number, and we left the line open for exactly eighty-six seconds before she terminated the call.

That was our own alibi. For all my talk about relying on the police, I'm not about to waltz in and volunteer the information that we've helped April abscond from a crime scene and spent the evening chasing after possible suspects—I'm not a fool, and I definitely can't afford any "misunderstandings" between myself and the authorities. Our story will be that April woke up beside Fox, called Peter, and then called me; pursuant to Race and Peyton's advice, Sebastian and I were already on our way out to South Hero when she reached me and I learned she was in trouble, and once we picked her up, we drove her straight back to town and the police.

I've got no idea if they'll buy it, of course—if we can somehow talk our way out of all the snags and conflicts that our fuzzy timeline will show, if the cops think too hard about what time we left the Atwoods' and what time we reached the police station—but it feels way safer than the truth. And I'm desperately hoping that it's the right choice.

While we waited for Peter to call back, we sat and watched through the broad front windows of Silverman's as the bleary-eyed late-night crowd shoved burgers and fries into their drunken, happy faces. All the while, resentment gradually consumed my gut like some kind of mold. It struck me that I'm always forgetting how, in spite of her occasional sweetness, April is still a Covington—and the Covingtons, to a one, think my mom and I are trashy, scheming lowlifes.

With the passion of a revivalist preacher, Peter has spent years spreading the gospel of my mother's moral turpitude, calling her a grasping, conniving tramp—and me the fruit of the poisonous tree—until he has managed to convince himself it's the truth. All my life I've had to deal with his relentless accusations, Hayden's unrestrained sadism, and the surgical strikes of Isabel's calculated, long-term vengeance. Only April has ever been willing to extend us the benefit of the doubt, but she is by no means immune to her father's influence. Sooner or later, his words find their way into her mouth.

I was still cursing myself for letting the Covingtons trap me in their web when Peter finally called back with the news that their lawyer was en route; I was still brooding over it as we made that uncomfortable left turn into the Burlington Police Department parking lot. But by the time I see Peter Covington himself, leaning against his S-Class Mercedes, his fine-boned face drawn into a dishearteningly familiar scowl, I resign myself to the hell I invited into my life by answering April's summons in the first place.

Before Sebastian even brings the Jeep to a standstill, April flings her door open and starts sprinting across the pavement toward our father, weeping like a hostage who's just been released from a besieged bank. Sebastian shoots me an uneasy look, eyebrows tented with worry. "Are you . . . I mean, are you ready for this?"

I'm not exactly sure which "this" he's talking about—dealing with Peter, or lying to the cops. Either way, my answer is the same. "Not even close. You?"

He doesn't reply right away, and when he does, he can't seem to look me in the face. "I didn't find you by accident tonight, Rufus."

My eyes widen and my stomach plunges. "Sebastian—"

"There's stuff I need to say to you."

"This is *really* not the time," I fume, feeling my back against a wall—one that's covered in spikes and slowly squeezing toward another wall, also covered in spikes. As if what he's saying is some kind of huge surprise. As if it isn't completely obvious that he didn't find me by accident at Lucy's party. He also invited himself along on this insane and borderline-criminal adventure, I noticed, without demanding any compensation for his trouble. Clearly there's something on his mind tonight, and I am terrified that allowing him to bring it up will reopen every last one of the hastily sutured wounds in my heart. Choosing the fire over the frying pan, I shove open my door. "I've got one crisis to deal with already. Tell me about it if I'm still alive when this is all over."

Four and a half weeks after Sebastian had surprised me at the Front Line *meeting with my first ever Actual Kiss, my feet were only just starting to touch the ground again. We'd become expert at finding secret ways to spend time together, stealing kisses in hidden corners and scheduling "study dates" at my house, where we'd microwave pizza rolls and then make out in my room for entire lifetimes. My mom figured out pretty quickly what we were up to, but she also knew that Sebastian was terrified of being "out," and so she walked the thin line of feigning ignorance while still finding excuses to insist I keep my bedroom door open whenever he came over.*

On a brisk day in March, after an especially boring away game the Ethan Allen boys' soccer team had played in Montpelier—which we'd covered for the Front Line*—we delayed our return to Burlington in order to go see a movie in a city where no one knew us. It was a proper date, with popcorn and handholding and no terrified jolting apart whenever we heard a noise, and I loved it. It was situations* *like those where we could just be ourselves, just be* together *without having to think about it.*

And yet I was *thinking about it; I couldn't think about anything else. The weight of our strange situation built slowly, like a trickle of sand that buried me bit by bit as the hours passed, snuffing out the happiness I'd initially felt. By the time the final credits rolled, I was depressed and off-center, lost in an ugly spiral of insecurity. Back in the lobby, I was feeling worse than ever when Sebastian steered me suddenly away from the exit without warning, pulling me into a photo booth set up alongside some arcade games.*

"I've been waiting for this all night," he murmured gruffly as he dragged me down onto the narrow bench beside him, sweeping the curtain closed. He pulled me in for a kiss, and I shifted back, moving his hands away from my waist, my neck. It only took him a second glance to register my expression. "What is it? What's the matter?"

"Why don't you want to be my boyfriend?" I blurted the question clumsily, surprising myself with how needful I sounded, and watched as Sebastian's shoulders sagged. Our relationship was not only undeclared, it was also undefined—a secret that didn't actually exist. We were like a tree falling in the forest with nobody around . . . and then maybe we weren't even really a tree to begin with.

"Rufus—"

"I just want to know why." I tried to sound firm, secure, but I could hear my own unevenness—my own weakness—and it embarrassed me. Two sentences in, and I was already losing the argument I had started. "You didn't mind being Lia's boyfriend, but you don't want to be mine."

"This is about Lia?" he asked stupidly, cocking a brow. "I told you—"

“It isn’t about Lia,” I returned with frustration, even though, yes, it was obviously about Lia—at least in part. “This is about . . . this is about us spending time together. It’s about this, right here, now.” *And it was about kissing in the alcove behind the theater, and hiking in the Green Mountains on weekends, and our Skype chats in the middle of the night, and the way he made sure our fingers touched whenever we passed things to each other at meetings for the newspaper. “This is about me not wanting to spend time with anyone else but you, and* you *saying you don’t want to be my boyfriend.”*

It sounded so pitiful that I’d have kicked myself in the face if it were physically possible. Sebastian raked a hand through his short, dark hair, his brow furrowing, and said, “Rufe, you know how I feel. I just . . . I don’t understand why we need to, you know, put some kind of label *on it, or whatever. Why can’t we just be what we are?”*

Because I don’t *know* what we are, *I thought, but did not say. Instead, I retorted, “Labels keep things organized. What’s wrong with labels?”*

He sighed. “I just spent the last year *wearing one of those—being someone’s boyfriend, dealing with all the drama—and I’m just kinda worn out from it. You get that, right?” It was a leading question, and I provided the nod expected of me, even though I* didn’t *get it. How could I? I had never been anyone’s boyfriend and couldn’t help taking it personally that his sudden need for a label-free existence coincided precisely with the advent of our relationship. I swallowed my words, not even sure how to speak them out loud, and Sebastian continued, “One of the things I really like about you—about us—is that there’s no pressure, you know? We can just be ourselves.”*

"But what do I mean to you?" I persisted, feeling smaller by the second and yet determined to at least not completely fail myself. I hated the way my voice shook, hated how much of my self-esteem actually depended upon his answer. When planning this conversation in my head, I'd envisioned myself resolute and in control, but here I was spiraling and trailing smoke.

"You know *what you mean to me." He moved close again, putting his hand back on my waist, squeezing. The scent of citrus and vetiver embraced me, and I felt my stomach go all gooey. "All the crazy CIA shit we do—getting hall passes at the same time just so we can kiss during school hours, just so I don't have to wait all day to do it? You know what you mean to me."*

I licked my lips, but I was like a fish on a hook, and he knew it. "I—I just . . ."

Sebastian put his other hand on my chest and shoved me against the wall of the booth. The air rushed from my lungs and warmth erupted in the pit of my stomach, flooding my extremities. I goggled at him helplessly as his hand prowled its way under my shirt, and when I felt his touch against my flesh, my skin knotted all over with goose bumps and I emitted an embarrassing whimper.

His lips grazed mine—not a kiss, just a promise—and he murmured, "This is the best part of every day, Rufus. This. You really have to ask what you mean to me?"

My willpower was running on its very last fumes, and it took all I had to whisper, "It j-just really m-matters to me. It feels like . . . I just need to know."

Sebastian exhaled, and put his forehead to mine, his eyes closed. For a long moment I held my breath, my heart beating so hard it hurt. I needed him to say the right thing . . . but if he didn't, what would I do? I wasn't sure I had the strength to walk away if he insisted on us continuing to Just Be Ourselves—on leaving me to always wonder why, if labels didn't matter, did it matter so much that we not have one?

Finally, he declared in a low, soft voice, "Okay, Rufe. If it matters to you, then . . . it matters to me. We can be boyfriends."

My heart literally expanded, like a balloon, and for a second I could swear I had started to float off the bench. "Are you sure? I mean . . . so, I'm, like . . . I'm your boyfriend now? Officially?"

*"Yes, dork." He laughed a little, amused by my enthusiasm. "You're my boyfriend now—*officially.*" Sebastian was quiet for just a moment after that, gazing into my eyes, and then he added softly, "I'd do anything to make you happy. You know that, right?"*

I was so overjoyed that, to mark the occasion, I insisted we actually use the photo booth for its intended purpose. We put our money in, planning to make a series of wacky faces for the camera—to have a strip of tiny pictures of us behaving like one of those perfect couples you see in the movies, all carefree and zany and loving life; but after the first pulse of the flash went off, Sebastian pulled me into his lap and started to kiss me.

His tongue slipped into my mouth, I wrapped my hand around the back of his head, and for three more bursts of light I simply lost myself in the electrical bliss of being his boyfriend.

10

MY FATHER SPARES ME BUT A SINGLE BALEFUL GLANCE BEFORE hustling April into the backseat of his Mercedes, where I presume that both Isabel and the family attorney sit, waiting to hear the full version of what they've been dragged out of bed for in the middle of the night. After Peter climbs in to join them, the slamming of his car door booms like cannon fire in the narrow, deserted parking lot.

"Rufus, wait," Sebastian calls out as I start heading from the Jeep to the doors of the station house.

"I told you I don't want to have this conversation right now," I hiss back in annoyance, making a point not to look over at the shiny black windows of the Covingtons' luxury sedan as I hurry past. If I know Peter, he's already working out some way to hold me responsible for April's predicament, and I'm eager to avoid speaking to him for as long as possible. With any luck, he'll be tied up with my sister and her lawyer until long after the police are finished with me. Whenever that might be.

"It's not that!" Sebastian breaks into a jog, grabbing my arm and stopping me a few feet from one of the pillars that support the triangular overhang above the building's entrance. When I turn to face him, I'm surprised to see fear in his eyes. "What's the plan, here? I mean, are we seriously gonna go in there and just start talking about murder? Should *we* have lawyers? And, I mean . . . are they gonna call our parents?"

The very idea of this last possibility seems to fill him with more dread than the whole going-in-there-to-talk-about-murder part, which surprises me a little. I sure as hell don't want *my* mom involved—she has more than enough to worry about, and getting her and Peter under the same roof will surely only result in at least one more homicide for the Burlington police blotter—but I can think of no reason why Sebastian wouldn't want his well-known and widely-respected father to come down and swing some influence.

Still, he's rigid with concern, his lips pressed together as he drills the question into me with worried eyes. An unwelcome wave of sympathy buries me. "We won't need lawyers," I say, almost sure it's true. "We're not even witnesses, right? We just picked April up. Our parents will only have to be present if they decide to question us, and they won't; the murder didn't even happen in this jurisdiction. Probably they'll just want to take our statements—what did we see, when did we see it . . . that stuff."

I am, of course, putting a very optimistic face on it. We're about to walk into a police station with blood on our clothes, and while we have an explanation, that doesn't mean they're just going to accept it. And if they choose to search me for any reason, I'm going to have a hell of a time explaining away Fox's drug money.

The truth is, sooner rather than later, our parents *will* be dragged into this—I know that—and I've got no kind of plan worked up for easing into that particular phase. Stalling for time is the best strategy I've got. Sebastian seems mollified by my arguments, though, because he gives me a weak smile. "You almost sound like you know what you're talking about."

My own smile is too weak to survive. "Peter's reported me to the cops before."

"That's because you're a complete psycho with a history of violent behavior." The disembodied and chillingly familiar voice comes from somewhere over my right shoulder, and I turn slowly, like a monster-movie extra just becoming aware that the shadow behind him is actually a sixty-foot-tall radioactive tarantula.

As I pivot, my body tensing up reflexively for fight or flight, Hayden Covington emerges from behind the support pillar, where he'd apparently been leaning and smoking all along, just out of sight. His blond hair combed back from his forehead, his polo shirt the same aqua hue as his eyes, he tosses a cigarette to the ground and stomps it out with the toe of a suede deck shoe before giving me a predatory smile.

"Hayden," I say cautiously, fighting against the urge to take a step back. Mentally, and at top speed, I replay the entire conversation Sebastian and I have just had, wondering if we've incriminated ourselves somehow. I don't think so, but Hayden has an uncanny way of *knowing* things . . .

"Faggot," the boy acknowledges me casually and then, looking past me, gives a constrained nod. "Bash. What the hell are you doing here?"

"Fox Whitney is dead," I blurt, and watch as Hayden lazily tugs a soft pack of cigarettes from the pocket of his khaki shorts and busies himself with lighting one.

"So I hear," he remarks uninterestedly. For a moment, I wonder what *he's* doing there. Either Peter made him come as a show of family solidarity for April, or he's here to take pleasure in watching his sister's life fall apart. Tucking his Zippo and cigarettes back into his shorts, Hayden takes a long drag, blowing the smoke out in a sideways stream that glows in the lights from the overhang. Then he fixes me with a flat, cold stare. "What the fuck's it got to do with you?"

"April was supposed to call me." Obediently, I launch into our cover story. "When I didn't hear from her, I got nervous, and Race and Peyton said she'd been upset when their party broke up, so I thought maybe I should go out and check on her."

Wordlessly, Hayden turns his interrogative gaze on Sebastian, who swallows audibly and states, "He didn't know where Fox's lake house was, but I'd been there before, so I . . . I offered to give him a ride." Seemingly aware of how weak this sounds, he adds, "I was worried about her, too."

"When we got there, it was . . . well, it was pretty bad," I conclude, watching the red ember on the end of Hayden's cigarette, imagining him flicking it at me—or grinding it into the back of my hand. I know he's not particular.

I'm not entirely sure why I feel the need to account for my actions to Hayden Covington, of all people. In part, I tell myself, I'm just taking advantage of an opportunity to rehearse the story we're about to go in and repeat to the cops; and in part, I figure it's also my safest chance to evaluate my older brother's behavior with regard to the news of Fox's death. In my opinion, he still qualifies as a potential suspect.

Lia told us that Fox had been "trying to do something shady" with the drugs he and Arlo were dealing—shadier than just selling them in the first place, I guess—and we knew from April that Hayden had been one of Fox's customers. It is in fact likely that some of the two grand currently stretching out my shorts pocket originally came from the blond sociopath who's staring me down right at this particular moment. And Hayden is not someone you pull "something shady" on. If Fox had been running some kind of scam and my older half brother was one of his victims, eleventy million stab wounds was actually Fox getting off easy.

Nothing I've learned specifically implicates Hayden, of course—and, with the money in my pocket and April about to speak to the police, it's thankfully none of my concern any longer—but my curiosity has nevertheless been aroused. Hayden wouldn't think twice about framing his little sister for murder; he doesn't care about her any more than he cares about anybody else.

The truth is, though, that I'm gabbling to my brother like a spineless subordinate because I'm *fucking scared of him.* He's barely two years older than me, and scarcely three inches taller, but he's got shoulders like the Lincoln Memorial and a cruel streak that makes Hannibal Lecter seem cuddly by comparison. "We just drove April back to town now."

"That," Hayden remarks in a smooth voice, blowing out a ring of smoke that wobbles up into the heavy night air like a poisonous jellyfish, "is a load of bullshit."

I feel the color drain from my face. Is our lie that obvious? "It's not."

"April was supposed to *call you*? Try again, shit-sack." Hayden steps closer, and I struggle not to flinch, but he smells my fear and smiles. "Why'd you really go out there? You one of Fox's customers? Or maybe you were buying for your mom. Was she too busy sucking dicks at the bus station to get it her—"

"She *was* supposed to call me," I insist stiffly, my mouth dry, my rage struggling to free itself like a dog chewing off its own leg. *Just breathe. Keep it together.* "It was about . . . my mom and Peter. They had an argument."

It really hurts to admit this out loud, after what he's just insinuated, but it's the official story we've agreed upon for the police. Amusement glitters in Hayden's cold blue eyes, and he bares his teeth in another self-satisfied grin. "Still begging for handouts, huh? Guess she's not turning as many rich tricks anymore, now that her tits are starting to sag. Too bad. Hey, tell her I'll fuck her if she cuts her rates in half."

A muscle in my jaw flutters, heat throbbing at my temples, but I refuse to take the bait. It would suit Hayden's agenda perfectly for me to take a swing at him in front of the cops, Peter, and their family attorney. I've long since lost count of how many times we've played out this scene: my older brother goading me into a fight, beating me into the pavement, and then telling his parents that I'd been the one to attack him. His toadying friends have always been happy to back him up, to swear that if Hayden fractured my jaw, he'd only done it in self-defense.

Peter, for his part, has never failed to use each occasion as a gleeful bludgeon against my mother, repeatedly threatening lawsuits, police intervention and, typically, my removal to some institution for violent and unstable youths.

When he finally went through with it, it was almost a relief.

I was in the seventh grade when Hayden broke my arm during a fight, and Peter immediately reported me to the cops for assault. Just for good measure, he also filed a lawsuit against my mother for pain and suffering, emotional distress, and—because my half brother had sprained his wrist pounding my face in—Hayden's medical bills. It was a preemptive strike, offense as defense, and it worked; broke and unable to fight back, my mom had no choice but to sign a one-sided out-of-court settlement wherein the lawsuit would be dropped if my mother relinquished all claims to future child support. We've lived in the incident's shadow ever since.

With effort, I ignore my brother's taunting and repeat, "It was pretty bad. April is kind of messed up right now."

"So's Fox," Hayden jokes crassly. I have no idea how to respond to that, and after a moment, he continues, "She say why she did it?"

"According to her, she didn't."

"I'll bet." He picks a fleck of tobacco off his lip. Then, "You actually believe that, or did she just figure out how to make you help her get away with it?"

"No," I answer unsteadily, the money in my shorts as heavy as a piano.

"You're lying." Hayden states it, flat and certain. "Hope you at least told her to wipe her fingerprints off the knife."

I gape at him in a silence just long enough to be telltale before I recover my wits and try to push past him, mumbling, "I have to give my statement to the cops."

"I asked you a question, faggot." Hayden grips my arm hard enough to leave a bruise, jerking me right back to where I was standing before. His eyes flashing like a warning signal, he growls through gritted teeth, *"Are you covering shit up for her?"*

"Leave him alone, man," Sebastian cuts in, stepping forward.

"I know how broke-ass you guys are," Hayden continues in a jagged undertone, his breath reeking of beer and his fingers digging into my bicep like he's trying to reach my bone marrow. "You see a way to make money, you take it, right? Finding my kid sister with a dead body's like a fucking blackmail payday for you and your trashbag mom—"

"Fuck you!" I exclaim, my face blazing, the world warping before my eyes. In my mind, on an endless loop, I'm watching Hayden's teeth explode into the night sky, scattering like fireworks. I want to hit him so badly I can taste it—literally—a coppery, brackish film coating the back of my tongue.

"Hayden, what the fuck is wrong with you, man? Let him go!" Sebastian actually reaches in and peels my brother's hand off my arm. I feel the lingering pain of his grip thud with each beat of my heart as my flesh rebounds, but I refuse to acknowledge it, won't give Hayden the satisfaction of knowing how much it hurts; I just stare bullets over Sebastian's shoulder when my ex maneuvers himself between us. "Nobody's getting blackmailed, and nobody's covering anything up, okay? Fucking chill out! What's your problem?"

"What's *my* problem? What the hell is *your* problem, Bash?" Hayden redirects, his tone hard enough to drive nails through cement. "What're you doing hanging out with this freak, anyway, driving him around in the middle of the night? What's *that* about?"

"I . . . we . . ." My ex-boyfriend retreats, facing down his own personal kryptonite. "We were at the same party, and—and I heard him saying he was worried about April and it got me worried, too. I was . . . worried."

"You were *at the same party*?" Smelling blood in the water, Hayden twists his mouth into a vicious grin. "How'd that happen? I mean, it sounds like something I should hear about. You guys are hanging out, driving around . . . now you're coming to the homo's rescue? I mean, *Bash*. Is he sucking your dick or something?"

"Some of us from the school paper were having a thing tonight," I interject, trying to settle the issue quickly, "and Bash is on the staff. It's not a fucking scandal that we were both there." Sebastian surprised me, putting himself at no small personal risk by intervening with Hayden, and I want to return the favor. Too late, though, I realize I've made a grave mistake.

"Oh. It was for the *ssschool paper*." Hayden mimics my voice, making my notable sibilance sharp enough to slice paper in half. " 'Bash, we're having a little *sssoiree* for the *ssschool paper*! *Sssay* you'll be there, oh, pretty *pleassse*!' "

"Stop it," Sebastian mutters irritably, but Hayden is only getting warmed up, mirth gilding the edges of his voice.

" 'Bash, I hope you like *sssausages* and *sssticky bunsss*, because that's what we'll be *ssserving* at our little *sssoiree*!' "

"Okay, dude, let it go!"

"Hey, *Rufusss*," Hayden continues gleefully, "is it true what they say about black guys? Do they have bigger *sssausages*?"

"*Fuck you*, man!" Sebastian finally snaps. With great force, he shoves Hayden, knocking my older brother back a few steps.

The atmosphere in the parking lot changes so quickly my ears pop, and I watch Hayden snap taut as a sail in a high wind. Suddenly, he and Sebastian are toe-to-toe, noses almost touching, muscles bunching under their skin. His voice lethal, my older brother snarls, "You better fucking watch yourself, Williams, and be careful who you mess with. I don't give a shit who your dad is, or how badass you think you are; I will fucking end you."

Staring helplessly from the side, I feel like a spectator at a round of Russian roulette. Sebastian doesn't have my history with the Covingtons, doesn't know that when you tangle with Hayden there is literally no chance you can win; even if a physical fight miraculously ends in your favor, a million-to-one chance, you still have to go up against Peter—the Final Boss in a rigged game that Sebastian has never played before. My ex-boyfriend is one swing away from getting that free night in the county lock-up that April has been dreading.

"We need to give our statements," I declare loudly. I sound like a coward, inventing excuses to duck out of a fight, but it is a known fact that the dignity you preserve by standing up to Hayden is never worth the price.

"Yeah, Bash." My brother stares dead into Sebastian's eyes, coiled and unblinking. "You better go and give your *ssstatement.*"

Like someone wrenching his tongue from a frozen lamppost, Sebastian steps haltingly back from Hayden, tacitly conceding defeat in their macho standoff.

"Hope he's making it worth your while, Williams," my brother calls out in a tone that sounds an awful lot like a threat as we walk to the doors of the station house. "And don't think this conversation is over."

Even after the glass doors have shut behind us, I can still feel Hayden behind me, like a tsunami about to hit the shore.

11

FOR LOTS OF REASONS, I DON'T WANT TO JUST MARCH RIGHT UP TO the desk officer in the lobby and announce myself there to talk about a murder—among them being that I have no desire to be listed in the dispatch as the person who reported Fox's death. It will invite too much scrutiny. I'm about to lie to the cops, and don't need them to be thinking about me every time they open the case file. Another reason is that I was dead serious when I told April it would be best if she does it—if she comes forward before she can be found out. Offense as defense.

Only, April's conference with Peter and their lawyer takes much longer than I expected, and so Sebastian and I just sit and wait in a clumsy silence, minutes piling up while we struggle to get comfortable on hard-backed chairs that might have been stolen out of a seventeenth-century dungeon. A television screen mounted behind the front desk is playing the local news at a low volume, the officer on duty dividing his attention between it and us. I do my best to appear guiltless and upstanding every time he looks our way, but my constant checking of the time and anxious glances out into the parking lot probably don't serve me very well.

Sebastian hasn't spoken a word since we walked away from Hayden, keeping his eyes focused moodily on his feet. The aborted confrontation has left a considerable footprint on his mental state, and I can't figure out how to brush over it—or if brushing over it is even the right way to handle things. I'm the only one of my guy friends who's even been in an actual fight before, and no one has ever tried to talk me through the aftermath. Everything I can think of to say sounds condescending and stupid in my mind, and Sebastian seems determined to remain mute, so I follow his lead and try not to feel bad about my silence.

But then my ex-boyfriend surprises me, his eyes snapping up to mine, suddenly alert. His voice electric, he hisses quietly, *"He was there tonight."*

"Huh?" I blink at him, confused by his seemingly abrupt change in mood.

"Hayden," he says urgently, and I chance a look back over my shoulder. I can no longer see my brother outside, but I feel him lurking nevertheless, a sinister disturbance in the Force. "He was there tonight—at the lake house."

"I know." I give Sebastian a quizzical look. "Race already told us that."

"No! I mean—" My ex-boyfriend drops his volume even lower, wary of the desk officer. "I mean later. Rufus, *I think he went back.*"

This gets my attention. "What? You mean . . . you think he might've killed Fox?"

"Maybe, why not?" His knee starts bouncing. "He's not exactly shedding tears over the guy's death, and those questions he was asking . . . they were a little too on point, right? 'Are you blackmailing her?' 'Did you tell her to wipe off the knife?'" He scratches a bug bite on his arm compulsively. "At first I figured they were just freaky-accurate guesses, but, like, why ask about those things—*those exact things*—unless he knows something?"

"But how? We didn't tell anybody, April sure as heck didn't tell anybody, and there was no one but the three of—" and I stop dead midsentence, my eyes going so wide it feels like they might fall right out of my face. "*Upstairs.* Sebastian . . . holy shit. *We never checked the upstairs bedroom at the lake house.*"

We stare at each other for several seconds, frozen in place, asking ourselves the same question: *Is it possible that Fox's murderer was actually in the cottage with us the whole time?* Like an out-of-body experience, I can suddenly see myself standing in the foyer again, tilting an ear up at that narrow, twisting stairway and listening for April. Had Hayden been up there instead, hiding, listening to our initial panic, our subsequent arguing, our ultimate agreement? We hadn't seen his car, but if he'd come back to the island intending to commit a murder, he might easily have parked it somewhere up the road, out of sight.

And then the moment passes, and I start breathing again, surprised to find my temples are damp with sweat. "No. There's no way the killer was still in there with us," I reason faintly, my lips feeling stubborn and cold. "It doesn't make sense. Fox was already dead when April called me, and it took us thirty minutes to get out there. If Hayden killed him, why would he still have been hanging around? Especially a half hour after hearing April call for help?"

"I don't know." Sebastian searches my gaze, as if he might find the answer there, and I realize—suddenly, inappropriately—

that it's the longest eye contact we've sustained since he dumped me. "Maybe they really were just wild guesses. Wiping away fingerprints is pretty basic, and Hayden . . . he talks a lot of shit about you and your mom because you don't have as much money as they do. Money's a really big deal to him, and he thinks it's the same for everybody. Maybe he just accused you of trying to get cash from April because if he'd been in your position, it's what he'd have done. Maybe you're right."

Sebastian has a point, of course—and a good one. Hayden is a mercenary prick who believes the rest of us are all just as bent as he is. But now my ex-boyfriend has got me thinking more carefully about that conversation. "Maybe I'm *not* right. He brought up the knife, Sebastian." I settle my mouth into a determined line. "But April never said Fox had been stabbed—all she told Peter was that Fox had been *killed*. He could've been shot or poisoned or run over or drowned in the lake, as far as Peter was aware, so *how did Hayden know there was a knife?*"

Sebastian doesn't get a chance to answer me. At that very moment, the doors to the station crash open and April appears. Pale and blotchy, her eyes swollen from crying, she's flanked on one side by Peter and on the other by Lindsay Wells, their attorney—whom I recognize from my own legal dustups with the Covingtons. Purposefully, the three of them march straight up to the desk officer, where April speaks in a faltering, scratchy voice. "My name is April Covington, and I need to report a m-murder . . ."

The dominoes fall somewhat quickly after the big announcement. April is whisked through a door, along with Peter and Ms. Wells, and Sebastian and I finally introduce ourselves to the relevant authorities. My ex-boyfriend is squired away immediately, but it takes some ten minutes before a dashingly square-jawed young policeman in a patterned tie ushers me down a series of corridors and into a small interview room.

Introducing himself as Detective Lehmann, he asks if I want coffee. I nod, and he leaves the room briefly, returning with a cup full of what seems to be lukewarm battery acid. I have to wonder if it's some sort of interrogation tactic.

I also kind of have to wonder if Detective Lehmann's foxy green eyes, slim-hipped physique, and unruly chestnut hair are also part of the same brilliant strategy—a charm offensive to tease out my secrets. The guy can't be much older than, like, twenty-four. Twenty-five tops. Immediately, I'm tempted to remind him that I'm above the age of consent in the state of Vermont, but I have a feeling that might weaken my position. Prudently, I remind myself that I'm about to lie to this man—this droolworthy cartoon prince of a man—and I need to keep my shit together.

Besides, he's a cop; he undoubtedly already knows the age of consent.

"So, Rufus," he begins, leaning back in his chair as if this were just a casual chat. "That's a cool name—I like it."

He spreads his legs a little, and I almost start to hyperventilate. Exhibiting tremendous self-control, I manage a neutral "Thanks."

"I always wanted a cool name. Mine is Conrad." He gives me an adorkably sheepish grin. "I hate it, but it's sort of a family legacy. Our *other* legacy name is Humphrey, though, so I guess I got off kinda easy, huh?"

"Sure," I agree, but his you-and-me Good Cop routine has just tripped my bullshit meter, and my guard begins to go back up by degrees. I'm used to authority figures trying to snare me in my own words, and I feel an instinctive mistrust of his pleasantness.

The time they kept me waiting for this little conversation comes back to me all of a sudden, and my shoulders go tense as I wonder if maybe the detective was checking up on me. Hayden was right: I *do* have a questionable history speckled with violent incidents, and it's not going to help me in this situation.

Every kid has temper tantrums, but as my friends in daycare and elementary school were growing out of theirs, I was growing in to mine. By the age of ten, my tantrums had evolved into howling frenzies, episodes of rage so ferocious that they scared even me; my anger was like a physical presence inside me, one that would swell so large, my body simply couldn't contain it any longer, and I would rant and flail and attack until I collapsed with exhaustion.

When my mom realized my issues were getting worse instead of better, she started looking into solutions. We went through a handful of mental health professionals and a slew of medications—from pills that made me paranoid and hyper to ones that made me numb and affectless—until we found the right mix. I haven't had a serious outburst in over a year, and the meds I'm on now help me manage my emotions without making me feel cut off from them; but my past is my past, and I'm not anxious to start babbling excuses for it to a man with police credentials.

Detective Conrad Lehmann folds his arms behind his head, his biceps straining against his tailored oxford shirt, and fixes me with a friendly look. "So, Rufus Holt with the cool name, why don't we start at the beginning. You tell me what happened tonight, in your own words, and I'll stop you if I have questions."

Clearing my throat, I do as I'm told, keeping my story as basic as possible. Liars often embellish, thinking little details are what give a tale its ring of truth; it is not so. Details are home to the devil, as they say, and every one you toss in becomes a trap to catch you out if you're not careful.

As I speak, though, running through our reimagined timeline—wherein our visits to Lia, Arlo, Race, and Peyton all come before April's call for help—my mind is wholly occupied with thoughts of Hayden. Is it really possible that he was hiding in the upstairs bedroom all along while we bumbled around on the ground floor? If he *had* murdered Fox, though, why on earth would he have still been hanging around the lake house when Sebastian and I arrived? Why wouldn't he have left immediately? Unless . . .

It hits me so suddenly that I actually stop speaking for a moment in the middle of my account, faking a coughing fit so I can buy a few precious seconds to think. *The money.*

Money's a really big deal to him. Sebastian has no idea how right he is. If Hayden went back to the lake house, murdered Fox, and then set April up to take the heat, he *still* wouldn't have gone anywhere—not until he recovered the cash he'd paid to his dealer earlier in the evening. No sense leaving it with a dead guy, right? I think about April's breathy, tremulous voice over the phone—*I need . . . I need help, Rufus*—and the loud blaring of Fox's music when we arrived; it's just possible that, if Hayden had been in another room, he might not even have heard April's call to me. He might not have been aware that anyone was on the way until Sebastian actually started knocking at the front door.

"Why didn't you call the police from the scene?" Detective Lehmann asks me suddenly, breaking through my reverie. I blink at him, thrown for just a moment, and he reiterates, "You found your sister shut up in a house with a dead body; why didn't you call the police right away?"

He sounds markedly less friendly now, but it's a question I've been anticipating. "April was really freaked out, and she phoned her parents first. They didn't want her talking to anyone without them present."

This has the benefit of being more or less the truth, but Detective Lehmann frowns anyway. "That sounds kinda strange, doesn't it? Why wouldn't they want her talking to the police?"

"Peter Covington is a lawyer."

He nods slowly. All cops understand interfering lawyers. "Did you know the victim, too?"

"Fox? Sort of. We're in the same grade, and he's popular."

"But you weren't friends?"

"No." I regret my tone the second the word leaves my mouth.

Detective Lehmann arches a brow. "You didn't like him."

Caught, I mumble, "We just . . . weren't friends."

"Why not?"

Now *that* is a loaded question. "Because I'm not popular. Because he didn't have any use for me. The only thing we had in common was our zip code."

"Did he pick on you?"

"He picked on everybody," I answer flatly, and watch the man chew on this for a moment, exploring it for alternate routes.

"So you're not going to miss him."

My body won't let me answer. I know how stupid it would be to lie—there'll be no minimizing it if he checks up on my story and finds out how much bad blood there really is between me and Fox's crew—but the truth feels too damning to admit, so I stare back at the detective dumbly until he speaks again.

"What time did you get to the lake house?" He poses the question in an off-handed way, but it's information I've already supplied, and I feel heat prickle under my arms. Maybe I should have lied after all—said anything to keep him from tugging at the threads of our story. I need him to dismiss me as a potential suspect and move on.

For a split second, I consider bringing up Hayden, putting them onto his scent; April is unlikely to mention him, having made no connection between his visit to the cottage and the events that transpired after she blacked out, so it might be down to me to make sure the cops consider him. But I have to let the notion go almost as soon as it pops into my head. How can I implicate my brother without compromising myself and April and Sebastian in the process? I don't even have a clear sense of motive yet.

Steadily, I meet Detective Lehmann's eyes. "We were already on our way out there when April called to tell me what happened, so I guess like maybe ten minutes after that?"

Lehmann nods thoughtfully. Then: "I've got to tell you, Rufus, something about this isn't adding up."

I go completely still. "Huh?"

"Earlier, you said that April called her parents first thing; so, if she knew they were already handling the situation, I guess I don't understand why she felt she needed to call you, too." It isn't a question, and I have no answer for it anyway, so I let him go on. "Why did she? If you and Fox weren't even friends, I mean?"

It takes every ounce of willpower I have not to look up or away while I scramble to think—telltale signs of bullshitting that he's no doubt been trained to look for. "She'd been drinking," I begin experimentally, my mouth so dry it clicks, "and she was freaking out. Some of her friends . . . well, okay, look—they were doing . . . some stuff at that party that was worse than just drinking, you know? And April was afraid of what would happen if her parents saw all of . . . you know, that stuff. So she called me. She was supposed to call me anyway, and she was really . . . I mean, she was freaking out! I guess she was hoping I could pick her up so her parents wouldn't have to know."

My pulse is beating so hard I'm afraid it's going to leave bruises, but Lehmann merely nods. "More serious than drinking, huh? What are we talking, here? Drugs?"

"I guess." I shift in my seat. "I'd rather not get into it, though. I wasn't at the party, so I don't know for sure what went on. You'd have to ask April."

"Was she using, too?"

My mind goes suddenly, terrifyingly blank. I hadn't intended to open the door to this question—had only done so out of desperation—and I truly don't know how to answer. April had sworn to me, convincingly, that she'd only had alcohol at the party . . . but I still can't bring myself to accept it. My uncle Connor had stayed with us for a few weeks while recovering from knee surgery the previous year, and so I know the difference between "drunk" and "fucked up on meds." I would bet every cent of the two thousand dollars in my pocket right now that April had been the latter when Sebastian and I found her at the cottage.

In the half second it takes me to trip over this seed of doubt, I've already missed my window of opportunity to give an innocuous answer; just enough time has now passed for a "no" to look like deception, an "I don't know" to sound evasive, and a "yes" to go without saying. I lick my lips again, preparing to blurt some kind of brilliant damage control . . . and am spared—miraculously—when the door to the room bangs suddenly open.

"What the hell is going on?"

To my shock, it's Peter, his face a familiarly livid shade of scarlet.

"Sir, I'm afraid you can't be in here." Detective Lehmann is on his feet in an instant, already moving to intercept my father. "These rooms are off-limits to—"

"What has he been asking you?" Peter demands of me over the detective's shoulder. "Did he tell you that you have a right to counsel?"

"Sir, you need to leave," Lehmann snaps sharply, his palsy-walsy demeanor gone in a hurry. "I am interviewing a potential witness in a sensitive—"

"'Interviewing,' my ass!" Peter shoots back, glaring at the hapless detective like he's trying to incinerate the man's soul with his eyes. "You're aware that Rufus is a minor? You have no right to interrogate him without notifying his—"

"This is not an interrogation; I am merely taking his statement, and there is no need—"

"'Taking his statement?' You've been in here for almost fifteen minutes! How long does it take to ascertain that he got a phone call from his sister, picked her up, and drove her here—to you?" He manages to make it sound like Detective Lehmann is not only incompetent but possibly also corrupt. To me, Peter barks, "Have you told him that much already?" Meekly, and somewhat dazed, I nod, and Peter nods back. "Good. Then get your things together. It's time for you to go home."

"Sir!" The beautiful detective is plainly aghast. "You have no right to—"

"I happen to be Rufus's father, as well as his attorney, so I'm afraid I have *every* right," Peter returns icily, "and unless you plan to arrest him for something, he is free to walk out of here any time he chooses. I won't have you exploiting his ignorance of legal process to pressure him. He's told you what happened, and that's all he's obligated to do. If you have any more questions for him, you can ask them through me." With pointed rudeness, my father produces a business card and tucks it into Detective Lehmann's breast pocket—the white-collar equivalent of *go fuck yourself.* "Also, for the record, I expect a copy of his statement to be forwarded to my office. If I discover that any part of it was coerced, I'm going to have your badge, *Detective*. Rufus, let's go."

I'm too stunned to argue, and don't know if I even have the wherewithal to try. As if under remote control, I rise to my feet and duck through the door, singed by the laser grid of white-hot glares that pass between the two men. I don't look up at either of them.

12

WORDLESSLY, I FOLLOW PETER DOWN THE EMPTY CORRIDOR LEADING back to the lobby, expecting armed policemen to jump out of nowhere at any moment and stop us from leaving the building. I still don't entirely understand what's just happened, and I'm not at all certain that Peter actually has the right to yank me out from under Detective Lehmann's nose like that.

It's not only Peter's intervention in the nick of time, though—saving me from an increasingly curious policeman who seemed to have caught the scent of my dishonesty—that has me so jumpy and off-balance. It's also the way that he authoritatively identified himself as *my father* in front of the detective. It's a biological fact that he has only ever admitted to in the past while under legal duress.

As grateful as I am to have been rescued from the interview before having had a chance to shoot myself in the foot, however, I'm not about to say thank you. I know Peter far too well to make the mistake of believing that his fierce performance of paternal concern has anything to do with my rights being abused. As if to drive the point home, my father stops abruptly in the middle of the narrow hallway, grabs me by the arm, and hauls me with him into a small unisex bathroom. Locking the door behind us, he then slams me—hard—against the wall. "What the *fuck* did you tell him?"

"Nothing!" Sixteen years of ingrained fear streak up my spine and race around my brain like a feral cat. "I said what you said—April called, we picked her up, and we drove her here. Let me go!"

His eyes bore into me like oil drills, the same dark gray as my own. We have the same wheat-colored hair, the same Cupid's bow mouth; I hate that I look so much like him. I hate that I have to be reminded of him every time I look in the mirror. Saliva gathering at the corners of his lips, my father snarls, "I know you had something to do with this. I don't know what, but it's got your stink all over it."

"I didn't have anything to do with anything! Now, let. Me. Go!" I shove him, and he shoves back harder, slamming me into the wall again and driving the air from my lungs. The room flips upside down and turns red, rage knotting suddenly together and throbbing in my chest like an alien spawn just below my heart.

"April is a good kid. Her friends are good kids—*respectable* kids," Peter rants on, clearly having no idea what he's talking about. "What did you do? There's no chance in hell you were invited to the Whitneys' lake house tonight, so what were you up to out there?" His face is lavender now, his teeth bared just inches from my nose. "You're the one who did it, aren't you? You killed that young man, and you've somehow talked April into covering for you—"

"April's *respectable friends* were dealing drugs, you stupid asshole!" I hiss back savagely, the pressure in my chest strangling my voice.

Peter blinks once, twice, and then actually shakes his head like a dog trying to cast off water. "No. No, that is . . . it's . . . disgusting, and you should be ashamed of yourself. Fox Whitney was a—"

"Fox Whitney was a *drug dealer.* Your daughter was dating a *drug dealer.*" I pronounce the words as sharply as I can, imagining the syllables as fists slamming into Peter's body. "That house looked like a fucking crack den when we showed up, and when we dragged April out of a *pool of blood* in Fox's kitchen, she was so damn stoned that even *she's* not sure she didn't—"

"That is . . . that is a *monstrous* lie," Peter gasps out. "How dare you—"

"The sheriff is probably real busy right now, bagging up about four hundred little white pills that were lying around at the *respectable* party April was having with all the *good kids* she runs around with—"

"You shut your mouth," Peter growls furiously, his face bright red. "I have had it with you and your underhanded mother trying to ruin my life, trying to sabotage my family and jeopardize everything I care about! I will get a copy of your statement from the police, and if I find out that you lied, that you . . . *did something* to put April in danger, I swear, I—I'll . . ."

He raises a fist halfway into the air, his hand trembling. In all the times we've faced off, all the times Peter has threatened me, physical violence has never entered the equation; he's bigger than me, his rages worse than mine, but I've never been truly afraid he might hurt me. Until right now, when I can see the depth of his loathing in eyes that look exactly like my own. He really wants to do it.

My voice embarrassingly small, I whisper, "Go ahead. Any lies I told, I told to protect April. But go ahead—give me a reason to call for Detective Lehmann so I can tell him what I really know."

It's a bluff—obviously—but Peter isn't so sure; and for all his talk about April being a "good kid," the doubt and fear that flash across his face tell me he honestly isn't sure that she *didn't* do it after all. In fact, he's terrified that she did.

He lets me go. Stepping back, his face pale, he sucks a breath of air through his nostrils and then stabs an unsteady finger at me. "You stay away from my family. I'll get a restraining order if I have to, but you stay away."

Then he storms out of the bathroom and back into the hallway, slamming the door shut again behind him.

I just stand there after he's left, trying to get myself back under control, quaking all over as tears clog my eyes and start to roll. The fear and anger that have been warring inside me are discharging like faulty wiring, and I feel like I'm going to be sick. I'm furious with myself for letting Peter push me to the point where I can't cope—humiliated by my impotence. I slam a fist into the space beside the light switch over and over until I feel the pain, until the drywall buckles and the skin across my knuckles splits and I have to wash the blood away in the sink.

As the water slips through my fingers, I think about just how much of my father is written into my DNA. I see him in the mirror every day—but it's what we share on the inside that casts the longest shadow over me. Every time my anger opens up, every time I feel it speeding through my veins, hear it thundering in my ears, it's one more reminder of Peter Covington. His influence works on me, unseen, like the moon pulling at the tides; and every day I struggle to remember that we are separate planets.

My knuckles stinging, I snatch up some paper towels, wiping my eyes and blowing my nose. Only then do I finally exit the bathroom.

Sebastian is waiting for me in the lobby, his eyes fixed on the television behind the front desk. He gives me a strange look as I approach, and I wonder if the stress of the past few minutes is as readable in my hot, blotchy face as it feels. Mustering my voice, I begin, "Are you done? Because I'm really ready to get the hell out of—"

"Rufus," Sebastian interrupts, his voice grave. "Look."

He directs my attention to the TV screen, where a local newscaster with great masses of hair is already in the midst of a report, peering earnestly into the camera. "—update on that house fire on Banfield Crescent. Fire Department officials are telling us that the blaze is now under control, and that early indicators suggest this was indeed a case of arson." The image cuts to a shot of a grandly gabled home, all peaked roofs and gingerbread trim, about a third of which is a rollicking inferno of bright orange flames. The newscaster's voice continues over the footage: "It was about two hours ago that the first calls came in to 911, reporting a fire in the high-end enclave of Banfield Crescent. Evidence suggests that the blaze began in the garage and spread quickly; by the time first responders arrived, much of this historic Victorian mansion was in flames." Another angle on the conflagration, menacing coils of smoke pouring up into the night sky, black on black. "Firefighters were shocked to discover *obscenities* spray-painted on the house's front door, an act of vandalism leading many to speculate that the fire had been set deliberately—a situation that officials are now calling 'likely.'" The shot cuts to a close-up of the whitewashed front door, the obscenities in question apparently so vulgar that they cannot be shown on television; digitally blurred out, they are nothing but a blobby, pinkish smear floating in space. "According to neighbors, the homeowners are out of town for the holiday, and attempts to reach them have so far been unsuccessful. Representatives of the police and fire departments are asking anyone with information to come forward."

"Dude." Sebastian grips my arm, tense and wide-eyed, as the newscaster drones on with pertinent hotline numbers. "Rufe . . . that's the Whitneys' place. *It's Fox's house.*"

"What?" I stare at him, trying to understand.

Someone set fire to Fox's house. It doesn't make any sense. It has to be related to his death; it strains credulity too far to suggest he might have been murdered and his house torched on the same night just by coincidence—but I still can't fit the two pieces together. The fire was first reported two hours earlier, which means we were probably just pulling up to the Atwoods' at the time. The blaze couldn't have been started *before* Fox died; but why would someone kill him at the cottage and then drive all the way back into Burlington and set light to his empty home? What would be the point?

I'm pondering the question, trying to remind myself that I've already fulfilled my obligation where the solving of this puzzle is concerned, when we step out into the parking lot again. It's just after two in the morning, the stifling heat of the day having finally abated, and the damp night air wraps around me like a tepid embrace. I'm hungry and exhausted, overjoyed at the thought of heading home; but as we start for the Jeep, I catch Sebastian glancing around, his eyes skittering between shadows.

"What?"

"I don't see Hayden." He makes the remark sound as casual as he can, and his forced nonchalance speaks volumes. "Guess he was just talking shit."

"He probably got bored and went home," I say. "You ask me, the only reason he was here in the first place was to fuck with me and enjoy April's panic."

Sebastian is quiet for a moment, and then mumbles, "I didn't know he could be like that."

"Really?" I cast him a sharp look. "Because he's never been like anything else with me, and he's never done much to hide it, either. Half the school hates him."

"Yeah, but . . ." Sebastian won't look up at me. "I always just figured people were jealous, you know? He's popular, he's . . . well, you know, he's *hot*, and . . . and I mean, sure, he makes fun of people sometimes, but . . ."

"But what?" I stop walking, determined to make him acknowledge me for this part. "But those people were losers, so they had it coming?"

"I didn't say that." His eyebrows draw together. "Don't put words in my mouth. Hayden makes fun of people, but it's usually just kid stuff, you know? Trying to be funny, to get a laugh." It's preposterous, and I feel a wave of insult cresting inside me; Hayden's version of "kid stuff" is sticks and stones with actual sticks and stones. But before I'm able to reply, Sebastian continues, "I guess I knew the guy had kind of a dark side, but he's always been cool with me. I've never seen him act the way he did tonight—to be that . . . intense. Is that . . . I mean, is that really the way he is with you? All the time?"

"Yes," I answer shortly, simmering inside, because of *course* Sebastian has seen Hayden "act the way he did tonight." He's seen *all* his friends act like that at one time or another. "Hayden is a freaking psychopath—like, a textbook one, with no actual conscience—and if you haven't noticed it before, it's only because you haven't *wanted* to notice."

And with those words, it finally hits me, and I feel like a moron. It's easy for Sebastian to be in denial of my brother's hateful villainy, because this is the first time he's ever been on the receiving end of it. Throughout the months we were dating, one of the things that terrified Sebastian the most was how his friends would react if they found out about us, what parts of his life would be upended or destroyed as people he cared about assimilated news they might not like. Tonight, for a few precious seconds, he lived his nightmare when Hayden turned on him, and now it's eating him alive.

Just like that, my anger begins to subside. I have a considerable storehouse of hurt feelings thanks to my ex-boyfriend, for reasons both legitimate and petty, but this is something I simply can't bring myself to hold against him. His blindness to how awful his friends can be is frustrating, but no one deserves to suffer Hayden Covington's ruthless schadenfreude; and how many times in the past did I ignore Sebastian's fears and blithely insist to him that coming out wouldn't be as bad as he feared? That he wouldn't endure exactly this kind of treatment? *I've* been just as guilty of willful blindness as he has, and out of the same selfish instinct to polish up an inconvenient turd.

"You know what? Never mind—forget I said anything." I

exhale wearily, rubbing my eyes. "I'm just exhausted, and I want tonight to go away. It's been a really shitty Fourth of July."

"No argument there." Sebastian gives me a meek smile of contrition, and we turn to head for his Jeep again.

There's no warning—no sound of an indrawn breath or a foot scuffing on pavement, no rustle of leaves or swish of fabric; we make it about two steps, and then a dark figure lunges at me out of nowhere, materializing from the void between two parked cars, and my life flashes before my eyes.

13

"RUFUS. WE NEED TO TALK."

I stumble backward, hands flying up in self-defense, my brain a typhoon of adrenaline as I blink uncomprehendingly into the darkness before me. The figure stopped short, abruptly, and only now finally steps out of the shadows. Dazed, I watch as moonlight deftly describes the harshly beautiful features of Isabel Covington—Peter's wife. Even at two in the morning, she is elegant: Clad in dark slacks and a silk blouse, her auburn hair tied back, she looks like she might be on her way to an afternoon business meeting. On a finger of her left hand, a diamond the size of a shrunken head glitters coldly, deliberately. April isn't the only thing Peter gave his wife in an effort to save their marriage.

My pulse starts to slow down again—but only marginally; just because Isabel isn't about to chainsaw me to death doesn't mean she's not a threat. "Whatever you have to tell me, I'm sure Peter already said it inside."

She doesn't even blink. "I doubt that very much."

"Okay, well . . . you can keep it to yourself, anyway." I keep my expression stony, even though my nerves are still crackling like Rice Krispies. "Peter already promised to get a restraining order, and I'm more than happy to go along with it if it means you guys will keep the hell away from me."

I try to step around her, but she moves like a cat—quickly, and with startling quiet for someone in spindle-heeled pumps. "What we have to talk about is more important than that."

Searching her face, I wonder how much disrespect I can get away with. Isabel has the capability to make my life truly miserable if she wants, and a long time ago I learned it was better to put up with infuriating insults than to give her an excuse to make her point in more consequential ways. But it's been a very long night, and I'm pretty much done being abused by the Covingtons. Coldly, I state, "I have to go home."

I push past her again and am almost to the back of the Jeep when she calls out, "I know everything that happened tonight, Rufus. The money April paid you, the visits to her friends, the fake phone call to establish your alibi . . . everything."

For the second time that night, I do a slow, horror-movie turnaround in that parking lot, cold all the way through with the frostbite of alarm. "What?"

"April told me," Isabel says simply. "Peter and Lindsay got out of the car for a private conference"—these two words, *private conference*, are shaded with a subtle disdain that suggests volumes—"and April gave me the whole story. We don't keep secrets from each other."

"Of course not." I could strangle April. Of *course* she told her mother everything. She's never been in serious trouble before, has never faced parental discipline, and has probably never been punished by anyone for telling the truth. She was either too naive to understand—or too apathetic to give a shit—what would happen to *me* when she laid all our cards on the table before Isabel. I taste bile. "So, what now? Are you here to threaten me? My mom already agreed to stop seeking child support. What else do you want?"

"You misunderstand me." Maddeningly, she's still completely unruffled. "Peter doesn't know anything about it. I could have told him—I could also be in there right now, telling the police. But I'm not." She waits a beat. "Aren't you curious why?"

"Not really," I lie stiffly, refusing to be baited.

"Because April's the one with her butt in a sling," Sebastian interjects, his reminder etched with confused agitation; he seems to sense that Isabel is up to something, but he can't figure out her angle. "If the cops find out what . . . well, what really happened, she's way worse off than either of us will be."

"Not entirely true, Mr. Williams," Isabel counters, vaguely amused. "April has a very, very good lawyer, and Rufus is under a lot of scrutiny right now by the school board. Probably more than his permanent record could withstand if charges were brought against him for withholding evidence, tampering with a crime scene, obstruction of justice—"

"*What do you want?*" A surge of unbearable rage spoils the meager contents of my stomach. Every time I think I've exhausted the supply of loathing I have for my father's family, I tap into a brand-new vein of it waiting to be plumbed—a dark harvest that burns my insides like poison. No one knows better than Isabel Covington how much scrutiny the school board has me under; she is their president.

Six months ago, I was hanging out in an alcove behind the

school one night with Lucy and our friend Brent, sharing a forty-ounce of disgusting beer procured for us by Brent's older sister. Ironically, we were only out there—where it was dark as hell, and the lake gleamed like graphite through winter-stripped trees—because it was the most desolate place we could think of to consume alcohol. Imagine our surprise, then, when a security guard appeared out of nowhere, flashing his Maglite around like a death laser and screaming at us to put our hands up.

Brent and Lucy got off with slaps on the wrists, but since I had actually been holding the bottle when we got caught—and because my name is *Rufus Holt*—I was brought before a very special kangaroo-court school board hearing, where all my prior sins were exhaustively catalogued. My fights with Hayden and his cronies; the time I busted Cody Barnes's tooth with that chair in the eighth grade; the time, freshman year, when my science teacher falsely accused me of cheating on a test and I got so upset, I hurled a ridiculously expensive microscope at a plate glass window, shattering both—they were all exhumed and picked over in front of me, like corpses found crudely buried in a basement crawl space.

In the end, I was given a week's suspension and two months' probation—along with the dire promise that *the school board would be watching me.*

"I want you to be fully aware of your circumstances, here. Given your background, I'm sure the board would feel compelled to review your file again in light of any police action against you," Isabel goes on, my red-faced resentment clearly warming the cockles of her heart, "and put some further consideration into whether or not Ethan Allen High is really the proper environment for a student such as yourself."

I'm so angry it feels like my eyes are bleeding. Paralyzed by wrath, I can't seem to move or even think clearly enough to speak—which is fine, as there exists no insult equal to the challenge of capturing Isabel Covington's coldblooded deviousness.

"Contrary to what you might think, Rufus, I don't hate you," she continues serenely, absurdly. "I'm sure you think I'm a bitch, but everything I've done, all the recommendations I've made to the board in the past, have been in your best interest. I believe you could do with a more disciplined setting than Ethan Allen offers, and I think—I hope—that someday you'll see I'm right."

"*What. Do. You. Want?*" I repeat, shaking all over and once more on the verge of tears. I cannot deal with this. I shouldn't *have* to deal with this; it isn't fair.

Isabel sighs, her nasty, self-satisfied smirk vanishing into the shadows. "I have a proposition for you."

"Huh?" I actually cock my head to the side, my mind-altering fury stumbling over its own feet as I try to process this statement.

"April did not do this." She declares it flatly, but an anxious line appears between her brows. "*Obviously*, she didn't do this, and what she's going through right now is . . . It's a nightmare. It's my worst nightmare." She squeezes her eyes shut, and for the first time in possibly ever, a glimmer of fragile humanity shows through Isabel's rock-hard exterior. Just as quickly, though, she banishes her fragile humanity back to the hell from whence it came, snarling, "It was that good-for-nothing Rossi boy, of course; his father is an alcoholic, his mother was a whore, and he's been a time bomb waiting to go off for years. I am certain the police will find the proof against him. In time."

This sentence has ended with a silent *but*, so I supply it. "But?"

"I know how bad it looks for April. The Whitneys are incredibly high-profile in this community, and the authorities will be under enormous pressure to close this case as quickly as possible." Her mouth tightens. "The Atwoods and the Forsyths . . . they won't care what the outcome is, so long as their precious little brats are kept in the clear, and I *know* how teenagers operate. Race and Peyton and . . . that Mexican girl, Lisa—"

"*Lia.*" Sebastian mutters his surly correction automatically.

"They won't want to say anything. Arlo Rossi is a *thug.* A violent *thug*, and he's had half the school cowering with fear since the day he started there." She might just as easily be speaking of her own son, and I wonder if she even sees the irony. "He was supposed to have been held back a year, but no one wanted him at Ethan Allen a day longer than necessary—and I mean *no one.*" She takes a deep breath. "The kids will be terrified of retribution from him and his knuckle-dragging friends if they speak out, and so they'll just hold their tongues and hope that April isn't convicted for something she didn't do. I cannot afford to be that careless."

I can't contain my sarcasm. "But April has a *very, very good lawyer.*"

"And she would be acquitted at trial," Isabel returns promptly. "Only—"

"You don't want it to go to trial," Sebastian concludes.

"It would be devastating for April. This is too small a town for her to survive the kind of spotlight it would bring her under, and her entire life would be—" She swallows the words, unable to finish. "The police will have to make an arrest soon; the Whitneys will see to that. And if they can't convince one of the other kids to turn on Arlo, April will be a sitting duck. Her life will be ruined."

"So what's your proposition?" I ask with toneless reluctance, sweating in fear of her answer.

"You know these kids." Her self-consciously cultured voice is almost imploring. "I am aware that they're not your friends, but you are their age, and they'll admit things to you that they won't say in front of an adult—certainly not a police officer, and certainly not in the presence of an attorney hired by their parents." Her hands flex open and shut, that massive diamond winking and spitting moonlight. "April paid you two thousand dollars to talk to these kids, to see what you could find out, and she said you believed they were lying to you."

"They were," I affirm carefully, taking an instinctive step back. The stench of blackmail is still thick in the air, and I still don't like the direction the wind is blowing. "But I can't even be sure they were all lying about the same thing."

"I will pay you," Isabel finally states, "to keep trying. The money April gave you is yours; I don't care about it, and insofar as it looks bad for her, I am happy for no one else to learn about it, either. But I will give you double again—an additional four thousand—if you can turn up evidence that exonerates April *before* the police are forced to make an arrest." She steps forward, her eyes flashing. "That is critical, Rufus. The deal depends on that condition. I will pay you, but only if you can provide something that preempts April's arrest."

I stare at her, open-mouthed. Isabel Covington is actually begging me for help. It's a deal with the devil—literally, from my viewpoint—but once again, the arithmetic is incredibly simple:

April's two, plus Isabel's four, plus the two thousand my uncle Connor borrowed last Christmas together equals the eight grand my mom needs to pay back the bank. *But is it worth it?*

I think about Arlo's gun and Hayden's powder keg of violent rage; Peyton's derisive sneering, Race's open hostility, and Lia's withering rudeness. It has been a hair-raising and wildly unpleasant night. Do I really want to go, once more, into that dismal breach? The answer is a resounding, and easy, no.

But then I picture my mom again—asleep in bed with her latest romance novel or self-help guide forgotten beside her—and this time I also see the pile of unpaid, unopened bills spilling off the nightstand and onto the floor. I envision April sitting in an interview room across from a scowling detective, trying to hold it together and tell the lies I scripted for her out of little more than a sense of self-preservation, and wonder if it's even fair of me to abandon her cause now.

Holding my breath, I meet Isabel's eyes with a silent prayer for some of that protection that's supposed to grace fools and children—at the moment, I feel like both. "Okay. It's a deal."

14

"RUFUS, ARE YOU FUCKING *NUTS*?" SEBASTIAN DEMANDS THE second we're back inside the Jeep. Isabel is already halfway to the police station doors, but I glance nervously in the direction of her sensitive ears anyway as my ex-boyfriend continues. "I mean, have you actually lost your damn mind? What the hell were you thinking?"

"I need the money," I mutter uncomfortably.

"How can you be sure she'll actually pay you?" He's becoming belligerent. "I mean, do you even *trust* that woman?"

"No." The glum admission doesn't make me feel any better. In my experience, most adults suffer from a crippling case of selective amnesia, prone to flare-ups any time they've made an inconvenient promise to someone under the age of eighteen. In particular, I've got absolutely no reason to think or hope that Isabel will decide to honor our arrangement if I manage to give her what she wants; after all, there's no one to hold her accountable if she chooses to screw me over.

On the other hand, about the nicest thing I *can* say regarding Isabel Covington is that she doesn't waste her breath. Peter, when he's caught up in the ecstasy of his rage, has a habit of guaranteeing hellfire he can't actually deliver; and half of Hayden's threats are deliberately empty, because he likes to keep his victims jumping at shadows. But Isabel is too obsessed with her own power to weaken it with empty saber-rattling. When she makes a promise, she follows through, and I just have to hope she'll consider it a matter of personal integrity to make good on the deal we've struck.

"Are you listening to yourself?" Sebastian is still upset, his large, dark eyes probing me angrily through the gloom in the Jeep. "Somebody murdered Fox, Rufus! *Murdered* him. Let the police deal with it! I mean, this was stupid enough before, when we were going around pretending we didn't know anything, but what do you think you're gonna do now? Show up at everyone's door and say, 'Hey, by the way, did you happen to stab Fox a million times and frame April for it?' "

I grit my teeth. "I don't know."

"You don't know," he fumes. "And you're just gonna, you know, *hope* that Maleficent Covington remembers to give you four grand when it's all over—*if* no one's killed you by then."

"Yeah, that's about the size of it," I snap back.

"Do you not even see that something is very seriously fucked up in the state of Denmark, here?" His tone is incredulous. "If Mrs. Covington is really worried about April's life being destroyed, why isn't she hiring an actual detective? She obviously despises you, Rufus; she didn't even bother to hide it! So unless she's got something up her sleeve, why the hell would she ask you to do this?"

"Lots of reasons." I count them on my fingers. "For one thing, a real private detective might cost her way more than four thousand dollars, and still not turn up anything; for another, if a legit P.I. found out about all the lies you, me, and April told the cops tonight, he'd have to report them or lose his license—and Isabel sure as hell doesn't want *that* happening; and for thirds, whether I prove April didn't do it or I get arrested or killed in the process, it's a win-win situation for the Covingtons."

"Oh, well that's just fucking *great*." He sounds disgusted. "What if she's planning to screw you? You told me yourself that she gets off on seeing you suffer; you don't even trust her, but you're willing to maybe put your life in danger because she *says* she'll pay you? How do you know she's not just jerking you around?"

"I don't."

"Well, then, what the hell, Rufus? Why did you agree?"

"Because. I need. The money!" I shout furiously. Sebastian's been to the tiny bungalow where my mom and I live—seen the beat-up old Nissan we share, the refurbished laptop I use, and my mom's shabby collection of flaking, secondhand paperbacks—but he has zero understanding of how deep our financial troubles go. It isn't his fault, but he simply can't relate. For Sebastian, a cash flow problem means he's spent his allowance and has to wait for the next installment. "We could lose our house, okay? My mom's business has been eating shit for years, and when Peter stopped sending support payments, she had to start using her savings to cover our bills. We're really, really fucked, Sebastian, and I can't afford *not* to take the chance that Isabel will deliver. I *can't*."

There's a thick silence, the shadows moving around us like

slime, and then he says the worst thing possible. "Shit. I'm sorry, Rufus. I had no idea—"

"Just drop me off at my house," I cut in roughly. I've put up with Hayden's bullying, Peter's contempt, and Isabel's manipulations; I'll be damned if I let Sebastian Williams pity me. "I can use my mom's car."

His eyebrows arch in disbelief. "You mean you're gonna try to go through with this ridiculous bullshit *tonight*?"

"When's a better time?" I challenge. "At least now I've still got surprise on my side. Once news of Fox's death gets out, and everybody hires a lawyer, I've got nothing. Whatever Isabel believes, none of those guys are going to talk to me unless they think I'm holding something over them. If I hit them with what happened to Fox, somebody's gonna have to fake a reaction, and I'm betting I'll know it when I see it."

"That is literally the stupidest plan I've ever heard."

Unfortunately, it *is* stupid. And what if it does turn out that Hayden is the killer? Not only is it too late to spring news of Fox's death on him and measure his response, but will Isabel still be willing to pay me if I only prove her daughter is innocent at the expense of her son? Still, it's better than the alternative—no plan at all—and so I state, churlishly, "Well, lucky for you, you don't need to worry about it. Just drive me home. You know . . . please."

Sebastian starts the Jeep, grumbling under his breath, but as he reverses out of the parking spot, he grunts, "That's idiotic. I'm coming with you."

"You don't have to do that," I return, exasperated. "You've done enough."

Sebastian slams on the brakes hard enough to make my

seat belt engage, and my heart jumps reflexively into my throat as the vehicle bounces to a sudden stop. His eyes smoldering, my ex-boyfriend glares at me from behind the wheel. "What the hell is wrong with you, Rufus? Do you really think I'd let you do this by yourself? When April gave you that money, I thought . . . I thought she'd killed Fox, and she was just trying to game you or something. But you could be walking into some serious, life-threatening shit, here, and I couldn't live with myself if I let you do it alone!"

"You don't have to—"

"*Fuck!* I *know* what I don't have to *fucking do*!" He exclaims furiously, smashing his fist against the steering wheel, and I stiffen in my seat. I've never seen Sebastian so angry. "I want to help you! Do you get that? One of these guys might've actually wasted Fox, and at least if there's two of us, they'll think twice before doing it to you, too. I should have said something the first time, when you agreed to take the money from April. It was completely insane, and I knew it, and I should have tried to stop you. But I thought if I—" He cuts himself off abruptly, eyes flickering with surprise, as though catching himself in the middle of something he didn't mean to say. Rubbing the expression away, he gives me a forlorn look. "Don't forget I'm part of this, too, okay? I found Fox, too; I lied to the cops, too; and I'm also worried about April. And . . . and you, too. You can't just shut me out."

"Okay," I agree awkwardly, chastened and unmoored by the feeling in his tone, disappointed in myself for not considering that he also has some emotions of his own invested in the search for the killer. Megadouche though he may have been in life, Fox had still been one of Sebastian's friends. "Um . . . I'm sorry."

My ex-boyfriend is silent for a moment. "You know, if Fox's

killer also set that fire at the Whitneys', the cops might clear April on their own."

Theoretically, he's right—only, according to the story we've given the police, April's time remains officially unaccounted for when the blaze was first reported. It would require some suspension of disbelief, but the cops might deduce that she *could* technically have killed Fox, stolen his car, torched his house as a diversion, and then driven back to South Hero. "All the more reason to get started now."

"So." Sebastian puts the Jeep into gear, gliding past the entrance to the police station and turning left onto North Avenue. "Where are we headed?"

Unable to help myself, I study his reaction out of the corner of my eye and answer, "Lia's. I want to know what Fox and Arlo were really fighting about. And I want to know why she lied to us."

"Me too," he admits. But he won't look at me.

A mist rose up from the lake while we were grappling with cops and Covingtons. It rolled through the streets of Burlington and turned the glow of streetlamps into thick smears of gold in the opaque night air. The blue glow is still flickering in the upstairs bedroom at the Santos house when we pull up to the curb, and in spite of the late hour, it almost seems as though Lia has been expecting us; it takes only one text from Sebastian—*Outside again. You up?*—and within seconds, the front door eases open and the girl is hurrying down the front walk for the second time tonight.

"What is it?" She whispers when she reaches us, but the annoyance that sharpened her tone on our first visit is gone; now, she sounds frightened. "What do you want this time?"

"Fox is dead," I declare, ready to pounce at the first sign of artifice in her reaction. To my surprise, she gives only a fluttering, distracted nod.

"I know." Her face is pale, the bruise like an inky paw print stamped on her gray skin.

"You *know*?" Sebastian stares at her.

"Hayden told me."

It's my turn to gape. *"Hayden?"*

"He was here. Just a little while ago. He said April did it—that April . . . that she stabbed Fox?"

It's a question, as if she can't quite believe it, but my insides sink like a torpedoed battleship anyway. What the fuck is Hayden doing? Apart from undercutting my admittedly crappy scheme to surprise everyone with the news myself, I can't fathom why he would want to spread this bulletin around. Is he deliberately trying to compromise April by telling her friends she's guilty? "He just showed up out of the blue and told you Fox was dead?"

"Yes. I mean, no—not exactly." Lia glances nervously up and down the fog-cloaked street like she's terrified my psycho older brother will emerge from the brume at any moment to punish her for talking. "He was upset, okay? He was *pissed*. He had an issue with Fox, but he said Fox was dead, so . . . so—"

"So he came to you?" I make my skepticism plain.

Lia swallows and gives me a strangely plaintive look. "Don't ask me to explain why—he wasn't making a lot of sense. He was really, really angry, and I thought . . . I was afraid he was going to hurt me. I mean, look what he did!" She holds her bare arms out, and in the diffuse light, I can see for the first time that she has new bruises forming, the flesh over her biceps darkening with the suggestion of powerful hands. "He *grabbed* me, started *shaking* me—"

"Hey, just take a deep breath, okay?" Sebastian steps forward, putting his own hands on her arms—gently—unconsciously supplanting Hayden's grip with his own. "You're okay now."

An unexpected wave of jealousy steals over me as I watch him soothe her injuries, watch her tilt her face to his with casual intimacy, their displaced chemistry palpable. They're not together anymore, and I know it now—hell, Sebastian and *I* aren't together anymore—but I feel a needle of crestfallen dismay stab into me anyway. Clearing my throat, I interrupt their moment. "Why did he come here, though? What did he want?"

"Money," Lia whispers quietly, like it's a dirty word. "He wanted his money back."

Sebastian raises an eyebrow in my direction. "The money he paid Fox earlier tonight? For the drugs?"

Lia glances up, startled by his knowledge, but after a beat she gestures a mute confirmation. Baffled, I ask, "Why did he think you had it?"

"I don't know!" She looks genuinely bewildered. "Like I said, he wasn't making a lot of sense. He just showed up here, calling my phone over and over until I agreed to come down, and the second I was out the door he was in my face—ranting and threatening and *shaking* me—"

"Why did he want his money back?" I interrupt, hoping to distract her with something concrete to focus on. "What was his issue with Fox?"

Taking a breath, Lia glances around again—and this time, so do I. Her anxiety is contagious. Licking her lips, she says, to Sebastian, "Not here. Can we . . . can we sit in your car?"

I get into the back this time, allowing Lia to have the front, and when the doors of the Jeep are closed against the sightless expanse of the night, she relaxes visibly. "You already know that Fox and Arlo were partners—or, at least, they were *supposed* to be."

"What does that mean?" I ask.

"I'll get to it. Basically, they had this system worked out. They'd get a shipment from their supplier, divide it up, and then sell it. Fox's customers were rich kids and college students and stuff; Arlo had a lock on basically everybody else. I mean, aside from our squad at Ethan Allen, they ran in totally different crowds, so working together made sense."

"Okay," I say, hoping this has a point.

"Once they sold everything," she goes on, "they'd give their take—all of it—to their supplier, who would bank it and pay them back their cut. I don't know exactly how much they were moving, or what their percentage was, but neither of them was really hurting for extra cash, you know?"

"So what did Fox do? Why did Arlo go after him tonight at the party?"

Lia's face hardens, her dark eyes flashing like obsidian. "Fox got fucking greedy, that's what he did. He wanted more money—as if he needed it—and thought he was such an untouchable badass that he could get away with pulling one of the stupidest, most dangerous scams in the book."

"What scam?" Sebastian asks, and Lia drags her hands through her hair.

"The big problem with white rabbits is that, you know, every now and then they make some people go completely berserk, right? Lady thinks her neighbor's turning into a dragon, so she runs him down with her SUV; or a dude jumps through a window because he's trying to escape a swarm of invisible robot hornets."

She purses her lips. "*Fox*—who barely passed chemistry last year—decided that he could fix the problem and make some serious cash under their supplier's nose.

"He had a thing about power. He wanted everybody to kiss his ass and bow down when he walked into a room, and it bugged the shit out of him that Arlo was the one who actually intimidated people. Fox insisted on being the point man with their supplier, so all the deliveries would go through him, because it meant he got to tell Arlo what to do. It made him feel like he was the one who was really in charge." Anger pushes color back into her cheeks. "This dumb-fuck plan of his . . . he didn't even ask Arlo if it was cool—he just went ahead and did it."

"Did what?"

She meets my eyes steadily across the back of the seat. "He cut the supply. He bought a pill press and a rabbit stamp from some shady Chinese company over the internet, he took an entire delivery of white rabbits from their supplier, ground it all down to powder, and then mixed it with . . . I don't even know. Baking soda and ketamine, or maybe GHB or fucking Ambien or something, I've got no idea—a bunch of depressants. Stuff he figured would mellow people out. Only, Fox is an idiot, and he fucked it all up! He thought he could double the amount of pills right under their supplier's nose, pocket half the take, and that no one would notice!"

"Oh shit," Sebastian observes, eyes wide.

"Yeah." Lia laughs. "'Oh shit.' Turns out, Fox's version of the white rabbit made people sick as hell, or it made them black out, or have fucking *seizures*. But Fox thought he could still get away with it. I mean, he had to try, anyway—it was either that or admit what he'd done, and volunteer to get his kneecaps pounded into gravel."

I slump back against my seat, my head whirling from the impact of Fox's mind-boggling stupidity. Burlington is a small town; there are less than fifty thousand people within the city limits, and only just double that if you include the outlying urban zone. Any kingpin who's bothered to claim our little strip of Lake Champlain shoreline as his territory would know in a heartbeat if extra merchandise suddenly hit the street. The scheme was breathtaking in its hubris and staggering in its ineptitude.

"So he bungled it," I summarize, "and he sold Hayden a defective batch."

"A thousand dollars' worth." Lia's tone actually borders on satisfaction. "Arlo's customers had started complaining, and he knew something was up because the pills looked different; but it wasn't until he found Fox's extra stash at the Whitneys' lake house tonight that he figured out what was really going on."

"And that's when they started brawling, and Fox threw Arlo out," Sebastian concludes.

"Yeah." She exhales, the energy that carried her through the account abating on a single breath. "I don't think you have any idea what kind of position Fox put Arlo in. He was moving those pills, too, you know. And even though he had nothing to do with Fox's dumbass plot, that doesn't mean his supplier will see it that way."

The cynic in me wants to say something sarcastic about her concern for Arlo, who has still been intentionally selling a notorious drug with wildly violent side effects. It's a little hard to feel sorry for a guy who accidentally got cut while living by the sword.

But, of course, the one who had been truly endangered by Fox's half-witted scheming was *Fox.* By my count, in one fell swoop he'd made three dangerous enemies: Arlo, Hayden, and whatever shady drug lord was paying them to fence white rabbits to high school students in the first place. The real problem is that, if I wanted to get my four grand, I was going to have risk antagonizing all the same people—and with potentially similar results.

"But why did Hayden come *here* looking for the money?" Sebastian asks. There's a secondary meaning to the question: We both know where Hayden's money is, and he's already come perilously close to guessing the truth about it.

"I told you, I don't know!" She tosses her hands up, exasperated. "He was barely speaking in complete sentences! He just kept saying that he wanted it back, and how 'Nobody cheats Hayden Covington,' and he said . . . he said he was going to get it one way or the other, even if it was too late to get it back from Fox." Her voice drops to an agitated whisper, and light spilling through the Jeep's windshield makes her eyes shine like gemstones as she states, "And now I'm worried he's going to go after Arlo."

15

"THE *LAST* PERSON WHO NEEDS OUR HELP IS FREAKING ARLO," Sebastian argues nervously as the Jeep rumbles over fragmented asphalt on the short drive to the Rossi home. "Not only is he just about the only guy we know who could possibly take Hayden in a fair fight, he's also got a fucking *gun*, remember?"

"Yeah, well. I won't pretend I'd cry about it if my asshole brother took a couple rounds to the face, but I've got a feeling Isabel will be more likely to pay me if I can stop him from getting his head ventilated." My response sounds as flip as I intended it to, but, truthfully, I'm just as on edge as Sebastian. I'm not at all interested in becoming collateral damage in a drug dispute, and I don't like the way the edges of Fox's death seem to bleed inevitably into ugly, menacing territory.

To compound my worries, I'm starting to become convinced that my older brother has more or less officially lost his feeble grip on mental stability for the night—that he's willing to do violence to anyone he thinks is standing between him and his money.

Arlo's gun won't scare him, as I believe that *fear* is something Hayden genuinely does not experience; and since the tattooed drug dealer obviously doesn't have what Hayden is looking for, there's every chance that we could be on our way to interrupting a very volatile confrontation.

Based on what Lia said, I'm even more certain that Hayden went back out to the lake house after his first visit earlier in the evening. Whether he'd been there when we were, I still can't be sure—but if he's going around town in search of his money, then it means he somehow knows it wasn't in Fox's possession, where he should by all rights assume it was. The minute April turned herself in, the Burlington PD undoubtedly notified the authorities on South Hero, who would have immediately sealed the Whitneys' property off as a crime scene; so then, at some point prior to that, my brother must have returned there and searched the place thoroughly enough to become convinced that someone removed his thousand bucks from the premises.

"Do you think Hayden did it?" Sebastian asks me after a moment, radiating anxious energy. "Do you think he killed Fox?"

"I don't know. He'd be my first pick, but . . . I don't know. It could have been . . . someone else."

Sebastian nods slowly. "You still think maybe it was Arlo?"

I mumble something, unable to give him a clear answer. I don't *not* think that; Arlo is Suspect Number Two, as far as I'm concerned. And I know I *want* it to be him or my brother. It would make my heart sing to see either of Ethan Allen's two biggest assholes go to jail for murder—and Hayden's arrest based on evidence I discovered would almost be worth the four grand Isabel would thereby never, ever pay me. The unnamed supplier also makes for an excellent suspect—albeit one that inarguably puts the water level of this pitiful investigation well above our heads.

The problem is, there's yet another person I want to suspect, as well. A sliver of resentment is lodged in my heart that I can't seem to ignore, no matter how hard I try, and it keeps calling my attention to two little molehills that cry out to be built into mountains.

Molehill the first: Lia hadn't been very moved by the news of Fox's death. Sure, she acted pretty rattled when we first arrived, but that was more about Hayden's threats than the news he'd imparted. The only emotion she exhibited with regard to Fox—one of her closest friends, who had just been murdered in a pretty awful way—was contempt.

Molehill the second: It was twice now that Lia had made a point of seeming to staunchly defend Arlo's character while simultaneously describing a perfect motive for him to want Fox dead. I can't figure out if this is a subliminal act of sabotage, like she believes him to be guilty and her conscience is making her betray him without her even being aware of it—or if maybe it's deliberate misdirection.

But the subject of Lia Santos is booby-trapped for Sebastian and me, and there's no point in pursuing it further until we've finished looking into Hayden and Arlo. One thing at a time. Out loud, I offer a feeble laugh. "Well, I know this for sure: I'll have a kick-ass '*What I Did on My Summer Vacation*' essay to write this year."

Sebastian smiles in spite of the ominous tension in the air. "'*How I Almost Got Shot by a Drug Dealer*,' by Sebastian Williams."

"'*How My Sister Bribed Me with Blood Money,*' by Rufus Holt," I rejoin.

"'*How I Learned That a Bunch of My Friends Are Actually Kind of Psychotic!*'"

"'*How My Family Is Full of Liars and Possible Murderers Who Still Call* Me *the Black Sheep!*'"

Sebastian pauses for just a moment, and then: "'*How I Finally Got Up the Courage to Tell My Ex-Boyfriend That I'm Sorry for the Way I Ended Things.*'"

The Jeep fills with silence, and I feel my smile flop dead on my face. With difficulty, I mutter, "Don't."

"Rufus, I—"

"I said, *don't*." I refuse to look at him.

"You have to listen to me," he insists quietly, and suddenly I can't wait to get to Arlo's house and face his rifle again. "The reason I came looking for you tonight was because I need you to know how sorry I am that I hurt you." His voice is thin and strange, and I can feel his eyes on me, and it takes all my concentration just to keep breathing. "I've done a lot of shitty things, Rufe, but the worst thing I've ever done was what I did to you. And I'm really, really sorry. I need you to know that."

It takes an inhuman amount of self-control to remain stoic, my throat tightening convulsively as memories explode open like letter bombs in my brain. My skin is hot and cold all over at the same time, and my eyes swim with tears that I'm quickly losing the strength not to shed.

"I told you I loved you," I finally whisper, the words ripping holes in my chest as they come out. It isn't fair. They should be ripping holes in *his* chest. But I'm the one who hurts; I'm the one who's suddenly crying. "I said, 'I love you,' and you stopped speaking to me."

By the end of May, the city of Burlington had erupted in brightly colored wildflowers, proof that nature was as thrilled as the rest of us that the school year was ending. After the final bell on of one my last Fridays as a sophomore, I asked my mom to drop me off near Church Street—a pedestrian-only stretch of shops and restaurants at the heart of town—and assured her I would get a ride home later.

It was only a ten-minute wait until Sebastian's Jeep turned the corner and slowed to a stop by the curb. My heart was already beating faster, my mind a whirl of warmth and anticipation, when he rolled down his window, fixed me with a smoldering, sloe-eyed look, and said, "Hey, sexy. Wanna lift?"

We'd arranged the rendezvous in advance, of course—another CIA maneuver allowing us to spend a few hours together off our friends' radars. Naturally, Sebastian had a party to attend that night, and I had promised Lucy some quality BFF time that would doubtless involve weed, nachos, and a Parks and Recreation *marathon on Netflix; but the afternoon belonged to just the two of us, and I couldn't wait.*

The Williamses lived in a rambling colonial within arm's reach of the Burlington Country Club, a house with two chimneys and about a million windows. Because of Sebastian's father's job with the athletics department at the university, and his mother's position as executive chef at this wildly popular restaurant just outside of town, it was no surprise that theirs was one of the most impressive homes on the block. The first time Sebastian had shown me inside, I'd walked around with the hushed reverence of a churchgoer, awestruck and humbled by the satiny granite countertops, the gloomy oil paintings, the museumy furniture. Everything was so sumptuous, clean, and expensive that I was afraid to touch it.

Sebastian's bedroom was magnificent; a converted attic with sloped ceilings and windows in three directions, it boasted a bed as big as a garbage barge and a private, en suite bathroom. It was up there that he led me that afternoon, as birds were singing and flowers were perfuming the air, and our relationship—though I did not know it yet—was already entering its final throes.

We put something on TV, but it was pretense—background noise to score the hungry look he gave me before he pressed his lips to mine, before he pushed me down into the rolling softness of his plump, white duvet and pinned my body beneath his own. I felt trapped, and it thrilled me—which terrified me, utterly.

It was something I'd been struggling with for weeks, maybe months. Sebastian had opened up a weak spot in me, slipped through my considerable protective barriers to a place where I felt helpless and insecure; but instead of reacting with alarm, I found that I liked *it. I liked how vulnerable he made me feel—a fact that both scared and excited me in equal measure.*

We'd been kissing for a while, his hips moving against mine until my entire body was sparking and overheated—on the verge of explosion—when he stopped suddenly. With an agonized exhalation, he complained breathily in my ear, "Fuuuck!"

"What?" I asked dizzily. "What's wrong?"

Sebastian sat up, his face flushed. "We need to stop."

"Why?"

"Becaaaause . . ." He blew out some more air, rubbed his

scalp, gave me a sly look. "I'm kind of . . . um. Close? And if we don't quit right now, it'll just be . . . uh, frustrating. If you know what I mean."

I nodded, because I knew exactly *what he meant. In our four months together, we had acted out this very scene several times, and it was getting harder and harder—no pun intended—to say our proper lines at the end. To go back to watching TV, or making a snack, or doing anything that emphatically did* not *involve our erections. More and more, I had trouble remembering why I was saying no in the first place.*

It was my choice; I was the holdout—the virgin. It wasn't that I didn't feel ready, exactly, and it certainly wasn't that I didn't want *to; lying there and looking up at him as the saffron light of the afternoon beat lazily through his dormer windows and swirled seductively in the air around us, every nerve ending in my body was screaming* yes. *What kept me putting it off was fear.*

Fear that it wouldn't mean the same thing to him that it did to me; fear that he might lose interest when it was over; fear that my protective barriers would break completely apart like autumn leaves if I let him that much closer.

The problem was, I already knew, that it was far too late to protect myself now. The thing I'd been most afraid of had long since happened: My barriers were toast, and my feelings for Sebastian were written indelibly beneath my skin. Gazing up at him, I took a breath, faltered, and then asked, "Do you h-have . . . a condom?"

"Really?" His eyebrows shot up, a surprised grin lighting his face. Then, almost instantly, his expression became careful, serious. "Are you sure? I mean, I don't want to make you feel like—"

"I'm sure," I answered before I could reconsider. I didn't want to reconsider.

What followed was nothing like it looks online. I was awkward and uncoordinated, my knees and elbows flailing about in places they weren't supposed to go, and a lot of stuff I'd expected to be sexy and cool was actually sort of hilarious and/or painful. But the experience was also electrifying and powerful and romantic—even when Sebastian had to turn off the TV because he felt like SpongeBob was judging us; and the fact that he was laughing and cringing right along with me made everything perfect.

Afterward, when we were lying together atop his duvet, his heart thumping against my back as a flowery breeze stirred the sweat on our skin, I felt a foreign happiness swelling in my chest. Bright, meaningful Words fluttered in my mouth like hummingbirds, and I had to keep my lips sealed to prevent them from getting out. With a sigh, Sebastian drawled, "That was . . . actually, that was kind of awesome."

I didn't trust myself to speak, so I giggled my agreement. But as he got up and crossed the room, hiding the condom at the bottom of his wastebasket, he paused for just a moment to look out the window into his backyard. The setting sun caught him, bathing him all over in such rich, warm light that it looked as if his body had been dipped in gold dust, and the Words burst from me before I could stop them.

"I love you."

They soared from my lips, straight up, and hung above my head like the sword of Damocles.

A lifetime of silence passed—shorter than a heartbeat, but long enough for me to see him flinch, long enough to know he'd heard me. And then he turned from the window, heading for the bathroom as if I'd said nothing at all, announcing broadly, "I'm gonna take a shower. Turn the TV back on, if you want."

The door shut behind him, and the sword plunged down, straight through my heart.

My statement feels radioactive in the silence of the Jeep, a spreading hazard that can no longer be avoided.

"You just disappeared. You stopped answering my texts and my calls, you stopped showing up at the *Front Line* . . . I had to hear from *Ramona fucking Waverley* that you'd dumped me." I swipe the tears from my eyes, but they just keep coming, hot and bitter. "You told the whole school that you were still in love with Lia, that you'd never stopped being in love with her. You should have told *me* that! You should have at least had the guts to tell me to my face that I was only a . . . a convenience. That I didn't even matter. You ass."

"Rufus." He sounds stricken, horrible, but I will not turn my face to his. "That's not how it was. I can't believe you'd think that."

"You know what? I don't care." I force steel into my voice, bite down hard against the thickness that betrays my anguish. For weeks I've told myself that the only upside of being ignored by Sebastian is that he'd never get to see how totally he'd destroyed me, that he'd never know how badly I've been hurting thanks to him—and now I've served the information up on a silver platter. It's all too much. "I don't give a shit how it was. You wanted to tell me you're sorry? Great. Mission accomplished. But don't wait for me to tell you it's okay, because I won't. I will *never* say that, because I don't accept your fucking apology."

"Ruf—"

"Stop the car."

"Are you fucking joking?" Sebastian is appalled. "Look, I know you've got a right to be pissed at me, but there's no way in hell I'm letting you go do this alone—go risk getting freaking *killed* just because you're super pissed at me and you don't want to give me the satisfaction of helping! You don't have to forgive me, but I still *care* about you, Rufus. I still have your back, whether you like it or not!"

"You need to stop the car," I reply shortly, "because we're at Arlo's house."

In fact, we're just passing it as Sebastian finally hits the brakes. Along the roadside, streetlamps leach rings of amber into the gauzy fog, soft irises embracing bilious, burning pupils—eyes that glare down at us as the Jeep bumps to a stop at the curb. Arlo's place remains in deep shadow, a case of black rot that threatens to infect the neighborhood.

Before I can get out of the car, Sebastian tries again. "Please—can you just hear me out for a second? We might be about to get shot or something, and I really need to tell you—"

"I'd rather just get shot," I fire back, trying to be as hurtful as possible. "You want to give me a bunch of excuses so that *you* feel better, and that's not my problem. I don't have to care how you're dealing with the way you dumped me."

With that, I shove open my door and march for the sidewalk. Sebastian sticks doggedly behind me, but I focus on tuning him out, trying to forget all the pain he's intent on stirring up. Fox's murderer is still out there—and so are four thousand genuine US dollars, ready to be claimed and sent to the bank, if I can just find a way to make sure April is in the clear. I need to keep my head in the game.

"Arlo?" I call out quietly but clearly in the heavy stillness, as soon as we enter the darkness beneath the towering oak. I want to avoid surprises—especially the kind that go *bang*—and announcing our arrival seems wise. "We're back—me and Bash. We're not looking to start shit or anything, okay? We just want to talk."

There's no answer. My voice is swallowed up by dense air, and I can hear nothing from the murky cover of the front porch. The silence is almost oppressive, the Rossi home seeming even more desolate than it was on our first visit. Glancing around, I take in the street, noting with relief that Hayden's BMW is nowhere to be seen. Maybe Lia's fears were unfounded.

"Arlo?" I approach the porch steps, Sebastian at my heels, and we start cautiously up them. The Rossis' door is just discernible in the charcoal smudge of darkness that yawns ahead. "Anybody home?"

The stairs groan under my feet, and twice I ask myself what the hell I think I'm doing—what moves I have planned for when I reach the porch and either find Arlo waiting for me with a rifle, or find *no* Arlo and have to decide whether I'm going to ring the doorbell and risk having to explain myself to the guy's father.

My concerns prove irrelevant. As I clear the top of the steps, I trip over something, nearly crashing into the front door before I narrowly regain my balance and look down. Arlo lies on his back at my feet, face placid and arms flung over his head as if he's just stretched out on the dusty floorboards to take a nap.

But he isn't asleep. I know it even before I notice the grisly, black fissure that gapes open across his throat like a second mouth—even before I catch the nauseating, metallic stench of blood that hovers in the air like a swarm of blackflies.

Arlo is dead.

16

JOLTING BACK, I SLAM DIRECTLY INTO SEBASTIAN, WHO HAS JUST reached the top of the steps behind me. He grunts in surprise. "Hey, caref—"

When his voice simply cuts off, plunging into ominous silence, I know he's seen the body. Tonelessly, I say, "Let's go."

"Is he . . . is he *dead*?" Pushing me aside, Sebastian stumbles forward, his eyes bright with alarm. "Oh *shit*—"

Without ceremony, I grab his elbow and drag him back again, stopping him before he can instinctively check for a pulse—before he can leave fingerprints at another crime scene. "Forget it. There's nothing we can do!"

Blood has gushed from Arlo's brutalized neck, streaking and mottling his inked torso, and it collects beneath him in a spreading, black pool. His eyes are half open, glassy, and vacant, like empty bottles or burned-out bulbs. He is clearly beyond saving.

Sebastian wheels on me. "We can't just—I mean, we can't . . . He's been *killed*, Rufus! Look at him! We can't just leave him—"

"We have to," I say, firmly and urgently. "I'm serious. Sebastian? We have to get out of here *right now*."

That finally seems to make an impression, and my ex-boyfriend's eyes widen even further, his voice hollowing out. "You think Hayden might come back?"

"I think we don't need to give the neighbors any more chances to see us and tell the police we were here."

"We're not even gonna call the *police*?" He pulls away as I start dragging him down the stairs. "Are you freaking kidding?"

"Do you really feel like explaining how we just happened to turn up at the site of a second murder tonight?" I challenge frantically, every fiber of my being itching to be back in the Jeep, halfway to anywhere else. "They're gonna find him any minute now, anyway, because April has to have already handed over Fox's guest list for the party. You think it won't look shady as hell if we're standing here when they roll up?"

He just stares at me, not wanting to understand. "We have to tell them about Hayden, Rufus. He's still out there, and apparently he's lost his fucking mind! What if he comes for you again? What if he goes for Lia?"

"Don't you get it?" I finally snap. "We can't tell the police why we suspect Hayden without telling them about the money—which means telling them when we *really* got to the lake house, and everything else that we lied about!" I hear myself, and guilt twists at my insides, followed by a rush of panicked adrenaline as time continues slipping away. "Look, I know it's my fault. It was my stupid decision to help April, even though we both knew I shouldn't, and now it's blowing up in our faces. I'm sorry. I am *really, really sorry* I got you into this; but here we fucking are." I take a deep breath, guilt twisting harder. "We can't help Arlo, but if you're right, and Hayden is going back to Lia's . . . well, then we need to get over there *now.*"

It hits him where I meant it to, his eyes sparking with fear, and he nods sharply. "You're right. Shit. *Shit*, we need to make sure she's okay."

Silently, he sprints across Arlo's yard, heading back for the Jeep, and I follow behind, tormented by mixed emotions. It's not my fault that Arlo is dead, but I *am* responsible for putting Sebastian in a position to lie to the cops; I was the one who took the money, not him, and he's risked a lot by covering up for me. I've been so angry at him for so long, but I've put him in an impossible situation that only seems to be getting worse.

Maybe I preyed on his feelings for Lia as a way of punishing myself, I reflect miserably as I climb into Sebastian's car and it jerks away from the curb. I knew his instinct to protect her would be the one thing that might override his desire to call the police; maybe I wanted to see him go all White Knight for Lia, because I needed to feel how much it would hurt. He used me unjustly, but I'm digging a hole that could bury us both, and that's something potentially far worse. Maybe I deserve a little pain right now.

Sebastian drives one-handed, shooting past parked cars with centimeters to spare, cell phone pressed to his ear as he calls Lia. I cross my fingers and hope that nobody is still awake to report the suspicious vehicle speeding away from the Rossi house, and listen mutely to the relief in my ex-boyfriend's voice as he gets his ex-girlfriend on the line. "Are you okay? Has Hayden been back?" He pauses, and then says, "I can't . . . look, we're on our way over to you now, and I'll tell you everything when we get there. Just . . . if Hayden does show up? Don't talk to him. Don't go outside, don't let him in, don't answer his calls. Just ignore him. No matter what. Okay? Promise me."

He hangs up, and a palpable silence once again vibrates around us, both of us too tense to speak. I want to put Sebastian at ease, tell him he's just jumping to conclusions. I want to tell him that Lia probably has nothing to be afraid of. But how can I? Maybe she does.

I wanted to be suspicious of Sebastian's ex earlier, but it's become increasingly evident that I might have to let that self-serving theory go already; in order to support it, I'd have to accept that she: 1) murdered Fox and framed April for it, but then tried to get us to believe that *Arlo* was the actual culprit all along, and 2) killed Arlo (to keep him from denying it?) and then tried to make it seem like Hayden did it. To get away with all *that,* she'll have to eventually kill my brother, too, and I simply don't believe she's that diabolical. It's not as if I actually trust her, and I definitely don't think she's been entirely honest with us, but I still haven't even figured out a motive for her to want Fox dead.

Hayden, on the other hand, has "two dead bodies and a heaping side of arson" written all over him. With an ego the size of an aircraft carrier, he long ago established a cult of personality at Ethan Allen, and he likes being revered; any sign of disrespect is a crime, punishable by cruel and unusual torture. Fox apparently forgot his place, and reminding him of it—with prejudice—would be par for the course as far as my demented brother is concerned. As his partner, Arlo was likely already doomed by association even before he inevitably failed to produce the missing cash. The only thing I can't quite figure out yet is why Hayden would burn down the Whitneys' empty home on top of killing Fox.

A superfluous house fire, however, is exactly the sort of thing you might expect from a pissed-off drug lord who needs to make an example of someone who's tried to scam him. I admittedly don't know a whole lot about drug runners, but it seems a pretty safe bet that any self-respecting kingpin would maintain a zero-tolerance policy about being cheated by his underlings. A bit of scorched earth—both literal and figurative, in this case—might go a long way toward encouraging the rest of the gang to keep in line.

Glancing over at Sebastian, I recognize anxiety in the set of his jaw, and decide not to share these bleak little observations. Two of his friends are dead now and, thanks to me, the lies he'll have to tell about what's happened to them are still piling up. Preoccupied with his fears for Lia's safety, he's probably not in the best place for more bad news right now, and I can tell I should maybe not mention yet that the night's agenda might also include rooting around in the private business of a homicidal drug lord.

The fact of the matter is this, I suddenly realize: I have to lose him, one way or another. For his own good, I have to figure out how to make Sebastian go home and let me finish this by myself. After weeks of wishing all kinds of terrible fates for him, the thought that he might actually suffer one because of me makes my mouth go dry. He's an ass, and I hate him; but I hate him because, no matter what I do, I can't seem to stop feeling fucking *feelings* for him. It sucks. It really, really sucks.

The Jeep screeches to a sudden halt, and I rebound against my seat, my heart jolting anxiously. Glancing up, I realize we're back at Lia's house, and as I catch my breath, Sebastian thumbs her a message. *We're here. Coming around to the basement.*

He doesn't wait for a response—just jumps out of the car and sets off across the lawn, darting for a narrow side yard. As I follow, once again trailing in Sebastian's wake, I shiver. The mist has thickened further, the air clammy and dense, and I feel it cling to my skin like cellophane. I can barely see onto the neighbor's property, have no clue whether the block is truly as deserted as it seems, and I pick up the pace.

Down a flight of concrete steps, illuminated by an outside light styled as an old-fashioned lantern, a door opens into a finished basement. Lia's waiting for us just inside, standing in the dark, her wide eyes shining eerily in the glow from her cell phone's display—evidently in the middle of texting Sebastian a reply. Thick carpeting swells under my feet as we enter, giving off the scent of a recent cleaning, and through the shadows I can make out the looming bulk of a widescreen TV, a plush sofa, and a pool table. The Santos family might not be quite as rich as the Whitneys or the Williamses, but they're doing a damn sight better than the Holts.

"What happened?" Lia asks immediately, her voice hushed but high-pitched, as though she's worried about waking someone. "Is he okay? Hayden didn't hurt him, did he?"

Sebastian doesn't answer right away, his hesitation presaging bad news, and when he does speak his voice is thick. "Lia . . ."

"Just tell me," she whispers.

Sebastian lets out a breath. "Arlo . . . he's dead, Lia."

Her phone's glowing display chooses that exact moment to time out, and her face is plunged into shadow. She makes a strange noise, something between a gasp and a cough, and a high, thready whine drifts out of the darkness. "*No* . . ."

"I'm sorry."

"*No, no, no, no . . .*" Lia's silhouette wobbles, she sucks in another strangled gulp of air, and then she drops altogether to the floor as though her legs have been swept out from beneath her. She begins to sob silently, her breath hissing out in convulsive bursts before being sucked back with a wet gurgle, and Sebastian gets to his knees to comfort her. Pitifully, Lia moans, "It doesn't make sense! He said it would be okay!"

My scalp prickles. "What would be okay?"

"He said not to worry, he said it would be okay." She rocks back and forth, her hands crawling through her hair. "He said it would be okay, he said he had a plan and everything would be okay. All I had to do was . . . was . . ."

"Was what?" Sebastian coaxes gently. "Lia, what happened tonight?"

She looks up, a bar of light from the window in the basement door illuminating the lower half of her face, making her tears shine as they slip down. Barely audible, her breathing still choppy, she confesses, "We went back."

"You went back. You mean, to the lake house?" In a flash, I'm down on my knees, too. "When?"

"After everyone left." She blinks miserably, her glistening eyes finally visible to me again as my own adjust to the dark. "Race and Peyton took off, and Arlo wanted to go back inside. He was really pissed at Fox, you know? He was so angry, I was afraid of what would happen, so I talked him down. I told him he'd better take me home, or he'd have to fight me, too. So he agreed, and we got on his bike. But . . ."

"But?"

"Halfway to town, he stopped. He pulled off the road somewhere in, like, Colchester, and just sat there for, like, a full minute. And I was like, 'What the fuck are you doing? Take me home!' But, instead, he turned back around and started for South Hero again." Her sobs have settled, but her voice remains choked as she goes on, "I was, like, *hitting* him the whole way, trying to make him stop, because I knew he'd decided to go have it out with Fox after all, but he just ignored me. He ignored me."

"What happened when you got to the cottage?"

"He was so pissed, he actually cut across the neighbor's property—like, off-roaded through somebody's garden and almost got clotheslined by a tree branch—because it was shorter than going all the way up to the actual driveway. We just about crashed into the Whitneys' water heater because he hit the brakes too late, and he didn't even apologize for almost getting me killed!"

In my head, I'm sorting the geography of the lake house, failing to picture the water heater. Sebastian beats me to the punch, sliding a meaningful glance my way as he clarifies, "So you guys came up on the side of the house? By the kitchen?"

"Yeah," Lia confirms dully. "And he started ranting about how it was 'time someone put Fox Whitney in his fucking place,' and how he wasn't gonna be messed with or whatever. I kept telling him to let it go, to forget about it, but he wouldn't! All he said was, 'If you don't wanna watch Whitney's candy ass get obliterated, then you can just stay fucking here,' and he left me with the bike."

"He went inside?" Sebastian's anticipation sounds as acute as mine feels. I don't know if either one of us still thinks that Arlo stabbed Fox—not anymore—but, then, none of the night's puzzle pieces seem to fit together cleanly.

Lia starts shaking her head. "He never made it into the house. He got all the way to the kitchen door, and then he just . . . froze.

Like, he just stood there, looking through the window, for . . . I don't know, thirty seconds? Maybe longer? And the next thing I knew, he was bolting back down the stairs and running for the bike again."

"What did he say?"

"Nothing! His face was totally white—like he'd just watched someone get eaten by a bear or something—but all he did was jam his helmet on and start up the bike like he was gonna fucking take off, with or without me. I barely got into the seat in time!"

"And you guys came straight back here?" I ask. She nods briefly, and the possibilities begin to swirl in my mind, a tight orbit moving faster and faster as I realize how few explanations make sense. "Did he tell you why he'd freaked out?"

Lia shakes her head again. "He said it was better if I didn't know. He said . . . he said all I had to do was not tell anybody that we went back. That the police would come around, asking about April and Fox, and that I had to just say we'd left when we left the first time, and that was it. He told me if I kept my mouth shut, we'd both be okay." Once more, she begins to weep. "He said it would be okay! He said he'd come up with a plan!"

The information is coming too quickly. "'A plan?' What do you mean?"

"He was sure that Lyle would come gunning for him because of what Fox did, and he—"

"Lyle?" Sebastian interrupts.

"Yeah. That's their supplier. Lyle."

"Lyle," I repeat, staring. "You don't mean . . . not Lyle *Shetland*?"

"Yeah, actually, I think that is his name." I feel two pairs of curious eyes probing me through the dark. "How'd you know?"

"Lucky guess." A dull ache pulses to life in my temples as I contemplate facing down even more of my past, my night turning into a clip show of every bad dream I've ever had. If I'm going to get killed for all this, it can't happen soon enough. "So, Arlo had come up with a plan."

"To get away from Lyle," Lia explains, "in case he wanted retribution. The guy's a loose cannon, and even though it was all Fox's fault, Arlo wasn't sure Lyle would believe it. He said there was someone he could get money from—enough to leave town until the dust settled, and he could prove to Lyle that Fox had screwed him, too."

I'm having trouble trying to pick which lead to follow first. "What do you mean, 'someone he could get money from?' Did it have something to do with whatever he saw at the lake house?"

"I guess?" The question stresses Lia out. "I have no idea—he didn't tell me *what* he saw! I mean, based on what he'd said, I thought . . ."

"You thought Fox was dead?"

"I thought *April* was dead." Her voice trembles. "I thought Fox had killed her, and that Arlo was gonna blackmail him. When you guys came here, saying she wasn't answering her phone, I was sure of it. But then Hayden showed up, saying *Fox* was dead and *April* was at the police station, and I . . . I—"

She breaks off, crying again, and Sebastian continues to murmur comforting words that I barely hear. It's possible, I try to tell myself, that when Arlo looked in through the kitchen door, he saw exactly what Sebastian and I had seen: Fox lying in a pool of his own blood, with his girlfriend collapsed beside him. It's possible he intended to blackmail April . . . but I don't think so. "Buy my silence" only works if the person you're threatening needs what you're selling; but April is so profoundly screwed by circumstantial evidence alone that Arlo's silence would be useless to her. A better plan would be offering to sell her a fake alibi.

Only that offer hadn't come in by the time Arlo pointedly directed us to the lake house so we could uncover the crime scene.

No. There is only one explanation; every way I try to add up Lia's account, the sum is always the same: *Arlo saw it happen.* He and Lia returned to the cottage just in time for him to witness his business partner getting murdered, and by the time they made it back to Burlington, Arlo decided to use his knowledge as leverage against the guy's killer.

Arlo had known everything all along.

17

A CLOCK TICKS SOMEWHERE IN THE DARKNESS, ALMOST MENACING against the soft undertones of Lia's grief and Sebastian's consolation, but my brain buzzes loudly enough to drown it all out. My brother is still my top suspect—and only Arlo Rossi would've had the balls to blackmail Hayden. The Covingtons have pockets deep enough to buy anything from a Brazilian vacation to a hollowed-out volcano in the South Pacific if the guy had been serious about wanting to escape Lyle Shetland's wrath.

Finally things are starting to come together in a way that makes actual sense. I still can't explain why my brother would stab Fox, frame April, and then later decide to torch the Whitneys' place—although it's possible the fire had been a message from Lyle's people after all, delivered just a smidge too late to be truly effective—but I can now easily picture how the scene at the Rossi home might have gone down.

Hayden and Arlo were united in their antipathy for Fox, and my brother is a master at exploiting the emotions of others; it's not at all hard to imagine him convincing his blackmailer that they were on the same side, that he honestly believed a payoff was mutually beneficial—two backs being scratched simultaneously. He could have made it sound sincere . . . all the way up to the point where Arlo dropped his guard, giving Hayden a chance to deliver a little payoff directly to the guy's trachea.

"When you two went back to the lake house," I ask Lia, "did you see any cars besides Fox's?"

She shakes her head with a loud sniffle. "No. We were on the other side of the house from the drive. And, anyway, I told you, everybody else was already gone—we passed them on the road."

"Before you doubled back, then. Did you and Arlo pass anyone going the other direction? Someone who might have been on their way out to the cottage?" I'm thinking of Hayden's deliberately ostentatious convertible—a great car for when you want people to notice you, and a lousy one for when you don't.

"I don't remember." Lia sounds bewildered. "I mean, no one else was invited, and I wasn't really—" She stops in midsentence, her eyes popping open. "You think maybe April had an accomplice or something?"

"April didn't have anything to do with what happened to Fox," I declare flatly, surprised by my own conviction. "She was set up."

I don't want to add much more than that, but to my chagrin, Sebastian tips our hand anyway. "What do you think Hayden would do if he figured out Fox had sold him a bunch of pills that didn't work?"

"You think—You think *Hayden* did it?" Lia stares, her eyes going huge. "Oh. Shit. Oh *shit*!" Without warning, she scrambles to her feet, her knee grazing my face as she rushes for the basement door, slamming the deadbolt into place with shaky hands. "He was here! He thought I had his money! What if he comes back?"

"Hey, don't freak out." Sebastian crosses to her, gently taking hold of her arms again. "You already told him you don't have it, right?"

"Well, yeah." She gives us both an indignant look. "I said if Fox didn't have it, then I sure as hell didn't know where it was! I'm not their fucking secretary or something."

"Okay, so he probably won't come back," Sebastian continues. He tucks a lock of hair behind her ear, and I taste something bad in the back of my throat. "If he does, just stay inside and don't answer your phone. In fact, don't answer it at all unless it's one of us. Call the cops if he scares you, and make sure he knows you're doing it."

Agitated, she gives a staccato nod. "Yeah. Yeah, okay." There's a loaded moment that follows, the clock ticking and the mist drifting sluggishly outside the door, a gray-gold haze caught in the glow of the lantern. Then, Lia peers up at Sebastian again, gazing through her long, dramatic eyelashes. "Can . . . can you stay here? Just in case? If he really does show up, I don't want to have to face him alone. Please, Bash?"

My heart goes through an ugly series of yoga moves, twisting and lurching as Sebastian meets her eyes, their profiles limned by the light behind them. I know I wanted to find some excuse to leave him behind, a way to keep Sebastian out of harm's way, but *this* is the universe kicking me in the nuts. Like I haven't suffered enough without having to watch them flip their relationship switch back to On Again right before my very eyes.

But the fact is that it's probably for the best, and I know it; not only is "guarding Lia" a job assignment Sebastian will no doubt readily accept, but—no matter what—I need to put some distance between us before his soulful eyes and sexy cologne completely undo all the hard work I've put into burying my feelings for him over the past week.

Sebastian, however, doesn't seem inclined to make my life any easier. Pushing Lia subtly away, he says, "I can't. Rufus doesn't have a car. I'm his ride."

"So what?" She gives me a look like I'm a vagrant, covered in my own filth, who has somehow wandered into her home by accident. "Call him a cab or something. Hayden's not out to kill *him*."

My sympathy for her is evaporating rather quickly, but in this, at least, we are sort of allies. "It's cool. I'm sure I can still get a Lyft back to my house, and I have the keys to my mom's ca—"

"No," Sebastian interrupts irritably, giving me a look that's part exasperation and part some other mood I can't quite identify. "We already talked about this." He turns back to Lia. "You'll be fine. Your parents are here, right? And your brother? Hayden won't pull anything with witnesses around—he's psycho, but he's not stupid."

Lia is no more pleased than I am by this weak brush-off, but she folds her arms across her chest and stops arguing. I'm going to have to find some other way to ditch him. In the meantime, there remains one piece of information I still need, and I face my ex's ex. "Arlo ever tell you how to get in touch with Lyle Shetland?"

Sebastian and Lia both turn to me with identically incredulous looks. Shaking her head, she asks, "I'm sorry, *what*?"

Simultaneously, Sebastian practically shrieks, "Are you *kidding*?"

"Hayden wants his money back," I explain levelly. "He didn't get it from Fox, and he couldn't get it from Arlo, so that's where he'll be headed next. Trust me—his parents raised him on a steady diet of 'I want to speak with your superior.'"

Lia actually starts laughing at me. "Lyle's not some dude in a sweater vest making shift schedules at fucking *Applebee's*, Rufus. He is a seriously bad guy, and he will turn you inside-the-fuck-out just for thinking you have the right to talk to him!"

"Fine. But do you know how to get in touch with him?"

"You're not listening to me." Her voice hardens as she grows annoyed by my cluelessness. "Even *Arlo* was afraid of this guy. Does that tell you anything? I mean, he will literally *kill you dead*, and it will not bother him one damn bit."

"I don't think he will," I rebut, sounding far more nonchalant than I actually feel. "Somebody just whacked two of his guys and shut down his business operations in Burlington. He might be happy to help set Hayden up for an arrest."

"Or else, you know, *firebomb Hayden's entire neighborhood*," Lia shoots back.

"Rufus." Sebastian approaches me, his face taut and his eyes serious, and he takes me by the shoulders. Nostalgic goose bumps erupt reflexively across my bare skin at his warm, gentle touch, and I struggle not to show him how much I like it. "What you're thinking of doing is insane. Like, *legit* insane. You say 'somebody' whacked his guys—well, what if it was Lyle? What if Fox and Arlo were already dead before Hayden got to them? This dude isn't gonna thank you for digging into his business!"

"Lyle wasn't behind Fox's death," I assert confidently. Sebastian tries to speak again, but I cut him off. "Arlo's plan was to get enough money to lie low until Lyle could cool off, right? Well, if he'd just seen Lyle waste Fox, then blackmailing him over it wouldn't exactly be a shortcut off the guy's shit list. It doesn't even make sense."

"You're just making guesses!" Sebastian glares. "Guys in Arlo's position turn on their bosses all the time—and they usually wind up just as dead!"

"Which Arlo would know," I rejoin, "which is why it makes even *less* sense that he would try to blackmail Lyle before turning to one of his many rich-ass friends for a loan, if he needed fast cash to get out of town."

"You have no idea what you're talking about." Lia is still laughing, but it's a sound like someone scraping rust off a drainpipe. "This whole conversation is ridiculous! Lyle is part of a fucking *gang*, you moron! If you go to him for any reason and start talking about shit that could get him in trouble, he will *break your legs off* and *beat you with them*!"

"No, he won't," I inform them both with a reluctant sigh. "Lyle Shetland is one of the few people in this city who actually likes me."

At some point shortly after the beginning of the eighth grade, I began to realize that the feelings I had for Eric Shetland had gone beyond regular friendship. Believe it or not, it took me sort of by surprise; despite all the jeers and jibes from Hayden and his friends, mocking my more feminine mannerisms, it had literally never occurred to me that I might actually be gay. But the fascinated rush when I was with Eric, the achy longing when I wasn't . . . it just became harder and harder to shrug off as the year wore on.

He was one of my best friends, and I was terrified that my secret might ruin our bond, but by the time spring break rolled around, the pressure inside me had built to a point where I simply couldn't take it anymore. I had to say something, I realized, or our friendship would self-destruct anyway.

It was early May before I got up the courage to tell him how I felt. Eric had come over to my house after school, and we were eating homemade pizza bagels and watching The Raid 2 *on Netflix, when I finally couldn't keep it in any longer. Pausing the movie, I turned to him and just blurted it out. "Um. I don't know if you've noticed me acting weird lately? But if you have, it's because, um, I think . . . well, I've realized that, um, I'm gay?"*

He froze, then looked over at me like he'd never seen me before. "Oh."

"Yeah. And . . . and also. Also. I think, also, that . . . I like you. Like . . . Like-*like."*

"Oh." Eric's face turned the color of a dead tooth, and a strange sound emerged from his throat. "Uh. Okay. That's cool. I mean, I'm not like that? But it doesn't bother me that you are." He looked fairly bothered, though. "Like, you're my friend and all, but I like girls. You know? Like-*like them. So, um, I'm not . . . into you. Like that."*

"Okay," I said, nodding like a slowly deflating parade balloon. I'd been prepared to hear that, but it still made something come painfully loose in my chest. "I get it. I just, I wanted to be honest with you. Because you're one of my best friends. At least, I hope you're still one of my best friends?"

"Well, yeah, sure." He inched subtly away from me across the carpet. "I mean, as long as you know that's all we are. Friends."

"Yeah. Of course." I looked at the space expanding between us. It was like the Atlantic Ocean.

The next day, I came in to school to learn that Eric had called Cody Barnes the second he'd left my house, and had reported everything I'd said; Cody, in turn, had alerted the entire rest of our class. The hallway was a shooting gallery, people pointing and whispering, popular guys coughing insults into their hands as I passed by, and when I reached my locker I saw that someone had drawn a squirting dick on it in black Sharpie. Things only got worse from there.

Cody was merciless with his taunting, his cruel names, his nasty jokes. He gave Eric plenty of grief as well: calling him my boyfriend, asking if I'd given him AIDS, and winding him up to the point where Eric finally announced—angry and panicked and apparently deadly serious—that he was thinking of reporting me to the principal for sexual harassment. Because I'd told him I liked him.

When I bumped into Eric in the hall on the way to our fifth-period math class, he shoved me as hard as he could into a bank of lockers, shouting, "Don't fucking touch me, FAGGOT!"

It was the end of our friendship, and in spite of Lucy's support and April's unexpected kindness, I still felt like a wad of used toilet paper by the time school let out. I was nowhere near ready to face my mom with the news of my day, so I rode my bike to the park instead, climbing up onto a picnic table where I stared out at nothing for a while. I was so preoccupied with my misery that I didn't realize I wasn't alone until someone called my name. "Hey, Holt! 'Zat you?"

Glancing up, I froze. Standing around a cluster of motorcycles in the parking lot was a group of hard-looking adult-type dudes in jeans and leather, their cigarettes glowing in the gathering dusk like the red dots of snipers' rifles; they exuded that kind of bored hostility that often portends mischief or violence, and I suddenly felt very alone. The tallest of the bikers, his shaved head a shiny, rose quartz dome, was ambling toward me. In a flash, I realized it was Eric's older brother, Lyle.

The guy was twenty-one, and even though he had an apartment somewhere in South Burlington, it seemed like he was at Eric's house more often than he wasn't. I'd heard about the kind of trouble Lyle got into—vandalism, shoplifting, drugs, fistfights. I knew he'd been arrested before, and that my mom didn't want me to hang out at the Shetlands' if Lyle had his friends over, but this was the first time I'd felt afraid of him.

He closed the distance between us in just a few strides, and I went completely rigid, suddenly sure that Eric had sent him; instead of being reported to the principal, I was going to be stomped into the earth by Eric's hell-raising sasquatch of a brother, from whom I didn't have a single chance of escaping on my little three-speed Schwinn.

"Heard you had kind of a shit day," Lyle grunted unexpectedly, plunking down beside me on the picnic table. Misinterpreting my startled expression, he added, "Small town. Rumors got nowhere to go but everywhere." He looked at nothing with me for a moment, while I felt like someone standing on a land mine, waiting for it to go off. Then he spoke again, contemplatively. "I don't know any homos, but I got nothin' against 'em. My thing is, as long as somebody's cool with me, I'm cool with them, you know? And I always thought you were a pretty cool little dude."

I nodded. Although, truth be told, I'd have nodded at anything he said. Disagreeing with Lyle Shetland was tantamount to suicide.

"You're the only one of Eric's friends I ever liked," he confided after another moment, surprising me yet again. "E's a pretty good kid, but he hangs out with all these rich pricks—and wannabe rich pricks—and he's startin' to turn into one of 'em." He looked down

at me sympathetically. "You and I got a lot in common, actually. We're both black sheep, and we both put up with a whole lotta crap, just gettin' through the day. But only the tough survive, and you got my respect for surviving, Holt." He stood up, jabbing a cigarette into his mouth, and offered me his fist to bump. "Life slings you shit sometimes, my man, and keeping your head up's all you can do. So hang in there. You ever get in real trouble, or need some punks beat down, you call me—I mean it. I don't like a lot of people, and I watch out for the ones I do."

And with a friendly wave, he was gone.

Eric got shipped off to some boarding school that summer—ironically enough, to get him away from his older brother's influence—and with him went the enduring reminder of my Coming Out story's more sordid details. That suited me just fine, thanks, and revisiting the whole, ugly experience for the benefit of Sebastian and Lia is not a proposition that holds much appeal. Instead, I sum up my connection to Lyle Shetland by saying, "He once told me that if I was ever in trouble and needed something, I could call him. Well, this sure looks like Shit Creek to me, and he's a guy with lots of paddles."

Sebastian gives me a beseeching look. "*Rufus.*"

It takes willpower to ignore the plea in his eyes, but I manage it. Turning to Lia, I ask, "Do you know how I can get in touch with him, yes or no?"

She tosses her hands up and lets them flap down at her sides in disgust, giving up on me. "He and his boys hang out at this dive bar over near the airport—"

"Lia!" Sebastian turns on her, aggrieved, and she gives him an insolent shrug.

"What? If he's got a death wish, I sure as hell can't stop him." She turns back to me. "The place is called Smokey's, or Smoker's, or the Smokehouse—something like that. It's in a strip mall off Route 2, behind this old gas station that closed down a couple years ago. There's a gross diner where they go after last call, right in the same complex. It's near one of those enormous dollar stores where they sell ugly bullshit and wonky stuff from China that doesn't work right."

"I think I know where you're talking about."

"Of course you do," she replies with insulting kindness.

"Rufus, this is nuts!" Sebastian is starting to sound desperate. "I don't care what this Lyle dude told you once upon a time! He is a dangerous guy, with dangerous friends, and you're asking for serious, murdery trouble if you go to him looking for favors!"

"You don't have to come," I answer briskly, shoving past him and making my way to the door. "You two stay here, lock yourselves in, and hide from Hayden in the dark. Meanwhile, April's at the police station, maybe about to get arrested for something she didn't do, and I promised I'd help her. So I'm going."

With that, I smack the deadbolt open and step out into the strangling golden mist that fills Lia's concrete stairwell like quicksand.

18

IT'S A PHENOMENAL EXIT LINE. UNFORTUNATELY, STOMPING OFF into the night all by myself to go hunt down a kingpin-slash-gang member is one of the stupidest things I've ever done, and I find myself regretting it before I've even made it out of Lia's side yard. Truthfully, I'm nowhere near as composed as I made myself seem when I was safely inside with the door locked. Way back then, confronting Lyle Shetland was just a notion—a preposterous one, which, through sheer stubbornness in the face of those doubting me, I convinced myself would work; now that I'm actually going to try to *do* it, every step I take feels like one more scoop of dirt piled into my own grave.

I can't even figure out exactly what I intended with my parting remark, which suddenly sounds petty, provoking, and self-congratulatory all at once as I play it back. *You two stay here, lock yourselves in, and hide from Hayden in the dark.* Did I really want Sebastian to stay with Lia and be safe? Or had I deliberately demeaned his courage so he would follow me? The fact is, I realize,

I want *both* to happen; and no matter which move he makes next, it's going to be the wrong one, and it's going to annoy me.

What the fuck is wrong with me?

When I hit the front lawn, the fog is rolling through the neighborhood as thick as grease, reducing the street ahead of me to a lonely smear of eerie shadows and ghostly light. Abruptly, I know precisely which option I *really* hope Sebastian chooses; and, seconds later, the sound of thumping feet behind me tells me he has in fact picked it.

"I think maybe you really do have a death wish," he grumbles when he catches up with me, glowering moodily.

In spite of how much I was just hoping he'd show up, I can't resist rising to the argument. "I told you, like, a million times that you don't have to come with me."

"I know what you told me—*I* told *you* that I don't give a shit. You're not getting rid of me." His eyes drop to a spot between my collarbones and his tone changes. "Look, I know you're angry with me. I know you . . . you hate me, and you're not going to forgive me. You made that really clear. But this isn't even about that. If you're walking into a lion's den tonight, then you're not doing it alone. Maybe you don't care if a drug dealer fucking wastes you, but *I do*. So, you know. Deal with it."

I struggle to come up with a response, but can't seem to. There are a thousand things I could say here, a thousand things I *want* to say, but each one is rigged with emotional explosives. Part of the problem is the way he seems to be looking at me, with serious, intimate eyes—the way he used to, when things were perfect; I'm afraid to not be angry, terrified of the slippery slope back into aching need for him that lies just beyond my terribly slender guardrail of resentment . . . but I'm just as afraid to push him away, because I *miss* serious, intimate Sebastian Williams so fucking much. And a greedy, lonely, traitorous quarter of my heart loves that he's looking at me again.

We make our way back to the Jeep through the dead silence of the neighborhood, the streets as still as a ruined civilization, and I try to shake off the creepy feeling of eyes tracking our progress. Wordlessly, Sebastian pulls away from the curb, heading automatically toward the airport, while I begin to think ahead—wondering what the hell I'm going to say when we reach our destination.

As if he's read my mind, Sebastian suddenly asks, "So what's the plan, anyway? I mean, we just walk into this shady diner where drug dealers hang out and go, 'Yo, who wants to help the cops arrest somebody tonight?' "

"I . . . haven't exactly figured that out, yet," I confess, not wanting to acknowledge just how close to the sun we might actually be flying. This is all improvisation, here, one foot in front of the other, and I know I'm putting an awful lot of faith in Lyle's memory. I haven't seen him in more than two years, and if he's forgotten about the little chat we had in the park, this mission will go from Risky to Kamikaze in a heartbeat. "I guess first we just see if he's there. If he is, we try to get him to notice me so that he'll say hi, and then we just sort of . . . you know, bring it up."

" '*Bring it up?*' " Sebastian's foot slips off the gas pedal. "You mean, like, 'Speaking of murdering two of your guys, that's what my brother did'?"

"Well, maybe not *exactly* like that, no—"

"And what if he doesn't notice you? What if he doesn't say hi? What's Plan B?"

"Um. We go talk to him, I guess."

Sebastian is quiet for what feels like a really long time, and then he says carefully, "I don't mean to hurt your feelings, but that's even stupider than your last stupid plan."

"I know," I acknowledge glumly. "But I don't have anything better."

"Oh fuck." Sebastian's shoulders slump. "We're going to die."

"We don't have to go through with it," I hear myself saying in return. "Maybe you're right. Maybe I should just . . . if we get there, and it seems really scary, we can always back out." I'm thinking about the previous winter, when I decided to get my ears pierced during my weeklong suspension from school. I made the appointment and biked over to the shop to get it done, took one look at the terrifying gun thing that was about to blast holes in my flesh, and fled outside again with a cold sweat pouring down my neck. "Believe it or not, I don't actually want to get shot and/or stabbed tonight."

"That's a relief." He lets out a grunt of friendly sarcasm, then glances over at me. "But what about what Mrs. Covington said, Rufe? You need that money, and if you give up, she might get you expelled. I mean . . . we have to at least try."

My face heats at the reminder that I made him aware of my mother's poverty—*our* poverty—but at least his look isn't pitying; it just seems like he cares. I think again about all the chances he's taking on my behalf, all the crazy, stupid things he's been helping me do, and I start to feel ashamed. There's something I haven't said yet—words he deserves to hear, but which have felt like a betrayal every time they've gotten near my tongue. Like I'd be selling out my pride while it's still fresh from being flayed alive. But I have to get them off my chest before I start hating myself.

"Thank you," I mutter stiffly, trying to sound as formal as

possible. "You know, for everything. For driving me out to South Hero and helping me with April, and for . . . for not making me do this by myself." It is so hard to say, and I hate how much it sounds like forgiveness—like I'm relinquishing any self-esteem I've salvaged from the smoking rubble he made of my heart. "And also for what you said to Hayden, back at the police station. And for this, now. I know I should've said it earlier, but I'm . . . I'm saying it now. Even if I'm kind of doing a shitty job. Thanks."

My face feels hot enough to smelt iron by the time I'm done speaking, and a pregnant silence fills the Jeep. The more the empty space drags out, the more I dread hearing what Sebastian is going to say in response, but at last he turns a familiar, wry smile at me and remarks, "It's cool. I mean, we're just gonna look for a drug-dealing motorcycle gang at a dirty strip mall behind an abandoned gas station in the middle of the night. What's the big deal?"

I actually laugh out loud.

The strip mall turns out to be pretty easy to find. I had a vague impression stamped in my mind of a grubby asphalt lot serving an L of run-down, single-story businesses—one with a massive sign reading DOLLAR BIN in violent neon capitals—that's darted past the window on the occasions when my mom and I have been headed to the airport. My memory is confirmed, in all its depressing glory, when we pull off the highway and glide up the wide boulevard toward our destination.

The fog isn't as thick this far from the water, and the shabby storefronts and light-up plastic signs suffer for lack of the dramatic, soft-focus effect that a little nighttime haze could have provided. There's some sort of construction going on in the lot, a freestanding structure rising from piles of rubble in a corner of the asphalt plaza—and a perimeter of plastic fencing spreads so wide around it that it blocks off the main entrance to the parking area.

Driving past, Sebastian pulls instead into the empty service station that looms on the corner—a weedy expanse of oil-stained paving, defunct pumps, and a couple of boxy, concrete edifices begging for demolition. Graffiti covers any surface wide enough for the writing to be legible, and the ground is littered with cigarette butts, used condoms, and broken glass. Sebastian turns off the engine, his headlights dying out, and I make a noise in the back of my throat. "You take me to the nicest places."

"Wait'll you see the Dollar Bin," he quips, and I giggle again. But even the easy humor hurts just a little bit.

"Are we leaving the Jeep here?" I ask, just to say something. "There's got to be another way into the lot."

Ahead of us is a small outbuilding—the gas station's restrooms—its painted metal doors padlocked shut; beyond that lies a short expanse of rocky undergrowth, which ends at the shore of the strip mall's asphalt sea, where the plastic construction fence forms a lattice against the glowing lights of what few businesses remain open. Among them are Suzy's American Diner, and, in what I hope is not some sort of omen, an establishment called the Smoking Gun.

"To be honest? I think I'll feel better with my car over here." Sebastian shoots me an uncomfortable look. "You said Hayden would probably come looking for Lyle, right? Well, dude knows my car, and it doesn't seem like he's in the mood to let bygones be bygones tonight. If we decide to make a quick retreat, I don't want to be running to the parking lot to find out that all my tires have been slashed and your bro is waiting there to finish what we started at the police station." Embarrassed, he gestures through the windscreen. "It looks like the diner's right there, anyway. Let's just cut across."

He gets out of the Jeep, and I follow, stepping over plants that shoot nearly ten inches high through fissures in the pavement. The building housing the restrooms reeks as though it has never been cleaned, and the cloying odor of a long-dead animal drifts on the thick air that fills the shadows behind it.

The undergrowth separating the service station from the parking lot turns out to be not just rocky but also filled with trash that lurks unseen in the swampy shadows, glass and metal scattering at our feet. Emerging at last before a length of the plastic fencing, which is anchored by upright supports every ten or fifteen feet along, we follow it toward the frontage of the strip mall. Less than half the businesses look like they're still operational, and every other window is cracked and clouded, the residue of signage lingering like tan lines.

Nearing the corner of the fenced-off work site, as we negotiate around a dented oil drum—half-full of dusty rebar and broken cinder block—we hear the sound of a voice raised in anger, and our feet stutter to an instinctive halt. Peering around the edge of the last upright in the row, gazing out on the darkened expanse of the parking lot and the dispiriting, electric bleakness of the storefronts, we see four people gathered together outside of Suzy's American Diner.

Lyle Shetland leans against a broad-shouldered motorcycle, arms folded across his chest. He's put on some weight since last I saw him—and grown some scraggly beard-like stuff that looks like something my mom once dredged from her shower drain with a wire coat hanger—but otherwise he's much the same: leather jacket, thick eyebrows, and a skull shaved to the quick. He's flanked by two other guys, one with a greasy-looking ponytail and the other with a black bandana tied across his forehead, both of whom radiate an aura of agitated subservience detectable a mile away; Lyle is clearly in charge.

Standing opposite them, red in the face with fury, is my older brother.

"—don't like getting ripped off!" Hayden is practically shouting, his voice reverberating off the glass front of the strip mall and bouncing in all directions. "You owe me a fucking grand, and I'm not leaving till I get it!"

"You need to calm the hell down," Lyle warns tonelessly.

"Don't tell me to calm down! You ripped me off, asshole, and I promise you I'm not an enemy you want to have."

Lyle barely moves, but his whole body seems to tighten somehow, a fireball contracting right before it blows. "I don't know what you're talking about, but you better watch your damn mouth when you speak to me."

"You. Ripped. Me. Off." Hayden repeats ferociously, jabbing a finger at the guy like he's hoping it'll hurt him from a distance. "I paid your boy a shitload of money for pills tonight, and they were fuckin' fucked up!"

My brother's loudmouthed aggression has an adverse effect on the ponytailed guy, who starts shifting and fidgeting, glancing around the empty lot to see if they're being overheard. I shrink back a little as Lyle answers, with deliberate caution, "I don't have 'boys,' okay? And if I did, they wouldn't be selling no pills."

"Don't fuck with me, man!" Hayden hisses. Reaching into the pocket of his shorts, he hauls loose a plastic bag that's filled with small, white tablets. "I got these off one of your guys tonight, and they're *bullshit*!"

He throws the bag at Lyle, who lets them bounce off his shoulder and drop to the ground. "I never seen those before in my life."

"Don't give me that!" Hayden spits. "I bought them off Fox Whitney about six hours ago. They're your shit, and everybody who took one got sick. One of the girls started flopping around on the floor, foaming at the mouth—we had to dump her outside the ER!"

Lyle seems to freeze, and his two henchmen exchange an agitated glance over the top of his shaved head. Ponytail does another survey of the parking lot then, his fingers twitching nervously, while Lyle eyes the bag of white rabbits with a dark expression. Finally, he growls, "I don't think I know a Fox Whitney. If you say he sold you some bad stuff, maybe you oughta take it up with him instead of fucking up my night."

"Yeah, I tried that already," Hayden replies smoothly, baring his teeth in a grin, "only I was a little too late. By the time I got to him, old Fox was fucking *dead*, and somebody had taken my money."

This time, Lyle straightens up, his back going rigid. "What did you say?"

"He's on a slab at the morgue, Lyle. Actually, both your boys are." Hayden squares his shoulders, finding security at last in his opponent's discomposure. "See, I figured Arlo must've iced Fox and swiped the cash, but when I went to see Arlo about it, it turned out he was fucking dead, too. So, way I see it now, either they both pissed off the wrong customer, or they both pissed off their boss." He plants his hands on his hips. "And, you know, I don't really give a shit either way, except that my money's still missing. So right now I'm thinking that since it was your boy who sold me bad product, and it was *you* who gave it to him, then *you're* the cocksucker who owes me a thousand fucking dollars. *Right. Now.*"

Lyle finally picks up the bag, examining it with a deep frown etched across his face. Wordlessly, he tosses the pills to Bandana Guy, who takes one out, studies it under the light, and then shakes his head definitively. "These ain't ours."

"*What?*" Hayden's face practically turns purple.

"The color's funny and the stamp ain't right." Bandana sounds deadly serious. Dropping the tablet into the bag again, he seals it up and tosses the cache back to Lyle. "I don't know where Whitney got these, but it wasn't our shipment."

"You heard the man." Lyle chucks the Ziploc at Hayden, who swats it away like a nuisance insect. "That junk didn't come from us, so I guess I don't owe you squat. Now, get the fuck outta here."

Hayden's chest starts to heave, his lips curling, and I can practically see the waves of heat distortion pouring from his eyes as he glares murderously at the complacent biker. "No, no, no—you do not play me like that! This is *your* merchandise, I got ripped off by *your* boys, and I want my damn money!"

"Go home to mommy and daddy, you little bitch," Lyle snaps. "We're done here."

"We're done when I say we're done!" Hayden shouts, and in one swift motion, he reaches behind his back, yanks something free from the waistband of his shorts, and draws it level with Lyle's head. "And we're not done until I've got my money!"

It's a gun. It is a *fucking gun.* And a half second later it has company when Ponytail draws a piece of his own—something enormous and nickel-plated—and thrusts it into the air at Hayden as though it were a sword. The armed biker shifts from foot to foot, so wired up that even his face starts twitching as he barks, *"Watch it, motherfucker!"*

"No, no, no." Sebastian breathes frantically into my ear, his fingers digging into my arm. "Oh, hell no. Oh *fuck*, dude, this is our cue to fucking leave!"

He starts backward across the pavement, stepping as quickly as possible . . . and then he turns around and crashes directly into the oil drum behind him. The rebar scrapes and clangs in the belly of the metal bin, rattled by the impact, and the noise rumbles out with the deafening resonance of church bells in a graveyard. Sebastian glances up at me, eyes like the fat zeroes on a time bomb, and I feel the atmosphere drop.

"The fuck was that?" Bandana yelps.

"Is it the cops?" Ponytail demands, his voice pitched almost to a shriek. "Did you set us up, you rich-ass punk? *Did you bring the cops here?*"

And that's when the first gunshot rips a hole in the night.

19

THE REPORT IS LOUD AND HEART-STOPPING—A MINIATURE thunderclap—and a burst of cold, primal adrenaline stokes my body. Simultaneous with the shocking *bang*, a hole erupts mysteriously in the thick plastic fencing to my left, and a fleshy, tearing sound sizzles through the vegetation to my right. I blink. *He's shooting at us.*

It takes a fraction of a second to happen, and as much time again for us to process the fact that *Ponytail is shooting at us*, and then we're off and running. Our feet pounding the asphalt, we sprint back up the length of the perimeter fence as more gunshots pop behind us. Glass shatters, people scream, bullets thump against metal, and my lungs burn as I veer after Sebastian, crashing through undergrowth and debris in a panicked retreat back to the abandoned service station.

I make it as far as the restroom outbuilding when another shot sounds, and the corner edge of the wall two feet in front of me explodes; concrete dust blasts from the fresh crater like a plume of volcanic ash, spraying into my eyes, blinding me. At the same moment, something sharp strikes my temple and I reel sideways, tumbling to the ground like a felled oak as the universe somersaults around me.

"Rufus!" Sebastian's voice has to navigate entire solar systems to reach my ears, but I feel his hands almost immediately as he hauls me to my feet. My eyes are gritty and raw, and I try to force them open, but they won't cooperate. Stumbling and gasping, I cling to Sebastian as we race crookedly across the gas station's tiny lot back to the Jeep, chaos filling the air like feedback.

He shoves me up into the passenger seat as I blink hard, trying to squeeze the dust from my watering eyes. They sting, my lids like sandpaper, and the world around me is barely distinguishable—a reflection in a fogged mirror. There are more gunshots, a motorcycle engine growls furiously somewhere, and then the Jeep rocks side to side as Sebastian vaults into position behind the wheel and slams the door. "Buckle up!"

He floors the pedal, and the motor gives a congested cough before roaring abruptly to life. Lurching forward, we jump the curb and crash-land on the street, rising up onto two wheels as Sebastian swings the vehicle around, steering back the way we came.

He shoots across lanes, the strip mall streaking past like a lit-up space station crashing to earth, and we make a beeline for the highway. We're almost there when another car overtakes us, flying so fast we might just as well be standing still; I recognize Hayden's BMW a second before its rear bumper smashes out one of the Jeep's headlights, my older brother careening in front of us and fishtailing up the on-ramp to Route 2. Startled, Sebastian swerves, missing the turn; instead, he punches the gas and shoots beneath the overpass just as sirens began to squall in the distance.

A sweaty mile later, he corners sharply into a residential neighborhood, jerking to a stop beneath a streetlamp. The night is almost deafeningly quiet now; no one seems to have followed us.

"Rufus?" Sebastian is staring at me, eyes wild, the gold flecks in his irises burning like caution lights. "Rufe, are you okay?"

I manage a dazed nod. My eyes feel like they've been scrubbed with a wire brush, but I can see again. My left ear is ringing, my temple throbbing hotly like a drumbeat, but I'm pretty sure none of the damage is permanent. "I'm . . . I'm okay."

"You're bleeding." He sounds scared.

I flip down the visor and looked at myself in the mirror. My face is pale, and dark blood oozes from an ugly gash above my left ear. "A chunk of cement got me, I think. When the bullet hit the wall—"

"No," he cuts me off urgently, pointing to my side. "*Here!* You're bleeding *here*!"

I follow the line of his finger and my eyes bulge, my stomach flopping over. My tank top is torn open on the left side, stained a deep crimson with blood that gushes from a jagged laceration just beneath my ribs. My brain feels like it's suspended in a jar somewhere, and I lick my lips. "I don't . . . It doesn't hurt."

In a flash, Sebastian drags the tank top off me, yanking it over my head and chucking it into the footwell so he can get a better look, his face gray and serious. The wound is ugly, the amount of blood nauseating, but it's clearly not an entrance wound. "It's not from a bullet," Sebastian declares, his voice actually wobbling with relief. "It looks like you cut yourself on something."

"Maybe a piece of glass, when I fell," I mumble distantly. The incised flesh looks puffy and grotesque, swollen lips drooling my life out.

"We need to clean it, like, *now.*" Sebastian fixes me with a look. "I cut my hand on old glass once, and it got, like, zombie-movie infected. I was on antibiotics for weeks." He punches open the glove box, digs inside it, and comes up with a bunch of McDonald's napkins and a small tube of hand sanitizer. "No lie, Rufe, this is gonna suck, so . . . you know. Try to think happy thoughts, okay?"

"Okay," I say weakly, staring in horror as he squirts a thick glob of jelly onto his fingers and the close air in the Jeep fills with the stinging aroma of pure alcohol.

Imagine someone tickling your ribs with a blowtorch, and you'll have the edited-for-TV version of my experience in having an open wound cleansed with hand sanitizer. I'm ready to hand over state secrets by the time Sebastian is finishing up, stuffing the gory napkins in a leftover Subway bag and capping the empty bottle of disinfectant. Peering down at his handiwork, I see a hot pink zigzag carved into my skin—a grotesque laceration that's embarrassingly small for how much drama it's caused. Still, every breath feels like a knife between my ribs, and it's an effort to remain stoic.

"You okay?" Sebastian arches a concerned eyebrow.

"I should have picked the zombie infection," I manage, blowing out through tight lips. "Is there going to be a round two, or have you finally run out of sulfuric acid?"

"All done. And I'm real proud of you, Rufe," he adds, with warmth. "You only called for your mommy twice."

"Oh, ha ha, fuck you." I can't help laughing a little bit, though. "How come I'm the only one who fell on dirty hobo glass? Life isn't fair." Taking one of the few remaining clean napkins, I wipe the blood off my temple. "At least I didn't take a bullet or anything. I guess I should just be glad I'm still alive."

"Don't even joke about that." Sebastian shudders, his eyes darkening. "When that wall blew up and you went down, I thought . . . I just thought—" He blinks, hard, and looks away. "Don't make jokes."

"You're right." The memory of actual bullets whizzing through the air, inches from my actual head, makes my palms slippery. "You have to admit, though: It'll make a great story to tell our therapists someday."

Sebastian looks back at me with an odd expression, like someone trying to smile for the first time in his life. Then, after a weirdly full silence, he leans across the center console and lightly touches my sensitized flesh, bending closer to have another look at the cleaned-up injury. "It's stopped bleeding, I think. And it actually doesn't look as deep as I figured. You better wash it again at home, though—like, with actual soap and stuff—and go see a doctor. You'll probably need stitches."

"Better than needing a coffin," I rejoin before I can stop myself.

He doesn't say anything, just looks up at me, and I become suddenly aware of how close he is—of how his hand is resting on my bare skin. Sebastian's eyes are deep and lonely, the air between us redolent of citrus and vetiver, warm from his body. The silence stretches out, and the longer he looks at me, the faster my pulse starts to beat. He leans up, his face moving in, and his other hand touches my chest—fingers hot against smooth muscle—and my flesh starts firming up everywhere, *everywhere*, goose bumps taking me like a plague. Softly, he murmurs, "Rufus, I . . ."

And then his lips touch mine, and my heart rockets up, down, up, and a Pandora's box inside of me springs open, releasing every treacherous emotion I've spent the past weeks trying to incarcerate. My guts twist in both directions at once, air pushing out of my lungs, until I feel myself starting to tear in half. I push him back as hard as I can, fresh tears springing to my eyes, and my body trembles all over. I can hardly speak. "*Don't.* Fucking *don't*, Sebastian. You have no right."

He stares at me, wide-eyed—looking scared and lost and ashamed—and I watch him struggle to say something. "Rufus. I . . . I d-didn't—"

"You know how I feel—how I *felt* about you," I whisper abjectly, my skin pulsing with the memory of his touch. "Maybe you were experimenting, or maybe I was just a rebound from Lia, I don't know, but I had *feelings* for you. You know that, and you're taking advantage of it, and that's *so* messed up!"

"How can you say that?" His mouth drops open. "How can you even think that?"

"How can I think anything else?" Tears come faster than I can wipe them away. "I loved you. I *still* love you, you fuck—You can't do this! You broke my heart and now you want to play with the pieces? It's messed up and I won't let you. *It's not fair.*"

I always thought it would feel good to get these words out, and yet I feel just as bad as ever, my misery a subdermal tattoo that cannot be removed. I try to tell myself the satisfaction will come eventually; but then Sebastian bends forward over the steering wheel, burying his face in his hands—and when his shoulders start to shake, I realize that *he's crying.* Choked, gulping sobs fill the Jeep, and I slowly petrify, caught in the crossfire of vindictiveness and shame.

Is this what I wanted?

I can find no words to say while he weeps into his hands, and so I just sit there—stiff and hot and embarrassed—and watch my fingers like maybe they'll do something to save me. Sebastian speaks again at last, his voice a tiny, broken whisper. "He knows."

"Huh?" I look up.

"He knows," Sebastian repeats mournfully, his face a quivering wreck of fear and distress. "He knows. About . . . about me. About us."

"I don't . . . Huh?" I think about the BMW cutting us off on the race to the highway; it seems evident that my brother escaped the gunfight at the So-Not-Okay Corral, and maybe Sebastian is afraid he recognized the Jeep when he hit us—deduced that we were the noisy spies who instigated the night's second round of fireworks. "Do you mean Hayden? Because I don't think—"

"My dad." He cuts me off with a convulsive breath, cheeks wet with tears, and I stare at him uncomprehendingly. "My dad . . . he kn-knows about us."

"What?" I still don't get it. *"How?"*

"He knew I'd been hiding something. He thought it was drugs." A dull, ironic laugh escapes from him, clogged with nightmares, and he starts trembling. "All the stuff I'd been lying about since February, the way I've been acting since . . . since we broke up? He knew something was going on, and he thought it was drugs. It's one of his big issues, and when they found white rabbits on campus at the university in the spring, he really went off the deep end." Sebastian pauses, staring down at his knuckles where they blanch in his lap. "Tonight he finally . . . he searched my room."

"No." My blood runs cold just imagining it happening to me—my mom reading the bawdy notes that Lucy and I scribble back and forth in Ms. Gibson's class, the mortifyingly erotic poems I wrote about my student teacher from freshman English, the

browser history I still haven't deleted from my laptop. I'd sooner roll down a freaking *dune* of dirty hobo glass.

"He found those pictures of us from the photo booth in Montpelier," Sebastian continues. "I was at Jake's place all day, helping him set up for his party, and when I came home to pick up my speakers, Dad was waiting for me. He had the . . . the photos, and when I walked in he, he just—" His voice stops, and he takes another breath, swallowing twice. "He started shouting. I've never seen him so mad before, Rufe. It was like . . . he was looking at me like he didn't know who I was—like he didn't even *want* to know."

Sebastian starts to shake all over, weeping uncontrollably, looking smaller and more vulnerable than I've ever seen him.

Clearing my throat, I ask, "So what happened?"

"I ran out." His voice cracks. "I was so scared, Rufus. For real, I've never been actually scared of my dad before tonight, but . . . if you could've seen him . . ." He shakes his head. "I panicked. I just turned around, ran out of the house, and drove away. He's been calling and texting for hours, and I've been too afraid to even check the messages."

"What are you going to do?"

"I don't know." He looks over at me like a terrified little kid. "What if he kicks me out? He's really serious about church, and he's always making my mom change the TV channel if there are gay guys on it . . . What if I go home and, like . . . and it's not my *home* anymore? I don't know what to do!"

Wracking sobs shake him all over, and I slide across the seat, pulling him into my arms. He collapses against me, pressing his face against my chest, and we stay like that for a long time. Holding Sebastian again feels wonderful and gut-wrenching all at once, and I try to keep my mind clear—try not to fall through the big trap door over my heart—but question marks swarm in the air, deafening and distracting, and when his tears finally ebb, I have to ask. "Sebastian, why did you still have those pictures?"

He had insisted on keeping the strip of photos from our date in Montpelier—those four little frames of us making out in an oblivious state of hormonal euphoria—and up till now I'd just assumed they'd been destroyed along with anything else that might remind him of our relationship.

"Are you serious?" Sebastian straightens up a little so he can look me in the eye, a pathetic, wrung-out smile on his beautiful face. He wrestles his mouth open, but no sound emerges, and he has to try again. "I was going to keep those forever," he whispers. "I look at them all the time, so I can remember how . . . how freaking *awesome* that day was—how actually happy I felt for the first time in forever." Then, apparently determined to say all kinds of things that make no sense, he continues, "Rufus . . . fuck. Don't you understand? I'm in love with you."

Suddenly, I'm back on the ground behind the gas station, winded and dizzy and totally disoriented. "I don't . . . I don't think . . . You can't—"

"I knew it that afternoon," he barrels ahead, afraid of losing his nerve—or maybe just afraid of letting me finish. "Actually, maybe I even knew it before we started dating—when you told me about the time you donated your birthday money to the Humane Society in the third grade. I thought it was so cute, and so . . . amazing. You're funny, and you're interesting, and you're hot." He blinks, shyly. *He* actually looks shy. "The reason I looked for you tonight, the reason I wouldn't let you ditch me, is because you're literally the only thing that made me happy, and I treated you like shit."

"Sebastian . . ." I can barely breathe.

"I'm so sorry," he goes on, his voice wavering again. "What I did *was* totally messed up. It's just . . . I kept telling myself that we were only fooling around, and that it wasn't serious, but when you said you loved me . . . when you said it *first*—"

"Oh," I say faintly.

"I had to either say it back, or run the other way." He wipes his eyes again. "And because I'm the world's biggest chickenshit, I ran. I couldn't even tell you to your face that I wanted to break up, because I was afraid of what I'd really say if I tried it in person."

My head starts spinning again, the recent past turning upside down so fast I can't keep pace with it, all my bitter certainties suddenly called into question. I've fantasized about this moment so many times—Sebastian tearfully admitting he'd actually loved me all along—but I can't remember any of my lines. "But . . . but, I mean. You went back to Lia. You told her you loved her."

"That was the second shittiest thing I've done to anybody. I wanted to believe it, so I told myself it was true, but the second we were official again I knew it was a mistake. Lia . . . we used to work, but now we can't even be in the same room without fighting." Pleadingly, he searches my eyes. "I did so much stupid shit, and I know I hurt you, Rufe, but please let me make it up to you. I'm not asking you to . . . take me back or whatever. I know how pissed you are. But can we please maybe just start over? Can we please go back to being friends? That's all I'm asking."

I swallow hard, my skin alive with some feeling I can't define, and try to sort out my words . . . but I have no speeches left; my pride still demands its pound of flesh, but the rest of me has lost the will to collect. From the moment I held him, or maybe from the moment he kissed me—or maybe even from the moment I left Lucy's house with him in the first place—I'd already started giving him a second chance.

"What if I do want to take you back, though?" I whisper, even more nervous than I was that time I asked him if he had a condom. More nervous than the first time we saw each other after our kiss in Mr. Cohen's classroom.

I'm not good at this stuff. I don't want any more bruises on my heart—but I no longer have the strength to pretend that I'm okay moving on without him.

He just stares at me like he's afraid to trust what I'm saying, and so I pull him haltingly closer. And press my lips to his.

20

IT'S MY FIRST BREATH OF AIR IN SIX WEEKS. WE KISS DESPERATELY, struggling through the gap over the center console and tumbling into the backseat, my wound screaming in protest as it scrapes across the rough upholstery. Sebastian's shirt pops a stitch as we fight it over his head, and then I lose myself in the thrill of being with him again. The night is a hunter, stalking us with realities we still have to face—Sebastian's parents, his friends, *my* friends—but we forget them all, clinging to each other and finding the rhythms I'd once thought were gone for good. Reality can wait.

Later, with his mouth nestled against the curve of my neck, after we've cleaned ourselves up with the last of the McDonald's napkins, he murmurs softly, "I love you, Rufus."

"You told me that already," I point out, but I'm grinning like an idiot, because hearing it again is amazing.

"Get used to it." His fingers creep along my sternum. "I'm going to say it over and over, because I can't believe how good it feels. I love you."

"I love you, too." It does feel good.

"And, you know." He props himself up on one elbow, peering down nervously. "I guess . . . there isn't really any point in my trying to keep it a secret anymore. You know? I mean, my dad knows, so it's like the shit's already hit the fan. How much worse can it get?"

It takes just a moment for his words to sink in. "You mean, like . . . are you thinking about maybe telling people? About us?"

"Why not?" He gives an indifferent shrug, but fear squirms furtively in his eyes all the same. "I mean, if he kicks me out, everybody's gonna know anyway, right?"

I struggle up onto my elbows, too. "Are you sure, though? I mean . . . all I wanted was for us to be together—to be *real* and stuff—but you don't have to . . . maybe we should wait and see how things go with your dad, before—"

"Rufus. I think I *have* to. Now or never, you know. It won't get easier, and . . . I don't want to lose my nerve again."

Judging by his pallor, I'm not sure he even has the nerve to lose, but I don't say so; instead, I put my hand on the firm planes of his chest, the smooth, brown skin warm and wonderful to the touch, and smile. "We can start easy—my friends first. And, you know, don't freak or anything? But my mom figured us out pretty much immediately."

It's an optimistic speech. The fact is, the future is still a terrifyingly blank slate. If Sebastian's dad really does kick him out, where will he go? He might be sent to live with relatives on the other side of the country; he might be dumped at a boarding school, like Eric Shetland; he might even be told that he can just kiss his financial support for college good-bye. There are about a million brick walls our current happiness could smack right into, fates that would obviate both his intentions and his nerve—but I choose to block them all out. I don't get a lot of Happy, and I want to enjoy it while it lasts.

Our peaceful moment is shattered right on cue by the sudden, loud *ping* of my cell phone, which fell from my pocket when we barrel-rolled into the backseat. I fish it out from a pile of debris in the footwell, take one look at the display, and shove myself upright. It's a text from April.

It's over. The cops are letting me go home.

Five minutes later, we're back on the highway, heading into the city again. It looks deserted, streetlights burning like candles in a cemetery, and Sebastian rolls the windows down to let cool air into the cab of the Jeep. I'm wearing one of his lacrosse jerseys, which he found wadded up in his trunk; it smells a little gamy, and it's covered in wrinkles—but that's still way better than being covered in blood, so I keep my mouth shut. Besides, wearing a shirt with his name on it feels really significant at this particular moment, and I pull it tight so that the letters press against my back.

"By 'over,'" he says, raising his voice to be heard above the slipstream of misty wind rushing by, "does she mean *over* over? Like, as in, they figured out who did it, and she's officially off the hook?"

"I've got no idea." I glare at my phone in frustration. "She didn't write anything else, and now she's not answering my messages."

"Do you think they could've arrested Hayden? Like, maybe they caught him fleeing from the strip mall after the shootout, and found some kind of evidence in his car connecting him to what happened to Fox and Arlo?"

"Maybe." I can't fend off a pensive frown. "You still think he did it?"

Sebastian cocks his head. "You *don't*? I mean, the dude is clearly homicidal, Rufe—and you had him figured for the killer even before he started trading bullets with a biker gang."

"I'm the last person who needs to be convinced that Hayden is a psycho," I aver, "but you heard him back there—he thought maybe Lyle was behind it all."

"Or maybe he just didn't want to admit to a bunch of armed drug dealers that he was out trimming their payroll for them. Would *you* go up to a guy like Lyle and say, 'Hey, bro, I just killed two of your boys! What do you think about that?' "

"No, but I only ever use the word 'bro' ironically," I answer and net a dirty look in response. "Seriously, though, why would Lyle care? Fox and Arlo weren't exactly his buddies and, as far as he knows now, they'd both been cheating him—whoever killed them just saved him the trouble. And even if Hayden wasn't thinking that far ahead, he obviously also wasn't even close to being afraid of Lyle. You saw him: He wanted those dudes to think he was this big, tough badass that they shouldn't mess with. If anything, you'd think he'd act like maybe he *was* the killer, just so they'd take him seriously."

Sebastian is unmoved. "None of that means he didn't do it."

"Okay, how about this: Apparently, my brother has a freaking *gun*. So why weren't Fox and Arlo shot? Why were they both killed with knives?"

"Knives are quieter."

"Okay, I'm going to ignore how creepy that sounded? And just point out that Fox's death didn't *need* to be quiet. Apart from April, who was unconscious, they were alone in the house, the place is practically in the middle of nowhere, Fox's music was blasting so loud we could hear it from the driveway, and there were fireworks going off all evening. Even if one of the neighbors did hear a gunshot, they'd have just assumed it was some asshole celebrating Independence Day in his driveway or something."

"That's still not—"

"My brother isn't a subtle guy," I interrupt with authority, "and Fox wasn't nearly as tough as he acted. If Hayden pulled a gun on him, Fox would've pissed himself and paid the dude back. And if Fox was stupid enough to call Hayden's bluff, my brother wouldn't have put the gun away so he could pick out a knife—he'd have either gone right ahead and shot him or, more likely, just stomped on his skull till it exploded like a fucking water balloon."

Sebastian thinks about this for a moment, looking for a counter-argument; but he knows the players even better than I do, and he has to realize that I'm right. With a troubled sigh, he finally concedes. "Okay. Fair enough. So where does that leave us?"

"I don't know." I look out the window, watching the fog thicken as we draw nearer to the water again. "Back at square one, I guess."

I'm still pondering this—thinking about Race and Peyton, the only remaining suspects we haven't spoken to a second time—when we pull up in front of the police station again. It's a destination we've gambled on, hoping against hope that we can catch April before Peter and Isabel take her home, and so I'm relieved to see her standing outside—alone. Leaning against the building's brick frontage, away from the lights of the overhang, she is at first only discernible in the darkness by the orange glow of a cigarette she holds in the fork of two fingers.

"Hey," I call out softly, after Sebastian has parked the Jeep and we're approaching her through the shadows of the almost empty lot. She still looks pale and drawn, but far more relaxed than she was when we first dropped her off. "What happened in there? Where are Peter and your mom?"

April drags on the cigarette for a long moment, the ember glaring as she evaluates us with strangely careful eyes. As she exhales, she pushes a hand through her auburn locks and states, "They're still inside. Talking to the cops. Or to the lawyer, maybe—I don't know. She's a total bitch, by the way."

"But what happened?" I repeat impatiently. "What did you tell the police?"

"What we agreed." She flicks some ash off her cigarette, her expression unreadable. "They kept saying my story 'didn't match up' with the one you guys told, but they wouldn't be more specific. I figured they were bullshitting."

It's a question, I realize. "They were. They must've been. I said exactly what we talked about, and then Peter sort of intervened, so the detective didn't get much of a chance to cross-examine me. I don't know if he believed it all, but I stuck to the script."

"I told them who my dad was, and they basically just took down what I said and thanked me for helping," Sebastian puts in. "The officer I spoke to played hockey for the Catamounts my dad's first year at the university. Being the son of Dominic Williams has its upsides. Sometimes."

"Well, anyway." April blows out another cloud of smoke. "I was in there for more than a fucking hour, saying the same stuff over and over again until they finally told us I could go because they didn't have enough evidence to arrest me. *Yet.*" She looks down at her hands. "I'm not supposed to leave town, though. It's so fucked up. This whole thing is so fucked up."

"Somebody burned Fox's house down," I blurt at last, wondering how long we have before Peter and Isabel come out and our time to confer is officially over. "Apparently it happened while we were going around and talking to everybody. As far as they know, you were still at the lake house, so they can't tie it to you."

April stares at me. "What?"

"And Arlo's dead," Sebastian adds. Her head swivels sharply in his direction, her eyes popping open wider. "We found him at his house. I guess he and Lia went back out to South Hero after they left the first time, and Arlo must've seen what happened to Fox. We think he was planning to blackmail whoever did it, only—"

"Then that's why they let me go." April gazes up at us, astonished. "It has to be. I mean, I was practically in jail—there's no way I killed Arlo and did whatever to Fox's house when they had me locked up in there. All that 'don't leave town' stuff was probably because they didn't want to admit they were wrong! Does this mean it's over?"

"Maybe." I can see hope making a desperate break for freedom in her expression, and I really don't want to be the guy to point out that relief is a little premature. There's no question in my mind that Fox's and Arlo's deaths are tied together, but who knows how long it could take the police to establish that fact—and to realize that April couldn't have been responsible? "Don't forget that what happened to Fox is technically in the jurisdiction of the South Hero police—"

"The Grand Isle Sheriff's Department," April corrects glumly. "They only mentioned it to me, like, eighteen times."

"Well, we'll probably have to speak with them, too—all of us—before they'll even think about officially clearing you."

"Awesome." April nods sarcastically, letting out a puff of smoke. Her eyes play over me, then narrow. "This is an interesting look. What happened to your other shirt?" Her tone is neutral, but I can see curiosity waking up in her eyes as she gestures at the jersey I'm wearing. There is, of course, actually a reasonable explanation for why I had to change, but I fumble my chance to give it; my first instinct is to look over at Sebastian, my cheeks turning pink with heat, and April reads deftly between the lines. "Wait. *WAIT. No. Way.* No way! You two aren't . . . I mean, *are you?*"

"It's not— Look, I had to change my shirt because—"

"It's cool, Rufe," Sebastian says quietly. "I told you I'm okay with it." He faces April, looking about as relaxed as a cat drowning in a toilet. "Um, yeah. Actually, me and Rufus are . . . you know. Um . . . together."

"Holy shit!" April claps a hand over her mouth, squeals, and does a weird little dance; then she tosses her arms out wide, and announces, "Welcome to the family!" Pulling Sebastian into a totally unexpected hug, she makes a conspiratorial OMG face at me behind his back. "I can't believe I didn't figure it out when we were riding around and you two were arguing like old ladies. My head must've been, like, two miles up my own ass."

"You had a pretty good excuse." My cheeks still feel ridiculously warm.

"Well, I won't tell anybody if you don't want me to," she swears. "We all know you guys are keeping enough secrets for me."

"It's okay." Sebastian takes a breath. "It's okay if you want to tell people."

And then all of a sudden, she seems to register what we said earlier. "Wait. You guys went back to Arlo's?"

"Yeah." For some reason, I don't want to tell her about the agreement I made with Isabel, so I just say, "We knew there was something Lia was holding back, so we talked to her again—and when we told her what happened to Fox, she finally admitted that she and Arlo had returned to the cottage after everybody else left."

"Apparently, Arlo saw something in the kitchen while they were there," Sebastian continues. "The reason we went over to his place was to ask about it, but . . ."

"But he was dead?" April predicts dismally, and Sebastian nods. My sister's forehead ladders with anxiety and she tosses her hands out, smoke twisting off her cigarette and melting into the mist. *"What the hell is going on?"* She rubs her eyes, and then asks, "Is Lia doing okay?"

"Yeah, more or less. She flipped when we told her about Arlo, but she was holding it together when we left."

"Did she know?" April studies our faces, her tone shrewd. "About Fox, I mean. If Arlo saw something, then he must've—"

"He didn't." I cut her off. "Or, she says he didn't. She heard it from Hayden."

"*Hayden?* Why the hell was he—" She interrupts herself this time, waving the question off into the night. "Never mind—I don't wanna know. Nothing about tonight makes any sense." Then, with a mirthless smirk, April mutters, "She must've been thrilled when she found out, though."

I frown. "What do you mean? Why would she be thrilled?"

April freezes up, flustered, like someone who's just been caught out. "Well, Lia wasn't exactly . . . She was really pissed at Fox tonight. That's all."

"Okay." My scalp starts prickling again. "Care to elaborate on that?"

April sighs unhappily. "Sometimes Fox and Lia rubbed each other the wrong way, you know? They'd bicker or whatever, and then get over it. But tonight . . ." She trails off, pursing her lips and glancing to the side. "Tonight she found out that Fox had been selling pills to Javi, and she kinda went apeshit on him."

"Javi?" Sebastian blinks so fast it's like he's trying to send a message in Morse code. "You mean 'Javi' as in '*Javier Santos*'?"

"Lia's brother?" I hazard.

"He's fucking *thirteen years old*!" Sebastian explodes. "He's in the *eighth grade*! Fox was seriously selling drugs to middle school kids?"

"I didn't know anything about it," April declares firmly. "Arlo was still pissed after he and Fox finished pounding on each other, so he told Lia the whole story, and she went fucking *bananas* on Fox; hitting him, calling him names in Spanish . . . the whole deal. Anyway, he just laughed her off. Told her to, and I quote, 'Go suck a few dicks and calm down.' That's why she made sure I knew all about what happened between Fox and Peyton. Another little secret Arlo had decided he didn't have to keep to himself anymore."

"April." I stare at her in disbelief, trying to figure out what the hell is going on behind those guileless blue eyes of hers. "Why didn't you tell us any of this? We were supposed to be trying to prove that somebody else might've done it—you paid me two grand to find proof that somebody else might've done it—and you didn't think to point out that Lia had a really good reason to hate Fox?"

"She was pissed off!" April exclaims. "That doesn't mean she killed him. She got her revenge by making *me* want to kill him, remember? If I'd told you about the one thing, I'd have had to tell you about the other, and that part makes me look guilty." She sucks in some air. "Besides, I was sure it was Arlo. *You* were sure it was Arlo."

I shake my head in disbelief. Her reasoning doesn't make sense, and there's a defensiveness in her tone that's causing my hackles to rise. "She had a motive, April. Why the hell wouldn't you want us to know that?"

"*I* had a motive, Rufus, remember?" she retorts sarcastically, chucking her cigarette to the ground. Then, squeezing her eyes shut, she leans back and exhales through her nose. "When I found out that Peyton had fucked my boyfriend, I really lost it, okay? I mean, *really*. Way more than Lia. I went for Peyton, just like I said, but after she ran out of the house—like a damn coward—I . . . I went for Fox, too." She opens her eyes and sets her jaw, defiant. "I threatened him. With the butcher knife."

"You mean . . ." I try to get my head around this. "You mean the knife we found in your hand when we got to the lake house tonight? The one that *killed him*?"

"Yes, obviously," April snaps in a harsh stage whisper, her eyes shooting to the door of the station, making certain we remain unobserved. "I told him I was gonna cut his balls off, and I made sure he believed me. Lia was the only one who saw me do it, though. She's the only one who knows. And I was afraid that if I sold her out—"

"—she'd sell you out right back," I conclude wearily. I feel like a dog tied to a stake, running in furious circles and never getting anywhere.

Sniffing, she adds, "And I *really* thought it was Arlo."

"You could've told us."

"*You* kept saying we had to go to the cops." She thrusts her hand at me. "I knew you didn't want to believe I was innocent, so the last thing I was about to do was tell you how I'd pulled that knife on Fox. I needed you to take me seriously."

We all eye each other for an unfriendly moment, and then my shoulders sag. Once again, she's got a point—the same rage that flows through my veins flows through hers, and I know exactly how far beyond reason it can push you. While crushed in the grip of my anger, I've raved, destroyed things, hurt people; if I'd heard the whole story, after finding her the way we did tonight, I might never have let her buy my assistance.

"Well, what's done is done," I finally remark, still unable to keep the acid out of my voice. "It's too late to go to the cops and change your story now."

"You know," she begins quietly, staring off into the swirling fog that turns Battery Park into a depthless, gray sea on the other side of the lot. "I'm not sure I even would. I think I'm kinda starting to realize that Fox was never who I thought he was. He cheated on me, screwed his best friend's girlfriend, sold drugs to kids . . . if Lia *did* kill him, I wouldn't blame her. And as long as I don't take the fall for it, maybe I don't even care, either." April faces me again, her gaze level and cold. "Maybe Fox deserved it."

21

SEBASTIAN DOESN'T SPEAK A WORD AS WE CROSS THE PAVEMENT and get into the Jeep; he doesn't speak as he turns the engine over, as he starts for the exit, or even as April waves good-bye, disappearing into the fog and shadows that thicken behind us as we drive away, the desolation of afterhours Burlington almost sinister in its totality.

Finally, however, the tension that fills the cab—heavy and unbreathable as wet cement—becomes too much for him to bear. "She didn't do it."

"Sebastian—"

"I'm telling you, Rufus: Lia. Didn't. Do it." We stop at a red light, and he turns to face me, his expression apprehensive but earnest. "I know stuff is . . . complicated for us when it comes to her—and I know that's my fault—but seriously. This isn't just me refusing to admit she's got flaws and stuff. She does. But I *know* her, Rufe; I've known her for a long time, and she's just not capable of something like this."

"We still need to talk to her," I answer him carefully. I've spent weeks resenting Lia, embittered by what I believed was Sebastian's happiness with her; but now that I have him back again—now that I know the truth of how he feels about me—I no longer experience a reflexive surge of ugly jealousy when her name comes up. For his sake, I even want to believe his assessment of her character . . . but I'm just not sure I can. "We need to hear what she has to say."

"What *can* she say?" he counters. "Fox was selling pills to her kid brother! Anybody in her position would've gone apeshit on his ass—so what? Lia's got a temper, but she's not *Hayden*. I guarantee you she ripped Fox a new asshole, put his secrets on blast, dropped the mic, and then walked out the door; that's her style. She's not a killer."

"According to Peyton, she was the last one to leave the house," I remind him, although I don't feel very good about it. "And we only have her word for what happened when she and Arlo went back there."

"Are you serious?" He screws up his eyebrows in irritation. The light turns green while he's staring at me, and when I gesture to it, he hits the gas pedal angrily. "You really think she stabbed Fox, staged the crime scene, and then just waltzed out and hopped on Arlo's bike? Or maybe when he went back to settle things with Fox, she ran in first and beat him to it."

"I don't think anything yet," I say as calmly as I can, trying not to become frustrated by the sarcasm in his tone. "I'm just observing the facts."

"Yeah, well, there are a lot of 'facts' that you're not observing. Like, how about the fact that Fox was banging Peyton, and that Race found out about it and tried to kick the guy's ass in half—and we still haven't done anything to rule him out. Maybe we should be going over to *his* place right now. Lia and Arlo passed him on the road; maybe he turned around after that and went back to the cottage before they did!"

"Maybe." I swear I don't want to argue with him, but he's making it extremely difficult not to. "But Peyton was behind him, remember? She'd have seen him if he doubled back, but she confirmed what Race said about the two of them driving straight to the Atwoods' house after the party broke up."

"She could be lying for him. She was sleeping with the guy's best friend—maybe she feels responsible for what happened, and thinks she owes it to Race to keep him out of trouble."

"She'd have to feel pretty damn guilty to help Race cover up a murder he committed. I don't see it. Not to sound judgmental or anything? But I'm not sure Peyton Forsyth is even capable of that much remorse. In the fifth grade, she literally stole a bunch of valentines from a disabled girl, and then had her mother complain to the school board when our teacher punished her for it."

"I'm being serious, Rufus."

"So am I!" I pick through my words. "Look: I agree that we still need to follow up on Race and Peyton, and if you say Lia couldn't have done it, I'll try to give her the benefit of the doubt—for you. But she's kept a lot of stuff from us tonight, and we need to get to the bottom of it before we can just scratch her off the list. That's all I'm saying."

The problem, of course, is that there's so much more to say.

Like how we only found Arlo's body because Lia sent us to his house; like how it was only after she knew *we* knew that the guy was too dead to confirm or deny her version of events that she told us about the return trip to the cottage; like how we also only had her word that she learned of Fox's death from Hayden—or that Hayden even went to her house *at all* tonight—and that he was the one who left the bruises on her arms. Said and done, for all we know, she got them while murdering Arlo.

It's definitely worth remembering that Arlo had been sitting on his porch with a rifle all night, apparently expecting trouble . . . and yet his killer managed to get close enough to slit his throat. How? There are a lot of reasons that math doesn't make sense, and only a couple of likely solutions. If Lia told us the truth about the trip back to the cottage, then for some reason Arlo had to have let his killer talk him into putting his weapon down; if she was lying to us . . . well, then, the only conclusion worth jumping to is that she's the murderer.

The idea doesn't please me. Sebastian and I are just starting over, and I really don't want Lia to be an obstacle between us again—I really don't want to kick off our reconciliation with another stupid fight. But the fact of it is, I can't help seeing a pattern of manipulation in the way that Lia has disclosed information to us. When we were clumsily fishing for motives for Fox's murder, she directed us to Arlo while making it seem like she was trying to defend him; then, once Arlo was dead, she openly directed us to Hayden. Maybe she'd even directed Hayden straight to Lyle Shetland, hoping that my brother would get himself killed and tie up all her loose ends for her.

Unable to say any of that out loud, I keep my mouth shut until we're at the curb in front of the Santos house again, both of us struggling for something neutral to say. Nothing appears to have changed since our previous visit, and Sebastian fires off a short text announcing our arrival, then falls into step beside me as we make our way to the basement door.

Lia lets us inside, barely allowing us to clear the threshold before slamming the door closed again and twisting the deadbolt into place. She looks terrible, dark circles expanding under her eyes, and I smell alcohol on her breath as she whispers, "What happened? Did you find Lyle? Did you talk to him?"

"Sort of. I mean, not exactly," Sebastian hedges uncomfortably, his body tense and his gaze aimed at the floor. Just like that, I realize that in spite of all his arguments in the car, he's got his doubts about her innocence, too. "Have you heard from Hayden?"

"No, thank God." Lia shifts from one foot to another. "What do you mean, 'not exactly'? Did you talk to Lyle or didn't you?"

"It's complicated." Sebastian scratches his elbow.

Lia seems to be waiting for more, but neither of us says anything, tension pouring in through the cracks under the door, our awkwardness hardening in place. Finally, she tosses her arms out. "*'It's complicated?'* I've been binging and purging my feelings for like an hour now, terrified that Hayden Covington was gonna show up and bludgeon me to death, and all you've got to say is *'It's complicated?'*"

"Why didn't you tell us about Javi?" Sebastian demands, and Lia jerks like he's just thrown a drink in her face. "Why didn't you tell us Fox was selling to him?"

"Because it's none of your business," she fires back savagely. "How dare you come here and ask—who told you, anyway? Was it Lyle? Was it *April*?" Her eyes suddenly go so wide, I'm afraid they're about to come flying out of her face like champagne corks. "Oh shit, did she tell that to the *police*?"

"Lia—"

"Javi is a good kid! He made one stupid mistake, okay? And

now they're going to think—" She cuts herself off, paces a tight 360, and then blurts, "April fucking threatened Fox with a knife, right in front of me! She said she was going to kill him for cheating with Peyton! If she thinks she can—"

"Why didn't you tell us about that?" I interrupt, startling her out of her tirade. "Hayden told you Fox was dead and that April killed him, but it was pretty easy to talk you out of the idea. If you knew she'd threatened to stab him, why didn't you say something about it?"

"I don't . . ." Her mouth flaps open and shut, and then she shakes her head in disgust. "Fuck you! What are you even doing here, anyway? You and April aren't friends, and you're barely even related. What the hell do you care?"

"You saw April threaten Fox with a knife," I persist, sharpening my tone, "and later, when you and Arlo went back to the cottage, you saw him look into the kitchen and shit his pants; but when I asked if you'd thought that meant Fox was dead, you said no. You thought it meant *April* was. Why? Why were you worried about her, when she was the one who was armed and dangerous?"

"Because," she fumbles, her eyes going totally blank for one long second. "Because Fox is, like, eight times her size, and she's built like a paper clip! She couldn't get a knife through a block of cheese, let alone some guy's chest."

"Why didn't you tell us about the fight she had with Peyton? Why didn't you tell us it started because you ratted out Peyton and Fox, and *that's* why the party broke up? Why did you leave all that stuff out?"

"Because . . . because of . . . Javi!" Lia turns to Sebastian, her eyes glossy and imploring. "You *know* him, Bash. He's not a screwup—he just does dumb things sometimes so his friends will think he's cool. It would literally kill my parents if my baby brother got in trouble because of drugs! I just . . . I didn't want anyone to find out."

I have to fold my arms to keep from launching into a sarcastic round of applause at her performance. "Oh, please. You didn't want to get *yourself* in trouble with the cops, is more like it."

Lia's head snaps in my direction, like a rattlesnake. "You know, you can get the fuck right out of my house."

"Just tell us the truth, Lia," Sebastian mumbles, and she takes a step back.

"Is that supposed to be a joke?" There's a decidedly nasty ring to the question. "Bash Williams is asking someone to tell the truth? How about *you* tell the truth for once? And you can start by explaining why Rufus is wearing your shirt, and why he's got a fucking hickey on his neck that wasn't there earlier." Too late, I clap a hand over my throat, and there's a dreadful silence, a clock somewhere in the darkness chipping time away like fragments of bone. Lia arches a brow. "Oh, I'm sorry—did you really think no one could tell? Did you honestly think I never noticed the way you *stared* at him in the hallways at school? The way your voice changed every time you said his fucking name?"

Sebastian's face goes utterly slack. "Lia—"

"Save it." She tosses up a hand. "You know, I was shocked at first. And then I was like, 'Damn, I guess that's just how it is—no wonder we didn't work out.' But then you asked me to come back to you. You *begged* me." Lia's voice breaks. "You told me you loved me, you *asshole*."

"I'm sorry," Sebastian whispers.

"You should've just told me that you're gay! I might actually have understood, you know. It's a hell of a lot easier to handle than 'I love you, only I really don't, so good-bye!' "

"It's not that simple." Sebastian's hands are shaking, and I want to hold them. "I mean, I'm not sure what I am. I don't—" He gives an anguished sigh, twisting the fabric of his shorts until the veins pop out on his arm. "You and me . . . we were real, Lia; I was into you for real. I never lied about what I felt when we were together, but I . . . when I'm with Rufus, it feels right. That's real, too. He makes me happy, and it's, like, I know who I am when I'm with him—who I wanna be. And I am so, so sorry, because I should've never said those things to you. It was wrong and . . . and unfair. I don't know how else to explain it. I was really scared, and I thought I could change how I really felt—about both of you—and . . . you didn't deserve that. I'm really sorry."

He's crying by the time he's finished, and with a start I realize that Lia is, too. "Fuck," she says, her voice raw as she backhands tears from her cheek. "Now I wish you'd just stuck with 'I love you, only really I don't.' It'd be easier to hate you." She lifts her chin, then, a flinty look in her puffy eyes. "I'm not forgiving you, okay? You're a shithead, and I'm not letting you off the hook. But . . . I get it."

There's a long, weird silence—our lives shifting and resettling momentously around us—as we realize that their brief exchange has fundamentally altered the way we'll all see one another from now on. Lia wipes her eyes, sniffles, and finally announces, "I drugged April."

"What?" I stare, almost hearing an actual needle scratch.

"That's the reason I didn't say anything about how the night ended—that and Javi." She slumps against the wall. "When she found out about Fox and Peyton, April lost every last scrap of her shit. She broke a bottle on Peyton's face, shoved her into a wall, and started screaming stuff; she pulled that knife on Fox . . . and then she threatened to call the police."

"She was going to report him for cheating on her?" I ask, confused.

"For the *drugs*, dumbass." She rolls her eyes. "She was in crush-kill-destroy mode, and she wouldn't be talked down from it—believe me, I tried—and *nobody* needed the cops to show up. We'd all been drinking; Fox, Race, and Peyton had been doing coke; and there were white rabbits everywhere. Even if we somehow got the place cleaned up, April was more than ready to narc anyway, just to see Fox burn. So . . . I spiked her vodka–Red Bull with prescription cough syrup when she wasn't looking.

"I kept her distracted until it kicked in, and then I left her in the bedroom. Race was already gone, Peyton split as soon as she knew April was out cold, and the second I managed to talk Arlo out of going inside to take Fox on again, we hit the road, too."

"What about Fox? Where was he during all this?"

She lets out an unpleasant peal of laughter. "He was making himself a fucking snack the last time I saw him." Wrapping her arms around herself, Lia explains, "April was dead to the world when I left her; that's why it didn't make sense to me when Hayden said she'd killed Fox. Honestly, right up to that exact minute, I was actually terrified that I'd overdone it—that maybe April had OD'd or something. *That's* why I didn't mention anything about the fight she had with Peyton. I thought that if something had happened to her, and that's why she wasn't answering her phone when you called . . ." Her voice ends in a choked squeak. "It would have been my fault."

Sebastian and I look at each other in the quiet that follows,

Lia's admission finding its place in the picture we're trying to assemble. It finally makes sense how stoned April seemed when we found her, yet how convincing she'd been when she swore she'd had nothing stronger than alcohol all night. It also fleshed out the rolling exits a little bit more: Race left after fighting with Fox, Peyton waited until Lia had defused April, and then my sister was abandoned—unconscious and alone—in the house with her boyfriend. So what had happened next? Who else returned to the cottage?

"I should never have shown her that video," Lia suddenly confesses, rueful. "It was all my fault."

"Video?" I repeat. "What are you talking about?"

She glances up at me, embarrassed. "The video of Fox and Peyton doing . . . you know." Unnecessarily, she demonstrates what she's getting at by making a circle with one hand and jamming a finger in and out of it with the other.

I do everything I can to prevent the correlated image from forming in my mind, but to no avail. "There was a video?"

"Yeah. Fox had recorded it on a hidden camera and sent it to Arlo; and when Arlo got pissed off, he showed it to me—and then *I* got so pissed I showed it to April." She shrugs guiltily. "It's why she wigged out."

"There was a *secret video* of Fox and Peyton?"

There must be something in my face as I stare at her, because Lia's brow furrows in confusion. "Yeah. You didn't know about it?"

I look from her to Sebastian and back again, my pulse picking up. "Have you heard from Race or Peyton at all? Have either of them called or texted you?"

"Both of them." She frowns anxiously, rubbing her arms. "Like, a bunch of times. And Ramona fucking Waverley's been blowing up my phone all night long, too, like I need to deal with *that* on top of everything else."

"Ramona Waverley?" I repeat, thrown. "How the hell is she involved in this?"

"She's not! She's just the biggest gossip in Chittenden County. Lord only knows what she's heard and who she's told it to."

"Well, what did she say?"

"I don't know . . . Bash said not to talk to anyone but you guys. I had no idea what was going on, or what to think, so I just ignored all my messages!" She tosses her phone at me, and I barely catch it before it smacks me in the face. "Look for yourself."

I pull up her messaging app, which shows three unopened conversations, along with the latest incoming missives from each sender. Race: *Text me as soon as you get this ok? PLEASE?* Peyton: *What the hell is going on tonight?* Ramona: *Girl call me ASAP about R+P I need this shit confirmed!! Or just stop by k? Working till suuuuper late.*

"R plus P?" I read out loud. "Race and Peyton?"

"I don't know, and I don't care." Lia sweeps her arms out decisively. "Why are they all writing me, anyway? What am I supposed to do?"

"Lia . . ." I don't want to scare her. Or maybe I do. Maybe I need to. "Hayden didn't kill anyone, and neither did Lyle; we overheard a conversation between them, and we're pretty sure they're in the clear. But that means it could be either Race or Peyton."

"What—?" She squints disbelievingly. "Are you high? Neither one of them could take Arlo! There must be—"

"They're the only ones left," I insist, "and we've got no idea how things went down when Arlo got killed. They might have outsmarted him somehow. Don't talk to either of them, don't answer the door if they come over, and don't go outside alone, okay?"

"What the hell are you trying to say?" She sounds immediately querulous and fearful.

"Lia, the first thing April assumed when I told her Arlo knew what had happened at the lake house was that *you* knew about it, too." I take a step forward. "Whoever did this apparently killed Arlo because of what he saw, and if they think he told you about it? *You could be next.*"

22

" 'DON'T GO OUTSIDE ALONE?' 'YOU COULD BE NEXT?' " SEBASTIAN recites my own words back to me when we're seated back in the Jeep outside of Lia's house, incredulousness writ large on his face. "Rufus, she's never gonna sleep again!"

"I just wanted to make sure she listened to me," I protest. "All the way over here you were saying maybe it was Race; well, maybe it was! She needs to know she can't afford to trust him right now—not if he killed Arlo for what he knew."

"If she's really in danger, then she needs to go to the police! I mean, we should be taking her there right now—"

"To say what?" I give him a frank look. "That we sorta think two kids from a couple of the most prominent families in town just might be on a murderous rampage tonight?" I toss my hands up. "Even if they don't laugh us right out the door, we'll have to explain a whole lot of dubious shit we did—like finding Arlo's body and not reporting it, for instance—and we'll have to tell them about the video, and the brawl that started after Lia showed it to April, which means letting them know that April was deliberately keeping stuff from them in her official statement."

"Who cares about that?" Sebastian exclaims. "You just said yourself that Lia 'could be next'—she needs some kind of protection!"

"It's not like the cops are gonna give her a new identity and move her to Bali! They'll just say, 'Thanks for the wild allegations and the total lack of evidence to back them up,' and send her home again." A moth swoops and darts around the streetlight above us, throwing monstrous shadows against the fog. "Don't forget: When April's story starts unraveling, *our* stories unravel, too; and the last time we checked in, Race and Peyton were covering each other's ass. Lia will sound like a crank, the police will start wondering what *else* we might be lying about for April, and the only two who will come out of it okay will be the ones with the corroborated alibis and the fancy lawyers."

"Fuck!" Sebastian smashes his hand against the steering wheel and shifts his jaw. "You're right."

Once again, I feel like shit. Everything I've said is pretty much true, but the real reason I don't want Lia sending the police after her friends just yet is because I need to be the one who does it. If I want a chance in hell of getting the four thousand dollars Isabel Covington promised me, I've got to follow her directive to the letter, and not give her a loophole to wiggle through. *Well, technically, Lia Santos was the one who got April's name cleared, so I'm afraid . . .*

Giving my phone a quick glance, I see more texts from Lucy, but nothing from my mom, and I breathe out a little sigh of relief. My curfew has long since passed, and if she wakes up and realizes I'm still out, my window of opportunity to resolve this thing is going to slam shut—hard. Fox's death won't make the headlines until his family is notified, and because Peter represented himself to the police as my dad, they probably won't bother contacting my mother; but Peter himself is another matter. To say he was furious when we parted ways would be an understatement, and it'd be standard operating procedure for him to call Mom and chew her a couple new assholes about me entangling myself with April.

Only he clearly hasn't done that. Yet. Maybe he took my parting threat to heart and wants to strengthen April's case before he provokes me into being honest with the cops; or maybe Isabel has prevailed upon him to leave my mom and me alone, buying some time so I can have a chance to deliver on the deal we've struck. Or maybe his heart grew three sizes when the police let April go tonight—I have no idea and can't afford to take anything for granted. Now, more than ever, I'm racing the clock.

I can pull it off. I know it. I can protect Lia, I can find some kind of evidence incriminating Race and/or Peyton, and I can give my mom the money we need to pay off the bank and save our house, all at the same time. Some damn how.

"We just need to prove Race and Peyton lied to us," I say, thinking out loud. "Maybe we can turn them against each other?"

"I don't understand why they're backing each other up in the first place," Sebastian grunts. "They were barely speaking to each other when we saw them." He looks over at me. "Which of them do you think did it?"

"My gut says Race, but with that video . . . I mean, it turns out Peyton's got a solid motive, too." My skull thumps against the headrest and I let out a weary breath. "Fox secretly recorded them together and then showed it to his friends. If she just found out about it tonight, it could've totally pushed her over the edge."

"That bloodbath at the cottage did sort of scream 'crime of passion,'" Sebastian agrees, "and there was no one behind Peyton on the road after Lia and Arlo passed her. If she'd turned around, nobody would have seen."

"But then why would Race be covering for her?" I rub my hands on my knees. "She cheated on him, but he'll lie for her anyway? Put his own ass on the line to keep her from getting busted for killing the guy she slept with behind his back?"

Sebastian fingers his car keys, metal and plastic clicking together. "So maybe it's like I suggested on the way over here: Race went back to the house, and Peyton followed. Either she saw him stab Fox and is backing his story out of guilt, or they somehow killed the guy together and formed a pact to protect themselves—mutually assured destruction."

"Let's hope it's the second one," I state. "The less they trust each other, the easier it'll be for us to get one of them to tell us what really happened."

Sebastian clicks his keys for another pensive moment, and then turns to me. "Look, I know maybe you don't want to hear this again, but I've got to say it: You don't have to do this. It isn't your job to save April's butt—especially now that there are lawyers and cops and stuff involved. I mean, maybe you've done enough, Rufus."

I swallow my first response. The embarrassment of having admitted how desperately my mom and I need Isabel's payout is still with me like a bitter aftertaste; I'm not getting into it again. But he's saying this because he cares about me—*he cares about me*—and so I manage a smile. "I'm not backing out now. I can't."

Sebastian nods, like this is what he expected to hear. "So where to now? Which one of them do we take on first?"

"Neither," I say promptly, surprising him. "I'm thinking first we take on the biggest gossip in Chittenden County."

"Ramona? You really think she knows something?" He screws up his mouth. "I mean, probably she just got wind of that video, if Fox was sending it around."

"Maybe," I acknowledge. "But then she'd be asking about Peyton and Fox, right? And, like, the timing . . . I mean, tonight of all nights she's desperate to confirm something she's heard about Race and Peyton? No matter what it is, I'd like to know about it before we go after them. We need all the ammunition we can get right now. You know where Ramona works?"

"Actually, yeah. It's a diner I eat at sometimes," Sebastian says, firing up the Jeep. "I gotta warn you, though: The food's disgusting and the ambience is worse."

"Just so long as it's not Suzy's American Diner, I'm in. I'll take gross food over twitchy biker dudes trying to blow my head off any night of the week."

"Got your heart rate up, though," Sebastian points out as he steers away from the curb. "Running from bullets totally counteracts mozzarella stick calories."

"Yeah, and getting hit by one makes them irrelevant. But as fad diets go, don't expect Oprah's endorsement."

A few minutes later, we pull into the parking lot of Silverman's—the same twenty-four-hour diner where we parked while April called Peter and asked for a lawyer. It's almost four thirty in the morning now, but still there are cars bathed in the electric glow of the building's broad front windows. Inside, the place is a throwback vision of Formica countertops, chrome trim, and padded vinyl seats, and—owing to its dirt-cheap menu and casino-style hours—it's incredibly popular with both Ethan Allen kids and the university crowd alike.

When we walk in the door, I'm instantly overwhelmed by the smell of breakfast sausage, maple syrup, and fried *something*, and I almost go weak in the knees. Looking around, I see no sign of Ramona Waverly, but the hostess—an ample woman with a tangerine bouffant and glasses like two hula hoops roped together in the middle—spots us immediately and starts heading our way.

And then I hear someone shriek my name. *"Rufussssssssss!"*

I turn around just in time to see a wild-eyed Asian girl bounding at me from the other direction. Launching herself into the air, she cannonballs into me in a body slam–slash–bear hug that knocks all the wind from my lungs and nearly takes me off my feet. It's my best friend, Lucy. Her hair is down, a dark mane of loose, bohemian waves that sweeps past her shoulders, and despite the late hour, her winged eyeliner is still just as perfect as ever.

"Holy poop, dude, I've been texting you all night long!" she exclaims, punching me in the arm. It's a typical Lucy Kim love tap—enough muscle behind it to draw up a welt I'll still have well into my twilight years. My children will be born with dents in their shoulders. "Where the shit have you been, anyway? You missed half my party!"

"It's a really long story," I say awkwardly, suddenly feeling Sebastian's conspicuous presence like a sunburn. "What are you doing here?"

"Hangover precautions," she explains. "Brent said he could drink me under the table, so I had to prove him wrong, and then we both barfed for like twenty minutes straight. So now we're soaking up what's left with potato skins." She keeps her eyes fixed on Sebastian through this entire account, and when she finally looks back at me I can feel her sharp gaze poking around in my cerebellum. "What are *you* doing here?"

"Um." I scratch the back of my head. "It's a really long story?"

"Mm-hmm." Lucy gives Sebastian a bright, friendly grin. "'Scuse us for just a second, okay? Best friend shit." She drags me about two paces away, still well within earshot, and stage-whispers, "You said you were ditching me for April, but then you come sauntering into Silverman's with *Bash Williams*, of all people, searching for midnight munchies and looking like the cat who swallowed the nine-inch canary. I think you owe me an explanation. And make it as graphic as possible."

"You know he can hear everything you're saying, right?"

"Shut up and start talking," she commands. "Is this what it looks like, or not?"

"It's . . . I mean . . ." I struggle pathetically, not even sure how to start. "Honestly, it's a really—"

"A really long story, I know," she finishes wryly. "Just tell me if this 'really long story' involves a 'really long' ride on Bash Williams's 'really long' d—"

"Lucy!"

"Your face is turning pink!" she declares triumphantly. "Your face is totally pink, Rufus, which means I'm right, and you just gave yourself away. You dirty little slut!"

"Lucy, seriously," I begin, but I can feel my face escalating well beyond pink and deep into Miami sunset territory.

"And when did we take up lacrosse, hmm?" she purrs, fingering the jersey I'm wearing. "I have to say, Rufus, I really like this look on you—it's so *masc 4 masc*."

"I'm ready to die now, Jebus," I declare to the ceiling, certain my face can be detected by infrared satellite. Sebastian, who overheard this entire exchange, has an expression on his face that's a mix of one half amusement and one half sheer, paralyzed terror, and I swallow a rush of nerves. "The thing is, um . . . maybe you're not, like . . . totally wrong?"

"I knew it!" She punches me again, in the other arm this time, and so hard she's probably bruised my bone marrow. "You are going to tell me everything, mister, and I want all the hot, juicy, throbbing details."

"You are such a gross pervert."

"That's why you love me." She boops my nose with tipsy affection, and then turns back to Sebastian. The hostess stands there, having reached us just in time to catch most of the humiliating things that were said, but the look on her face suggests only jaded disinterest as Lucy declares, "They're going to sit with us."

"It's okay," I say quickly, suddenly thinking it might be better for Sebastian to get to know Sober Lucy before he gets to know Drunk Lucy. Both versions of my best friend are hyperactive and inappropriate, but at least the former is two percent less likely to intentionally embarrass me. "You and Brent were already doing your thing and hanging out. We weren't even planning to st—"

"There is not a chance in H-E-double-penetration that you're wriggling out of this one," she assures me pleasantly, "so just suck it up and park your skinny butt at our table."

She marches me across the restaurant, Sebastian following behind and staring in wide-eyed fascination as Lucy manhandles me into a chrome-frame chair at a four-top, where Brent Bosworth is already seated. Lanky and pale, Brent is too uncoordinated to be much of an athlete but too cute to be a total outcast; lucky for him, girls tend to think his perpetual, clumsy-footed bumbling is adorable. A giant platter before him shows the remnants of their potato skins, and two chocolate shakes as thick as Play-Doh are packed into tall metal cups that anchor the table. My best friend plunks herself down across from me and gestures graciously for Sebastian to sit by my side.

"We've finished eating," she says, her voice musical and exaggeratedly polite, "but we would love to keep you boys company whilst you dine."

"Hey, bruh," Brent says to me, shooting a paranoid look across the table at Sebastian, his experience with Ethan Allen's ruling class about as awesome as my own. Calling me "bruh" was an ironic joke that he started up freshman year, and which very soon got completely out of hand; now it seems as if he's totally lost the ability to refer to me as anything else. "Where've you been all night?"

"Brentford James Bosworth!" Lucy exclaims in mock horror. "That is an extremely personal question! Are they not entitled to their privacy?"

"My middle name is Ezra," he returns. "And my first name is not Brentford."

"I know that, but Brent Ezra Bosworth sounds like a leprechaun's curse," she complains back. "I fixed it for you. You're welcome."

"Where have you been all night?" Brent asks me with desperation, like he's barely holding on to his sanity after a night alone with Lucy. It's all bullshit; Brent has been madly in love with my best friend ever since she kissed him on New Year's Eve, but he's so certain she'll reject him that he's refused to make any kind of a move in the months since. He's a neurotic mess, and in some ways perfect for her; but Lucy likes an intellectual joust,

and Brent's obvious—almost obsequious—devotion frustrates her. There are times I suspect the current status quo is really the best for everyone.

"Rufus was just getting ready to tell us about his evening, actually," Lucy says pointedly, resting her chin in her hand.

"Um." I scratch the back of my head again, the lacrosse jersey suddenly like a wool blanket as my body temperature climbs. I'm nervous about outing Sebastian, even with his permission—but still more nervous about how Lucy will react when she finds out what I've been keeping from her. There's far more at stake here than the simple question presumes. Under the table, I feel Sebastian's hand sneak into mine and squeeze, and I swallow a gulp of air. "So . . . uh, yeah. Bash and I are . . . kind of . . . together. Like, as in boyfriends."

"Gasp!" Lucy exclaims out loud, gaping at me in a way that's simultaneously teasing, happy, and interrogative; it's all vicarious excitement edged with the faintest glimmer of hurt. Just like that, I can tell she's wondering how long I've been holding important details back from her. She banishes the look quickly, though, and scoops up her chocolate shake. With a signature lack of tact, she asks Sebastian, "Do any of your sportsball friends know yet? Are they shitting themselves over all the assholey things they've said about gay people for the past, you know, ever?"

Sebastian squirms a little bit, his hand tightening on mine. "Uh, actually, none of them really know yet? So I'm not sure how they're gonna react. I can guess, maybe. I mean, there probably will be some self-shitting."

My best friend processes this for a moment, and shifts her jaw a little. Setting down the chocolate shake, she wipes the moisture off her fingers and states expansively, "Well, if Rufus likes you, then you're probably too good for them anyway. And as long as you keep him happy, you're welcome to hang out with us."

"We can't play sportsball," Brent admits with effort, visibly putting aside his instinctive distrust of the athlete in our midst, "but between the three of us, we could probably recite every line of *Scott Pilgrim* for you."

"And if you *don't* keep Rufus happy," Lucy continues, twirling a butter knife rapidly around in her fingers like one of the Teenage Mutant Ninja Turtles, "I will be selling your organs off on Craigslist. Just so you know."

"Duly noted." Sebastian straightens up a bit, eyebrows in a high arch. "Now, when you say *'Scott Pilgrim'* . . . are you talking the movie, or the graphic novels?"

"Um, are you *freaking kidding*?" Brent practically squeals. "The graphic novels, bruh, they're *epic.* I mean, how could they leave the 'stark, existential horror of Honest Ed's' out of the movie? Bryan Lee O'Malley is a damn genius!" In a stagey voice, he quotes, " 'I need some kind of, like, last minute, poorly-set-up deus ex machina!' "

Slapping her palms down on the table, Lucy chimes in gleefully, " 'I had sexual relations with your mother! Your mother was not that good in bed!' "

" 'Let's be friends based on mutual hate,' " I submit—a personal favorite.

" 'You listen to me,' " Sebastian fires back, beaming. " '*I'm* the one who tells you what your mom says, okay?' "

The four of us giggle stupidly for a moment, and then Lucy snatches up her milkshake again. "Okay, I guess he's all right."

At that moment, a waitress sidles up to our table, her reddish-blond hair tied back in a collapsing knot of thick curls. Of all people, it's Ramona fucking Waverley. "If you guys don't keep it down, you're gonna wake the other customers."

With a sardonic expression, she gestures to an old man who has passed out, face-first, in a plate of toast at a nearby table. Contritely, Lucy offers, "Sorry, Ramona. We promise to use our Inside Voices."

"Puh-*lease* don't!" Ramona casts a greedy, conspiratorial smile around the table, silently claiming membership in our disjointed clique without waiting for permission. It's her signature move: skipping all the History and Trust Building stages of friendship and going straight to Familiar Intimacy. With a flourish, she produces a check and places it facedown between Lucy and Brent. "There you go, guys. Pay that when you're ready, but take your time—you're the most exciting thing that's happened in here for hours, and I'm still on till six. Graveyard shift sucks, am I right?"

"'Specially if you're a vampire," Lucy replies cheerily, shoveling up some of her shake with a long-handled spoon.

"Hey, Bash." Ramona's eyes glitter like a hungry raccoon's as she turns them on my boyfriend. I swear she even licks her chops a little. "Guess there's a whole lot of drama going down tonight, huh?"

"You're talking about Race and Peyton," Sebastian hazards in a neutral tone. It's a thin line he's started walking, here; Ramona, like all gossips, treats information as power—and an uneven exchange of it will not be in her best interests. If we ask her flat out what she knows, she'll shut down faster than my crappy laptop every time I get to the—*ahem*—good part of an adult-type movie clip online.

"It must be really tough on your group, huh?" Ramona goads with overbaked sympathy. "Like, everybody taking sides and whatever?" Misinterpreting Sebastian's hesitation to answer, she sighs. "All right, I get it: You don't want to blab. At least just say if they're officially broken up or not. You can tell me *that*."

"Uh . . ." Sebastian, it turns out, is total crap at the gossip game. "How much do you know about it?"

I almost groan out loud as, predictably, Ramona's eyes narrow. "How much *is* there to know?"

This vaudeville routine could go on all night, I realize, so I head it off at the pass with an abrupt announcement. "Fox Whitney is dead."

Ramona, Lucy, and Brent all react in unison. "*What?*"

"It's a really long story," I say, with a look to my best friend, "but that's what was up with April tonight. We had to take her to the police so she could make a statement. They just sent her home a little while ago."

"A *statement*?" Ramona grabs a free chair from another table, dragging it noisily across the floor, and plops down next to Brent. "So, when you say he's *dead*, what you mean is . . . ?"

It's a leading question, and I shake my head. "You first—what have you heard about Race and Peyton?"

"Okay, okay!" Her curiosity is too piqued to hold out. "It's not what I *heard*; it's what I *saw*." She leans forward and we all mimic the move unconsciously, like a bunch of spies in a made-for-TV movie. "So, it was early on, like, not long after my shift started. You know—when everybody else was out partying?" There's a faint rebuke in her tone, which we all choose to ignore. "Anyway, I'd only been on for like an hour or so, when guess who stomps right through that door, *alone*, and orders an herbal tea?" She scans our faces, waits a beat, and then announces, "Peyton."

"How did she seem?" I ask carefully.

"*Super* upset. Like, her face was all blotchy and swollen from crying and stuff, and, I mean, she ordered an *herbal tea* for Pete's sake—it's a total cry for help. Like, either she's ninety years old, or she's in emotional free fall, you know? Anyway, she just sat there, messing with her phone for about fifteen minutes, and then all of a sudden *Race* walks in." Ramona straightens up importantly. "And, I mean, they were obviously not expecting to see each other, because he takes, like, two steps through the door, catches one glimpse of Peyton, and I swear it was like the start of a brand-new fucking ice age. Race spins right around, not a single word, and storms out again. Peyton *chases* after him—*literally*—and they totally just get into it. Waving their arms around, shouting at each other in the parking lot—like *really* shouting—and then they just . . . took off."

"Together?" I ask.

"At the same time, anyway. They both had their own cars."

"Did you hear what they were saying?"

"Um, if I had, would I be asking?" Ramona counters deprecatingly. "They always play the music too loud in here." She pouts in a way that can only be described as aggressive. "But it was *clearly* an epic fight. They were both totally red in the face and, I mean, they looked pretty dunzo to me." She fires a beady-eyed gaze at Sebastian, seeking confirmation—but I'm not "dunzo" with Ramona Waverley just yet.

"What time?" I demand, and I must sound like a lunatic, because Lucy, Brent, and Ramona all raise their eyebrows at me. "I just mean, you know, about what time did Peyton get here? Do you remember?"

"Well, I didn't, like, check the clock or whatever . . ." Ramona pauses gratuitously, letting me pay for my eagerness. "But it had to be about ten thirty, maybe quarter to eleven? And Race came along fifteen, twenty minutes after."

Sebastian and I stare at each other, and I feel abruptly more grateful than I ever thought possible for Ramona Waverley and her great big mouth. More than an hour elapsed between the time that April's outburst prematurely ended Fox's Independence Day party and the occasion whereupon Peyton and Race arrived—separately—at Silverman's Diner. Just like that, the biggest gossip in Chittenden County has handed us exactly what we've been looking for: proof that Ethan Allen's cutest sophomore couple were lying through their perfect teeth when they said they'd gone straight back to the Atwoods' together after leaving South Hero.

23

FEELING OBLIGATED TO COMPENSATE RAMONA FOR THE VALUABLE information she provided, Sebastian and I offer a heavily redacted version of the night's events over a fresh basket of fries. Another wave of guilt steals over me as I feed lies and half-truths to Lucy one more time, but I promise myself that once the night is behind us—when everything is settled and I'm four thousand George Washingtons richer—I'll tell her the whole story.

As it is, unable to account for the real reason Sebastian and I want to leave almost the second we're done eating, I let my best friend's prurient imagination supply the missing details. As we head for the exit, Lucy calls out, teasingly, "Good night, boys! Don't do anything I wouldn't do!"

Before the door closes behind us, we also hear Brent's sarcastic reply. "What kind of advice is that? The only two things you won't do are eat cilantro and watch anything starring Gwyneth Paltrow."

"Dude," Sebastian exclaims as soon as we're in the relative

privacy of the parking lot. "That's it—that's what we needed! We can show they were lying now; we have to tell the cops!"

"We can't—I mean, not yet. What we just found out . . . it's nothing that'll make any difference to the police."

Sebastian bridles. "Race and Peyton *lied*, Rufe! Their cover story is a load of crap!"

"They lied to *us*." It's an important clarification. "We don't even know if the police have spoken to them yet, or if they're still using the same story. Our big Gotcha won't mean dick unless we know their lie is on the record first. They weren't expecting you and me to come asking for a timeline of their evening, so they might have just made a sloppy mistake in the heat of the moment; but they'll realize that Ramona will remember seeing them—*especially* if they were fighting. By the time they sit down with their lawyers and then talk to the authorities, you can bet they'll have some way to account for everything."

"But we can't—" Sebastian tries to check his frustration, but it clearly gets the better of him. "You don't know that for sure. If they weren't trying to hide something, they wouldn't have pretended they'd gone straight to Race's house from the party in the first place. We *know* they lied to us, and we've got to explain it to the police! Maybe they'll understand—"

"Understand what?" I spread my arms. "It'll be our word against theirs, and they'll just say they didn't want to tell us about Silverman's because their fight was none of our business. And don't forget the cops have a freaking *file* on me, and that they were second-guessing everything I said tonight! I really don't need to give them any more excuses to dissect my original statement."

Sebastian claps both hands to his head and lets out an

exasperated wail. "This is insane! It's in-freaking-sane, Rufus. I mean, what the hell? We know they're lying, but we can't do anything about it?"

"The *police* can't do anything," I counter. "But we wanted to try turning them against each other, right? Well, maybe this is our leverage. Quick—don't think, just answer. Which one of them is more likely to cave here: Peyton or Race?"

After a fractional hesitation, he decides, "Race."

I consider his answer. It makes sense; Race isn't especially smart, and if we can convincingly act like we know more than we really do—or maybe take a page from the cops' playbook and tell him that Peyton is already telling people that he did it—he might actually believe us and crack under the pressure. "Race it is."

We start for the Jeep, the fog even denser than when we arrived, the air around us as tangible as sea-foam. The temperature has dropped considerably since the stifling heat of the early evening, and clammy moisture causes the skin on my bare shoulders to pebble with goose bumps. Sebastian's arm brushes against mine, and he takes my hand again.

"Your friends seem pretty cool," he remarks after a nervous moment.

"Was that okay in there?" I ask, a little worried. "Like, are *you* okay? You're having kind of a Big Deal night, I mean."

"We're both having a Big Deal night." He gives me a fleeting grin that belies the anxiety I know he must be feeling. "It was sort of scary, I guess. Being, like . . . *out* all of a sudden. Trying to figure out what that even means. It's like I'm walking through a room in the dark, and I've got no idea where all the furniture is, you know? Like I don't know what people are gonna think when they look at me anymore."

“Lucy and Brent liked you, I could tell,” I assure him automatically, even though I know it isn’t what he means.

“They accepted me. For you.” The correction isn’t bitter, but almost affectionate. “Your friends are weird as hell, Rufe, and kinda nerdy, but I like them. For real. And seeing how you are when you’re around them . . . it was cool. It was sorta like . . . I don’t know. Meeting a part of you I didn’t really know before?”

“A good part?”

“A really, really cute part.” We reach the back of the Jeep and stop, and Sebastian slips his arms around my waist, pulling me into him. His touch, and the scent of his cologne, warms me to my fingertips as he murmurs, “You’ll have to let me know what kind of stuff Lucy *would* do, by the way, because I’ve got some things in mind that might surprise her . . .”

He brushes his lips over mine, gently, and my breath catches; and that’s when we hear the sound of feet scraping against asphalt, startlingly close. I barely have time to glance up before a broad silhouette sweeps out of the fog on the other side of the Jeep, coming toward us and closing in fast. We jolt apart and stumble back, rising onto our toes to run . . . but then we freeze in place, dumbstruck, as the shadowy figure comes to a halt mere feet away and a recognizable face emerges from the swirling mist.

It’s Dominic Williams—Sebastian’s father.

“D-dad?” Sebastian’s voice is strange and foreign, his eyes like bottomless pits, and almost instantly his hands begin to tremble again. “W-w—what—”

“What the hell do you think you’re doing out here?” Mr. Williams barks in a sharp voice, solid as a wall before the translucent haze that blurs the night. I stare, unmoored and unsure what to do. “Are you out of your mind?”

"I was—" Sebastian falters, almost swaying on his feet. "I d-didn't . . ."

"I've been calling you all night long, Sebastian!" The man clutches his cell phone in a tight fist, so hard I half expect the casing to crack. His gaze darts to me, burning with suspicion and something else—fear, worry?—and then back to his son again. "What the hell is the matter with you? You think you get to make up your own rules, now? Choose when you get to listen to me? *Where have you been?*"

"I . . . I—" Sebastian's attempt at speech ends in a swollen gulp, his skin waxy looking. "I don't . . ."

"I didn't raise you like this," Mr. Williams exclaims, cords standing up along his neck. "To show this kind of disrespect? To . . . to drop a bombshell on me and then *walk out the door*—to disappear for hours and not come home? It's five in the morning! What the hell do you have to say for yourself?" Sebastian tries to speak, but no words come out; he gags with fear, the sound ugly in the soft stillness around us, and Mr. Williams adds, "Your mother thought you were lying in a ditch somewhere! I had to talk her out of calling the damn police!"

"I'm—I'm s-sorry," Sebastian forces out in a choking whisper. Tears roll down his cheeks, and finally the world turns red, my face molten with rage.

"Don't apologize to him; he should be apologizing to you!" I take a crooked step forward. It's stupid and inappropriate, and I'm dimly aware that I'm only making everything worse; but the only two things I'm actually any good at are losing control and screwing up my life by antagonizing powerful adults—I'm finally in my milieu. "You're the one who should be sorry—*you're* the one who should be ashamed," I shout at Mr. Williams. "Sebastian's a good person! If you're too fucking stupid to see that, then maybe there's something the matter with you."

"Rufus, *stop*," Sebastian pleads, horrified, and before I can ignore him and launch into a second round—to say to Mr. Williams what I'm wishing I'd had the guts to say to Peter at the police station—I feel his hand on my arm, and I look over at him.

Beyond the stormy fear in my boyfriend's eyes, I see a sort of resolution, and it makes my jaw snap shut with a click. This is the moment Sebastian has been running from all night, and now that it's caught up with him at last, he's decided to face it—and whatever happens, he's the only one who can fight this battle. If I really want to help him, I need to keep my mouth shut for once.

Turning to face his father, his tone as hollow and fragile as a rotten log, Sebastian says, "I didn't come home because I d-didn't . . . I didn't know if you'd want me there anymore."

His erratic breathing fills the stuffy silence around us, and Mr. Williams blinks, his mouth dropping open; gazing at Sebastian with dark, confused eyes, he takes a moment to find his voice. When he does, it sounds strangely rough. "You . . . didn't know if I would *want* you there?"

"You were s-so . . . so mad at me," Sebastian states thinly, his hands opening and closing. "I know you're dis-disappointed—"

"I never—" Mr. Williams covers his mouth and shifts, sucking air through his nose; then, dropping his hands to his hips, he hangs his head. It takes him a moment to speak. "I wasn't . . . I'm not mad at you, Sebastian, I—"

"You broke Mom's bowl," Sebastian whispers. "You threw it."

"I was . . . I was *upset*." The man tries to make it sound as if there's a clear distinction. "I didn't mean—that doesn't give you the right to just *leave*—to disappear like that! It's not acceptable behavior. This isn't something you can just . . . *drop* on me and then walk away. You can't expect me not to have a reaction."

"You *threw* it!" Something catches in Sebastian's throat. "You were so angry, and I thought . . . I didn't . . ."

"Sebastian—" Mr. Williams begins, but his voice thickens so much that he has to stop. "I would never turn away from you—not ever. You know that. You *have* to know that. Nothing you could do would ever make me . . . *reject* you. Nothing. I love you, no matter who you are, or . . . or what you do with your life. That's a fact. And you'll always be welcome at home. It's *your home*."

"But you *said*." Sebastian struggles to breathe, struggles to keep it together. "You *said*. You said it was *wrong*."

"I said some . . . some very stupid things," Mr. Williams admits with difficulty, seeming suddenly aged. He rubs a hand over the burnished dome of his shaved head. "I grew up in a very religious household. Your granddad was a pastor, and he taught me a lot of uncompromising things early on, about what's right and what's wrong, and I . . ." He peters out, giving his son an exhausted look like he's run out of gas, and he changes tack. "You know, there are some openly gay athletes on a few of the teams up at the university now, and I've learned a lot from working with them. I respect them—we respect each other—and not so long ago that's something I wouldn't have thought possible. And I thought that meant I'd finally moved past some of the things I once believed—the things I was raised on. But when I saw those pictures . . . when I realized what they meant, what you'd been keeping from me, I just . . ." He shakes his head helplessly. "A lot of old feelings came back in a heartbeat. Feelings I'm not proud of. And I didn't handle myself very well."

"I didn't m-mean for you to . . . to find out like that."

Mr. Williams is silent for a moment. "But is that what's going on, Sebastian? Are you gay?"

"Maybe?" My boyfriend can only offer an honest shrug, still unable to fully articulate the boundaries of his sexuality, perhaps not even aware of where exactly those boundaries lie; whether he's bi or pan or heteroflexible—or something else. There's no litmus test for this stuff, and you can't exactly weigh yourself on the Kinsey scale. For now, it could be that "maybe" is the clearest and most accurate answer he knows how to provide. "Can you . . . can you handle that?"

Seriously, thoughtfully, his father asks, "What do I always tell you about family, Sebastian?"

"Blood is always thicker," my boyfriend answers quietly, somewhere between a question and a statement.

"Blood is always thicker," his father repeats with solemnity. "And you're my blood. You're my son, and I love you no matter what, Sebastian. I don't want to be the kind of person you feel you have to hide yourself from. If you can be a little patient with me, I can handle anything." Mr. Williams then puts on a brave smile, and gestures awkwardly in my direction. "So Rufus is really your . . . is he your, uh . . . he was the one in the pictures."

"Oh, um, yeah." Sebastian looks at me, as if surprised to see me standing there, and offers a nervous gesture. "Dad, Rufus is my . . . my boyfriend."

"It's nice to see you again," I offer inanely, and then Sebastian's father and I share what will probably go down in the record books as History's Most Awkward Handshake, considering how pointedly rude to him I was just minutes ago.

"I hope that maybe we can start over." Mr. Williams, it seems, is some kind of a mind reader. "This wasn't exactly . . . it's been a rough night, and I haven't shown myself to my best advantage; but anyone who makes my son happy is important to me, and . . . and it looks like maybe the effort I plan to make for him extends to you, too."

"I'm sorry for what I said," I manage, embarrassed, feeling only slightly more comfortable than that time I had an open wound cleaned out with hand sanitizer.

We step apart again, a tense silence falling over us like a fireproof blanket, until Sebastian clears his throat and asks, "Does Mom know?"

"I told her. You know she's way better about these things than I am." Mr. Williams flashes a wry slice of a grin. "You think my temper tantrum was scary? You should've seen the one she threw when she found out I smashed her bowl."

"Is she mad?"

"Not at you," the man answers quickly. "Well, maybe a little, because you've been gone so long. But not about anything else. She'll probably shout at you for a while when you get home, but then she'll hold on to you until you're about forty." Soberly, he then adds, "You do need to come home, though, Sebastian. You're not in trouble—I promise—and we'll have a big family talk tomorrow about everything. But we should all be in bed right now."

Sebastian nods, and clears his throat. "Okay. I will. I just . . . Rufus doesn't have a car, and I'm sort of his ride tonight, so I have to . . ."

"Okay." Mr. Williams rubs his arms as if noticing the damp chill in the air for the first time. "Drop him off, but then come straight home, all right? And maybe text your mother, so she can stop panicking? I don't want her to send me out after you again."

"I will," Sebastian promises. He hesitates for just a moment, and then asks, "How did you know I was here, anyway?"

"Funny thing. I expected you'd be halfway to New York or Montreal or somewhere, and that I'd have to get the state police and the feds involved. Wasn't until about thirty minutes ago that I remembered there's a GPS system in your Jeep, and I used the antitheft tracking function to figure out where it was."

Sebastian looks down at his feet, mumbling, "I'm sorry I scared you guys, I—"

"Let's forget about it." Mr. Williams shifts uncomfortably. "I scared you first, and Rufus is actually right—I owe you an apology. I'm sorry. I wish I could do this whole night over again, but . . . instead we start clean tomorrow. Okay?"

Sebastian nods his agreement and, after a quiet pause, Mr. Williams steps forward and draws his son into a hug. Feeling suddenly intrusive, I glance away to give them a little bit of privacy, studying the bright lights of the diner's facade.

"I love you, Sebastian," Mr. Williams says gruffly, and Sebastian murmurs a reply that's lost to me. After a moment, I hear them step apart, and I look back in time to see the man give my boyfriend's chest an affectionate thump with his fist, and then turn around to head for the other end of the parking lot. Over his shoulder, he calls, "I'll see you at home. Soon, okay?"

"Okay," Sebastian replies, his voice rocky and strained but filled with relief. Together, we watch in silence as Mr. Williams turns first into a gray shadow, and then vanishes altogether into the mist, leaving us alone again.

24

WE SIT QUIETLY IN THE CAB OF THE JEEP AS MR. WILLIAMS FIRES up his car, exits the lot, and turns out onto the road, his taillights glowing softly through the smudge of pre-dawn fog. I hold Sebastian's hand in mine, clutched tightly over the center console, and I watch him carefully as he stares out the windshield in a sort of daze. The event that just transpired was so significant that there proves almost nothing to be said about it, no easy words to boil it down or sum it up.

After a long moment, Sebastian finally looks over at me, his face completely unreadable. "Everything is different."

"I know."

"My whole life . . . it's—"

"Been rebooted, with additional software," I finish for him, sounding anxiously optimistic. "You're Sebastian 2.0 now. You just have to get used to the improvements. Are you . . . How do you feel?"

Sebastian shakes his head. "I don't know. I'm . . . scared still.

I mean, I'm happy, I guess, but I'm also sort of totally freaking out. Does that make any sense?"

"It makes perfect sense." It's a feeling I remember from my own experience—that terrifying death-drop when my secret was out, when I was no longer in control of that part of my life. "But this is huge, Sebastian. There's some bumpy stuff at first, but it doesn't take long for it to get better. And, I mean, the hard part is over now, right? And your dad actually wants to make an effort for you."

"Is the hard part really over, though?" Sebastian's dark, expressive eyes are full of doubt. "My dad's always been like my best friend, Rufe. We talk about everything. What if we can't anymore? What if this is too weird for him? What if he's just not ever able to look at me the same way?"

For just a moment, his anxiety conjures up some inappropriate envy in me. Peter and I have never talked about anything personal, never been anything remotely approaching "friends." He must know that I'm gay—either April or Hayden would have certainly brought it up at some point—but I have no idea how he feels about it. I doubt he's ever spared a single thought for what it meant for me to come out. I'm over being hurt by him . . . but I can't stifle that shameful pang of jealousy when I see how important Sebastian's relationship with his father is to him.

But Dominic Williams is not Peter Covington, and I know my boyfriend doesn't have to be afraid. "He will. Everything might not be the same as usual right away, but I swear he will. You heard him, Sebastian: He loves you. He wants things to be like always just as much as you do. You guys just have to get past this part first, that's all."

My boyfriend nods, although he doesn't yet appear wholly

convinced. "I feel like I'm on stage and nobody taught me my lines."

"Totally normal." I search his face—his dark lashes, his full lips, the smooth contour of his cheek swooping down into his jawline—and say softly, "I love you."

"Thank you, Rufus." He gazes at me, expression serious. "For staying with me. For cursing at my dad." A smile flickers across his half-lit face. "Thanks."

"Cursing at dads is my signature move," I remark dryly. "Just ask Peter." Then, with some selfish reluctance, I ask, "Does this mean you're going home now?"

"Not until we get some answers out of Race and Peyton." Off my surprised expression, he adds, "I promised to have your back, Rufe, and I'm sticking to my word. I mean, it sort of sounds like any trouble I get into tonight will be kind of a write-off as far as my parents are concerned."

"Wow." I give him a sly grin. "Sebastian 2.0 lives on the edge. I like it."

"Sebastian 2.0 does not have a frigging clue what he's doing anymore, so take advantage of it while you can," he answers with a lopsided grin. He's about to say something else when his cell phone interrupts us, chiming loudly to announce an incoming text. Then it chimes again, and again, and Sebastian frowns with concern as he fumbles it out of his pocket. "It's Lia."

The messages are brief and frantic.

Race keeps texting me what do I do?

He says he wants me to MEET with him! He won't stop writing!

Seriously, Bash, text me the fucking fuck back, I'm freaking out! What if he comes over here?? What if he tries to fucking stab me??

"We've got to nail this down *fast*, dude," Sebastian breathes worriedly as he types out a reply, his words appearing in all caps as he thumbs them in, admonishing her to ignore Race and make sure her doors are locked. "This isn't right. She's losing her shit, and we can't protect her unless we—"

"*Stop!*" I order him suddenly, the urgency of my command startling the both of us. His thumbs freeze in midsentence, and he glances up at me with wide eyes. Licking my lips, I say, "Don't send that message. Delete it. Tell her . . . tell her to write him back and say she's willing to meet with him. Right now."

Sebastian wrinkles his nose, staring at me in disbelief. "Rufe, are you nuts? Race might be the freaking *killer*."

"I know. That's why we're going to meet with him in her place."

He regards me for a moment. "You know, Sebastian 2.0 might not know what he's doing, but he sure as hell knows he doesn't want to go get his throat cut."

"It'll be two against one," I point out, "and even if he is the killer and he does have a knife on him, he'll have to realize Lia wanted us to intercept him. We tell him flat out that she's expecting us to call and tell her we're safe and sound after the meeting is over, or she's going to the cops. He won't try anything."

Sebastian thinks about it. He looks like he still wants to argue, but eventually he offers a trepidatious nod. Deleting the draft of his message to his ex-girlfriend, he sighs, "I really, really hope you're right."

Me too, I think, wiping my sweaty palms on the Jeep's upholstery.

Just more than fifteen minutes later, the two of us walk side by side down a desolate stretch of road south of town, trees lunging out on either side of us, our footsteps like cymbal crashes in the silence. Ahead of us lies Fernwood Park, a vast expanse of lakeside acreage—and the isolated location Race has chosen for the clandestine meeting he thinks he's having with Lia.

My experience with Fernwood Park is limited, seeing as my last visit was for Field Day in the sixth grade, and so I only have a distant memory of the place—of boxy metal barbecue grills that looked like they'd never been cleaned; weathered, wooden picnic shelters that smelled of tar and resin; and vast, uneven fields spreading between thickets of pine, birch, and maple trees. My vague recollections include the hazy impression of a necklace of rocks surrounding the shoreline, guarded over by weeds and willows, from beneath which the waters of Lake Champlain slowly carve out soil by increments. There's a modest parking lot as well, but at this early hour it's off-limits, a metal gate chained shut across the entrance. We're forced to leave the Jeep ridiculously far away.

The tense drive out from Silverman's actually took us right by Banfield Crescent and, unable to resist my own morbid curiosity, I instructed Sebastian to turn down the tony avenue so I could see where Fox Whitney once lived.

The air reeked of damp soot and scorched plastic, a hot, sweet stench that left an afterburn in the base of my throat. The remains of the once-stately Victorian mansion, dark and abandoned and ringed with caution tape, stood back from the road like a self-conscious leper. Here and there, intricate woodwork had survived, but still the house appeared totally unsalvageable—a ruined husk remaining upright through willpower alone. Everywhere there were charred timbers and smoke-blackened brick, windows blown out by heat and then haphazardly boarded over, and the garage and roof had been utterly skeletonized by flames. Even the lawn bore the scars of fire, strange loops and lines branded into the earth as if a family of electric eels had been mating on the grass.

Across the wide, whitewashed front door, scarlet letters spelled out the multitude of Fox Whitney's sins in bold, streaky spray paint:

LIAR
COCKSUCKER
DRUG DEALER
RAPIST

"'*Rapist*'?" I read out loud, alarm staining my tone as I began to wonder if there were dimensions to the guy's murder we hadn't even considered yet. Sebastian gave me a bewildered shake of his head in response, his expression making it clear this was something he knew nothing about, and then he turned the Jeep around again.

As we drove away, I thought about the Whitneys. Someone must have gotten in touch with them already; they had to have learned what had happened to Fox and about the arson that claimed their home. I wondered if they were already on their way back to Burlington—and what they would do when they got here. They had two addresses and nowhere to live, one house a hollowed-out wreck and the other a blood-soaked crime scene where their youngest son had been murdered. How could they face either?

Now, as we step up onto the curb, skirting the padlocked gate of Fernwood Park and crossing the empty lot to the grassy expanse beyond, I try to steel my nerves. Before us stretches a gray bank of obliterating fog, punctuated only by the distant burn of an amber lamp that marks an emergency phone lost in the gloom. It's 5:20 in the morning, and high above us the sky is a gradually fading indigo, stars winking out one by one; where we stand, however, light only reaches us as a whisper of blue in the dark pall of densely gathered mists.

"I wish we'd brought a real flashlight," I remark, mostly to break the thick crust of tense silence as I use my phone to illuminate a mounted placard showing a map of the park. Walkways squiggle hither and yon over the simplified diagram, and I attempt to figure out which one of them we're supposed to follow.

"*I* wish we'd brought a Doberman," Sebastian mutters. "Or maybe a couple of Navy SEALs."

Secretly, I have to agree. I can think of only one reason Race might want Lia to meet him all the way out here, and it's not because he thinks she's *rilly, rilly cute*. I still need that money from Isabel, but I've put so much effort into convincing Sebastian—and myself—that we have to see things through to the end that I sort of lost my sense of how much danger we could actually be in. Glancing back the way we came, I hazard, "You were right before. We don't have to do this, I mean. We can always call the police and tell them—"

"No." Sebastian interrupts decisively. Off my surprised look, he continues, "Look, Sebastian 2.0 can probably explain away coming home late after dropping off his boyfriend—I'm pretty sure my dad won't want to press me for details—but lying to the cops could result in some serious house arrest. Or regular arrest." A symphony of frogs and crickets trill around us, underscoring how alone we are. "You were right before, Rufe: strength in numbers. He can't take both of us, and it's like you said—we need solid proof if we want to make sure this ends tonight."

"Look on the bright side," I suggest, turning away so he can't see how anemic my smile is. "Maybe Race wants to meet with Lia because Peyton did it and he needs help deciding whether he should turn her in or not."

"Actually, I'm pretty sure the bright side is 'Maybe he won't even show up.' "

It's a simple, if stressful, hike to our destination. The knowable universe has shrunk to a terrifyingly small circumference, landmarks only discernible within about ten paces, and every object beyond the obscuring curtain of fog is an armed and dangerous murderer until proven otherwise. Sebastian put the pedal to the floor on the drive from the diner, determined to arrive early in case this was a trap; but the truth is that we've got no idea what we might be walking into—we have no idea where Race had texted Lia *from*. For all we know, he's already here, waiting and watching . . .

"There," Sebastian whispers suddenly, and I nearly leap out of my skin.

Before us looms an elongated picnic shelter fronted by an *in memoriam* plaque dedicating it to "Jane and August Tidwell"—it's the meeting spot Race identified in his text messages. Knobby pinewood supports hold up a pitched roof, the beams of which no doubt host a biblical plague's worth of bats and spiders; and while three sides are open to the elements, a brick wall at the far end masks the plumbing for connected bathroom facilities.

But my knowledge of this wall is distant memory, not direct observation; the shadows and fog render the murk inside the shelter impenetrable, so concentrated I can't see to the back of it. There's no way to tell what lies hidden inside, no way to disarm my imagination. Fresh corpses, a bloodthirsty killer, or just a few warped, sticky tables and some forgotten trash abandoned by a bunch of drunken holiday revelers—anything is possible. Yawning before us is a black hole, containing everything and nothing all at once.

"Hello?" I call apprehensively into the void, and my voice bounces back to me. "Race, are you in there?" Water drips somewhere out of sight. "Lia sent us."

There's no answer; even the crickets are silent now. Sebastian and I exchange a nervous glance, and I step forward, edging past a dingy wooden column and squinting to sharpen my vision. I sense nothing, hear nothing. Tables butt out of the dark emptiness before me, their planks rough and uneven with age. Could someone be standing back there? Is someone breathing? My tongue feels like a scrap of dried leather in my mouth. "Lia knows we're here, okay? So if you're thinking of trying something—"

"Rufus!" Sebastian's voice comes with the harsh, staccato urgency of a hammer striking glass, and I swing around instantly. *"Someone's coming."*

He stares in the direction from which we arrived, the spiked limbs of birch trees and evergreens reaching for us like fingers emerging from a swamp. Out of the blue-tinged haze before us, a form begins to congeal—a figure trudging through the damp grass, steps almost soundless, footfalls deadened by the close, heavy air. I scramble to Sebastian's side, my pulse thudding in my temples as the new arrival takes on shape and solidity: a bulky sweatshirt with the hood up; head bowed, hands jammed into pockets; long, slim legs.

"Race?" I call out sharply, telltale anxiety pitching my tone high, and the figure stops abruptly. We stare at each other across an empty patch of grass, my hands tingling as adrenaline throttles my heart, trapped by our mutual apprehensions. "This is good—that's close enough. Whatever you wanted to say to Lia, say it to us instead."

My words fall on deaf ears, the figure taking two more steps forward. Sebastian and I both tense—preparing for what, I'm not sure, because we never make it that far. As we watch, the person before us reaches up, pulling back the sweatshirt's hood to reveal a cascade of blond ringlets and a pair of sharp green eyes that glint in the scant light.

It's Peyton.

25

FOR A MOMENT, WE ALL JUST STAND THERE, THREE PAIRS OF EYES reflecting the same mix of confusion, mistrust, and disbelief. Finally, she demands, "What the hell are you two doing here?"

"What the hell are *you* doing here?" I sputter, too nonplussed to come up with anything snappier.

Peyton's wary gaze darts between me and Sebastian, then drifts over the yawning cavern of the shelter behind us, her weight passing from one foot to the other. She looks like she's trying to make her mind up about something. "I'm supposed to be meeting someone."

"Lia?" Sebastian challenges, evidently wondering if maybe Race and Peyton are both responsible for Fox's death after all—and conspiring to cover it up. I look at what she's wearing: an oversize Ethan Allen lacrosse hoodie, baggy track pants, battered tennis shoes. Did she dress like her boyfriend deliberately? Or am I reading too much into a slouchy outfit she threw on over her pajamas for an early morning rendezvous?

"Why the fuck would I come all the way out here to some abandoned, bug-infested shit-swamp on the dark side of nowhere just to talk to *Lia*?" Peyton retorts, and it would take a logarithmic equation to express the amount of scorn she's managed to pack into so comparatively few words. "I don't even *like* Lia."

Sebastian wrinkles his nose. "You're one of her best friends."

"So? What's that got to do with anything?"

"Peyton, if you're not here to meet Lia, then who *did* you come here for?" I ask impatiently.

"None of your business."

"Hello? Are we not all standing in the middle of the same bug-infested shit-swamp at five thirty in the morning?" I toss my arms out. "Just give us an answer, okay?"

"*Fine*. I'm supposed to be meeting my boyfriend, all right?" Even in the silvery morning shadows, I can see her cheeks turn pink. "Is that all right? Is that okay with you, Rufus?"

Sebastian and I share a curious and uneasy glance, and I lick my lips. "Why did Race ask you to come to Fernwood Park?"

"I don't know!" Peyton starts fingering the coiled blond waves that spill over her shoulders, a gesture that radiates insecurity and makes me feel strangely ill at ease. Peyton Forsyth is someone I grew up resenting quite comfortably, as throughout my adolescence, I could always count on her to make the cruelest and most cutting of verbal attacks. Knowing how protected she is by her popularity, how little chance there is of any successful retaliation against her, she's never shown any mercy or expressed even an ounce of remorse for her bullying. In fact, I've never seen her exhibit a single iota of vulnerability at all until this very moment. Tugging unhappily at a lock of her hair, she mumbles, "He wouldn't tell me why. Things are kind of . . . he's really mad at me right now, and I was just glad he was willing to see me at all."

I nod slowly. "We heard about the fight you guys had."

"Great." Her hands slap down at her sides. "So the whole fucking world knows." She fixes me with a venomous glare, waiting for further remarks, but I just let the silence grow until she feels the need to fill it again; when she does, though, it's only to turn the tables. "So why are *you* here? And what does Lia have to do with it?"

Sebastian and I exchange another glance, a silent debate passing between us about how much we should share—or if there's really any reason to hold back—and then he reveals, "Race wanted Lia to meet him here, too, but she was scared. So she asked if we would come instead. He didn't say anything to you about her?"

"No," she replies, bewildered. "No. I mean, it was a text—when he told me to come out here, it was in a text—and all it said was, like, 'Meet me at the Tidwell Pavilion in Fernwood Park,' period. I'd been calling and texting him for hours and it's the only thing he's written back." Peyton does a frustrated turn, scanning what little we can see of the surrounding area, then jams her hands back into the pockets of her hoodie. "I don't understand any of this! Why did he text Lia? Why did he ask her here? And what the hell do you mean, 'She was scared'? Scared of what?"

For what feels like the millionth time in a few short hours, I deflect a loaded question with an explosive statement. "Fox Whitney is dead."

The explosion is a dud—again; Peyton merely draws in some air and looks away. "I know. I heard."

"You *heard*?" I ratchet my eyebrows up a little, analyzing her tone, and then offer my blunt assessment of it. "You don't seem very broken up about it."

"Oh, screw you, Rufus Holt!"

Sebastian puts a hand on my arm, a tacit suggestion that Bad Cop isn't the right way to approach Peyton Forsyth. He's probably right, but I can't imagine approaching her any other way, so I hold my tongue and let him take the lead. "Who'd you hear it from?"

"Does it even matter?" She tosses her hair. "You still haven't answered my question. What's it got to do with Lia?"

Sebastian deflects as well. "Arlo's dead, too."

Her mouth drops open. "What? How do you—?"

"He was killed a few hours ago. We don't know if the police have found him yet, but . . ." Sebastian looks over at me again. "We saw him. It happened at his house."

Peyton lifts a fist to her mouth and shakes her head, then wrings out her fingers with a fierce twisting motion. Through stiff lips, she insists, "This can't be happening."

"Arlo and Lia went back to the lake house after you all left tonight," I jump in, seeing Peyton's guard down and wanting to press the advantage. "Arlo had it in his head to finish the fight he'd started with Fox, but they were too late. Lia says whatever he saw in the house freaked him out so badly that he drove them all the way to Burlington again before he was willing to talk about it."

Peyton squeezes her eyes shut. "I don't understand what you're saying."

"Arlo saw what happened to Fox." I spell it out. "And from what he told Lia, it sounds like it gave him the incredibly stupid idea to blackmail Fox's killer. Long story short, we're pretty sure that's why he's lying on his porch right now with a happy face carved into his neck."

"Arlo sold *drugs*," she points out, like I'm an idiot, but the muscles in her shoulders have gone stiff. "If he's dead, it's probably because of that."

I narrow my eyes, taking in how tense she is. Peyton apparently really doesn't want to believe that Arlo's death is connected to what he saw at the lake house, and it seems pretty clear why. "There were six people at that party tonight, and only four of you are still alive; April was with the cops when Arlo got his ticket punched; and now Race wants you and Lia to meet him in the middle of a deserted park, a million miles from anyone who might hear you scream, at five thirty a.m. Any thoughts on that?"

I don't even make it to the end of this little summary before a shudder crawls ineluctably up my spine. The obscuring closeness of fog lends an impression of intimacy to our little gathering, but we've got no idea what lies just past the thick scrim of vapor hanging in the air—or how far our voices are carrying. Where *is* Race, anyway?

Peyton steals my attention back, shaking her head again, lips clamped into a thin line. "You don't know what you're talking about. Is that what Lia told you? That Arlo saw Race—?"

She can't seem to finish the thought, and I save her from having to try. "She's not sure what Arlo saw. But something tells me you are."

Her face pales a little. "What's that supposed to mean?"

"You and Race lied to us tonight." I notice a flicker of something in her eyes. Doubt? Fear? "He said you two went straight from the party to his house, and you backed him up; but it was bullshit. We know you guys were fighting, we know you left

South Hero separately, and we know you ran into each other at Silverman's later—actually, not long before we came over to the Atwoods' place to ask about April. Nobody knew Fox was dead yet, so why were you two already covering for each other, Peyton?"

"We weren't," she insists impossibly, her voice faltering.

"Stop lying!" Sebastian is as fed up as I am, his nerves equally strained.

"I'm not! I mean, I thought . . . I mean—" She breaks off, clapping both hands over her face, and a muffled sob emerges through her fingers. We wait her out again, resisting the heartstring tug of her emotional display, and eventually she pulls herself together. Thickly, she mumbles, "You just . . . you don't understand."

Sebastian shuffles his feet uncomfortably. "So explain."

She looks up, peering from one of us to the other. "I wasn't covering for him. Or, at least, at the time, I didn't know that's what I was doing. I thought . . . I thought he was covering for *me*. Okay?"

For a moment, it's so quiet I can hear the water dripping behind me in the sightless depths of the picnic shelter. "What are you trying to tell us, Peyton?"

"You have to . . . you have to understand what happened between me and Fox, first," she says beseechingly. "If you know Race and I were fighting, then I guess April probably told you about the video? Well, that whole thing wasn't just some spur-of-the-moment attack of hormones, okay? Fox and I . . . it was sort of inevitable.

"Fox always had a thing for me—even back in middle school," she continues, wrapping her arms around herself. "Our moms are best friends, so he was always around and . . . I don't know. Eventually I developed a thing for him, too. Not a crush, but like . . . a *thing*. Like we kinda wanted to push each other down the stairs, and we also kinda wanted to make out at the same time." She shrugs. "But, you know, Fox didn't want anything unless he couldn't have it—and there wasn't anything Fox Whitney couldn't have. Everything he ever asked for he just *got*, and he completely took it for granted.

"He was so used to being the best: the best looking, the best athlete, the *favorite*; and people fell all over themselves to please him, because everybody wanted him to like them—even adults. Even teachers sucked up to Fox." The corners of her mouth tick upward in a thorny smile. "I was probably the one person he knew who *didn't* kiss his ass, and it drove him up a wall."

"Okay," I say obligingly, marveling at the fantasy version of Peyton Forsyth that's being described to me. As if Sebastian and I, and everybody else she's ever met, haven't watched her whole clique toady after Fox Whitney every single day since practically kindergarten, as desperate for his approval as the less popular kids.

"Fox's big problem was girls." Her tone is authoritative and cold. "I mean, beyond just the fact that he was a lying shit-sack who stuck his dick into anything he could, he had a *problem* when it came to girls—like a mental problem. Ask yourself something: What's the one trait all Fox's girlfriends have had in common?"

I eyeball this question over to Sebastian, because we're talking about his friends here, and because my apathy regarding Fox Whitney's love life—prior to finding my sister soaked in his blood, anyway—cannot possibly be overstated. My boyfriend shrugs, and guesses a theme at random. "They're all hot?"

Peyton rolls her eyes. "They have *no self-esteem*. They're just a bunch of thirsty hoes who *threw* themselves at him. They all knew his reputation for burning through girlfriends; they all knew they'd get tossed out like yesterday's trash as soon as he got bored; but they begged for it anyway, because being Fox Whitney's flavor of the month is still better than being *nobody*." She looks right at me as she says it, daring me to defend April's honor. "Fox loved it. All these girls worshiping him? He *lived* for it. He couldn't date a girl unless she proved that she would completely debase herself if he told her to—but, of course, once she did, it was over. He'd be done, because he'd have lost all respect for her. I mean, how can you possibly respect someone who doesn't even respect herself?"

"But you were different?" I predict, hoping to urge the narrative of this Very Special Episode along. Her account drips with the earnest self-importance of a reality show confessional, and it's taking all my concentration not to roll my eyes.

"I wouldn't play his game, and it pissed him off. Half of his 'relationships,' or whatever you want to call them, were just sad attempts at making me jealous. He seriously believed that, one day, I'd come crawling and begging for him like all his other conquests, because he'd literally never encountered a girl with an actual backbone before." Peyton gives a complacent shrug. "So, to teach him a lesson, I started dating his best friend. I mean, truth is, Race and I have been together for almost a year now? But my real long-term relationship—maybe my only real relationship—was with Fox."

"So what changed?" Sebastian interposes quietly, and Peyton's lips purse.

"Me and Race. When you get down to it, that's what changed. Maybe I only got with him in the first place in order to make some kind of a point, but . . ." She shrugs again, uncomfortably.

"You know, Race and I actually make sense. We have a lot in common, our families know each other, and we have fun together. Usually." Peyton shifts, rubbing her forehead. "I think Fox started to realize that I was getting . . . you know, serious about my boyfriend. That the triangle was finally turning into a real triangle, for once. And he couldn't deal.

"He started dating April, and he really tried rubbing my nose in it, but I honestly couldn't be bothered anymore. I ignored him. And when that didn't work . . ." She looks down at her feet, her shoes wet from the slippery grass. "One day, totally out of the blue, he was just a complete ass to me at school, and we had our first actual fight in years. Next day, Friday, he comes up to me, tail between his legs, and says, like, 'I'm sorry I've been a dick lately, but there's something kind of important going on and I need to talk to you about it.' He wanted me to come over after school. I was supposed to hang out with Race, but I'd never seen Fox so . . . so actually *needy* before, so I said yes. I made up some stupid excuse to get out of my plans, and then after cheer, I went to the Whitneys'."

She keeps her eyes down, words rushing out of her mouth like she's trying not to taste them. "Turned out Fox wanted to talk about *us*—our 'thing.' And he said all the stuff I'd been wanting to hear for years: how he was pretty sure he loved me, but had been too scared to admit it; how he was crazy jealous of Race; how it scared the shit out of him that I might actually be happy with another guy." Peyton glances up, tears in her eyes. "His parents despise each other; it's why he's so fucked up about relationships. All Mr. and Mrs. Whitney do is fight, but they won't get divorced because they'd rather be miserable than admit failure. Their marriage is just one big power struggle, and Fox grew up thinking that's how it was supposed to be—that the point of a relationship is control."

"Is this going somewhere?" Sebastian finally asks, evidently as exasperated by Peyton's dramatizing as I am.

"Yes, *asshole*," she snaps ferociously. "He told me he loved me! He told me he wanted to be with me, and he didn't care about the consequences. He actually fucking *cried*. So . . . so I let him take me up to his bedroom, and—"

"And we've already heard about the video, so let's skip ahead," I suggest quickly.

"I avoided Race Saturday and Sunday, trying to figure out how the hell I was going to tell him we had to end things because Fox and I wanted to be together." Peyton sounds more subdued now, but something dark embroiders her tone. "Fox texted all weekend, too, saying how he couldn't wait to see me again, how everything was going to be different. And then I got to school on Monday, and . . ." Her voice falters, and she looks up at the sky, swallowing. "And the second he saw me, he jammed his tongue down April's throat and started groping her ass. Right in front of me. And he leered at me over her shoulder, with this shit-eating grin, like he was so fucking proud of himself. He was *gloating*."

Unhappily, Sebastian ventures, "You mean—?"

"I *mean* that he fucking *played me*," Peyton snaps so hotly I'm surprised the fog doesn't burn off around us. "I *mean* that it was all bullshit—every last word! He'd finally figured out which buttons to press so I'd roll over for him, and that's all he'd ever cared about. Everything he'd told me was a lie, and he wanted me to know it; he *needed* me to know that I'd let him turn me into just another meaningless notch on his fucking belt. I'd thought we had this twisted mutual respect, all *Cruel Intentions* and shit? But no. Fox never respected me. And he wanted to make damn sure I couldn't respect myself anymore, either." Viciously, she scrubs the tears from her cheeks.

"I'm sorry," I say.

"Screw you." Her hostility is reflexive. "Like you actually give a shit." She drops her defensive posture, though, shoulders slumping wearily. "Anyway, after a week of this crap, Fox comes up to me in the hall again and says, dead serious, 'My parents are gonna be out late, so why don't you come over again?' I might have blacked out for a second, I was so outraged—like, I was *this close* to frying his balls with my stun gun when he finally tells me about the video. He said . . ." She squeezes her eyes shut, and her breath catches. "He said . . . 'You're gonna cancel your plans and come over to my house again, Peyton, or I'm gonna make sure Race knows what a fucking slut you are.' So I had to. I didn't have a choice."

More water drips behind me, and the distant sound of a passing train clacks and whispers in the air. Sebastian looks horrified. "Peyton . . ."

"*Save it.* The point is, he had something on me. He could have ruined my whole life whenever he wanted to—gotten my boyfriend to dump me, turned my friends against me, my *parents*—and you can bet your ass he'd have been happy to do it. He knew he could get away with anything, and that without my friends and my . . . my *status*, I had nothing. I *was* nothing." Peyton sniffles loudly. "He had me on the hook, and for weeks I was just his on-call whore. He made me say things and do things . . ."

She seals her lips together, like she can't bear to go on, and my skin crawls just thinking about what she's described. "You must have hated him."

"You're damn right I hated him." Her answer is prompt and

savage. "I wanted him to fucking *die*, and I'm not sorry at all that he did. I wanted to kill him myself—tonight—when I found out he'd been showing that disgusting video to his disgusting, perverted friends!"

"I don't blame you." I mean it, too. We seem to be closing in on the heart of the matter at last, but the picture before me isn't wholly clear. Is all this the build-up to a murder confession? Peyton had more reasons to loathe Fox than I ever imagined, but pieces of the puzzle remain missing. I still can't understand what's going on with Race. Why did he lie for her, and why did he set up this bizarre meeting in the first place?

"I didn't even get to hit him." Peyton's hands knot into fists. "Fox, I mean. April coldcocked me, all hell broke loose, and then I was running out of the house before I even knew what was happening. When Race finished trying to pound Fox into the floor, I was *sure* he was coming for me next, but he'd barely even look at me. He just got in his car and took off. I was afraid to follow him, but I was terrified not to, so as soon as Lia said she'd made sure April wasn't gonna call the cops, I went after him."

"And what happened?"

"I never caught up." She shakes her head dismally. "He was going too fast—I'm not even sure I ever saw his taillights. I was crying so hard I could barely breathe, though, and somewhere on the way back to town I just . . . *snapped*. I just snapped."

"Peyton . . ." I step forward, mist threading around my arms, slipping through the ventilated fabric of the lacrosse jersey. "What did you do?"

Her eyes are glassy and wet, her chin trembling, and it takes several tries to force the words out. In a squeaky whisper, though, she finally manages. *"I burned down Fox's house."*

26

THE FOG SEEMS TO CONSTRICT, DRAWING IN CLOSER, AND THE three of us just stand there like a taxidermy display. I've been an idiot. "You . . . You're the one who torched the Whitneys' house?"

"I didn't do it on purpose," Peyton sobs helplessly. "I was so upset I couldn't think straight! All I wanted to do was teach him a lesson. It was . . . Thanks to him, everybody knew my secret, and I wanted to make sure everybody knew his secrets, too! His parents just ignore all the shit he gets up to, and I wanted to do something they couldn't pretend not to notice anymore; I wanted to make sure that Fox would finally be held accountable for all the things he's done!"

"So you *burned down his house*?" Sebastian stares at her, aghast.

"It was an accident!" she screeches. "I just . . . I busted a few windows and spray-painted some stuff on his door. That's all I meant to do. That was the plan. I mean, I didn't even *have* a plan, but that's all I was thinking."

"'Liar, cocksucker, drug dealer, rapist,'" I recite.

Peyton gives me a startled look, but then she nods slowly. "Yeah. I wanted it all big as life, so his parents couldn't avoid it, so they'd have to ask Fox to explain himself." Swallowing hard, she continues in a tremulous voice, "But then I started thinking, you know, what if he had the door painted over before they got back from New York? He had enough money that he could easily find some guys willing to do a last-minute job, even on a holiday. And *then* I thought, maybe I could write it on the lawn—like, burn it into the grass? Then there'd be no way he could hide it.

"So that's what I did. I spelled stuff in the grass with a gas can I keep in my trunk and I lit it up, and then I just—I don't know!" She tosses her hands out. "I must've, like, the gasoline must've dripped or something, because the fire just went *everywhere*, and I'd left the can in the driveway, and it fucking exploded! The garage went up *just like that*, and it was, I mean, the whole thing was burning, *just like that*!

"So I took off. I was so freaked out that all I could think to do was pretend it had never happened. I changed my clothes, I washed every part of me that smelled like gas, and I went straight to the diner, thinking . . . I don't even know. That if I could act normal enough, nobody would think I could be behind what happened to Fox's house."

"And then Race showed up."

"I wouldn't let him get away that time. I chased him to the sidewalk, and I begged him to hear me out; he didn't want to, but this time I followed him all the way home, and I *made* him listen to me. I told him the whole story—even what I'd done to the Whitneys' house. He was so pissed, he'd barely even look at me. He just sat there." She takes a deep, shuddering breath. "I needed him to know how sorry I was. How much I'd already paid for trusting Fox." The sound of the train dies away in the distance, the rhythmic clacking dissipating into nothingness. "I was so sure he was going to turn me in, but then you guys showed up, and he told you we'd both gone straight back to his place after the party. I couldn't believe it."

"You didn't arrange that in advance?"

"No! I was shocked when he said it. I thought . . . When he lied, I thought it meant he'd forgiven me. I thought, at the very least, it meant he still wanted to protect me, and that maybe we still had a chance." She rakes her fingers through her hair, blond curls writhing like snakes. "But you guys kept asking questions I was really afraid to answer, so I left; and I kept texting Race, trying to thank him—trying to see if he still wanted to be together—but he never wrote me back. Not once. Not until a little while ago."

I take another step forward, my scalp and the backs of my ears prickling. "Peyton . . . did Race kill Fox?"

"He must have," she whimpers back. "It had to have . . . He lied for me, because I was his alibi. Because he knew I'd back him up. It's the only thing I can figure now." She shakes her head tearfully. "I had no idea. I didn't even know Fox was dead, I . . . I only put it together later. He lied because covering for me meant I'd be covering for him."

I look over at Sebastian, who meets my gaze, grim-faced and ill at ease. Peyton said she never caught up to Race on the drive back to Burlington; what if that was because the guy had pulled into a driveway and killed his engine after Arlo's bike passed, and then waited for Peyton to go by before doubling back?

How he might've managed it is pretty much irrelevant, though;

with everyone else's moves accounted for, there's no one left but Race. He must be guilty. Glancing around us, I become aware of how much time passed while Peyton was recounting her story, dawn spreading over Fernwood Park in inexorable degrees. The sun must be above the horizon by now, but the oceanic fog surrounding us is still an endless bruise, only gradually relinquishing the pale purples and blues of early morning. The prickling in my scalp takes on a new intensity. Race is at least fifteen or twenty minutes late now. *Where the hell is he?*

"Peyton," Sebastian says, nerves rubbing his voice raw, "you need to tell all this to the police."

"Are you nuts?" Whatever hypnotic state she was in that had compelled her to bare her soul, she just snapped out of it. "I'm not turning myself in for fucking arson—it was an *accident*!"

"Then tell them that—it doesn't even matter!" Sebastian takes a sharp breath. "Don't you get it? You're the only one who can implicate Race in Fox's death—you're not safe until you tell the cops what you know!"

"I'm not going to prison for something I didn't even mean to do," she insists vehemently, not even listening, "and if you guys say anything about all this, I'll deny it! And how am I in danger, anyway? I'm Race's alibi, remember? He wouldn't hurt me."

"For fuck's sake," my boyfriend mutters through his teeth.

"Are you delusional?" I squint at her. "Peyton, you're only his alibi if you're willing to *cover up a murder*! And that means that you're also the only one who can prove he *doesn't* have an alibi. Look around"—I gesture at the swarming mists, the limitless blank that engulfs us—"and ask yourself what the fuck you're doing out here! Ask yourself what your pissed-off boyfriend needs to tell you that's so important he doesn't want to say it over the phone or in front of witnesses!"

"You said he also asked Lia to come," she argues weakly.

"Of course he did—he thinks Arlo told her what he saw when they went back to the lake house!" I expel an angry sigh, try to will my nerves to settle their clamor, try to sound calm. "Look, Peyton. As far as Race is concerned, you and Lia might be the only two people left alive who can tell the police what really happened to Fox—especially after he *slit Arlo's throat to shut him up*—so are you honestly willing to bet your life on the chance that the reason he tried to lure the two of you out here is so you could coordinate your fake stories?"

"He wouldn't hurt me." It's almost a question.

"Yeah? How's he feel about Lia?" Sebastian interjects, his voice sharp and hot, forcing her to look him in the eye. "He got any reason to think she'd lie for him after he killed Arlo? Because something makes me doubt it."

She bites her lip miserably, her expression torn—caught between having to accept what we're saying or trusting what she'd rather believe; and just as she opens her mouth to speak again, she's interrupted. From somewhere frighteningly close, somewhere just past the point of visibility in the mist, there comes a rustle of leaves and an abrupt *thud.*

All three of us whirl, briefly pinned in place by fear, our eyes huge as we stare into the gray-blue void spreading around us—and then we spring into motion at the same time. I turn and lunge for the picnic shelter, taking cover in its stubborn shadows with Sebastian a half-step behind me, my heart thudding so hard I can feel it in my jaw. Peyton, on the other hand, spins on her heel and takes off at a dead sprint in the opposite direction, vanishing almost instantly into the fog.

"*Peyton!*" I hiss, but it's no use; the soft shush of her track pants brushing together dies out, and the hazy morning fills again with an unbearable, moody silence. Sebastian moves closer, as if to prevent me from going after her; I don't intend to—stepping back out into the open now could be suicide—but I want to, and the conflict burns in my gut. *She's* the way to end this; she is the key to not only stopping Race, but maybe also saving my house from the bank. *But if Race is out there . . .*

"What the fuck do we do?" Sebastian breathes almost silently in my ear, apparently thinking along the same track. Even the dark gloom of the shelter won't hide us for long if Race comes looking; but running off blindly into the expanse of the park—where we can't even see fifteen feet in any direction—won't be much safer.

"I don't know," I mouth back. Seconds tick by as I wait for something to happen, each moment an agonizing eternity, and cold sweat rolls down my back. Straining my ears, I listen for the sound of footsteps, breathing . . . but all is deathly quiet.

Agitation roughens Sebastian's voice. "Do you think that was Race?"

"I don't know," I repeat, frustrated by my own indecision. If it *was* Race, did he go after Peyton? Or is he waiting for us to come out of hiding, so he'll have a better shot at sneaking up on us? And what if it had just been, like, a clumsy skunk falling out of a tree? How long are we really prepared to just stand around like a couple of assholes while we wait to see if we're about to die? "We have to get out of here."

"Okay." Sebastian nods, but he makes no move to leave the

protective darkness just yet, his eyes reflecting the weak, gray light that seeps in under the angled roof. "She's . . . Peyton will probably go straight home. Maybe we can catch up to her."

"No." I wipe sweat off my lip, still listening to the silence. "We have to go to the police now. It's time. It's way past time."

"But unless Peyton comes with us—"

"We don't need her. If we report exactly what she told us, word for word, it'll be enough for them to round up her and Race both. We know they didn't prepare their alibis together, so no matter what they say to the police, the details won't match. It's not perfect, but it'll divert suspicion from April—and once Race is in the spotlight, it'll be too late for him to go after Lia or Peyton or anybody else. Everyone'll be safe."

"Okay," Sebastian says again, sounding indescribably relieved. "Okay."

"On the count of three, right?" I inch forward, moving to the edge of the shadows, on the precipice of a milky-blue oblivion. "One. Two. *Three.*"

We charge out into the fog, knees churning, feet coming down hard on the knotted ground as we race in what I hope to be the direction of the parking lot. I'm operating purely on instinct, and as soon as the picnic shelter dissolves behind us, a tremor of anxiety ripples through me. Without visible landmarks, we're like the victims of a capsized ship, swimming aimlessly and just hoping to find land.

We sprint past an unfamiliar flower bed, a stand of birch trees, and a forlorn picnic table etched with graffiti and decoupaged with bird crap. The amber beacon of the emergency phone blazes like St. Elmo's fire somewhere in the distance ahead of us, and I correct course to the left. Air whistles past my ears, my shoes slip in the damp grass, and my lungs burn as frantic nerves gobble up my oxygen faster than I can suck it in.

Then, the grayness before us darkens and solidifies, a barricade of trees materializing out of the mist like Brigadoon, and we skid to a panting stop. I start to turn, so I can look behind us—convinced I'm about to see Race flying at us out of the gloom—but Sebastian grabs my shoulder and gives it a tug.

"Over there," he gasps. *"Parking lot!"*

Without waiting, he takes off again to the left, where a telltale border of concrete wheel stops is just barely discernible at ground level, a family of alligators lying patiently in the grass. I hurry after him, but we slow to a cautious walk the second our shoes hit the paved lot, fragments of rubble and damp grit scratching the hard surface with intolerable volume beneath every footfall. With each sound we make, I feel increasingly vulnerable.

Suddenly, Sebastian draws up short, and I collide with his back. His voice is high and stiff as he forces out, "Holy shit, dude."

Rising out of the mist before us, glistening with a delicate sheen of moisture and faced away at a daring angle in the center of the lot, is a sleek white automobile. Tracks crushed into the grass show where the vehicle jumped the curb, neatly circumventing the padlocked gate that guards the entrance to the parking area, clambering over the low wheel stops. I take in the car's dramatic spoiler and the dark, angular lines painted along what's visible of its side panels, and my heart launches so far up into my throat that it bounces off my uvula. *It's Race's Camaro.*

"He's here," Sebastian says tonelessly, shoulders taut and raised. "That *was* him. *That was him, Rufus.*"

"Where's Peyton?" I ask worriedly, eyeing the car as if it might explode. It felt like eons passed while we stood alone in the picnic shelter after she ran off, but it could only have been a few minutes before we followed after her, and this is the only way out of the park; she must have come by here. What did she do when she saw the car? Keep running? Stop to look for her boyfriend, convinced they were still on the same side? *Did she even make it this far at all?*

"Shit. *Shit.*" Sebastian swings around, eyes doing a nervous dance. The Camaro's rear windshield is tinted, impossible to see through, the black glass like a portal to some lonely hell. *Is he in there?* "We need to get the fuck out of here. We'll get to the Jeep, and we'll call the police."

I nod my mute agreement, still trying to burn a see-through hole in the rear windshield with my eyes, finally eager to trade my problems up to a higher authority. Only, that's when I notice something that makes my heart stumble in my chest and a strange noise escape from my mouth. "Sebastian, wait."

"What? What is it?" Clearly anxious to keep moving, he stops long enough to follow the line of my arm as I point, to see what I've spotted: a fold of soft, gray fabric protruding through the thin seam where the lid of the Camaro's trunk meets the body of the car. Sebastian shakes his head. "That's . . . it's nothing, Rufus. Come on—"

"It's Peyton's hoodie."

"It *looks* like Peyton's hoodie," he corrects, fear mounting in his eyes, "which looks like a million other hoodies. Every player on every sports team at Ethan Allen has one that same color—including Race. He's probably got a whole stack of 'em jammed in that trunk. It doesn't mean anything."

"She might be in there," I whisper, unable to move. "We have to—"

"To *what*?" He gets in front of me. "Haul her ass out and carry her half a mile to the Jeep? If Race comes after us, we'll never get away from him! If she's hurt, she needs the police, Rufus; *we need to get the police*."

"She might be dying, or—"

"And she might be already dead with a knife in her face!" Sebastian exclaims, his voice rising to a point where it almost cracks, and I can't resist the urgency in his tone; he's not just arguing with me at this point—he's practically pleading for me to listen. "It could even be a trap—think about it! We need to get the hell out of here."

He's right, and I know he's right. If that *is* Peyton in there, the odds she's still alive are tremendously slim. The car is motionless, the air silent—nobody is kicking and screaming for help in the trunk. Leaving without so much as checking feels wrong, but wasting time is a risk we can't afford. I let Sebastian pull me around the vehicle, but the driver's side window drags my gaze as we pass, and I cast a fearful look inside, terrified that I'll see Race grinning dementedly back at me.

He isn't there. The window is open, and the car is empty. But something catches my eye anyway: the dull gleam of a metallic object resting on the passenger seat, caught in a square of pale light cast down by the burgeoning dawn. When my brain computes what I'm seeing, I freeze in my tracks again. There are a million possible explanations. *It could mean anything. It* doesn't *mean anything.* And yet . . .

"Come on, Rufus!" Sebastian halts when he realizes I'm not behind him anymore, glancing back with exasperation and concern. I barely hear him. Moving to the Camaro, as if in a trance, I grab for the door handle and give it a try. It's unlocked. The interior lights pop on, and I hear Sebastian stifle an incredulous yelp at the same time that my suspicions are confirmed. "*Rufus, what are you doing?*"

He makes it back to my side just as I find the trunk release and activate it, the lid popping open with a muted *clunk*. He practically bounces from foot to foot, his eyes darting frantically around the empty parking lot, on the lookout for a killer, but he follows me anyway as I step to the back end of the car and look down. My stomach drops, but it's my boyfriend who gulps a shocked breath of air, taking in what we've discovered, and blurts, "What. The. *Fuck?*"

27

CURLED UP IN THE TRUNK, DRESSED IN BATTERED TENNIS SHOES, track pants, and an oversize lacrosse hoodie—his hands and feet bound—is Race Atwood. And he isn't moving.

"I don't . . ." Sebastian stares, his face blank and uncomprehending. "I don't understand. This doesn't make any sense."

"Yes it does," I say numbly, squeezing my eyes shut, the image already burned into my mind. Race's skin is pallid, his eyes closed, his mouth sealed with tape—at a glance, it's impossible to tell whether he's alive or dead. His hands are bent awkwardly beneath his chin, and the red stain on one finger is dark and ghoulish under the sulfurous lights of the trunk. "It does make sense. Go look at what's sitting on the passenger seat."

Sebastian circles back to the driver's side door, still hanging open, and peers into the vehicle. "It's a can of spray paint. So wh—"

The minute the words are out in the open, he makes the connection. His eyes meet mine, his lips parting in surprise, and I turn my gaze back down to Race. To the finger dyed the same vivid scarlet hue as the words emblazoned across Fox Whitney's front door: *LIAR. COCKSUCKER. DRUG DEALER. RAPIST.*

When we were talking to Race and Peyton earlier in the night, I'd been thinking about blood, *looking* for blood—and I'd seen it in that split-second glimpse of the guy's fingertip. As if Fox's murderer could have washed away every trace of the crime except for that single one. But spray paint won't come off with just soap and water, and if Race had hooked his finger too far over the nozzle of the canister when he was using it—

"This still doesn't make any sense," Sebastian insists flatly, his expression stricken. "*Peyton* burned down the Whitneys' house—she told us! I mean, her story . . . she couldn't have made that up."

"She didn't. The story was true." I can picture her face again perfectly, her frightened expression, her trembling chin. "It just wasn't *her* story. It was his. Race is the one who went to Fox's house; Race is the one who accidentally set it on fire. Peyton is . . . Peyton—"

"No." Sebastian shakes his head, unwilling to believe we were so duped.

"She played us. She didn't know what Lia knew, and she needed to find out if Arlo had said anything about her. She knew that if he *had*, Lia would ignore her calls, so she texted from Race's phone instead. Because of that, and because . . ." I shoot him an uneasy look. "Because if Lia had to die, the phone records would implicate Race."

"No way. No way, Rufe, that's nuts. You saw her when she was telling us what happened tonight—she was losing her shit! Peyton's not that good of an actress!"

I'm just about to speak when a voice interrupts from somewhere behind me, and my heart all but lunges out of my chest and runs away down the street like a spooked horse. "Peyton is better at a lot of things than people give her credit for."

I pivot, and there she is: standing on the other side of the Camaro, having emerged from the heavy fog as silently as a cat, her green eyes hard and glittering. She appeared so quietly, it occurs to me that she could easily have been shadowing us this whole time, matching us stride for stride as we stampeded through the park in our flight from the picnic shelter.

"I'm a fucking *great* actress. You should've seen the performance I gave Arlo tonight."

"Peyton," I begin, intending to say something brilliant and persuasive; but my brain rusts to a complete halt as I stare at the frightening emptiness in her expression.

"This can't be real—it doesn't make sense." Sebastian still refuses to believe, his eyes traveling from Race's prone body to Peyton's cold, serious face. I can tell by the way her right arm moves that she's holding something, but her hand is hidden from view behind the Camaro. I imagine a giant butcher knife, and the four-thousand-pound car between us suddenly seems ridiculously insubstantial. Sebastian is scowling, frustration and fear catalyzing his anger. "Race didn't have anything to do with it at all, did he? You killed Fox and then torched his house, and . . . and then—"

"No." I force myself to think it through, to focus and clear my mind—*take a breath and step back*. "Peyton snapped, just like she said, but she went back to the cottage to get her revenge—not the Whitneys' house. She knew April was out cold, because Lia told her about the cough syrup, remember? Race didn't hear that part. *Peyton* was the only one who knew there'd be no witnesses—and that there'd be somebody to frame." The air feels swollen around us, pressing in close. "Race was the one who spray-painted the

Whitneys' door, and he must have told Peyton. Maybe he demanded that she cover for him. Maybe he said she owed him an alibi to make up for cheating with Fox."

Peyton nods slowly, mechanically. "He was really scared. He drove away as soon as the garage caught fire, because he was sure that it was going to spread to the rest of the neighborhood. He was still panicking when I ran into him at Silverman's—it's the only reason he told me as much as he did." Her tone is affectless, devoid of feeling, and it makes my stomach roll. "When he said I had to lie for him, I honestly thought the universe was sending me a sign that I'd done the right thing by getting rid of Fox. I mean, I was freaking out about it, and then an alibi just . . . dropped right into my lap."

"You're not making sense!" Sebastian blurts. "The door said '*rapist.*' We saw it! Why would Race write that if he didn't know Fox was blackmailing you to . . . to *do* things for him?"

Peyton releases a brittle laugh that sounds like someone prying open a sarcophagus, and which is approximately six thousand times scarier than when she was showing no emotion at all. "Do you have any idea how many girls Fox Whitney has gotten drunk or stoned and then taken advantage of? He was a disgusting asshole. Race knew even more than I did the kind of shit Fox got up to. Maybe if he'd told me some of it, I wouldn't have fallen for Fox's crap."

She aims a resentful look at Race's motionless body, still folded awkwardly into the limited space of his trunk, and I begin to sweat as I wonder what Peyton intends to do next. Between the two of us, Sebastian and I can certainly overpower her . . . but if she *does* have a knife, then the cost of trying might end up being higher than we can afford to pay.

Clearing my throat, I venture, "You killed Arlo because he tried to blackmail you, and you killed Race because . . . what? He figured out why you were so eager to lie for him? Where do you think this is gonna end, Peyton? Are you planning to bump off everyone else who was at the party and just hope the cops think that April was teleporting back and forth across the city all night on a murder spree?"

"Race isn't dead," she counters pedantically. "Yet." She spares her boyfriend another look, and I can swear that this time I almost see regret form and disperse in her eyes, a storm that won't quite break. "It didn't have to be this way. Nobody else needed to die tonight, besides Fox. I didn't want to hurt anyone else."

"But Arlo forced your hand," I prompt, eager to keep her talking. We could run. Peyton does track, and I know she's fast, but she couldn't chase us both if we went in different directions, right? "He saw what happened up at the lake house, didn't he?"

"He saw me dragging April into the kitchen. He thought she and Fox were both dead." She rolls her shoulders, the joints popping loudly. "I don't think he gave an actual shit about either of them, but he was terrified of Lyle Shetland, and he figured I could pay him enough that he'd be able to blow town for good, if he had to. He wanted ten grand. In cash." Peyton smiles then, her teeth sharp as a picket fence. "I showed up at his house dragging a duffel bag filled with magazines and shit, and the dumbass actually believed it was the money. Like, how the fuck did he think I got my hands on *ten thousand dollars* in the middle of the night?"

"And he let you get close enough to cut his throat."

"He told me to back up while he opened the bag, but I rushed him when he bent down to unzip it, and I stun-gunned him. Cutting his throat was the easy part."

"But there was still Lia—and Race," I supply, my mouth feeling dry. The problem with running in different directions is that whomever she *did* decide to chase could easily die before the other managed to get help—and the nearest point of actual safety is the Jeep. There'd be no hope of losing her on a half-mile sprint, and stopping to unlock the car door would be an invitation for her to start with the stabbing. Splitting up is just as risky as trying to jump her.

"I didn't have a choice," Peyton declares firmly. "Race, that stupid douche—he changed his mind! After I dealt with Arlo, I went back to Race's house so we could work out our story, but by that point he'd seen the news about the fire, and he was losing it. I mean, he had a total meltdown—crying, laughing, the whole bit—and he started saying he had to turn himself in. I tried to talk him down, but he wouldn't listen. He figured Fox would know he'd done it, and he'd be busted anyway, so he might as well just confess." She heaves a weary breath. "So I told him why he couldn't do that. Why I needed him to stick to the fucking story we'd already told you guys."

"He didn't take it well?"

"He did not." A faint, creepy smile slithers across her lips. "I had to use the stun gun again, just to keep him from calling the police, and then . . ." She shrugs listlessly. "Then it was too late to take chances. I can't let him tell the cops about me, so . . . he has to die, too."

"Peyton, listen to yourself," Sebastian implores, his voice rising again as he tries to cope with what she's saying. He thrusts a hand into the damp air, fingers splayed, his body tense as a coiled spring. "This is . . . it's insane! It's *fucking insane.* Two people are dead already—isn't that bad enough? You don't have to kill anyone else!"

"I don't *want* to, all right?" she snaps back fiercely, eyes blazing. "This actually isn't a whole lot of fun for me, Bash. That wasn't all acting, when I was crying earlier? When I was pretending I burned down the Whitneys' house? Killing Fox . . . it was *awful.* It happened, like—it was—even when I was doing it, I couldn't believe I was doing it, and, and it was . . . *awful.* I barely kept from puking." Her throat flexes at the memory, and her chin jerks forward. For a moment, I think she's going to puke right in front of us, but then she swallows and grits her teeth. "But Fox Whitney was a human colostomy bag. He was a misogynist dickhole, he blackmailed me for sex, he wiped his ass with his friends, *he sold drugs to kids* . . . Just tell me he didn't deserve it."

"I—" I want to argue with her, to turn this conversation around . . . but what can I say? Fox Whitney really was a terrible person. Murder is wrong—I mean, *obviously*—but I'm not going to miss the guy. I can't offer anything more than empty platitudes about right and wrong anyway, and I'm not sure those will make much of a difference to her at this point. But I have to say *something.* I have to try.

Peyton isn't acting anxious or desperate; on the contrary, she's controlled and steady, seeming not the least bit worried we might get away from her—and that makes me cold with dread. The unbeatable team of nerves and my smart mouth conjure up some words at last.

"Peyton, I've hated Fox a hell of a lot longer than you, but somehow I managed to not kill him. Maybe you could've given *not killing people* a try?"

She rolls her eyes, annoyed. "You are such a sanctimonious shit, Rufus, you know that? I mean, keep it up, really—you're making what comes next a whole lot easier."

Sebastian grabs my elbow and pulls me closer, protectively, his eyebrows drawing together. "You don't have to do anything, Peyton. And you can't kill all three of us. Lia's expecting us to tell her what went down tonight—in person—and if we don't do it soon, she's gonna call the police!"

"And by the time they get here, I'll be long gone, and all their loose ends will be wrapped up for them," Peyton finishes complacently. "Race's dad will be getting back from Washington in, like, half an hour, and when the cops show up to ask where his son is, he'll be finding a convenient suicide note on Race's computer that confesses to everything." She gives us a little frown, more disappointed than regretful. "I really . . . I almost thought it was a good thing that you guys showed up here instead of Lia. You already seemed pretty sure Race did it, and I could tell you bought my story. I thought maybe I could let you go to the police and back me up—tell them I burned down Fox's house, and let you support my alibi. But Race needs to die *here*. It's what I wrote in his suicide note, and it's too late to go back and change it without getting caught. Maybe if you guys had kept walking. Maybe if you hadn't looked in the trunk. But . . ."

Her face goes blank again, her eyes as cold and empty as Pluto, and I hold my breath instinctively. Sebastian's fingers tighten on my arm, and I can tell he senses it, too—something is about to happen; we're all out of time. Whatever move we're going to make, we have to make it *now*.

And then Peyton lifts her right arm, and I see what she's been keeping just out of sight. All the pressure levels in my body change; my stomach drops, my lungs rise, and my heart suddenly feels as if it's beating in the center of my brain.

In her hand is Arlo's rifle.

28

IN THE EAST, THE SUN IS FINALLY STARTING TO MAKE ITS PRESENCE felt, daylight asserting itself in shades of white and silver that displace the mist's dreamy blues and purples; but Fernwood Park remains an endless swamp of turbid air and wet grass nonetheless, trees looming like shrouded sentries as we struggle past them with our cumbersome burden. Race's legs feel surprisingly skinny in my arms, but his upper body keeps slipping from Sebastian's hold, and—to Peyton's escalating aggravation—he and I have to stop frequently to rest and switch places.

The stakes changed pretty drastically upon the reintroduction of Arlo's rifle. If we could somehow get away from Peyton, escape and lose ourselves in the fog before she could take proper aim, we'd have a chance at hiding from her—perhaps; but she seems well aware of this fact, and trails just far enough back to be out of arm's reach while still keeping well within sighting distance. She handles the firearm like she knows what she's doing, and it makes me think twice about saying *fuck it* and trying to run anyway.

Besides, I can't make a move unless I know Sebastian will also be safe, and there's no way to confer, to plot. We have to bide our time—we have to hope there's enough time *to* bide—and wait for a clearer opportunity to present itself.

The first thing she did, once the barrel of the weapon was out in the open and we all knew exactly where we stood, was instruct us to put our cell phones on the ground and stomp on them until they shattered. Then we were ordered to pull Race out of the Camaro's trunk and, supporting his weight between us, march him off into the pale abyss of Fernwood Park in order to meet our collective doom.

"Race is having a lot of problems, you know, dealing with his guilt over killing Fox and Arlo?" Peyton explains conversationally as we maneuver the limp body past some misshapen statue, a freakish homunculus of cast bronze that had evidently been placed in memory of one Wilfred Stanhope—a backhanded tribute, if I've ever seen one. "There's a whole lot of stuff about remorse in the note he left on his computer. He's starting to think maybe he just doesn't deserve to live after everything he's done. He hasn't made up his mind about whether Lia's going to live or die, and he's not sure if he'll be making it home from the park tonight. He's real fifty-fifty on the whole thing. Poor guy is really losing it."

"Sounds like you thought this through," I comment sourly.

"The rifle was sort of a happy accident," she admits, sounding pleased with herself. "I didn't know Arlo would be armed—not for sure—and there were a million ways that little scenario could've gone sideways on me. But it didn't. And when he was dead, I figured he didn't need a gun anymore, so I took it. Now, when Race uses it to whack you guys, and then himself, it'll prove he was at Arlo's."

I look down at poor Race—a guy I never thought I'd ever think of as "poor Race"—and feel a little sick to my stomach. His skin is sweaty and pale, dark veins showing across his eyelids in spidery lines, and I wonder what she did to make sure he'd stay unconscious for this long. Somewhere, she has to have screwed up—left evidence connecting her to these murders. She's wearing gloves to keep her prints off the rifle, but her hair tumbles loosely over her shoulders; she might easily have shed long, telltale strands of it on Arlo's body, or Fox's. Not that it would exactly be damning, since she spent half the night partying with the pair of them.

In any event, it'll be pretty useless to Sebastian and me, whatever might or might not turn up in a police lab, months or even years after they find us dead in a grove of pine trees with Arlo's bullets clanking around in our skulls.

"We need to stop," Sebastian says gruffly, as Race begins to slip out of his hold again, sagging lower and lower to the ground. My boyfriend is walking backward with his fingers hooked beneath the unconscious guy's armpits, and the awkward task makes his steps short and difficult. "My hands are starting to cramp."

"So the fuck what?" Peyton fixes him with a peevish look. "You won't have to worry about it much longer. Suck it up."

Sebastian comes to an immediate halt, glaring daggers of flame at her, his jaw clenched so tightly I can see his pulse throbbing in his neck. "I'm about to drop him, so we'd have to stop anyway."

For once, I'm not the one about to rage out; powerlessness in the face of impending death is causing Sebastian's anger to metastasize, and I realize as I look at him that if a "clearer opportunity" doesn't present itself soon, he's going to try something to turn the tables. Or maybe he already is. I watch Peyton reposition the rifle, running her fingers impatiently along the stock, and I speak up. "We should switch places again."

"You're stalling," Peyton snaps, "and I'm sick of it. Keep moving."

"I'm not stalling." Sebastian growls through his teeth, eyes blazing. Race is drooping lower and lower, the fabric of his sweatshirt twisting and bunching under his arms as my boyfriend struggles to hold on. "This isn't fucking easy, okay!"

"I got him in the trunk all by myself, and you two pussies can't even carry him a hundred yards together?"

I glance around, wondering if that's really how far we've come. Clearly intimate with the terrain, she's been guiding us nonchalantly through the park—presumably back to the Tidwell Pavilion, where she initially intended to confront Lia—but we're taking a different route than before, and I have no real clue where we are. Across from me, Sebastian bends down and drops Race defiantly to the ground at his feet. "If you wanna take over, be my guest."

"Are you fucking for real?" Peyton gives him an incredulous stare and then lifts the rifle. "Pick him up!"

"Why don't you go to hell, Peyton?"

I'm still holding on to Race's bound ankles, scrambling to figure out if I need to defuse the situation or help Sebastian provoke Peyton even more—when I feel the unconscious boy's feet twitch. Then they jerk, violently, kicking out of my grasp and smacking down onto the ground as Race's entire body begins to shake and jolt. A wet stain blooms in the crotch of his track pants, spreading quickly down his leg; his back arches, his neck goes stiff, and his eyelids flutter, exposing nothing but ghastly white.

Peyton recoils, staring down in shock as Race writhes and

flexes in the grass, the sharp smell of urine filling the close air. "What the hell?"

"What did you do to him?" I ask. The boy's skin is the color of congealed fat, and a gurgling noise sounds in his throat. To Sebastian, I say, "Quick—get the tape off his mouth!"

"Stop!" Peyton jerks the rifle up again, but her expression betrays fear and growing insecurity. "Leave it where it is."

"He's having a seizure, Peyton," I shout with mounting impatience. "He could swallow his tongue, or choke to death on his own barf! How're you gonna work *that* into your handy suicide narrative?" She doesn't respond, but the rifle drops a few inches, and Sebastian immediately leans down to remove Race's gag. "What the hell did you do, anyway? How much voltage does that stun gun pack?"

"It's not—I mean, I just zapped him the once, and he was only out for a couple of minutes!" She's flustered and unnerved, watching her control of the situation swiftly evaporate. "When he was coming around, I made him drink a glass of water with some white rabbits dissolved in it—to relax him. Usually they just relax him! Like, make him happy and goofy and . . . and easy to handle? And I thought, I mean, with all the stuff in the news about them, if they turned up in his system afterward, it would make it more believable that he'd killed a bunch of people!"

My mouth snaps shut, and I glance back at Race. Sebastian, looking seasick, has rolled him onto his side while spasms rock the boy's torso and pungent, foamy liquid oozes from his mouth. "You gave him some of Fox's stash, didn't you?"

"Yeah, so?"

"'So?' It was *poisoned*, Peyton!" She stares at me, alarmed, and I realize that she had actually missed that entire revelation.

She'd been out in the hot tub when Arlo confronted Fox about the doctored pills and probably knew nothing of their unintended side effects. "Fox cut the white rabbits with something, and—you know what? It doesn't even matter. Race might die from this, okay? You'll never convince anybody that he shot us and himself—not when they do an autopsy and find out he was having a grand mal fucking *seizure* at the same time!"

"N-no." She shakes her head vehemently, her face white. "You're lying."

"I'm not." In her eyes, I can see she believes me—or thinks maybe she should—and her gaze darts to the boy jerking and twitching on the ground. I cut a glance to Sebastian, and he stares back at me with a look as loud as a thunderclap. His lips are clamped shut, but I hear him screaming in my mind, asking the same question I'm asking myself: *Is this it? Should we wait longer? Can we afford to?* I pour more poison into Peyton's ear. "You fucked up, and it's game over, so you might as well just help us get him to the hospital! Maybe if you save his life, the cops'll take it into account."

She keeps shaking her head, but the rifle dips another few inches as she stares uncertainly at Race, chewing her lip while he convulses and she tries to think of some new workaround—some way to alter her plan and still forge ahead. It's as distracted as she's ever going to get, I realize, and so I blank my mind and lunge.

As I leap forward, I reach for the weapon, envisioning the barrel in my hands—anticipating the force it's going to take to wrench it out of her grasp, and how the action might throw me off-balance; I have to be prepared for that. I *am* prepared. My heart is throbbing, heat scratching at my chest, my throat, my face, and I channel all of it into the strength of my will.

There's too much ground to cover, though. Peyton sees me coming before I'm halfway there, and the barrel jigs up again, the sight swinging toward me just as I put my hands out to grab it. Sebastian shouts, my fingers close around cold metal, and the rifle goes off; the bullet probably misses my face by an inch, but heat and pain radiate through my palms as all the sound in the world vanishes in an instant, replaced by a piercing, insistent ring.

Peyton loses her footing, and the rifle is ripped from my numbed hands as she stumbles backward and falls, dropping hard onto the slick grass and twisting away. I don't try again. I've got a split-second choice to make—dive after her, or turn and run—and she's already scrambling to right herself, finger still on the trigger. My close call scared me a hell of a lot more than I think I'd care to admit, and my bladder doesn't have the integrity for a second attempt.

"*RUN!*" I scream, spinning around, every muscle in my body suddenly alive, my nervous system blazing like a fire in a coal seam. I spring over Race's body just as Sebastian—already on his feet—falls into step beside me, and we bolt together into the fog. I've never run so fast and felt so slow, the gun at my back making every stride nightmarishly inadequate.

The rifle cracks twice, hideously—the noise expected, and yet simultaneously so startling that Sebastian steps wrong and falls, skidding several feet on his shirtfront. I help drag him up again and we keep going, veering left, afraid to look back. Peyton shouts, and we pour on more speed.

A butterfly garden appears ludicrously before us, the entrance a whimsical arch of willow branches woven through with tendrils of ivy, and we plow down a slender path, twisting between beds of echinacea, zinnias, and milkweed; we cut right as we emerge on the other side, careening down a shallow slope, skirting a massive tree stump and blundering headlong into a forest of waist-high cattails. The earth squelches under my feet, and I realize that we've reached the water's edge, a doleful tree with drooping branches bending over as if admiring its reflection in the lake.

We hunker down, cold mud seeping through our clothes, insects and worms crawling over our exposed flesh, and we wait. Lake Champlain is eerily calm at our backs, flat as a mirror, the mist hanging above it like smoke. Minutes pass and we don't move—we don't dare—listening for the sound of Peyton's footsteps, refusing to believe we've lost her. *Have we?* Even without a visual, she could still have easily heard us; panting and gasping, our feet slapping the ground as we fled the business end of the rifle, stealth had not been our main objective.

But as three minutes of silence becomes four and then five, it seems obvious she isn't out there. If she'd been anywhere close behind us, she'd have already shown herself; she doesn't have the luxury of time to lie in wait for us to emerge—not with the clock ticking on Race's life, and her clean getaway dependent on finishing this business before Mr. Atwood can discover his son's alleged suicide note and send the authorities out here to find him.

"Okay," I whisper at last, my lips so dry that the skin across them feels tight. "Okay. We should move. I think . . . I don't think she saw where we went, but I feel like a fucking bull's-eye just sitting here. We should go before she doubles back or something."

"Rufe." Sebastian shakes his head, looking pale and worried. "I'm staying here."

"The sun's up, though. If the fog starts to lift, we lose our cover, and it's our only advantage!" I have to convince him; there's no way we're splitting up now. "We can make it to the Jeep, I know we can."

"No. Rufus—"

"Listen, if we stick to the edge of the park, where there are trees and stuff—"

"No." He says it so forcefully I fall silent and just stare at him. He winces, his dark lashes fluttering, and mumbles, "I'm saying I think I need to stay here, Rufe. I don't . . . feel so good." He pushes himself up into a sitting position, and panic wraps around my throat like a noose when I see his left flank soaked in blood. Lifting his shirt, he reveals an ugly furrow of ragged flesh, raw meat exposed where Peyton's bullet carved a channel across his skin, and I feel my gorge rise abruptly in my throat. "I think . . . I think she hit me."

Tears spring to my eyes instantly, bile stinging the inside of my nose, and my voice is like a busted harmonica—seventeen tones all at once. *"Sebastian—"*

"It doesn't actually hurt all that bad," he says, a dopily proud smile on his beautiful face. "But I'm kind of a little bit dizzy?" He shakes his head. "I think I need to stay here. I'll just slow you down—"

"Sebastian, no, no, no." Air rattles as I suck it in, my lips wet with tears. I feel like I can't breathe. I try to make the universe reshape itself, to make Sebastian's wound as insignificant as the one on my own flank, but I can't. I want to trade. *This is wrong, all wrong.* "You *can't* stay here—we have to get you to a hospital! Put your arm over my shoulders and I'll help you—"

"Rufus—"

"I'll *carry* you," I sob as he shakes his head, looking terrifyingly beatific, like a martyr who's already accepted his fate.

Digging into his pocket, he wrestles out the keys to the Jeep and pushes them into my hand.

"You know how stupid that sounds?" He cocks a brow, still relaxed, still flirting with me. "Get my car and go for help—I'll be okay. It'll be better for both of us if I stay here and just . . . you know, rest."

I kiss him, because I don't know what to say—because I can't take him with me, and I can't stay, and because suddenly I cannot possibly kiss him enough. Pulling the jersey over my head, I bunch it up and press it to his wound, making him flinch. "Hold this here, as hard as you can for as long as you can. *I mean it.* It'll slow the bleeding, okay? Promise me."

"I promise." He gives me that dumb grin again, eyes traveling drunkenly over my naked torso as his thumb traces my bottom lip. "You're so beautiful, Rufus. I love you. I love saying that. I love you."

"I love you, too," I whimper, overwhelmed, sandbagged by debilitating emotions I'm not accustomed to. I'm used to being alone and angry. I'm used to fighting back and wrapping myself in a protective shell of combative resentment. I'm used to distrusting people and second-guessing their motives.

I'm not used to *this*—this wretched feeling of needful love and utter, paralyzing helplessness. This feeling that for the first time ever, saving myself just isn't good enough. I kiss him again, then again. And then I leave him there.

29

THE RETURN TRIP TO THE PARKING LOT IS AGONIZING. EVEN adhering to my own simple plan—following the shore until it gives way to dense woods, and then trusting that the trees will lead me back to my destination—I feel totally lost, my confidence destroyed by the pressure I'm under. I'm so shaken, I can't even be sure I'm heading in the right direction, that I'm not actually going deeper into Fernwood Park instead of out toward the road.

The fog is dissipating much faster than I expected, and the added visibility unnerves me; every sound I hear sends me scrambling into the trees to hide. Even so, I move as quickly as I can, risking the attention-grabbing crack of twigs underfoot and the rustle of bracken at my ankles, determined to save Sebastian before it's too late. I have to believe that he'll be okay. *He has to be okay.*

After what might have been five minutes or five hours, I abruptly find the parking lot spreading out before me, like a lake of fire I'll have to cross to reach the road. This is where Peyton was the last time, waiting for us, knowing that it's the only way out. I hesitate, breathing hard, anxious sweat prickling my scalp and under my arms, and look in the direction of Race's car. It's still where it was, just visible in the slackening mist, an apparition against a hazy backdrop of faded gray. *Is she there?*

She'll know that, short of diving into the lake and swimming north, our two best options for getting help are the Jeep or the emergency phone. It's plain to me that the phone is too risky, an obvious trap with a bright yellow light that would make it real easy for Peyton to pick me off while I stood there trying to figure out if the damn thing even works anymore. To hedge her bets, though, she'll probably be on the opposite side of the lot—close enough to the phone to watch for shadows, close enough to the road to listen for footsteps.

My eyes riveted on the front end of the vehicle, watching intently for any sign of life, I step cautiously over one of the concrete wheel stops and start creeping toward the road. My heart pounds, my steps as loud in my ears as bones breaking, and my fingers tingle painfully with a surplus of adrenaline. I'm halfway across before I realize she's heard me—before a deafening *crack* rips apart the humid morning air and a bullet shreds its way into the trees behind me. Peyton's silhouette materializes at the far end of the Camaro, rifle held high—but by then I'm already at a full sprint.

I tear across the pavement as the rifle barks out a second report, another tree taking the hit as my innards churn and fizz, going haywire from the overload of panic. I jump the next wheel stop and narrow grass verge in a single bound, stumbling off the curb and into the street as I land. Pivoting left, I race up the empty roadway, arms pumping, my lungs already in pain.

Half a mile to the Jeep. Give or take. Half a mile that might as well be a half-marathon. I keep expecting another bullet, wondering if it'll knock me off my feet or if I'll even notice it at all—they say you don't hear the one with your name on it. Maybe I'll just blink out, defiantly alive one second and a sad memory the next, a flame guttering and then gone.

Believe it or not, it's the sound of metal scraping against concrete—a car chassis thumping as it rolls over the curb and settles on the even road—that serves as my first reminder that Arlo's rifle isn't the only weapon in Peyton's arsenal. There's a rumble as the Camaro's engine devours some fuel behind me, tires growling like a pack of angry dogs as they begin chewing hungrily at the pavement, and the lingering fog flares white around me when high beams come on at my back.

My heart coughs, my feet stumble, and I go dizzy with fear as rubber shrieks brightly and the car lurches forward. There's nowhere for me to go. The road is barely two lanes wide, bordered on both sides by steep ditches filled with black water—moats that disguise a treacherous bounty of sharp rocks and dirty needles. Even if I want to climb down the embankment and splash across one, I'll only find myself thrashing through a dense maze of trees and chest-high shrubs on the other side. I'd make it about five feet before Peyton pulled up and blew my head off. If I try to use the trench as a secondary escape route, I'll be a duck at a shooting gallery. *There's nowhere to go.*

Swerving right for no reason, I hear the Camaro's engine getting louder, tracking me, closing in. My throat is sandpaper, my eyes reeling at the sight of my shadow leaping and shrinking against the mists as the headlights bear down. My shoes graze the lip of the ditch and I balk.

I turn around. The front end of Race's car rushes at me, picking up speed, and I dive sideways at the last second. Time slows as the metal monster zooms by, so close I feel hot wind against my legs—so close my shoe clips the side-view mirror as it rockets past. My body flips over, flung away by the glancing blow, and I flail wildly in the air.

I crash-land hard on the pavement, my knee ripping open with a blinding burst of pain, and I roll to a turbulent, agonized stop on the opposite side of the road. My head spins violently, my body stinging all over, and I gulp down frantic mouthfuls of air. The Camaro's brakes engage fiercely and it skids, spins, and screeches to a halt at an angle, its engine panting; then, after a fractional pause, Peyton puts the vehicle into reverse, straightening out—readying for another try. Whimpering out loud, I shove up on shaky arms and shakier legs, deep scratches crosshatching my bare torso, and I stagger back into a pitiful, limping run.

I'm heading for the park again, not thinking, just afraid—reduced to a primal state of sheer terror. Peyton revs the engine, bringing the tires to a frenzied, stationary spin, keeping the car in place while she patiently waits for me to give her enough room to build up some real speed. Loping hopelessly along the verge of the road, I sense the dark, evil-smelling water in the trench below, pain breaking through me like a jackhammer every time I put weight on my injured knee. Through the haze of pain and tears, I hear Sebastian's voice in my head again, talking me down from one of my feral, mind-wiping rages: *Take a breath and step back.*

Peyton releases the brake, and the car leaps forward with a triumphant squeal, tires humming gratefully as they're finally set loose. I stop and turn—exhausted, bloodied, weak—and watch with a hollow feeling as the coupe surges at me. There will be no death-defying jump this time; I'm lucky to still be standing at all. The air parts between us, Peyton's malicious grin flashing behind the wheel . . .

And I take a step back.

The verge drops away beneath my foot, and I fall, my nerves amplifying to a queasy, nightmarish frenzy as I plunge through limited space to a hard destiny. The stream running through the ditch gives me a cold, shallow embrace and my back smashes down on a bed of sharp stones, bottle caps, and long, pointed twigs that puncture my flesh like candles sinking into a birthday cake. My head strikes against something, light strobing behind my eyes, and I inhale a mouthful of oily, fetid water.

Peyton slams on the brakes again, but she's too late; the pavement is slick with dew, and Race's tires can't bite down fast enough. The car wobbles and fishtails . . . and then shoots over the edge of the road. Trapped and dazed, I watch the underside of the vehicle as it jumps the ditch just past where I lie, the Camaro's headlights firing against the sturdy tree trunks that wait for it.

The sound of the collision is deafening—a hideous detonation of glass, metal, and plastic collapsing in the blink of an eye—the car flipping up and swinging wide, tossed sideways by its own momentum. It bangs down hard, the quarter panels raking loudly against the trees, and finally settles at an angle in the ditch. The air reeks of gasoline and oil and heat, and I drag myself up from my watery berth like a zombie freeing himself from the grave.

I think I half expect Peyton to somehow kick her way out of the wreckage like the Terminator, rifle aloft, still determined to finish things; but my fears are unfounded. In her haste to run me down, she never put on her seat belt. Struggling to stand on feet I can't even feel, I see where she rocketed halfway through the windshield—where she now lies sprawled across the Camaro's hood, blood and glass decorating her hair, her body ruined.

Peyton Forsyth is dead.

ONE MONTH LATER

"I HOPE I'M NOT INTERRUPTING ANYTHING," MY MOTHER SAYS with an ingenuousness that is not the least bit convincing. Two minutes earlier, Sebastian and I had been making out on the floor of the living room, our shirts cast aside, and I was very excited by the telltale hardness I felt against my hip when he shifted subtly on top of me. Then the front door rattled and popped open, my mom calling out an improbable "Yoo-hoo, it's just me!" and we'd scrambled to dress and reorganize ourselves in the thirty seconds that passed before she sauntered into the room with a sly grin on her face.

"No, Mrs.—uh, Genevieve," Sebastian stammers nervously, his face adorably flushed with embarrassment. "We were just watching a movie."

Mom takes in the TV screen at a glance. "Ooh, *Friday the 13th*! This is part . . . seven, right? The psychic girl who throws stuff around with her mind?" She flops down into our easy chair, settling herself and giving Sebastian a broad wink. "You don't mind if I join you guys, do you? Part seven is my favorite."

I offer her a resentful scowl, my erection practically making a slide whistle noise as it deflates beneath the popcorn bowl I brilliantly used to disguise it when she made her entrance. On the screen, Jason—the hockey-masked killer—impales the teenage protagonist's mother with a scythe, and I announce pointedly, "What a coincidence—this is my favorite part."

Sebastian nods vigorously, too preoccupied with his attempt at acting casual—pressing an old copy of *Elle Decor* across his lap, like that's fooling anybody—to notice my sarcasm. The nice thing is, he's still sitting right next to me, our legs brushing together as we pretend to be engrossed in a movie we've both seen about a billion times. It's taken a while to get to this point, where he doesn't reflexively pull away whenever someone catches us touching or holding hands, and the feeling is good. I like the closeness—the not having to worry anymore about how people will react.

After I crawled back up onto the road that night, broken twigs jutting out from my bloodied flesh like a botanical experiment gone hideously awry, I somehow managed to stumble all the way to the emergency phone and call 911. The first responders wanted to put me into an ambulance the second they saw me, but I refused; first, I led them all the way to where Sebastian was lying among the reeds—gray-faced and unconscious but still breathing—and then I collapsed.

Sebastian, Race, and I were all taken to the same hospital; all three of us were questioned thoroughly by the authorities, and all three of us were ultimately sent home. I don't know what version of the night's events Sebastian told the cops—if it even matched mine in the slightest—but I doubt it mattered. The entire affair was a PR nightmare for the authorities, with several notable families involved in a high-profile scandal of drugs and murder and arson, and we were handing them a closed case on a silver platter. Three eyewitnesses and a dead suspect made the case open and shut, and I think they were relieved to turn a blind eye to all our lying and dissembling.

"I thought you were supposed to be meeting with a potential client or something," I say to my mother, hinting rather obviously that she should leave again.

"I am," she answers, "but I had a few minutes, and I thought I'd stop at home first to see how my boys were doing. I know you can't cook anything that doesn't have microwave instructions, so I got some of those frozen pizza rolls you two like so much. That way I know you won't starve to death."

"Ha ha." I roll my eyes.

"You two have any plans for the evening?"

"Sort of?" Sebastian looks around the room at nobody in particular. "My friend Jake is having a birthday party tonight, so we thought, uh . . . you know, we might go to that. If that's okay?"

Many of Sebastian's friends have actually been pretty cool with the news that he's dating a guy—less so with the news that said guy is *me*, as I had predicted, but we're working on it. Jake Fuller is probably Sebastian's best friend these days, and as the self-coronated Party King of Ethan Allen High, he's already guaranteed us a few opportunities—like tonight—to road-test public opinions on our relationship. With my worst enemies at Ethan Allen out of the picture for good, attitudes toward me are proving more malleable than they've ever been before, and guys who've passively made my life crap in the past are actually willing to speak to me in a pseudo-friendly way all of a sudden. It takes all my strength of character to be grudgingly civil to most of them, but, like I said: We're working on it.

As soon as Race was released from the hospital with a clean bill of health, he went straight into seclusion, moving to his grandparents' house in Maine to weather the media storm surrounding the events of Independence Day. From what Sebastian's heard, the Atwoods are seeking out a private school near Portland that he can enroll in come the fall. In similar news, Hayden has also decamped from Burlington for the foreseeable future, and I have to say I'm relishing every minute of a life without him in it.

Two days after reports of the shootout at Suzy's American Diner made the news, Peter and Isabel decided to bestow upon their eldest a suspiciously convenient late graduation gift of a six-week European vacation. Hayden left on the first flight out, and is by now no doubt brawling outside nightclubs in Ibiza or drinking himself blind in Prague. If and when he eventually returns to the States, he'll be bypassing Vermont altogether and heading straight to college in Massachusetts instead. According to April, Lyle's boys still ride by their house every few days anyway, just in case the prodigal son should make an unexpected return.

April herself is in a very weird place. Of her former clique, Lia is the only member left—and the two of them can barely look one another in the eye after everything that's happened. My sister was exonerated by the law, but her reputation at Ethan Allen has been permanently tainted, and so she'll be attending a private school in the fall, too, just like Race. She's made no secret of the fact that she'd also like to leave the state to do it, but Isabel has flatly refused on the grounds that it would look like running away.

In the meantime, without her popular clique to count on, April's taken to texting me more and more often—and even inviting herself along when my friends and I hang out. It's a turn of events that never stops feeling bizarre to me—but, somehow, it actually seems to work. Most of the time. There's no way Peter approves of our associating, if he's even aware of it, but he handles his daughter now even more lightly than he used to. April doesn't always seem to enjoy the downgrade in her social status, which is not a huge surprise, but I think she's learning that being an outcast comes with the liberating privilege of not having to worry about your image so much.

"A party sounds like fun," Mom says insincerely, her eyes on the TV while her mind is clearly still back in early July, "but, you know, I'd appreciate it if—"

"If I come home no later than midnight," I supply automatically, "and wake you up if you're sleeping, so you know I'm not out getting murdered somewhere. I will, I promise."

"You know, when most kids say sarcastic shit like that, they make it sound like their parents are paranoid neurotics," my mother points out dryly. "Somehow, you don't quite pull it off."

I make a face at her just as a knock sounds on the front door, and Lucy Kim barges into the house without waiting for a formal invitation.

"Hey, Mom!" my best friend calls to my mother melodiously, bounding past her and hurling herself across the sofa like she belongs here. Which, let's be honest, she really does. "Hey, dudes. What's goin' on?"

"You know, Lucy, it's the funniest thing," Mom says with a theatrically pensive expression. "If I weren't absolutely sure my son and his boyfriend knew it was against house rules, I would almost swear I'd caught them in the middle of 'Netflix and chill' a few minutes ago. But they promise me that they are just watching a movie."

Lucy widens her eyes and pulls her mouth down in an "oopsy" face, and then says, very chipper, "Rufus would never dream of violating a parental boundary, Mrs. Rufus's Mom. Why, I remember the time I wanted to try that soda pop stuff I've heard all the kids talking about, and Rufus said, 'No way, Jose,' because soda pop leads to fornication—"

"Oh my gosh, *okay*—I surrender!" I exclaim. "I apologize for *almost* Netflix-and-chilling, all right?" Burying my face in my hands, I moan, "I should never have introduced you two."

"Too late," Mom says brightly, rising to her feet and straightening out her clothes. "Anyway, I suppose I should probably go and meet that client. Cross your fingers, because this could be a big fish." Leaning down, she ruffles my hair affectionately. "See you later, kiddo. Have fun at your party." At the door, she tosses back over her shoulder, "And, just so you know, I'm *not* going to go sit at the end of the block for a while and wait to see how long it takes for you to get rid of Lucy."

Lucy and I *both* roll our eyes as the door slams shut.

My final showdown with Peyton resulted in two cracked ribs and a series of incredibly gnarly flesh wounds, and for a while there, my body was a Frankensteiny road map of damaged skin held together with stitches and staples. They gave me a course of nuclear-powered antibiotics at the hospital, and then kept me for a couple nights while they waited to see if I would develop some kind of horrible infection anyway. In all that time, my father did not bother to send me so much as a get-well-soon card; but on my last day, I did receive an unexpected visitor in the person of Isabel Covington.

She kept her remarks brief and to the point, offering up a terse "Glad to see you're feeling better," and then informing me—in the manner of a business associate imparting news of vaguely promising figures in the latest quarterly projections—that the police had officially cleared April of any wrongdoing in Fox's death. “She wanted to come see you, but I didn't think that would be appropriate.”

And then, into my hand Isabel pressed a blank envelope containing four thousand dollars—cash—before walking back out the door without another word.

When I presented my accumulated six grand to my mom a few days later, she was nearly speechless. I told her not to ask where it came from, and she didn't. Probably, she assumed I'd stolen it from Fox or Arlo, or maybe off Peyton's dead body—or possibly that it was hush money from the Atwoods, Whitneys, or Forsyths. All I knew was that if she learned most of it came from Isabel, she'd never have touched it; so I kept that detail to myself, Mom paid off the bank, and the wolves were gone from our door.

As for Peter, the man has spent the past few weeks working overtime to un-sully the Covington name and distance it from the scandalous events of the Fourth of July. He's made sizeable donations to several notable charities; he managed to get himself quoted in no fewer than three different newspaper articles about the dangers of teenage drug abuse; and he wisely refused to take on a wrongful death suit against the Forsyths organized by Fox's parents. More importantly, he never filed that restraining order against me and seems to have grudgingly accepted that I was in no way involved in Fox's death.

“Hey, um . . . so I kind of gave Jake Fuller your phone number?” Sebastian says to Lucy, peering up at her on the couch. “I believe I'm supposed to tell you that he thinks you're cute. He hasn't called you yet or anything, has he?”

“As a matter of fact, I *did* get a text from him the other day,” Lucy remarks. “It says . . .” She draws up the messages on her phone and reads aloud from the screen. “*Sup?*”

"Jake's . . . not very smooth with the ladies."

"No, I dare say he's not."

"Any chance you want to come to his birthday party tonight?" Sebastian wrinkles his nose. "I'm supposed to make it sound like I thought of it myself, like you can come or not come and it's no big deal, but I think he really wants you to come."

"That depends." Lucy swings up into a sitting position and eyes my boyfriend smartly. "I don't suppose Mr. Fuller has ever mentioned feeling like an ass for calling me a 'fag hag' in the eighth grade and then laughing like it was a hilarious insult?"

"Uh . . . no."

"And I don't suppose he's ever apologized for implicitly calling Rufus a fag, implicitly reducing me to Rufus's sidekick, or implying that there is somehow something wrong or shameful about enjoying the company of The Gays?"

"Uh . . ." Sebastian starts to panic in the face of Grammatically Accurate Lucy, which shows that he's definitely developing an accurate sense of her danger zones.

"Well, you may tell Jake Fuller that if and when he is ready to apologize and have an adult discussion about these issues, I am willing to listen."

Sebastian makes a strange face. "I don't think you realize just how clueless Jake is. If I tell him all that, the only thing he's going to hear is that he maybe has a shot."

"Arrrgh, *boys*." Lucy flops back on the couch, disgusted. "You're all so stupid and dumb. Life would be so much easier if you weren't so freaking hot."

"Tell me about it," Sebastian says, ruffling my hair.

I punch him in the arm.

ACKNOWLEDGMENTS

This book started as just an image in my mind—of a boy finding his sister at a murder scene in a lonely lake house—and I've got a lot of people to thank for what it took to bring Rufus, Sebastian, April, and their friends (and enemies!) out of my head and onto the pages you're holding.

To my exceptional editor, Liz Szabla: thank you for loving this story as much as I do, for knowing when the characters needed an extra push or two, and for always making my work stronger. I'm already looking forward to our next endeavor together! And to my amazing publisher, Jean Feiwel: thank you, once again, for letting my dreams come true by turning this story into an actual book.

To Molly Ellis, my lifesaver, combat trainer, and publicist: thank you for being The Actual Best literally all of the time. I could not have made it this far without you! To Caitlin Sweeney, marketing magician: you were one of my earliest champions, and I'll never forget it. Thank you for everything.

To be frank, my extended Feiwel and Friends/Macmillan family is peerless. My deepest gratitude to Rich Deas, Mandy Veloso, Kim Waymer, Allison Verost, and Jon Yaged for all that you've done to see that my Pinocchio became a real boy; and many thanks also to Brittany Pearlman, Ashley Woodfolk, Heather Job, and Kelsey Marrujo (and Emma Mills, Marissa Meyer, Anna Banks, Kami Garcia, and Leigh Bardugo!) for making my Fierce Reads experience an absolute pleasure.

My marvelous agent, Rosemary Stimola, has been the Gandalf to my Frodo: giving me her counsel, wisdom, and trust, and always, always helping me find my way. Thank you, again, from the bottom of my heart for all you've done—and for answering all my emails, no matter how frantic or bizarre they get!

So much gratitude, also, to my debut crew, the Sweet Sixteens—you guys gave me a YA family and taught me so much. A million thanks to Kristin Cast for her support and generosity (and for sharing my love of *Drag Race*!) And all my love and respect to the bloggers and booksellers—in particular Stacey Canova, Jennifer Gaska, Angie Mann, Susan Rowland, Vee Signorelli, Eric Smith, Nena Boling-Smith, Rachel Strolle, Katie Stutz, and Heidi Zweifel, all of whom I owe a special debt—who have befriended me, talked up my work, and/or saved my butt at BEA (you know who you are). This industry is lucky to have people like you.

My friends and family have put up with a lot of my breathless panicking over the years—and even more of my half-baked, sardonic one-liners—and I want you guys to know how much I appreciate it. To my support systems in L.A., Michigan, Phoenix, Chicago, and beyond: you guys keep me going, and I thank you for it.

To Tapani Salminen and Erkki Mäkelä: thank you both so much for years of generosity and friendship. I wrote this book while living on Hämeentie and finished my own edits of the manuscript on my birthday at your house, so this story is inextricably woven into the time we shared with you during our years in Finland. Paljon Kiitoksia!

And, once again, I have saved the best for last. Uldis, this book will find us in our thirteenth year together. From the Valley to Hollywood, from Hollywood to Helsinki, and from Helsinki back to the Valley, our own story is full of thrilling adventures and surprising twists. I can't wait to see what comes next. As a wise sage once said, "The rest is still unwritten!" Es tevi mīlu, Ulditi.

Thank you for reading this Feiwel and Friends book.

The Friends who made

WHITE RABBIT

possible are:

Jean Feiwel, Publisher

Liz Szabla, Associate Publisher

Rich Deas, Senior Creative Director

Holly West, Editor

Anna Roberto, Editor

Christine Barcellona, Editor

Kat Brzozowski, Editor

Alexei Esikoff, Senior Managing Editor

Kim Waymer, Senior Production Manager

Anna Poon, Assistant Editor

Emily Settle, Administrative Assistant

Mandy Veloso, Production Editor